MW00776563

Copyright © 2020 Viktor H. Strangewayes
All rights reserved.

Cover and Book Design, Vaal'bara Historical Society logo, and all contained works are covered under registered copyright. This volume has been typeset in Adobe Garamond Pro, Antro Vectra, Helena, Courier New, Kingthings Trypewriter, Sinister Sam, and Informal Roman.

No part of this volume may be reproduced in any form, magical or otherwise, or by any electronic or mechanical means, including information storage and retrieval systems, without permission in writing from the author. The only exceptions provided are to a reviewer, who may quote short excerpts in a review, or through a Coadjutor device, which cannot help but to record its environment and that which it comes in contact with.

Printed on the Planet Earth using Native Materials.

First Edition Text: March 2020

ISBN - 978-1-952529-12-2

DISCLAIMER AND / OR LEGAL NOTICES

This volume is a work of Forgotten History & Factual Magic. Names, characters, places, and incidents are, in most cases, part of our past, but may have since been altered due to lifeforms capable of manipulating or traveling through time. Any details pertaining to actual persons, events, or locales currently residing within this timeline were accurate at the time of publishing but may no longer coincide with accepted real world data.

All authors, inventors, or the works they have produced, which may be hinted at or included within this volume, were added only as informal references or documented due to their proximity to involved characters. Any such parties should refrain from interpreting their inclusion as inferred support for actual Magic, time travel, or other anomalous actions.

While all attempts have been made to verify the information provided within this publication, neither the author nor the publisher assumes any responsibility for errors, inaccuracies, or omissions in any details regarding the use of Magic and/or time travel. This volume is not intended for use as a source or guide for such activities. Caution is advised while endeavoring to reproduce similar effects.

This is Volume Three of a continuing saga,
picking up after Chapter 43 of:

The Vaal'bara Historical Society
- Volume Two -
The First Fall of Lord Marris

"One step into the unknown is an adventure not soon forgotten."

~ Aurthur G. Ma'lorean

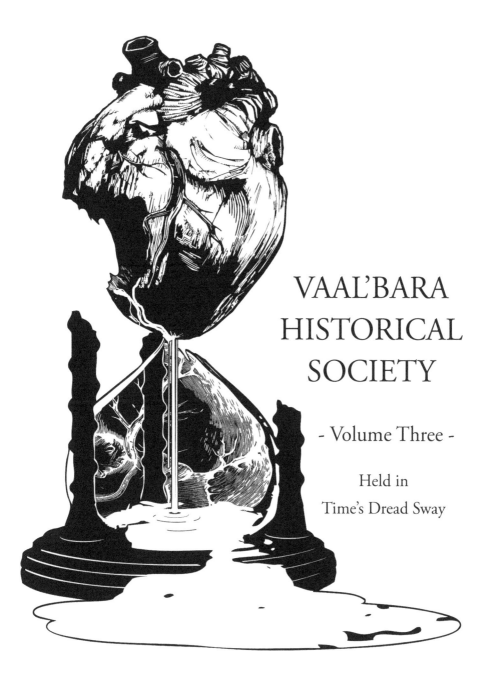

VAAL'BARA HISTORICAL SOCIETY

- Volume Three -

Held in Time's Dread Sway

Composed by:

Viktor H. Strangewayes
& Laurence P. Cromwell

While reading this historical account, you will come upon four symbols which serve to inform you of specific events:

You are being notified that a period of time, whether it is a few minutes or a few days, has passed without the narrator reporting what has happened.

You are being notified that the narrator has stepped through a portal or has been teleported to an entirely different time or location.

You are being notified that a letter or document has been written, and you are reading or being read what is inside it. It will be accompanied by a second, complimentary symbol marking its end.

You are being notified that the narrator has been thrust into a vision and is experiencing events outside the current timeline. It will be accompanied by a second, complimentary symbol marking its end.

PROLOGUE

Two weeks passed by, the computer open and drained of life, spilled coffee permanently staining my carpet. Finding myself incapable of coping with the events that had taken place, I tried my best to fill the time with other activities in an effort to blot out the imagery poisoning my brain. Unfortunately, sleep, the activity I needed most, appeared elusive. Each night, while I lay upon my pillow, rest would creep in around me, only to be repelled by the story I had been told. Fatigue was nothing compared to the virus-like narrative, which pushed itself deeper and deeper into my subconscious.

I was not the only person haunted by how the tale had transpired; Laurence, before his departure, had unraveled in both his composure and his objective. Unlike him, however, I did not know how the entire story concluded, and that information troubled me. How he escaped, what had happened in the billions of years between then and now - it was all a grand mystery to me.

One might assume that something so vivid, so stressful, should be left alone, buried and forgotten in the mental fog that accompanies time, but that option was beyond my grasp. Whatever spellwork laced Laurence's story only seemed to increase in its potency as the days passed. Every hour that ticked by, further smothered my thoughts in a blanket of obsession.

Unable to hold the words at bay any longer, I turned on my laptop and began to type. Upon pressing the first letter, relief flooded through me in waves, but it wasn't until many chapters had been written that I came to terms with how sickly I had become. What I once believed was a spell which emphasized the vivid imagery brought on by Laurence's words, appeared instead to be a virus - a literary virus - and I was its carrier. He had, in effect, passed it on to me, and my only hope of survival was to copy those same words down onto my computer.

Absently I wondered if Laurence was not only a carrier, but also afflicted by it.

Was he, too, unable to live without spreading the tale to others? Would those who read my volumes in the future also find themselves unable to control their compulsions to spread the tale? Of course there were no answers to be found, but it didn't matter. The words, at long last released, would spill out until every last one of them had been freed and I was unshackled from their grasp.

That night, my fingers sore from typing, my eyes blurry from the artificial lighting of my computer screen, I succumbed to exhaustion. But restful sleep I did not have, and only a few hours passed before I was awoken by sickness not unlike that of food poisoning. The pattern continued until, finally, the last keystroke was entered. My eyes becoming heavy, I slumped backward in my chair and did not rouse from slumber until well over a day had passed.

When consciousness returned to my stiffened body, it was dark. Unaware of how long I had been asleep, I stumbled to the sink and leaned forward to drink directly from the tap. I was dehydrated and famished; I had drunk seldom and refrained from eating entirely until the volume was complete.

After a basic meal, composed of food I could prepare quickly, I began to consider what the second volume's completion might mean. Somehow Laurence had known when the first had been finished. Would he also be alerted in regard to the second, or did his breakdown mean he would never show up again? Only time would tell, I supposed.

I wasn't at all certain I wanted to see him again. His words had weakened me. His behavior had caused me great distress. What then of his return? Was it worth continuing on with him? Was it worth learning more, if only to slip further into sickness and possible insanity myself?

It turned out I had no say in the matter. As I rose from the table, my empty plate in hand, I was startled to find Laurence once again sitting where I had last seen him, his arrival unannounced. Dropping the plate, I let out a yelp before composing myself. Picking crumbs of food from the floor, I shot him a glare.

"Not yet," I replied to a question he had yet to ask. "This is too soon. The second volume made me sick. I need time to recover."

Laurence tilted his head to the side, appearing to consider what I had said. His gaze seized me, his eyes forcing me to stare into their depths, unable to turn away.

"The second volume is complete," he stated resolutely.

"Yes, it is, but I need time before we start again. I'm not feeling-"

My words were cut off as I found myself teleported to the chair opposite Laurence.

Leaning forward, he studied me. "You became sick from lack of writing. Unlike typical conversations, where details come and go according to fatigue, my words are retained in your brain absolutely. You cannot hold so much information in the forefront of your mind for long. You need to release what you have heard far more quickly from now on. Abstaining from writing will only threaten your life."

I didn't respond, choosing silence over dispute. Laurence was not requesting my assistance; he was informing me of how I would cope with the next volume. And frankly, I had no intention of resisting his demands, as he possessed powers far superior to my own. Considering I had no abilities at all, any user of Magic would have bested me, but he was the one I had to deal with face to face, and I did not want to anger him.

Crossing his legs, Laurence propped his hands on top of his knee. Taking note of the coffee stain on my carpet, he frowned. In an instant the spot vanished, but he continued to stare at the area anyway.

"I must apologize for my behavior during our last session, Viktor. I can be a bit… *passionate* at times. You see, when I started this tale, I informed you that Jillian Winters was whom my thoughts resided upon most often. It was an honest admission - they still do - but it would seem I was not ready to divulge those thoughts just yet without emotion attached to them. Pain is powerful, but regret is far more dangerous." He risked a brief glance up toward me. The power held within his eyes was, for the moment, completely gone. "Keep your eyes open," he repeated quietly.

I nodded in reply but otherwise did not interrupt. As I had suspected, whatever was contained in the next volume was agonizing for Laurence; it had affected him deeply. Although he appeared ready to share those experiences with me, I wasn't about to risk saying something which might cause the collapse of his composure a second time.

Seeing my compliance, Laurence turned toward the window, as he had done before. Watching his body briefly rock backward, I imagined the imagery contained within his mind contacting him like a rolling wave of water. Slowly, as he submerged himself into it, his lips parted and he began to speak.

CHAPTER *forty—four*

-A PORTAL PAST BY-

Vael'ehn's words resounded over and over in my head.

*"Whatever useless purpose you were created for, you have obviously failed it! You will remain here with the knowledge that your mission was an utter and complete failure. Your savior is dead, you have lost everything, and you did **nothing** to stop me!"*

Evil or not, Vael'ehn was correct; everything we attempted up until that point *had* failed, allowing him to pull off the impossible. The sword had been restored to whatever insane, dark power it had possessed in the past, and Jack, the only person who could influence Mor'dresh in a positive way, had just died.

Everything unraveled so fast…

Watching helplessly as humanity's only hope was snatched out from under my eyes, being held in place by an unknown spell without the ability to break free - there were no words to describe the emotions flooding through me.

If only I had more experience with Magic, perhaps I could have stopped Vael'ehn.

Did I try hard enough? Should I have somehow pushed harder?

Had I been the key to our potential success?

Was I the sole cause of our failure?

A thousand questions ran through my mind, but all had one thing in common: they were pointless. The events had occurred as they had, and in life there were no do-overs, no second chances. That was, unless a person was willing to remove himself from his own timeline to correct those wrongs for everyone but himself. Ironically, we had just failed at that very task. We had squandered our second chance.

But who is to say a person only gets one attempt at righting a wrong?

I paused, baulking at the absurd thought. It felt far too convenient to be possible.

Is it really that simple? If I was willing and capable, could I just go back and try again? Just... travel backward through time and have a "do-over?"

By going back in time once already, I had been removed from my future timeline - that was, unless the crystal protected me from such dangers. But removing myself from a second timeline could have consequences far beyond what Wenton had warned. For all I knew, my form hadn't been created to endure such a thing. Traveling backward again could break the potential link I might have had between my body in the future and my mind in the past.

Trying this a second time could force me to forfeit my body, or even vanish altogether...

And if I do die, will I wink out of existence altogether, or arrive as a lifeless shell, allowing all of this replay again, exactly as it just had?

Has this scenario already played out an infinite number of times, with my death causing each and every one of those repeat performances?

Is there a pile of dead crystals waiting for me in the past?

The thought was mind-boggling, horrifying even, but I had to admit, the upside was certainly promising. My survival could buy Jack a chance to correct his demise. If I was to survive the time-traveling trip intact - if such an act were even possible, given my limited skillset - there would be a second version of myself waiting on the other side. Jack would have *two* crystals to help him overthrow Vael'ehn.

But, what if we both maintain a link to the same body? Will one of us die when I arrive in the past?

If we both survive, what about the future? Two versions of the same person surely can't occupy the same human form; that's for certain.

And why should my duplicate get to return to my body instead of me? He's the one who fails at his task, and I'm the one taking the risk to save Jack again!

The thought was honest, if a bit selfish.

If it comes down to me or a copy of myself, and only one body to fill, what will happen?

What if, upon my arrival, he has the same thought?

*What if he considers me **his** duplicate?*

Deep down inside, I knew the answer: if push came to shove, I'd pick myself over a prior, lesser version. Even so, I decided to ignore the question until it came up again - *if* it came up again.

The real topic of importance right now is our mission, not myself.

Whether or not Jillian was being completely honest, whether or not she had a hidden agenda, I still felt compelled to save her, if given the opportunity. So too was I compelled to make sure Jack's death was brought on by natural causes instead of a corrupted sword. And of course Vael'ehn had to be stopped before he could carry out his plans.

He cannot be allowed to tear this planet apart.

The only uncertainty remaining was whether it was possible to achieve any of what I deemed necessary, given my limited experience with Magic. It was just as likely I might be forced to continue on from where I was, accepting the casualties that had taken place. For all I knew, there really *was* nothing I could do to change events, however little I wanted to admit that.

I'd have chosen just about anyone over myself as this world's last hope.

In an effort to give myself a moment to think, I turned my attention toward the cave. My surroundings were invisible, lost in a sea of darkness - a black that made my eyes feel as if they were suffocating. Vael'ehn had made sure I'd have nothing to distract me from my mistakes, and he had done a sufficient job. I was truly alone, and the nothingness of it all pressed inward on me.

No, I can't let him gain another victory while he's not even present. Who am I to be scared of the dark?

I had at least figured out how to create my own illumination. I had done so before while following Jack and Vael'ehn; it would be no different in a cave.

Or would it?

As I tried to gather the light around me, I realized the folly of my prior spellwork: there was no light to gather, no source to pull from. My spell did nothing without first being provided with light to accumulate.

I'm such a fool; this will never work! I might as well have asked the rocks to turn into lightbulbs!

As I scoffed at the silly notion, several rocks along the edges of the cavern flashed into existence before plunging the area into darkness again. The idea might have been brought on by sarcasm, but deep down, some part of me was being honest; I had wanted the light to come from somewhere other than myself. Subconsciously I must have deemed the rocks worthy of light, if just for a split second, and they had responded to my will.

Astounding...

Having seen the location of the few stones which had revealed themselves, I pictured them exactly as they had been, glowing like bubbling glass over a bulb. Knowing that I created in reality, what I had imagined in my mind, allowed me to focus. Although still nervous, the knowledge that it was possible made me feel like I could attain results that much easier.

The idea that rocks were unable to glow no longer occurred to me. I simply believed that rocks could glow, and I was not disappointed. The exact rocks I had manipulated by accident before flared back to life. As if I had pulled a blanket from my head, the darkness was chased away. Before me lay the dimly-lit interior of the cavern.

Besides the macabre pile of decapitated corpses covering the ground, and the portal platform that Vael'ehn had destroyed, the room was barren, leaving me nothing to inspect from where I hovered. Ignoring the entrance that Vael'ehn had sealed up, there was only the one side passage to venture into, making my choice of where to proceed far easier, even if it did seem fruitless.

If that passage had also led out of the cave, Vael'ehn would have sealed it as well.

Still, it might contain something useful to me.

As I drifted down the tunnel, I was rewarded with a small alcove, something I hadn't expected to see. More cramped than Thaddeus' secret room had been, there was only enough space for a miniature desk and bookshelf, both of which were sparsely covered. Among the writing utensils, odd rocks, and stacks of paper, lay a scroll. Its seal already broken, it had clearly been read and cast to the side. Reaching out with my mental powers, I pulled it to the middle of the desk and unrolled it.

Father,

I have returned from the future and altered it as you requested of me. Mor'dresh and its victim should now return to you as you have deemed necessary. Consider the task completed.

I, however, have decided to amend my own plans for the future. I am no longer interested in overseeing the day-to-day vexations that have befallen our Empire. Two of our Capital cities have already toppled due to continuing battles with the Retrogrades; the last is not far behind. The wall has slowed their progress, but they are persistent and, if nothing else, innovative. No matter what we do, they seem to breach our defenses every time.

I have decided to leave the ruling council in charge of all matters and visit the tournament instead. They have extended a formal invite to me for many years now, and I feel it is finally appropriate for me to accept. Whether or not I will participate or simply spectate, I have not yet decided. Either way, by the time you find this I will have begun my journey.

I no longer wish to be associated with the Empire, Mor'dresh, or any of the changes which will soon come to pass due to the actions we have taken. If you care about my well-being, you will respect my choice and leave me be. I wish you all the best, and whence our paths cross again, I hope it will be under different circumstances than these.

For times to come, for times having passed, and when we've gone, may our accomplishments last.

- V -

V!

This letter was written by the same author; the handwriting is the same!

But Vael'ehn's son is Varek…

Varek is V!

I was stunned. Before me lay proof of something I'd never have considered. It was almost impossible to comprehend. Not only did Varek seem to be interested in a neutral existence, peacefully participating with the other territories, but he also appeared to be interested in aiding us - at least, it appeared that way based upon the contents held within his prior letter to me.

However, the revelation that Varek had traveled to the future, intent on changing events at Vael'ehn's request, only created more questions.

Was Varek the time-wizard?

I hadn't gotten close enough to him on the Long Road to verify his identity for sure, but I felt comfortable making those same assumptions. He had gone to the future to alter it, he had worn black and gold robes, and inside the vision, he had questioned whether or not I was his father spying on him; it was all the proof I needed.

Is this letter the reason Vael'ehn decided to murder his own son?

Had we unwittingly lost an ally in our fight without ever having met him?

That being said, the answer in regard to whose side Varek had been on wasn't as obvious as my first reaction made it seem. Varek had clearly guided me by altering my future, but he had also prevented Jillian from being restored by killing Renault, taking the books we needed, and leaving behind a dangerous tome on Necromancy. It was hard to believe those choices could have been performed with good intentions.

Did he know something I don't?

Were Renault and Jillian casualties for the greater good?

Varek had consciously allowed the sword to escape to the past *and* find its way into Vael'ehn's hands again. That action alone was almost impossible to justify. Even if he *did* wash his hands of the plot, its results were lying on the floor, deceased in the other room. Vael'ehn was out rampaging, and that was, in some part, thanks to Varek. Perhaps he had meant well, but he was dead, and Vael'ehn had won. If I was able to head to the past, I might further reconsider his intent, but the letter changed nothing; my task was still the same.

But how do I travel back in time without guidance?

Ironically, Varek, the person who could have offered the most aid to me regarding time travel, had already died.

Is there someone else I can seek out for information?

The idea of teleporting out of the cavern came to the forefront of my mind. If freed, I knew I could seek out Wenton's help. If anyone, he might be willing to travel to the past, as his future counterpart had already volunteered for such a task.

No, that's a foolish idea; Wenton is likely already dead. I've seen how much Vael'ehn hates him. Wenton will be the first on his list to die. For all I know, with the sword's power, Vael'ehn has passed right through the tournament's barrier and slain everyone inside.

Vael'ehn would waste no time in destroying *all* threats to his revolution. With every ounce of power he had once wielded and then some, he had no reason to hide. For my own safety, I needed to assume everyone I had met so far was already dead. Even if they weren't, it wasn't worth the risk to find out.

And Vael'ehn isn't stupid; he will have placed wards to prevent my escape. Even if I somehow bypass them, he'll be alerted, and I'll be recaptured immediately.

There were no present options left to explore which ended well for me.

I can't escape, I can't hide, I can't fight, and anyone I've met is in Vael'ehn's direct line of fire.

My situation made the need for a portal through time all the more necessary, but I had no reagents and no knowledge of spells, and without a portal room, there would be nothing to guide me.

Drifting out into the main cavern again, I stared down at the shattered crystal, which had obliterated the runic platform below it. Vael'ehn had done a thorough job. He knew I'd use it to escape. Although I was weaker than him, I was also something he couldn't quantify. I might have been easy to control, but I also appeared to be indestructible. He certainly couldn't allow me to run free.

*I know **I** wouldn't want me around if I were in his position.*

I thought back to the crude portal room I had built back on the battlefield.

Can I repair the one in front of me?

My construct was nearly disastrous in quality, but it was still complete, for all practical purposes. In contrast, the one before me was nearly obliterated.

If the portal backfires and proves to be faulty, who knows what will happen to me. Jumping through an erroneous portal might cause my story to appear in one of those books written about horrible Arcane disasters.

But then again, do I even need a portal room?

Someone with real skill wouldn't need such a superfluous contraption to aid in their casting. Mages all over the planet created portals without visiting special rooms or tossing handfuls of crystals on the ground. It was clear the portal room was only for people lacking confidence or experience. Even the mantra I recited on the battlefield had been vague at best.

I might as well have said, "I summon a portal to where Vael'ehn traveled to, because that is what I want to do!"

Immediately the area before me flashed to life, a tear in reality opening before my eyes. The explosion of Magic startled me so badly I launched backward, the idea of Vael'ehn diving through to assault me a second time proving far more terrifying than expected. But the portal snapped shut just as fast as it had formed, my sheer terror likely forcing it closed.

I stared toward the empty space where the portal had opened, shaken by what its appearance meant.

I could have caught up to Vael'ehn instantly…

That might have been my one chance to stop him!

If I had a mouth I would have laughed out loud at my audacity. Jumping in front of Vael'ehn was like playing chicken with a train. I could bluff all I wanted, but when push came to shove, I had no chance of winning. I might have been invulnerable to his powers - at least for the time being - but my own abilities were nothing compared to his. Worse, Vael'ehn frightened me, which took a toll on my ability to perform.

Even so, despite my fears, I had again managed to create a portal just for the sake of needing one. I hadn't questioned whether or not it was possible; I required a portal, and it had appeared.

I can't believe it. I summoned a portal without any aid at all…

But why should I be surprised? Isn't this what I have been preaching to myself all along? Isn't that why Vael'ehn and Wenton praised Jack?

Anything *is possible if a person truly believes.*

My success caused a similar effect to that of the "rock bulbs" just minutes prior. Without realizing it I had inadvertently made another crucial leap in confidence. As my nerves recovered, I found myself less concerned by the creation of portals - even those traversing time itself - and far more interested in where I would choose to go after creating one.

I have to select the most advantageous time period, and that means defeating Vael'ehn before he has the sword, before he becomes invincible.

Thinking back to the time when I had first entered the cave, I considered what my reappearance in the middle of that drama might change. Jack had already been manipulated by Vael'ehn. In fact, Vael'ehn was prepared for me; he knew I'd appear.

It would turn into another situation just like the letter and the Oculus.

Considering those prior attempts to correct the past filled me with fear - fear that the sword might use the reset to its advantage again. Whatever choice I made, Wenton had said Mor'dresh would use *my* memories to learn of the future.

"Objects of Power are semi-aware and can both sense and communicate with one another. Their power ripples through time and space like stones tossed into a pond. The ripples, when close enough, collide, interact, and transfer information."

Sadly that meant my plan *relied* on the sword. Any changes it made to the timeline could result in a person arriving in a different place, taking a different action, even living or dying. I was hoping Mor'dresh, a corrupted artifact, would allow events to proceed as they had, despite showing little prior inclination to do so unless it benefited its situation.

And I would have no idea if it viewed my choices as beneficial until it was too late.

It was a terrible strategy, a desperate strategy, but one not entirely without merit; Wenton of the past had also indicated there was hope.

"In my opinion, it is the sword itself which allowed him to take it…

…My heart wishes to believe there is some piece of Kaldre'shen deep down inside it that isn't corrupted, something which recognized Thaddeus for who he was and what he represented…"

Through me, Mor'dresh would learn of its final corruption, but it would also learn of its potential salvation. It would see our intent, and that could play on whatever small part of it remained uncorrupted. I had no choice, it *had* to work; Vael'ehn destroyed every other avenue to my success.

I just have to pray that the good inside the sword is enough to combat what Vael'ehn wants it to become. If it likes what it sees after Jack dies, we're all done for.

But at what time do I choose to reveal that information to the sword?

I thought back to when we arrived at the citadel. Vael'ehn was already advancing with his troops. He somehow organized an army against us in less than a day and, again, had delayed me when I went through the portal onto the battlefield. Any additional help I could provide would likely be minimal, but I could at least stop him from manipulating my prior self into allowing him admittance.

But he would have a plan in place in case no one spotted him. My meddling in time could cause that battle to end far worse than it had, for all I know.

And what if my portal can't make it through the Citadel's defenses? Vael'ehn himself couldn't do so. I could find myself floating outside, helpless and alone.

I have to be sure. If my plan has potential weaknesses, I have to treat those weaknesses like fatal flaws.

I thought back to the tournament. There were so many people in attendance, I couldn't count them all. Armed with my foreknowledge, and protected by the barrier, we could feign like we were proceeding as usual, act like we were playing into Vael'ehn's hands, but spring our trap on him at the last second when he was most vulnerable.

That's what Wenton had originally wanted before Jack botched his plans.

But how can I distill all the information I've learned? I have so much trouble communicating! It would take me forever to write it all down for them.

And Vael'ehn could simply read Jack's mind and learn of our new strategy!

That means Jack can't interact with Vael'ehn after I explain everything. If he finishes the tournament the way he did, he'll become depressed and want to leave.

What will happen if I reveal that Jack causes an accident? Will they cancel the tournament or force him to continue on?

Will the new test he's subjected to be altered? What happens if he causes another tragedy?

If they cancel the tournament, what will happen to the others? I saw them in my vision; they must be important. I'd be changing their future, too.

No, this is way too complicated!

Vael'ehn had played everything out to his advantage at every turn, and it wasn't just by chance; he was an incredible adversary. There was no reason to believe luck would guide me through my quest, at least not anymore. I needed to devise a plan neither he nor the sword would be capable of manipulating.

How do you fool the person who thinks of everything, while hovering right in front of him?

How do you manipulate a sword which instantly learns how everything plays out?

It would be far more preferable to be removed from their presence altogether, but that would mean-

Again, my mind returned to the idea of creating a clone of myself. I had considered it an inevitable consequence of my time travel - one where the remainder of the timeline counted down with two crystals participating together instead of one. In truth I didn't have to relive *any* of the events I already knew would play out. I could do whatever I wanted, *go* wherever I wanted. My duplicate could be a tool for my benefit by remaining ignorant of my presence.

Why not reside in a different location, participating in a separate activity? How better to fool Vael'ehn and the sword into believing everything is going as planned than to allow it to go as planned while I manipulate other events from the outside?

That being said, I was also well aware my options for communication with others were limited. I certainly couldn't waltz up to the tournament or the citadel and request aid. I'd be risking capture by Mister Haemond or Jacob, who might not understand what I represented.

If I get captured or nullified before managing to share my story, then Jack and my prior self will keep going as they had before.

I considered meeting Wenton when he was alone, but his Magical room might be booby-trapped, and who knew what would happen to anyone it snared. Waiting in the Castle of Confusion was also just as terrifying; it would likely pull me into an endless maze for the rest of my life. And that was only if I could penetrate the tournament's shield in the first place, which seemed doubtful.

The only way to control everything is to work by myself, but how can I possibly manipulate anything without being detected? The only places I've gone so far are trapped, protected, hidden, or accessible by Vael'ehn and the sword!

And even if I do arrive in an isolated, safe area, will the sword remain ignorant?

Wenton said Objects of Power exchange information "when close enough." How far away do I have to be to break that line of communication?

In order to be completely sure, I'd have to arrive at a time when the sword wasn't present at all. And the sword had arrived long before I ever started my quest, before I was even inserted into the chest.

I mean, the only time Mor'dresh wasn't present was after Jack killed Wenton and ran through the portal, leaving me alone with-

Jillian!

The entire time, Jack and I had been so set on saving her, but in reality, we had no idea where she had gone. Better yet, *the sword* had no idea where she had gone. Either by chance or by my own determination to stop Jack, I had followed him instead, but she had traveled to an entirely different location.

Who better to help me? Who better to listen to me? Who better to speak for me? Who better motivated to intercept Jack and convince him to change his plans before he meets his demise?

The idea was brilliant. In one motion I could not only track Jillian down and make sure she was safe, but also tackle the issue of Vael'ehn, keep the sword in the darkness, so to speak, and aid Jack from a completely different angle.

I'd even have Jillian at my side! With her strength and Magical ability, we might make an even more effective team than Jack and I had been!

A team…

A horrible thought occurred to me: I had no idea whose "team" Jillian was on. The few visions I'd experienced involving her had taught me she repeatedly lied to everyone around her. She had not only been tainted by Demons but had also gained access to hidden Magical knowledge - knowledge which could have helped Jack. Instead of sharing that information, however, she kept everything to herself, and I couldn't be sure why.

Can I trust her?

What are her true intentions?

Did she even travel to the same time period we had, or is she currently playing out some other piece of long-forgotten history?

There is only one way to find out: I have to go back to the future, to before she jumps through the portal, and chase after her.

My surroundings changed so fast, it took me a moment to comprehend what happened. I had expected to plan some lengthy conjuring ceremony; some tiresome deed which consumed all of my strength; some overwhelming struggle to transport myself forward to where I had last seen Jillian. Instead, the concept of what I truly wanted had barely occurred to me before playing out in real time without my consent.

In the blink of an eye, I found myself back at Wenton's bookstore. I hadn't created a portal; I had simply *arrived*.

Crying out in her horrible, decrepit voice, Jillian faced a tableau I could never have forgotten in a million alternate timelines. Cackling filled the air as Jack threw back his head and laughed. There, next to the portal, lay Wenton's severed body, blood spreading across the floor.

Immediately I knew I had made a mistake. The gaze of Mor'dresh turned upon me, its intensity threatening to suffocate my senses. I found myself overwhelmed by a sickening feeling brought on by knowledge of my absolute failure.

I've lost. My plan didn't stand a chance. I have to start over from the beginning, again battling a sword armed with knowledge of our future.

That is, if Mor'dresh even allows this to continue now that it knows the truth.

Distraught and terrified, I called out to the sword.

Mor'dresh, please. Ignore me. Ignore what I've done.

Time slowed as Mor'dresh pressed its oily, shadow-laden words into my mind, repeating what it had said minutes before killing Jack.

Much can be seen in the darkness, which cannot be found in the light.

The shadows sense the cries of the lost, which ripple through time in all directions.

Five must die to break the night.

I found myself incapable of managing a response, instead trembling in place, waiting to be seized by the sword's immense power.

The gaze of Mor'dresh drifted away, seizing upon Jack instead. It was no chance happening; the sword had me dead to rights, and it knew it. Yet, somehow, it had chosen to ignore me, chosen to give me the one chance I needed.

But for what reason?

I wasn't daft enough to assume its choice was based on compassion, but I had no time to consider what its motivation might be, as time once again pulled itself from its shadow-induced lethargy.

"Oh, I see now! That was *you* in my backyard," Jack called to the body of Wenton. "Well, half of you, anyway. At least ya didn't stumble through *another* portal!" He continued to laugh at the grim display, but a voice from behind caused him to clamp his mouth shut and scowl.

"Jack, look at me," Jillian commanded, her voice a harsh mixture of necrosis and something not of this world. "Look at me and *stop* this."

Focusing downward, I stared at the back of Jillian's head. Whether for good or evil, she had undergone a horrific transition which had destroyed her life. Seeing her in that state caused a peculiar thought to wend its way into the forefront of my mind.

If Jillian had lived at Jack's house, had stared out at his backyard, had known what lurked there, why did she allow Jack to dig up the chest?

Wouldn't she have known the damage it would cause her?

Did she make a mistake?

Did she think she could overpower the sword?

Seeing her just inches from me, I couldn't resist. I needed more information before making my next decision. Slowly I glided forward, covertly brushing against Jillian's elbow.

With a sound similar to a whip crack, I appeared in front of a doorstep, the scene in front of me shifting without transition. Plain, red, windowless - I had no idea what the door represented or where I had arrived. A diminutive, egg-shaped portal shimmered to life. As soon as it had formed, it expelled a small basket before snapping shut with an audible clap. Less than a foot before me lay the proverbial orphan in a basket.

Screaming in agony or terror, I wasn't sure which, the baby seemed not at all comfortable with its transition from one location to the other. But I wasn't as concerned with the babe as I was with what had accompanied it. Inside the basket, wedged under the corner of a pillow, lay a grimoire I never could have forgotten: *Magic: Manipulation & Mastery.*

Is that Jillian as a baby?

But who would do such a thing? Varek?

Does Jillian even know?

As my mind spun, attempting to decipher the new revelation, the door opened to reveal a young couple, their expressions changing to complete bewilderment as they, too, laid eyes upon the child. But as they did so, a curious thing happened. As if a spell had been cast on all three - and perhaps it had - the baby stopped crying, and the couple's mouths went slack.

Slowly the woman turned to her companion and stared up at him. "Theodore, it's our baby," she stated in a dull voice, devoid of any inflection. "We have such a wonderful child. We are so fortunate to have such a miracle in our lives."

Turning his head toward her, Theodore responded in a similar, emotionless voice. "Yes, Susan, how blessed we are to have such a magnificent child."

The couple retrieved the basket and closed the door, apparently accepting the baby as their own. Left alone on the front step, I motioned toward the door, but had no time to pursue the strange new family, as the vision quickly dissolved around me.

I returned to Wenton's library with a dozen new questions. The purpose behind Theodore and Susan's peculiar actions or Jillian's point of origination would have been incredibly useful details to learn. As usual, the answers I desired most were almost intentionally absent. But the vision *had* informed me of something important: Jillian never found her Magic tome; it was given to her as a baby. That meant she hadn't stumbled into Magic; she was *born* into it.

But whose child is she?

Jack denied Jillian in a dark, corrupt voice. "I am no fool, demon. I will not face you. You will be given no power over me."

Jillian bent her head to the side, trying to catch his distant gaze in hers. "Jack, look at me. *Now*. This isn't you, but you're in there… *somewhere*."

The command was laced with disturbing Magic. I felt myself being compelled to follow her instructions.

Jack also seemed obliged to meet her glare. His vision clearing, he staggered unsteadily before looking back down. "Goodbye, Jill," he whispered.

Jillian, still fighting the effects of the time shift, paused for a moment to steady herself, but the delay was one second too long. Before she could react, Jack turned and leapt through the portal.

Extending down from my past self, the portal had been filled with a wash of dark shadows, images of a once-foreign locale shimmering inside it. From my new perspective, I could see that the man by the campfire had indeed been Vael'ehn. I could see the hill where Jack and I had arrived inside the Kaap'vaal Mountain Range. But within seconds, the portal flashed to purple, transitioning to an abandoned city I had no recollection of.

Is that where Jillian traveled to?

"You keep that damned thing open for me, crystal!" commanded Jillian, launching toward the portal with startling speed.

This time I didn't hesitate; my objective was clear. I gave chase, hitting the portal milliseconds after her. As I did so, I turned my attention up toward my clone. Struggling to hold the portal open, desperate to figure out where Jack and Jillian had gone, he hovered above me. I found myself awash in the emotions I had experienced in the past. Confused, naïve - his abilities were, in many ways, insufficient for what he was about to encounter on the other side.

The sense of how I had once felt gave me pause. I had often considered myself ill-prepared for my entire journey, but staring at my duplicate, I couldn't help but reflect upon how much I had grown since then.

If only he knew what I have become.

Am I now what I need to be?

Have I gained enough power to make a difference?

I suppose only time will tell…

CHAPTER  forty-five R

-LOST LIBRARY-

On the other side of the portal, much to my excitement and relief, I arrived next to Jillian. Behind us the portal exploded into a shimmer of purple sparks. I hadn't had time to think about what might have happened had I popped out next to myself on the hill, or worse, next to Jack at the campfire.

What if Vael'ehn had caught me and thrown me into that lantern...

The thought made me shiver; thankfully, that had not been the case. Whether through luck or design, we had arrived in the abandoned city depicted within the portal. Why it would have brought us to that location, I couldn't say, but at least I had caught up to Jillian.

So this is where she had begun her journey while I was off with Jack.

I wonder how events had turned out for her.

I suppose I'll never know; I've already destroyed that timeline.

I could finally say that Jack, Jillian, and my past self were all alive and relatively safe. For the moment, that was all that mattered. I had bought myself a hefty amount of extra time to learn and grow, given us a second chance, and assured the safety of Jillian in just one move.

For once I feel as if I've done something right.

I wished I could have arrived earlier to save Wenton, but had I the presence of mind to do so, it could have complicated matters. The sword had been determined to force his demise, and my further presence might have created too many variables to allow me to be of any help. Instead, Jack and I were in one location, Jillian and I were in another; we were dividing and conquering.

*Besides, if I manage to repair history, Wenton may never **be** killed.*

Now I just have to find out where and when we are in relation to Jack so I can formulate a timeline to follow.

Turning my attention to our surroundings, I could see we had arrived inside a dusty, drab library, which must not have seen living eyes for a very long time. Tables had been flipped, bookcases knocked over. Hundreds, if not thousands, of books lay strewn about the area, ruined and torn. The entire room had been covered with such a thick layer of dust, it appeared as one monotone color of gray. With every slight movement that Jillian made, her feet kicked up billowing clouds of particles, which sparkled dimly in the moonlight.

High above us stood the remains of tall, shattered, stone-framed windows and broken archway roof supports. The windows and roof, ruined and decomposing, only hinted at their prior design. Rain, snow, and animals were free to come and go as they pleased. It must have been a sight to see long ago but, oddly, it still managed a different type of beauty in a post-apocalyptic kind of way.

"Jack!" Jillian called as she began to pace through the room, kicking up more dust. "Jack?" Turning her attention first toward the floor and then toward the surrounding area, she shook her head; her footprints were the only disturbance marring the otherwise perfect blanketing of dirt and dust. At last, she took notice of my form floating behind her. "He's not here, is he?"

I shook to the left and right.

"Do you know where he went?"

I waggled back and forth in a gesture of uncertainty. While I knew where Jack was, I still didn't know where that location was in relation to us.

"Maybe?" she guessed. "Do you-"

Jillian bumped into a table leg, dislodging an entire coating of debris, which had come to rest on the broken table top. Particles billowed up into the air, blotting out our view. She waved her hands in front of her face in an effort to clear her vision, but she appeared to be immune to coughing due to her condition.

"We should get out of here," she finally concluded.

Realizing that I could *do* something, as opposed to simply floating and watching, I focused on the dust, much as I had in Vael'ehn's tent. Rising from the floor in one massive blanket, it drifted to the edge of the room before rolling itself into a neat pile, far from our feet.

Jillian turned and stared at me, her disconcerting eyes wide in surprise. "Was… that *you?*"

Yes, yes it was.

"Wow! Count me impressed. I had no idea you could do *anything* like that. I thought you just... you know, flew around, more or less."

She hadn't meant to insult me, but the statement stung more than it should have. Even so, I couldn't help but admit she was right; I *had* been a useless, floating piece of glass. But I had grown in my abilities since I started the journey - substantially so.

Focusing on the newly-cleaned stones, which comprised an ornately-designed floor pattern, I considered a new option for communication.

I've purchased us a moment to rest. Before things get too hectic, I should explain myself and what has happened. But I need a form of communication befitting someone of my abilities. If I can travel through time, I can do more than bounce and wiggle.

Imagining a Magical writing utensil before me, I began to draw on the stones a brief summary of what had happened thus far. Slowly but surely, an unseen finger swooped back and forth along the rough surface, revealing before us a complete but brief synopsis of what had transpired in glowing purple letters.

```
             I am not who you think I am.
      I came from after Jack went through portal.
           We went back in time - black portal.
          Met Thaddeus - Thaddeus is Vael'ehn.
           Vael'ehn is evil owner of Sword.
                Sword's name is Mor'dresh.
     Met 3 friends - 2 died because of Mor'dresh.
          Went to tournament - met 3 more friends.
             Found Wenton alive in the past.
        Jack had accident - killed people - sad.
        Jack won tournament - went to Citadel.
            Had battle with Vael'ehn's army.
        Jack trapped by Vael'ehn - went crazy.
              Jack killed more people.
            Jack murdered by Vael'ehn.
              Vael'ehn took Mor'dresh.
          I went back to future to find you.
           Followed you through purple portal.
              Not sure to where or when.
       We need to find tournament before it ends.
             Jack and Wenton will be there.
```

A bit hasty and brief, but much better than another Yes and No session.

Her brow wrinkling, Jillian studied the writing for nearly a minute before responding. "So, you followed Jack through the portal and ended up somewhere back in time. You then met Vael'ehn, who lied to you about his identity. And if I understand, you ran into a *past* version of Wenton, but a lot went wrong after that, and Jack died. Then you went back in time again, from your perspective at least, returning to the future. You followed me through the portal I chose instead. Now, we've traveled somewhere - a different location than Jack, possibly a different time too. But you're interested in making your way back to that place you first went so we can meet up with him and Wenton there. Is that right?"

I scrawled "Yes" and "No" upon the floor before tapping the *Yes* section. That was, word for word, exactly what had happened, and I couldn't help but be amused by her summary. My message had been brief, but her deduction skills were astute.

Now let's hope we're in the same time period as Jack.

Jillian frowned. "I can't believe Jack *died*. If it wasn't for you telling me we still had a chance, I… I think I'd have just given up. But I have to say, that was smart of you. You two failed, but you decided to make another attempt by finding where *I* went instead of battling it out with the sword." She gasped. "But you… you must have created another *you*. Do you understand what you did? You're *also* with Jack right now!"

I again tapped down on *Yes*. I was fully aware of the implications my actions had wrought.

Jillian shook her head. "*Wow*. I mean, thank you. I don't know what that means for your life, but if you hadn't been willing to deal with those consequences, Jack would still be dead right now. That means everything to me. I would hug you if I could."

I wasn't about to decline. Staring upward into her ghastly yet somehow beautiful eyes, I found myself lost in their gaze. Gliding forward, I met both Jillian's embrace and a vision - two things I eagerly wanted to experience from her.

Transported away from where I desperately desired to linger, my eyes opened to reveal a small office. I had appeared behind the shoulder of a woman I hadn't seen before, at least not from that angle. In front of us the door opened, and Theodore and Susan, Jillian's unwitting foster parents, walked in with her in their arms.

"Hello, you two!" exclaimed the woman below me. "I see the family is getting along great as usual," she added with cheer evident in her voice.

The pair nodded, seeming only slightly muted by the spell's handiwork. "Yes, it is. We love our daughter," they said in unison.

Seemingly unconcerned by the strange tandem response, the woman began to rummage through a drawer full of folders.

Is she affected by the same spell?

Tapping a stack of papers on the table, she laid them out before the couple. "Well, as you know, the requisite year has passed, and both your home review and background checks have come back to me with no issues listed. All we need are your signatures here, here, and here, and we'll be all set!"

The pair nodded and signed the paperwork eagerly, if not a little rigid and mechanical.

Leaning backward, they both nodded. "We are a family now, as was intended," they again said in unison.

"Yes, you are, and no one can separate you!"

As I stared down at the signed paperwork, trying to figure out what purpose the Magically-induced adoption had been implemented for, the brief vision faded around me.

Finding myself back in Jillian's embrace, I slowly drifted away to study her again. The two visions I had witnessed were easy to interpret; someone had seemingly manipulated her since she was born, and I was slowly gaining a better perspective on what had happened. Whoever transported Jillian to Theodore and Susan's house was clearly intent on guiding not only her but those around her.

And considering the book she was transported with, that means the responsible party is deeply involved with demons.

The obvious answer was Varek. In a prior vision I had witnessed him explaining to Renault that the changes to Jillian needed to happen. He was clearly a proponent of her zombie-like features coming into play. That being said, Varek didn't exactly exude demonic qualities, either. It was entirely plausible that he had no idea of Jillian's run-in with demons before she was attacked by Mor'dresh.

Perhaps, in a way, he was manipulated, too.

I couldn't help but feel like we had all been manipulated into shaping Jillian's life. The contrast between how she had once appeared and what she had turned into was startling. We had gained some progress on restoring her, but a pair of attempts to rectify events by sending notes to the past had degraded those results. She was not quite as "alive" as she should have been.

Worse, the effects brought on by the woman that Jillian had consumed in the Passageway seemed to be wearing off already. The fire of life still burned within her odd eyes, but slowly her body was transitioning back to a corpse. Part Magical zombie, she would be required to consume another victim soon to retain her self-awareness. However, in doing so, she would further aid her conversion into demonhood by feeding her body the souls it craved.

When she finishes transforming into a demon, will she continue to decompose?

My gut told me *no*. She appeared to be suffering from one affliction which would cure the other in time. When it completed its work, however, I had no idea what I would be left with.

Will the demon side of her consume her human memories?

Wenton had indicated as much in a prior reality.

Wrinkling her brow, Jillian gave me a strange look, as if something had just occurred to her. "You know, you said you traveled to the past through that portal, and you clearly participated in a long series of events with Jack once there, but something just hit me: the future is still the same." She frowned. "Or have I changed since you last saw me? Was I normal before you traveled back?"

I couldn't help but silently stare into Jillian's uncertain eyes. The question was one that, somehow, I hadn't considered; one that could have ruined everything I intended. I had left Vael'ehn rampaging across the countryside, set on destroying the entire planet. For some unknown reason, his plans hadn't come to pass. Not only that, everything was as it had appeared - or was at least *very* similar to how it had appeared - when I left the first time.

But how is that possible?

I had made a mistake - a *horrible* mistake. I had considered my plan a success, yet I had missed the biggest pitfall of all. From that point onward I knew I had to be more careful, more masterful, with my strategy. Luckily for me, someone had saved the day, someone had taken care of the weakness in my plan, and I only knew of one person who would have gained the knowledge to do so.

Myself.

Before traveling through the portal with Jillian, I had felt strong emotions as I stared upward at the prior version of myself. I had interpreted them as stemming from the remembrance of a past experience, but that might not have been the case.

Wenton indicated my crystal was an Object of Power. What if I was receiving the thoughts and emotions of my duplicate as I passed under him?

What if he, too, received information from me, just as the sword had?

What if, armed with that knowledge, he was able to counteract Vael'ehn's plans - at least as far as preserving our standard timeline was concerned - and we were already living out its results from his intervention in the past?

The truth was, I had no way of learning the answer, nor was I even certain if that was how the past and future interacted with one another. I was beginning to see how complicated time-travel could become, but I had more pressing matters to tend to than speculating on the cause of something that had already taken place.

If my duplicate is involved, I have to trust he is off doing his part without creating any impediments to my success. It's up to me to correct the rest of the timeline. I have to protect Jillian and bring her to meet up with Jack and the others.

No matter what I had done before, no matter how Vael'ehn had been defeated, Jillian's corruption remained, and Magic was still missing from the future. I had begun to figure out how our Magically-devoid existence came to pass, but that didn't bring me any closer to correcting it.

Righting those wrongs will bring history back into alignment.

Drifting down to the floor, I began to write.

You were the same before I traveled back.

The other version of myself must have countered Vael'ehn's plans or contacted someone who could help maintain the timeline.

The rest is up to us.

Jillian stared down at the words. "Wow, this-" She shook her head. "This feels like I'm really late to the game. So, you're saying Vael'ehn will be defeated, after he gains the sword, through some action taken by a duplicate of yourself, but only because you've traveled back to the future and just created him? But we're already experiencing those effects even though…" She shook her head again, as if she was having trouble picturing such an action. "Wait, that's too much. Don't bother explaining that right now. What… what are you setting out to do with me, now that *we're* in the past?"

She doesn't understand how important this part of the plan is.

```
        We will save Jack. We will heal you.
        We will bring Magic back to the future.

        And we will make sure those changes
        don't prevent Vael'ehn from dying.
```

Jillian managed a smile. "So we won't need to achieve anything difficult, then," she teased.

Turning her attention to the abandoned room, she let out a thoughtful "hmm" sound as she began to study her surroundings.

"I wonder why we were brought *here* though. You said there were two places depicted inside that portal you made, and Jack passed through the other one. Was the other version of you responsible for sending us here?"

I touched down on *No.* The truth was, I couldn't be sure, but I felt certain that, if a version of me had been involved in the choosing of locations, I'd have left myself with something more than a heap of unanswered questions.

Perhaps if we go outside or locate a map, I can find my bearings. The Tournament is the most popular event in the world; if this time period is correct, it must be documented on maps.

"Maybe some of these books are Magical," Jillian considered, interrupting my thoughts. "They might be able to tell us where we are."

She pulled the Apperception Oculus out from under her shirt and held it up to her eye. It was, of course, the one she had removed from Renault; Jack had worn the one we sent back through time. I had forgotten about the duplicate. It hadn't been long since those events had occurred, but it certainly felt like it. So much had happened since then, it seemed as if I were recalling a distant memory.

This is good luck. If we hadn't sent the Oculus back in time, Jillian wouldn't have had one for her own use. She would be completely lost, with only a mute to guide and communicate for her.

I shuddered at the thought of having to navigate the world around us without an Oculus to translate speech. I hadn't needed one myself, clearly due to my form, but copying down everyone's words for translational purposes would have been far too impractical.

Good luck indeed!

Jillian stalked around the room, snooping about with the Oculus pressed to her face. It twitched back and forth, mimicking the movements of her actual eye. Lifting tipped bookcases and righting overturned tables, she explored every nook and cranny. Even so, she came to the same conclusion my own Magical vision already had.

"There's nothing useful here, is there?" she queried, glancing over in my direction.

I touched down on *No* before gliding to a pair of giant doors, which marked the only way into or out of the room, save for levitation. Made of wide, solid planks of wood, they were taller than any man and double arched at the top. Riveted metal filigree, now heavily rusted and pitted from ages of neglect, ran up and down their length in large, spiraling curves.

Jillian followed up from behind, her hand extended. She had intended on grabbing one of the ancient rings hanging from the door, but her boot caught the edge of something resting on the floor. Turning her gaze downward, she eyed a thin book, which appeared far newer than the ruined ones littering the room behind her. Bending down, she picked it up and wiped off its cover. A title had been hastily scratched into the leather.

"*The Fall of Vael'curion Dahr'krest*, by Varek'ehn Dahr'krest," she read aloud.

Jillian motioned to toss it to the side, but I swept down, mentally snatching the book from her grasp. She may not have known who Vael'curion or Varek'ehn were, but *I* certainly did.

Soon, Varek will be murdered and Jack will take on his identity, but for the time being, he is still very much alive.

Vael'curion was also the very person whom Vael'ehn used to be. The book before us seemed to tell the tale of Vael'ehn's descent into madness, possibly from Varek's perspective. If I had let Jillian pass it by, I may have been ignoring the most important clue we would find on how to defeat him.

But why is it here?

It struck me as strange that Varek had not only written a book on his own father, but that it had been directly in our path, inside a room we had been teleported to by Mor'dresh. In my experience so far, events like that couldn't possibly be a coincidence.

Varek must have written his name on the cover for a reason. Was it to let us know we could trust him, show he was working against his father?

How would he have known that I would be the one to read it, that I'd go back in time after following Jack? Or was this meant only for Jillian?

Is he working against the sword by countering its decision to follow Vael'ehn?

Yet Mor'dresh let me pass through Jillian's portal. It must have wanted me to come here.

We need to read this book before moving another inch!

Jillian gave me a strange look as she watched the book bob up and down in front of her. "This is important, then?"

Pushing the book toward her, I opened the cover to reveal the first page.

Nodding, she began to read the quickly but ornately scrawled text.

"Vael'curion Dahr'krest, it is with heavy heart and hesitant hand that I speak these words," began Ty'berus Forensound, leader of the Forgotten Order. "I hereby strip you of your rank and your power. I cast you out of our presence and sentence you to..." Ty'berus took a deep breath and sighed. "...death by surceasance." The verdict finished, he slammed his fist against the podium.

In response, five peers surrounded Vael'curion, their faces shrouded from view. "It is done," they called out in unison from under their hoods.

Vael'curion fell to his knees as a powerful ward was drawn in the air by each, leeching his power from him like blood seeping from a thousand wounds. On his forehead they drew a single symbol, preventing him from using Magic ever again.

He felt weak, alone, and scared. The stripping of power was far more crushing to one of the Order than even the sentence of death. Anyone could use Magic in those times, and members of the Order were no exception; each of them had been imbued with power far greater than the general populace could even conceive of. To be stripped of that power was to be left with less than nothing.

As the five turned and took a step away from him, most of them his friends just days prior, Vael'curion began to weep.

"How could so much have happened to me in such a short period of time?" he thought to himself. *"Just days ago, I was the favored candidate in the upcoming election for the Ruling Council, and now... now I am nothing."*

Two days prior, Vael'curion awoke from a nightmare with a start. His clothes sopping wet with sweat, he swung his feet over the edge of his bed. A series of heavy breaths followed. Wiping his face, he tried to calm himself. What a horrible dream it had been, indeed.

He had imagined he was leading a squadron of troops through a fiery green portal to wage war against a legion of Dghem'oni battling across a ruined, desolate world. Black ichor and limbs flew from Dghem'onic corpses as the Order carved a path of destruction through their ranks. It seemed there was no stopping the group of men, but before long the war began to take its toll.

Soon he found himself alone, his fellow companions either slain or separated from him. The Dghem'oni advanced further and further until he had neither room to swing his sword nor the mental strength to cast a spell. Forced to the ground, he cried out for help as they began to tear him apart.

Just as the light of life began to fade from his eyes, as if responding to his plea, the Dghem'oni halted their attack. Vael'curion looked upward to see who his savior was, but what he beheld drained the blood from his face.

There before him stood their commander - a giant, black-skinned abomination with long wicked horns, and claws so razor sharp, just a prick might send him to his grave. The Dghem'on lord threw his head back and cackled as looming, ominous wings unfurled behind him, blotting out the sun.

Vael'curion boldly addressed the monster, despite his waning strength. "You may slay me, Dghem'on, but our Order *will* find you - find you and destroy your kind!"

The Dghem'on lord's laugh grew even louder. It bent down so their faces were only a few feet apart. Raising its taloned hands to his head, it pulled off a great ebon helmet, revealing a hideous mockery of a human face. Large white fangs stretched upward from its grinning mouth, contrasting with its blackened skin. Burning green orbs, devoid of pupils, bored into Vael'curion's own eyes, chilling his soul.

"Slay you?" the Dghem'on lord responded in a deep voice, its distorted mouth so full of sharp teeth it had trouble pronouncing the Xahl'thari words. "Why *ever* would we slay... our own flesh and blood?"

Grabbing the fallen warrior by his helmet, the Dghem'on lord summoned a small, enchanted piece of fruit. Pressing it into Vael'curion's mouth, it forced the poor man's jaw to close until he had no choice but to swallow. Grinning, the Dghem'on lord pulled Vael'curion up to its blackened face.

"Savor it, warrior. It is the last of the harvest," it said menacingly.

Astoundingly, Vael'curion's wounds started to close, and his bones began to mend. But his mouth became dry, and a hunger formed inside him.

Carrying Vael'curion back to the small, flickering portal his men had come through, a pair of Dghem'oni pressed him through just seconds before it blinked out of existence. As he fell to the ground on the other side - the only Xahl'thari warrior to have made it back safely - he heard the Dghem'on lord's voice call to him.

"Only I can show you how to relieve your hunger, warrior. I will see you… again…"

Vael'curion sat on the edge of his bed, his eyes growing wide in horror and recognition of who the fallen warrior was. He knew it had been no simple dream; not only was it far too real, but it also explained the horror he had beheld as a child. It was a vision of his father, who had died when Vael'curion was very young.

When he was just a boy, a group from the Order arrived in his village and burst into the home he shared with his recently widowed, pregnant mother. His father had gone missing weeks prior. He had died in glorious battle, or so she had told him. The Order, however, had shared a different version of events, claiming that she had been tainted by Dghem'onic forces. The creature residing inside her was an unnatural heir, one who was prophesied to bring about a scourge which would not only destroy the Order but the entire planet.

So it was, before Vael'curion's own bleary, tear-filled eyes, that the Order bound his mother with a series of spells and removed her from existence. Horrified, Vael'curion turned to run, only to find himself captured by the powerful hands of Lord Ty'berus.

Regarding the young boy, Ty'berus told him of the might and wrath of an evil horde called *the Dghem'oni*. Although once a noble race of creatures, they had consumed pure Magic, making them wildly powerful. Over time, however, their continued consumption had distorted and perverted them, erasing all signs of what they had once been. Forever addicted, their only purpose was to consume Magic and destroy that which they could not devour.

If left unchecked, the Dghem'oni's consumption would allow their numbers to increase, slowly destroying all who remained uncorrupted. The only force keeping them from succeeding in that very goal was a small group who fought valiantly against them. A secret agency, known only in whispers and stories, fought an invisible war against a foe that most had no belief in.

The Forgotten Order, as they had come to be known, had slain every Dghem'on who managed to arrive on the planet Xahl. And it was because of the Order's effectiveness that the Dghem'on lord had come up with a sinister plan. His forces would lure some of the Order through a portal, leading to their home world of Dgh'em. In doing so, many would perish, but one simple objective would prove its worth: the capture of a Xahl'thari man. That man would be beaten, broken, and forcibly fed Magic, making him dependent on its power. Then, he would be sent back to Xahl to unwittingly corrupt the Order from the inside.

That man had been Vael'curion's father, Thar'ceron, who had once fought for the Forgotten Order, but had since been discharged due to an odd sickness. Unbeknownst to Vael'curion's mother, Thar'ceron had been destroyed just minutes prior by the Forgotten Order upon finally learning the truth: his sickness had been brought on by a dependency on the consumption of Magic.

The Order had recently learned the truth from a captured and tortured Dghem'on, who had come through a portal to locate Thar'ceron. The Dghem'on reluctantly divulged that Vael'curion's father was prophesied to have an heir who would not only bring about the end of the Forgotten Order, but also unite the Dghem'oni in victory over the Xahl'thari. The story, of course, did not sit well with the Order, and they moved swiftly to thwart it, killing his mother and, in turn, his unborn baby brother, who they believed was the heir.

But Ty'berus saw something special in Vael'curion's eyes that day. He vowed to raise him as his own and teach him a multitude of secrets, ensuring that even after he passed away, no Dghem'on would survive to threaten the Xahl'thari again. And so Vael'curion returned with Ty'berus and the others of the Order to grow and train to become one of them.

At first Vael'curion did so in a secret bid to avenge his mother and brother, but as time progressed, he realized the folly of his thinking. The Order had been correct to destroy his mother and the abomination growing inside of her. Had it been him in Ty'berus' place, he swore he'd have done the same; the Dghem'oni were too much of a threat to the Xahl'thari and their planet to allow them to live.

But that ordeal had taken place many years ago, and both Ty'berus and Vael'curion were old men, having lived past ninety and sixty years respectively. Even so, Vael'curion barely looked to have passed twenty years, and despite whispers to the contrary, most people assumed his youth to be a blessing brought about by an unfaltering faith in his Magical abilities. In fact, Vael'curion's appearance was the main reason he was being considered for promotion to the Ruling Council: they all considered him a good omen.

However, upon experiencing the nightmare he had just witnessed, Vael'curion suspected otherwise. He leapt from his bed and raced to the lavatory. There, he lit a candle and peered down into the still, glass-like water of the wash basin. Staring back at him was the same face he had seen in his dream - a mockery of a human with fangs and burning eyes. Vael'curion screamed at the visage he beheld, but in an instant it was gone, leaving behind only unnatural, green-tinged, brooding eyes.

Members of the Order poured into the small room to find out what had happened. One by one, as they gazed into his possessed orbs, they clasped their hands over their mouths and gasped in horror at what had befallen their friend and comrade.

Soon, Ty'berus himself arrived. His shoulders slumping, he released a drawn-out sigh. "When we sought Thar'ceron out those many years ago, he told me his eldest son had not been tainted. It would seem the truth has been shaded from my gaze, as I have raised you as my own. I do not blame him; he did what he could to save his lineage. What happened to him must have transpired years before we assumed it had." He shook his head. "It matters not. What was not completed then will be completed now."

Vael'curion was pained by what he heard. "Ty'ber, what do you speak of, my friend? You are first to me, even before my own father. On this very night, I have learned that there is a hidden danger inside of me, a dark force yearning to consume, but we can *surely* cleanse it or, at the very least, use it to our advantage. You and I possess the power within us to do so! You know what I believe. It is still *I* who stand before you. See me for who I am."

"Of course I see you for who you are!" bellowed Ty'berus. "Do you think this does not tear at me from within? It matters not whom you have been, nor what you have done, but what you will become. There is no stopping this now; it has awakened inside you! Before long you will forgo your convictions and lose your memories. The teachings you have learned in this secret place are clear and absolute; you know what you are and what *must* be done."

Vael'curion had no way to refute the words which had just been spoken to him. Despite slaying dozens of Dghem'oni throughout his years, he appeared to have been infected by the sickness his father carried. He, too, should be put in chains. For that reason, he did not struggle when they summoned Magical restraints and led him away to await trial and sentencing for his heritage.

It was by those convictions that Vael'curion still refused to struggle as they led him to his death. But as he walked slowly toward the gallows, a dark, familiar voice spoke up inside his head.

*"Are they any better than **you**? Those who profess to be **pure**, slaughtering a pregnant woman, only to leave her **child** behind? Slaughtering a hero because of his **heritage**?"*

By exhaustion or delirium, Vael'curion regarded the voice out loud, as if it were a person walking next to him. "They are not better; they are just and righteous, and they will protect us from evil."

*"Vael'curion... were you aware, neither your brother nor your mother contracted the hunger to consume Magic? They were both **innocents**. They were slain **unjustly**."*

Tears welled in Vael'curion's eyes as he listened to the revelation, but he pushed them back. "Then they died in my place, and I am guilty for far more than my sentence. I deserve a thousand deaths for what I truly am."

The voice only grew louder. *"How many **women**... how many **children**... how many people have you **saved** by your skill with a weapon... by your **faith** in Magic? They admit that you are **exceptional**... that you should be a **leader** amongst them... that you are the **best** of them. How many innocents will now **die** because you are no longer there to **protect** them?"*

Upon hearing the words, Vael'curion stopped. The men holding his chains tugged in a vain attempt to force him forward.

"Stop talking to yourself and move!" they growled.

"It does not matter," Vael'curion whispered. "The evil live, the good die. The good live, the evil prevails anyway. I am living proof of that. Everything is hopeless."

The voice continued on and so did Vael'curion, proceeding toward his death.

*"There is no **hope**. There is no **good**. There is no **evil**. There is only the **truth**, the power of **life** and the power of **death**. Those who will **live**, and those who will **die**."*

Vael'curion walked up the steps to the middle of a pentagon-shaped frame. Crafted from imbued stones and carved with intricate Arcane runes, it had one purpose: he would be Magically vaporized, completely erased from existence. Nothing, no one, would be able to pull his soul back from the dead, for it would no longer exist on any plane of reality.

Staring upward at the framework he was being bound to, Vael'curion closed his eyes. "Do I deserve to live?" he asked the voice.

*"**You** are the one who will decide **their** fates. You will live to deal **death** to those who **deserve** death. On this day, you have been given a **gift** from your **god**. You now hold the power to **destroy** within your body. Open your eyes and breathe deep of that which you have become."*

Vael'curion opened his eyes as the restraints were being tightened around him. Corrupted Magic - Magic that was not of the world in which he lived - began to dance within his body, sparking through his muscles and crackling along his fingertips. Feeling the power consume the wards which had restricted his abilities, he laughed out loud.

As the platform swung away, Vael'curion was left to hang in mid-air, the Magically-enhanced bindings pulling taught as his weight bore down on the device. But just as the runes began to glow, his restraints rotted, cracked, and crumbled to dust. Falling through the air, he landed on the ground, the impact shaking the earth around him.

The gathered group of Order members gasped at what had just taken place.

Calmly Vael'curion stood up and addressed them. "You have all been judged by your god - judged and found *guilty*," he announced in a voice not altogether his own.

Raising his hands, the stone pentagon levitated into the air above him. Moments later it shattered. Shards of glowing stone flew in all directions, impaling those who weren't swift enough to create shields. Following after, a dark wave of Magic exploded outward from Vael'curion. The entire crowd screamed as their skin was incinerated by shadowy flames, their bodies burning until all that stood was a macabre group of lifeless, desiccated skeletons. In unison the screaming stopped, and the bones clattered to the ground in heaps.

Vael'curion stood at the center of the destruction, laughing, the only one left alive. He turned to see the lifeless bones of Ty'berus on the ground several paces from him. Walking over, he picked up the blackened skull and stared into its empty eye sockets.

"I am coming for everyone you have ever loved, my old friend. Your wrongs will be their wrongs. Your sin will be their sin. None shall know the history of the Forgotten Order. They have *all* been judged and found guilty."

Dropping the skull on the ground, Vael'curion crushed it with his boot before walking away. Pausing for a moment, he turned to regard the carnage behind him.

"Whom shall I worship for my salvation?" he called out.

One word returned to his ears like a whisper on the wind: *"Roth'Roh'Kah..."*

Suddenly, Vael'curion was overcome by a presence behind him. Turning, he beheld a vision of the giant, sinister Dghem'on lord from his dreams. Kneeling, he shook in terror.

"P-p-please let me serve, my Lord. I am not yet ready to leave this place. All who killed my family have been judged, as you said they would be. I have work to do. Let me slay them all in your name."

"I am Roth'Roh'Kah, leader of a thousand legions, Consumer of Magic, Destroyer of Worlds, Terror in the Darkness. You will pave the way for my glorious arrival and eternal reign!"

Vael'curion fell to his knees, his forehead touching the ground. "Yes, my Lord. I will do as you say."

"I have foreseen the future, my son. There shall be a great tribulation on your planet. A race of giants will blanket your shores for as far as you can see. They will wipe out all who reside here like a plague. You shall say nothing. You will wait until their arrival and stay your hand as they lay waste to the masses.

"Your race will hide like cowards and run to those around them who still hold power. They will turn to you to lead them against their foes. Play upon their desperation. They will give you anything... **everything**. *In their time of greatest need, they will craft a weapon unlike anything you have ever seen, and you will accept it graciously.*

"Lead your race to their new land, and destroy your enemies, for they will be as fodder beneath your boot heel. Use the power you have gained on this day to sway your weapon's will. Bend it until it has been reforged in your likeness. Let your people become weak and supple in their following years. Extend your life beyond what all others have been given. Consume all around you until you have gained what is required to prepare the way for my glorious arrival."

Vael'curion stared up in awe as he beheld his new god.

"Yes, my Lord. I, Vael'curion Dahr'krest, shall usher in your reign."

The Dghem'on lord reached down and cast a spell upon Vael'curion's forehead.

"At the proper time, you shall resign the name of Vael'curion, for you will not lead your people through danger. You shall be known as Vael'ehn, for you will bring about the End of those you have led. Now go forth into this world and remember not your history. Remember not what has taken place here. Remember not the tasks I have given you.

"As the future reveals itself, the convictions planted in your heart will compel you to act as you have been told. You will be convinced the course you have taken will culminate in the correction of a flawed and destined-to-fail regime. That your actions will result in the rebirth of your race. That the civilization guided by your hand will be powerful, pure, and eternal."

Vael'ehn fell backward, landing upon the ground. With his impact, an immense blastwave of Shadow Magic radiated out from him, tearing through the entire city. The earth shook and buildings dissolved. Fires erupted all around. In seconds the secret city of the Forgotten Order was razed to the ground, and all who had once lived within its walls were wiped from existence.

His eyes closing, Vael'ehn fell into a coma. There he lay for days, surrounded by rubble, while his body slowly recovered from the immense effort.

At long last, dazed and confused, he awoke and stumbled to his feet. Gazing out at the scorched, barren earth around him, he gasped.

"What… what is this place? What happened here?

CHAPTER

forty-Six

-COLLAPSED COLOSSEUM-

Jillian snapped the book shut. Unease filling her eyes, she stared down at the cover, tracing the hastily-scrawled writing with her finger. Strangely, the book had taken on a vivid, almost vision-like quality as she had read the words, at least in my eyes. To her, however, it appeared to have been nothing but a story.

"Is this true? *Was* Vael'ehn's father turned into a demon? Did he also-" Her eyes flitted toward the mark on her forearm, giving her pause.

I neglected to answer either of her questions for I, too, had been stunned by the revelation. It appeared Vael'ehn *had* been tainted by the demon from my visions. Having already met the man, he clearly hadn't been transformed into a demon, but that also seemed to be part of Roth'Roh'Kah's plan - to keep him ignorant until the appropriate time.

*Vael'ehn has not only threatened the safety of the entire planet but has killed Jack and many others. Even so, having his mind manipulated into the service of a demon while being kept unaware of the horrible event; having his genes mutated into a corrupted state... that means Vael'ehn is... **a victim?***

I couldn't bring myself to comprehend the enormity of it all; one brief story had changed my perspective in a matter of minutes. The campfires where Vael'ehn had laughed and cracked jokes, the attempt to save Jack's life, the comments after Jack's death when Vael'ehn admitted to liking Jack - those could very well have been fractured parts of his real personality creeping through.

In addition, Vael'ehn's corruption meant Varek could have been, and likely was, tainted as well. He would have realized such a story would incriminate him, but he had shared the information anyway. Announcing his identity as the author must have therefore been intentional.

But why this location in particular?

Varek, like his father, was clearly methodical, and his actions premeditated. Both the book and the pair of us had been left there for a specific reason, and I had to know why.

Even more peculiar is the spelling of-

Jillian gave me an impatient look. "*Was* or *wasn't* he a demon?" she repeated.

Her words almost forcefully pulling me from my next topic of consideration, I couldn't help but feel compelled to answer. Swooping down, I touched *No*.

"So he had a tainted family tree and was being manipulated, but hadn't changed." She considered for a moment. "Have you met the author?"

I answered in the affirmative despite the truth. I didn't know Varek, but I knew *of* him. Jack had used his identity, I had read two pieces of his correspondence, and Vael'ehn had killed him.

Might this book be the real reason Varek was killed by his own father?

Had he divulged sensitive information regarding Roth'Roh'Kah, which had somehow triggered a subconscious defensive reaction by Vael'ehn?

"When did you meet him?" Jillian queried. "You didn't write his name on the floor. Was he one of the friends you met? Why would he leave this book here? Or was it someone else? And how would they have gotten here before us? For that matter, how did they even know we'd be coming here?" Her inquiries went on and on without a pause for me to catch up.

I immediately regretted the answer that had led her down that path. Jack had always asked blunt, almost singular questions. Yes and No were often accepted at face value. Jillian, on the other hand, seemed sharp, contemplative, and unable to accept basic, one-word answers. Anything I left out or failed to clarify was something which would clearly be brought up time and time again. I had a feeling my communication skills were about to be tested.

My mind drifted back to Varek's account. Although Jillian was still focused on his agenda, I had moved on. She had missed what might prove to be the most important clue written within the story - not because she had ignored it, but because she hadn't been privy to something Vael'ehn had let slip in my prior timeline.

In his story regarding the history of our race, Vael'ehn briefly made mention that the *Earth* was called Dgh'em. He said the Xahl'thari would come to adopt it as their home world. They would change the name of their race to *the Dghem'oni*, which would later be replaced by *Human*. Though, he indicated the Xahl'thari hadn't begun to make that transition yet.

Jillian assumed logically that the word *Dghem'on* was an older version of the word *Demon*; they did sound similar, after all. Truthfully I had almost passed over the word choice myself without thinking twice. But I could not force myself to move forward while assuming it was a coincidence.

Why then would Varek's story refer to demons as Dghem'oni if the two had nothing in common with each other?

Did the Dghem'oni originate on Earth and assault the Xahl'thari through portals from here?

Is that how the Gor'tier chose their next target and eventual home? Did they learn of the Forgotten Order's struggles, travel here, and destroy the Dghem'oni?

It would certainly be ironic for the Gor'tier to defeat the greatest enemy of the Xahl'thari, inadvertently giving the Xahl'thari time to recuperate, rebuild, and seek revenge.

Then, to have future generations of Xahl'thari adopt that name after identifying Dgh'em as their home, inadvertently mocking the Gor'tier's greatest mistake for the rest of time...

Well, that would certainly be a suitable and hilarious end to that story!

Of course I couldn't help but speculate, but I felt I was so close to the truth. I was just missing a couple crucial details which would have allowed me to unearth another secret buried within our past. Sadly, I didn't have time to pantomime every one of my theories to Jillian, nor was I about to cover every inch of the room in scrawled purple writing. I decided I'd figure out more on my own before bringing her up to date.

Drifting over to the door, I knocked on it several times.

Time to go.

Jillian stared at the door and then back at me. "You don't know? Or maybe it's just too much to say? Is it something I need to know right now, before we leave?"

In response I simply knocked on the door again; we had to keep moving. I had no idea how far away from Jack we had been placed, and I needed to find out before I informed her of anything else.

Sighing, Jillian reached for the weathered ring, which had been hammered to the face of the door with large, mottled rivets. Pulling backward, she strained against the ancient, rusted hinges. Slowly the door groaned and began to move as she forced it against its will, her unnatural strength overcoming its stubbornness.

I expected to see the world outside as the door crept inward, but we were instead greeted by a dark wall of stone - evidence that we were in what remained of a much larger building. Moving out through the doorway, I took it upon myself to illuminate the area. Accepting that I needed no light source to absorb beforehand, I created my own brilliance from nothing.

The wall in front of us was revealed to be part of a truly massive hallway, which led left and right from our position. With a vaulted roofline, rivalling the height of even the most ornate cathedrals, the hall extended onward for what seemed like forever until it curved enough to pass out of sight.

Situated along both walls, standing opposite each other, were tall, dark pillars, most of which had toppled to the ground. Positioned in between them were statues of what could only be described as champions - giant stone representations of various beings in triumphant poses. Most had fallen or been crushed by adjacent pillars, but a few still remained.

Jillian walked up to one such statue. The being depicted had been so well covered in unusual armor that it was hard to tell what he or she might have looked like. In its right hand hung a giant shield, some sort of repurposed creature's shell. Five rows of three spikes protruded from its dented surface.

No doubt it was used offensively just as much as defensively.

In its left hand, the statue extended a giant weapon. I had deemed Captain Jacob's sword almost comical in size when I had first seen it, but the statue's armament put it to shame. Even stranger, the weapon appeared to be organic, possibly made from the rippled carapace of a colossal bug. A disturbing, alien-like eyeball bulged from its center.

I wonder if it moved around like an Oculus...

Jillian walked up to a plaque at the base of the statue and wiped off what had to be centuries of dust and debris. Squinting through the Oculus, she read aloud.

Citadel Vizier Var'lok Klakk'Klarn
- Xxokk'kkla -

Widely hailed as the only champion to rise from the Xxokk'kkla, Var'lok won fifteen bouts in the Ring of Blood before finally being defeated and slain by Mul'bock the Bone-Breaker.

We recognize Var'lok's life and gladiatorial accomplishments with this statue. May he forever be remembered with honor.

The statues seemed to be representative of people - or beings - who had died in ritual gladiatorial combat of some sort. There may have been a gladiator arena close by, but considering the condition of the hall, I doubted it was still in use. And I felt that was a good thing; after inspecting the immense suit of armor that Var'lok had donned, I in no way wanted to run into Mul'bock the Bone-Breaker.

After scanning through the text again, and appearing to re-read it in her head, Jillian spoke up.

"Zoke-cloke-cla? Zo-cluck-cluck-la?" Her face scrunched as she attempted to decipher the pronunciation of the odd race. At last, she shook her head, accepting she would never know for sure. "I guess this is some sort of hall surrounding an arena, but it's all abandoned. I wonder what happened here." She stared up at Var'lok and shook her head. "Weird. Well, there's no answers on this plaque, and Var'lok isn't talking. Let's move on."

She turned her attention back to the hallway and continued walking onward.

After a few dozen repetitive sets of broken pillars, it became obvious that the hallway did indeed keep curving in an oval. I suspected Jillian had the right idea; we were circling the arena we had read about. Eventually, on our right, we came to a smaller arched hallway, which led out onto a rubble-filled colosseum floor.

"So it *is* an arena, then," Jillian concluded. "Might as well take a look. I bet we'll just walk in a circle if we keep going."

As we walked toward the center of the coliseum, we passed what had once been smaller doorways, nearly all of which had collapsed due to either age or damage - I couldn't be sure. Finally, a few dozen feet before the hallway ended, we came upon one which still seemed intact.

Jillian immediately perked up; the idea of a mysterious door was clearly of grand interest to her.

"*Oh!* Let's check inside! We need to investigate *everything*. After seeing how important that book was, I don't want to risk missing another clue."

Nevermind that it might be treacherous.

Despite any potential dangers, she was correct; we needed to search for any information we could possibly find. Clearing my mind, I prepared for what we might encounter behind it.

Reaching out, Jillian pushed against the heavy door, but it wouldn't budge. Harder and harder she shoved; no matter the effort, it barely even creaked. Considering its age and frailty, its refusal seemed impossible.

Wait a moment. What was the first thing I learned about locked doors from this time period?

Gliding up to the door, I tapped on the wood and iron panel where I imagined a lock might be installed. As sure as the night leads to day, a socket appeared before our eyes, identical in every way to the ones I had disarmed several times prior.

Jillian gasped. "How did you know it would do that?"

Seeing no reason to explain, I slid inside. Feeling no response, I attempted to turn the socket anyway. My actions were rewarded by one loud clack.

Noticing the sound, Jillian again pushed against the door with little result; time had seemingly frozen its hinges, too.

"Didn't you unlock it?" she asked, turning to regard me.

I motioned in the affirmative, which caused her to frown.

"Fine, we get in the hard way."

With all her might, Jillian let out a disturbing growl before kicking the door. Instead of opening, the brittle wood exploded under the force of her powerful blow, peppering the area beyond it with debris and sending billows of dust back in our direction.

Jillian didn't wait for the dust to settle, instead opting to leap blindly into the room. For all I knew, she was capable of seeing where she was heading; she had never made it entirely clear what the extent of her powers were.

As the dust settled inside, I took note that the room hadn't been touched in quite some time. To the right of where Jillian stood, sat a table covered in various medical utensils, needles, and bottles. A good portion of the vessels had been shattered by the door debris. Had they still held liquid, their contents would have coated the room, but the fluid seemed to have dried up long, long ago.

Above the table hung ten or twelve larger devices resting on hooks, all of which appeared grizzly in purpose or design. I couldn't tell if they were used for advanced medical procedures or for interrogation and torture.

Depending on the person holding them, I suspect it could be either.

Across from the table stood three man-sized iron coffins. The coffins to the left and right had both been opened, revealing their sinister intent. Their interiors had been lined with rows of thin needle-like spikes from chest to toe. Anyone trapped inside would have been impaled and bled to death, if not instantly killed. I needn't have speculated, though, as the stones underneath the closed coffin in the center were coated with a large dark stain.

Dried blood.

Jillian also stared down at the evaporated puddle, a grim expression crossing her already gruesome features. As her eyes rose upward to meet the casket, she shifted her jaw around in an inhuman way before speaking.

"There's something in there; there has to be." Turning to regard me, she raised her brow. "You know we've gotta open it. That corpse could have something Magical on it, something which might tell us where we are." She motioned toward the Oculus hanging around her neck.

I wasn't looking forward to what we might find, but I had to agree with her. Every item that could yield anything at all should be investigated.

Seeing no objection, Jillian stepped forward, gripped the side of the iron lid, and pulled hard. The hinges groaned with every inch of progress, ages of rust crumbling off of them until what was left finally shattered. With a loud boom, the lid landed against the ground and fell forward onto Jillian. Despite stumbling backward, she braced herself and heaved it to the side. It landed on the ground with a hollow, almost bell-like sound.

I found myself completely taken aback. The lid had to have weighed an incomprehensible amount, but she had dealt with it handily, as if it were only reasonably heavy.

Moving an object with Magic is one thing, but seeing such a petite girl hoist an immovable object with her bare hands is quite another!

Jillian's expression pulled me from my thoughts. She stared into the casket, her mouth agape in surprise. As I, too, turned my attention toward what had been revealed, I was not disappointed. Nothing could have prepared me for what I beheld.

Inside lay a naked, withered corpse, completely impaled by spikes. From his shoulders down, long, pointed pieces of metal protruded from lethal wounds, dislocating bones and penetrating organs. But the damage caused by the torture device was to be expected; his condition, however, was not. Although pale, wrinkled, and not altogether human, the corpse had not been dead long. Still moist and supple, its flesh appeared as if it had been dead for a week at most - at least, that's what I imagined week-old flesh might look like.

His body still looks fresh.

"Wow, he still seems... *fresh*," Jillian commented, duplicating my sentiment.

She prodded a finger into the meat of his shoulder, which was far more than I would have had the courage to do. The flesh made a squishing noise, causing fluid to squirt out from around a nearby spike.

The action was just enough to dislodge the corpse. The body, no longer pinned from the front by an opposite set of spikes, slumped forward. Still slick with fluid, it slipped off the metal behind it and, with a meaty thump, hit the floor, creating a gruesome pile of flesh.

Jillian frowned and turned to leave. We had disturbed the resting place of some poor soul unlucky enough to be recently thrown into the contraption. Worse, with no personal effects, there was nothing to be learned from his body. But as I, too, drifted away, something wet slopped against the floor, catching our attention.

Behind us, the corpse had begun to shudder, its outstretched arms grasping blindly upon the stone floor. Slowly, strength found its way into its grey fingertips, and they steadied themselves. With a rattling, sucking noise, the lungs filled with air from the myriad holes in its chest cavity, and a gruesome face tilted up toward us. Opening its mouth, it appeared ready to speak, but before it could utter its first words, the corpse lurched upward, vomiting black fluid all over the ground.

After expelling an alarming amount of the oily substance, it turned its head back toward Jillian and opened its eyes. The unsettling appearance of its disturbing black orbs was only enhanced by its dark, sunken eye sockets; they twitched back and forth, intelligently eyeing both of us.

Flashbacks of the undercroft below Wenton's lab ran through my mind. When Jillian had been reanimated by the dragon heads, she too had come back to life in much the same fashion. Her resurrection had been only seconds before she lunged for Jack, intent on consuming him. Again, I found myself faced with something similar, something potentially just as dangerous.

This is the work of Necromancy.

Should I destroy this poor soul before it has a chance to attack?

To our surprise, it was the shambling corpse who broke the silence.

"Dreyl'vyn Glaas of the Cimmerians, ready to serve," it mouthed breathily, the air still sucking from its chest wounds.

Jillian stared down at the odd form, her brow raised and inhuman eyes wide. Saying nothing in response, she was surely just as disturbed and taken aback as I had been.

Dreyl'vyn, as he had identified himself, appeared just as insecure. Filled with uncertainty, his black orbs continued to twitch back and forth between us.

"Dreyl'vyn Glaas of the-"

Jillian, composing herself, managed to respond. "I heard you the first time, sir, but we aren't who you think we are. At least, I don't think we are."

Dreyl'vyn's eyes trailed downward, first to Jillian's clothing and then to her hands, before regarding her face again.

"You are... out of your cell. Flee before they punish you. I will say nothing."

Jillian's brow knitted together into a confused expression; she obviously thought the man was mistaken.

"No, you don't understand; we aren't who you think we are. My name is Jill, and there's no one else in this building. I just freed you from that... torture device you were in." She pointed toward the metal casket.

Dreyl'vyn glanced at the coffin, then turned his head to survey the room, his eyes lingering on the debris-covered table.

"Did the champions revolt?" he asked. "This room is damaged. Items are missing and ruined."

Jillian's confusion turned to that of frustration. "I don't understand what you're talking about, Dreyl'vyn. I just arrived here - wherever *here* is. To me, this place has been abandoned for what looks like a long time, but it doesn't seem like you've been in that torture device very long at all. Who put you in there?"

Dreyl'vyn appeared bewildered by the question but did not respond. Instead, he hoisted himself up and stood for a moment, seemingly unaware or unconcerned by the dozens of wounds still oozing black fluid from within his body. Slowly, cautiously, he stepped toward Jillian and began to inspect her face. To her credit, she did not move despite her uncomfortable expression.

"Anomalous. Inconsistent. You are similar but not the same. You are *not* one of us," Dreyl'vyn concluded.

Jillian frowned. "No, I wouldn't think so. I'm a human from a different place, or time… or both, I'm not quite sure. Who are you?"

"I am Dreyl'vyn Glaas of the Cimmerians."

"I know that," replied Jillian curtly. "Who are the Cimmerians?"

Attempting and failing to take a deep breath, Dreyl'vyn walked past Jillian toward the table.

"We are the mist walkers, the dark people, those who move between the shadows, the bloodless ones, the faceless, the immortal - a thousand names for a race few understand." He turned back toward her, his expression still passive and cold. "Whatever you call us, we are slaves - once to build, twice to fight. Long ago, we had our own world called Cimmur. It was laid waste by the Crotgar before we were brought here. Perhaps you have heard of their race?"

Jillian shook her head. I, on the other hand, knew far too much about them. The Crotgar were what the Gor'tier had called themselves, and they had been the ones to destroy Xahl. Apparently they had destroyed Dreyl'vyn's world as well. Despite my knowledge, I did not respond. The strange man before us might not have been aware of my sentience, and I was intent on keeping it that way until I found out more about him.

Dreyl'vyn continued. "The Crotgar were a race who traveled from planet to planet, consuming all they found. They captured us and forced us into labor on each new planet they conquered. Here on this world, they stayed; for what reason, I cannot say. We were put to work, shaping it to their tastes.

"Then, another race arrived, and a war began. The Crotgar were murdered by the thousands. The new race did not seem interested in our people, so we slipped away into the wilds. Soon, the sky filled with odd colors and lightning. Large earthquakes began. Volcanoes and towering waves tore the world apart. We survived where many could not, endured where many perished.

"Ages went by in solitude before the race who had started the war came in contact with us again. Some say those who destroy my persecutors are indeed my savior, but once a battle is over, I am certainly proof that a savior can turn into yet another persecutor. The Xahl'thari is what they called themselves, and they may have taken the Crotgar from us, but they did not delay in tearing apart our culture and destroying our lives.

"Under heavy guard, they trained us in the arts of combat and threw us into this ring to fight champions from other races, far and wide. Our regenerative abilities make us the perfect fodder to be cut down over and over. What better than a training aid that rises after every instance it is struck down?"

The Xahl'thari enslaved Dreyl'vyn's race and forced them to fight?

I find that hard to believe.

Dreyl'vyn turned to regard the shattered bottles and debris littering the table. Reaching out, he grabbed a fistful of what appeared to be red sand and rubbed it into most of his wounds. Instantly they shrunk, sealing themselves from the inside. He looked down, seeming unsatisfied with the results; most of the punctures still remained as indented scars.

"Incredibly stale," Dreyl'vyn observed. "I see there is truth in your words; I must have been inside my chamber for a substantial duration."

Without looking back toward us, he proceeded to walk out of the room.

Shaking her head as she watched him, Jillian flapped her arms down toward her sides. "Guess we're following *him* now," she commented, stepping through the ruined doorway.

We caught up with Dreyl'vyn and made our way out onto what was left of the colosseum floor. The football stadium-sized arena appeared as if a hundred bombs had gone off on top of it. Most of the earth had been churned up or was missing altogether; the rest blanketed the thousands of stone risers which filled the massive structure. Most of the seats had been broken or damaged, leaving little to resemble what it had once been.

Back in its day, I suspect this was quite grand.

Dreyl'vyn moved along a side wall and began to busily rummage through large heaps of stone.

"It may still reside here," he grunted, hoisting a huge rock slab over his shoulder. Its impact caused it to sink into the soft soil behind him. The stone easily weighed hundreds of pounds.

It was odd seeing a pale, emaciated, and completely nude man throwing gigantic rocks every which way. I had to admit though, he seemed impressive standing there. Dreyl'vyn had somehow already regenerated a large amount of body mass and grown much taller. With every toss, his muscles swelled, and he became more and more imposing. Before long, I was staring at what I knew to be a true gladiator, a colossal killing machine honed for one purpose alone.

Walking up beside him, Jillian began to toss boulders to the side as well. Although the ones she chose were far smaller than Dreyl'vyn's, they should have been much too large for her to manage.

"What are we looking for, if you don't mind me asking?"

"We are searching for my armor: Loh'Mach, the Unrelenting. Unless someone has taken it, it should be-" He lifted a long, flat piece of stone, revealing a partial set of armored plates, which had been pressed into the ground. "Loh'Mach. It remains here."

Continuing on for a few minutes longer, the pair had soon revealed all of what Dreyl'vyn had sought after. Amongst the rubble lay a black and red set of armor, covered in riveted, sculpted plates of metal. Deep gouges and dents marring almost every surface, it bore the signs of many battles. Even so, it seemed strangely unscathed by the rubble that had landed on top of it. That stood as both a testament to how resilient the armor was and how strong whatever hit it had once been.

I wonder if Dreyl'vyn ever had to fight Mul'bock.

Dreyl'vyn stepped back from the armor, pushing Jillian along with him. His large hand nearly covered her entire chest.

"Come forth, Loh'Mach, your master calls you," he rumbled in a commanding voice.

As if they had taken on a life of their own, the pieces began to rattle before dragging themselves toward each other. A swirling fog appeared, lifting the armor into the air. Coalescing into a human-like form, the armored wraith stepped toward Dreyl'vyn.

Turning, the giant faced away from the enchanted armor. Appearing to shift out of phase with our reality, it continued to walk through him until the pieces had positioned themselves in alignment with his form.

"Let us be one again," Dreyl'vyn called to the armor, causing it to fully phase into being around him.

Imposing, immovable - he appeared at least as intimidating as the statue of Var'lok had been.

Wait… I've met him before!

I may not have known what part Dreyl'vyn had to play in our group, but I was almost certain I had seen him in my visions. In attendance with Wenton and the others at the demon's funeral, he silently stood in the corner, his colossal form mostly hidden by a hooded garment, so tall his head brushed the rafters.

He may be shorter and far more wrinkled, but it's definitely him!

Before the tournament had ended, I worried that meeting Walther, Modera, Cindee, and Dael'yan meant my vision would soon come true, and Jack was about to die. I hadn't realized that I was apparently witnessing a vision from an alternate time period - a time period where I had gone back and taken a second portal with Jillian.

Secretly I had assumed in the back of my mind that my time travel might mean we wouldn't come into contact with that demon after all, that we might not encounter the final battle which ended Jack's life, but I had been wrong; the danger was still present. I now knew that Vael'ehn, unaware of being manipulated, was in league with Roth'Roh'Kah. And that meant a constant threat of being assaulted by demons.

But Jillian wasn't in that vision, which is what had masked the truth, leading me to believe my meeting was likely to occur far earlier. In reality, I still had time before it took place. But anything could happen between now and then. Dreyl'vyn and I could very well end up meeting the others without her unless I stepped in to change things.

The vision is a warning. If I don't shape the future the proper way, Jillian could die. I have to stay vigilant. Finding Dreyl'vyn is very important. Now I know I'll be successful in locating the others. Until then, Jillian is in danger.

Stretching his gauntleted hands out toward another pile of stones, Dreyl'vyn closed his eyes. As if it had been desperate to meet the call of its master, a massive hammer with a large red gemstone head exploded outward from the pile. Swiftly gliding through the air, it drove itself into his hands, clanging against the metal armor. Spinning it around, Dreyl'vyn latched it onto his back with the practice of a warrior who had endured countless years of combat. His task complete, he turned to regard us.

"I am ready," he stated matter-of-factly, his expression stone-like and passive.

Jillian seemed surprised by the statement. "Ready... for *what?*" Dreyl'vyn towered over her by nearly two feet, forcing her to incline her head.

"To leave this prison. Wherever your destination is, it is a better choice for me to travel there than it is to stay here." He spun around slowly, observing his surroundings. "Whatever happened in this place, it is over; there is nothing left. My fellow Cimmerians may be captives, they may be free, but they are *not* here."

Dreyl'vyn turned his eyes down toward Jillian's clothing before looking back into her eyes.

"You are and are *not* a Cimmerian. A kindred soul perhaps, a spirit trapped inside a foreign body. You are new to this land; you should not be traveling through such a dangerous place, wearing thin garments such as those. Come, before we leave, let us find you something more appropriate. The females were housed across the way."

They made women fight here too?

The idea surprised me. Cimmerian women were likely giant, imposing, and scary, to be sure. But again, the idea of women being forced to fight in gladiatorial combat didn't seem to fit the Xahl'thari agenda.

Who would wield enough power, enough of the negative Magic one would need to not only control Dreyl'vyn but an entire race of immortals just like him?

Before my mind finished the question, I had already settled on the answer.

Vael'ehn.

After trudging over a large heap of rubble comprised mostly of the arena floor and pieces of the stands, we made it to the opposite side. There, the damage was lesser, and everything seemed more or less intact. Inside a tunnel identical to the one we had entered from, Dreyl'vyn kicked through the first door. Within stood three similar coffin torture devices, but all were empty. He repeated the process for five more identical rooms. Fortunately, he found no other survivors suffering the same fate as he had.

Eventually we arrived at a reinforced metal door - one which appeared nearly impenetrable. Dreyl'vyn withdrew the massive hammer from his back. Lunging forward, he struck the mighty door. His weapon drove into the metal as if it were nothing, causing it to crumple inward on itself. Stowing his weapon, he barreled through what was left, using his immense bulk as a battering ram. Watching him move so swiftly, he appeared more to me as an armored rhinoceros than a man, his impact completely removing the damaged barrier from its hinges.

As we moved in behind him, a room full of armaments was revealed to us - armaments fitted for women. A full dozen suits stood on forms, still intact, with three others strewn across the room after being hit by the door.

Dreyl'vyn strode up to the biggest, thickest, most impenetrable looking set he could find. "This is nothing compared to Loh'Mach, but it has many layers and will do well in combat. It is a worthy choice."

Jillian gave the bulky heap a skeptical, almost saucy look. I couldn't help but laugh to myself. The suit of armor was so large, she might have been better off wearing a refrigerator topped with a bath tub. Instead, she made her way to a minimal set, which lay folded in the corner. Made mostly of leather, with steel patches attached to a few of the surfaces, it still seemed sturdy. Luckily, it appeared to have been skin-tight for whoever had worn it prior. Once on, the pieces were only a size too big, and their many buckles corrected most of the issues.

Dreyl'vyn nodded his head. "Yes. Good. That is worn underneath."

Jillian turned around, and shot him an odd look. "This isn't armor?"

Dreyl'vyn cocked his head to the side. "No, it is not armor. Those anchor points keep the armor centered on your body as you move. A weapon such as mine would not be halted in the least by undergarments such as those."

Jillian laughed out loud. "So it's gladiatorial underwear?" She laughed again. "Well, is it better than the clothes I'm wearing underneath it?"

"Of course it is. Your clothing is not fit for *any* task."

"Would it take blows from weapons lesser than yours?"

Dreyl'vyn looked down at the tiny suit of what Jillian had coined gladiatorial underwear, and studied it. "A couple, perhaps, if you could stand your ground."

"And wouldn't I be more agile in this than in *that?*" She pointed over at the giant set of refrigerator armor.

Dreyl'vyn turned to regard the gargantuan set. "Yes, you would be quicker, but far… softer."

"Then this will do nicely. You can't damage what you can't hit. Besides, I'm not some sort of Amazon warrior princess. That stuff would be way too clunky, even if I *could* carry it."

I think you're selling yourself short.

Dreyl'vyn seemed confused by the reference, but nodded anyway, accepting her reasoning.

"So, did you receive your fancy armor from winning so often?" Jillian inquired, changing the subject to Dreyl'vyn's armor, which had clearly been enchanted.

Dreyl'vyn looked down at the armor comprising Loh'Mach and paused for a moment before returning his dark gaze to her.

"As I gained strength and ability, I became a valuable asset, but make no mistake; I was given this armor to keep me subdued. It was bound to me, and it protected me, but I could feel its true intent; it resisted whenever I considered leaving this place."

Jillian seemed confused by the statement. "Then why bother wearing it? You're free now." She wrinkled her lip. "Wait, did you *seriously* stop yourself from leaving by putting it on again?"

"I have used these armaments for many years. They are as much a part of me as this body I occupy. To leave without them would be impossible for me to comprehend." Dreyl'vyn motioned toward the destroyed colosseum. "Loh'Mach now urges me onward. What once was, no longer is. I am a prisoner no more."

"Let's hope so," Jillian replied, eyeing the armor with uncertainty.

Turning, she took notice of a cabinet built into the back wall of the room. Once opened, it was revealed to house a large rack filled with row after row of smaller weapons. Given the size of what Dreyl'vyn preferred to use, they were likely side arms, only used if the combatant's main weapons were knocked away.

Dreyl'vyn also eyed the contents of the cabinet. "You have a penchant for agility; I expect you would rather not use weapons such as mine." He pointed to a row of several razor-sharp daggers, which hung from pegs. "Would those suit your tastes?"

Jillian didn't respond; she had already picked up a small chest, which could have easily been overlooked. Inside she found a set of complex mechanical fingertips, which appeared far too large for her. As she slipped one over her finger, however, it ratcheted, reducing in diameter until it became snug. After fiddling with the mechanism for a few moments, she found that by balling her hand into a fist before quickly extending her fingers outward, she could articulate the devices. Once activated, they released sharpened talons.

Her eyes growing wide in recognition of what the weapons were, it took Jillian no time at all to don the entire set. Turning and waggling her fingers, she more resembled some sort of clawed, animalistic predator than a human, at least in my eyes. The way she leapt and sprinted, saw in the dark, her inhuman strength - the weapons seemed to fit her far better than swords or daggers would have. From the wild gleam in her eyes, I could tell she agreed.

With Jillian suited up and prepared for battle, Dreyl'vyn seemed far more content with her appearance. Why he was so concerned for our safety in an abandoned colosseum, I couldn't say, but it kept me on edge. Extending a tree trunk-like arm, he motioned toward the door.

Exiting the armory, we turned left and headed toward the outer ring. I expected it, too, would be lined with statues of famous gladiators from the past.

Perhaps this set will display female warriors.

Instead we were greeted by a gigantic, seemingly bottomless hole, where the floor of the wounded building had given way, making the area completely impassible. Beyond it, the wall and roof of the structure were also missing, revealing a dark, cloudless sky.

Dreyl'vyn walked up to the edge of the crater, causing bits of debris and rocks to crumble inward. They made no noise as they plummeted into the darkness, lending further credence to my impression that it was deep indeed. Strangely, he stared down into the void, his gaze transfixed, as if he was fascinated by something.

"Dreyl'vyn, be careful; you're heavy," Jillian called.

"Is it not curious to you?"

Jillian walked up next to him, cautiously peering downward. "What do you mean? It's probably a sinkhole, revealed by an explosion or something."

Dreyl'vyn didn't respond right away, instead staring deeper into the abyss.

"One push, one slip - a man could be sent downward without ever expecting it. He would simply vanish, never to be heard from again. To have an end - is it not curious to one such as you?" he repeated before turning to leave.

"Call of the void," Jillian whispered.

Dreyl'vyn did not respond, instead choosing to head back the way we came.

Her eyes flitting toward me, she frowned. "Sorry, it's a French term. It means *call of the void*. It describes dark thoughts you have that you don't actually intend on acting upon."

She used the same words twice.

Apparently my crystal automatically translates French too.

Watching Dreyl'vyn walk away, I couldn't help but wonder if such a term applied to his state of being. He may very well have considered acting upon those urges. After all, he was immortal and, for one reason or another, his circumstances had clearly given him a fascination with the idea of death.

I suppose the never-ending life of a slave turned combatant might be quite painful to endure.

As we continued back across the wreckage of the arena floor, Dreyl'vyn asked what felt like a thousand questions pertaining to just what exactly had happened. We, of course, could not answer any of them. Just as frustrating was his lack of knowledge on Vael'ehn, Wenton, or anything else which had transpired. His race was often kept in solitude or impaled in horrible devices when not out in the arena.

I can't even begin to imagine such an existence. No wonder he thinks about death.

Dreyl'vyn did, however, listen patiently to Jillian's own summary of why we were there - or rather, why she suspected we were there. She had only a few details to explain why Vael'ehn was the lead role in a demented plot involving an evil sword.

But as Jillian recounted the information we had garnered from the book written by Varek, I realized that the "plot" Vael'ehn had concocted wasn't really why we were there. In fact, it might never have existed at all. The whole idea Vael'ehn had contrived about recreating his own world was useless drivel, seeded into his brain so neither he nor anyone else would uncover his true purpose.

In truth, the demon lord planned on opening a portal to make his way through into our plane of existence - an act that seemed quite difficult for him to accomplish. Not only had the Forgotten Order kept him from entering Xahl, but even Jillian and I had managed to keep him at bay. Likely, countless others had thwarted his attempts throughout the universe as well.

Clearly, the demon lord needed a very large portal - one far bigger than a man - and no one to prevent him from passing through it. Vael'ehn would never make his way back to Xahl; he would instead unwittingly provide Roth'Roh'Kah with the incredible amount of Magic required to bring his plan to fruition.

I wonder, if Vael'ehn was brainwashed into doing something he has no desire to do, would it be possible to correct his mind, use him against the demon lord?

The thought led me back to Jillian's condition. She, too, had been seeded by some sort of demonic power. Whether or not that was the same as having a demonically-tainted father, I couldn't be sure. If I could somehow prevent her from changing further, or send the condition into remission, that knowledge might prove to have an application toward Vael'ehn as well.

And if I can convince Vael'ehn that he's been the pawn in a scheme to destroy everything he values, I can pit him against the demon lord himself.

I could recruit the most powerful person on the planet for our cause!

Dreyl'vyn's surprising response to Jillian's summary distracted me from my internal monologue.

"If this *Wenton* has spoken true, the weapon you refer to sounds like that which was used to crush my prior captors. That same weapon was also used to enslave my race. Its power is beyond you. Whether or not you come in contact with your mate again, you will most certainly perish along with him."

The statement was blunt and emotionless, but it was also wrong. As Jillian stared up at him, black tears welling in her eyes, I swooped in to set things right. I needed to stop Dreyl'vyn before he continued on with his demoralizing summation, sending Jillian into a downward emotional spiral; she was my only hope to correct the past.

As I neared, the giant plucked me from the sky and brought me up to his pale grey face. Disturbing, black, pupilless orbs regarded me with suspicion.

"What is this object that follows you around? It is different from others I have seen."

Jillian wiped her eyes, leaving smears of black across her cheeks like mascara.

"I've been told that it is neither a Coadjutor nor an Obli'tahr, and *both* at the same time." She smiled to herself. "That sounds like a riddle from *Alice in Wonderland*. But uh, it has a friend of ours trapped inside. He's been very helpful."

"I have no knowledge of those terms, nor have I heard that tale," Dreyl'vyn replied, squinting as he examined me more closely. "I see no one inside it; it appears your friend has escaped his prison."

Jillian's smile widened. Dreyl'vyn's literal translation of someone being trapped inside was certainly amusing.

"No, I mean, his *spirit* is inside it. You can't see it."

Dreyl'vyn turned his gaze back upon the crystal. "When a man dies, he is gone. Fear of death causes entire civilizations to search for immortality. I know how you both must feel. Trapped inside a shell for eternity - this world has no equal for our imprisonment."

As Dreyl'vyn released me, I thought about his words. I had never considered that, in my new body, I might have inadvertently gained eternal life. Some might gape at how fortunate I had become, but as I looked into Dreyl'vyn's horrifying yet tired eyes, I could see that an eternity was an awfully long time indeed.

Jillian spoke up. "You seem pretty focused on death, Dreyl'vyn - like it's a blessing to finally die - but you're free to do what you want now instead of being trapped. Perhaps you can find something to enjoy, like a hobby - something to do instead of wishing you were dead all the time."

Dreyl'vyn stared at her for a long while before responding.

"Throughout what mortal beings would call *my lifetime*, I have seen *many* beings come and go; our race does neither. We…" He seemed to struggle with the words. "…*are.*"

Jillian regarded him with an expression of disbelief. "You *are?* You're… saying you weren't born? You're immortal in both directions through time?"

"*Immortal* is acceptable, but still insinuates that we defy death." Before Jillian could respond, he attempted to explain. "Corporeal lifeforms appear to be ruled by their *time*. Everything they do or say or think ultimately travels back to what is left of their time. But that is not how *all* beings experience life. Even so, their minds can only imagine it as a linear progression. They are linear beings."

I thought back to my time spent with Jack and Vael'ehn on our walk out to the hill inside the crater. He had attempted to explain that time might not have a beginning and an end, that it might be an infinite circle. The being standing before us was apparently living proof of that concept.

Or, at the very least, he believes he is.

Jillian nodded, as if that explanation made some sort of sense to her. "But then, how are you here with me? Aren't you experiencing time like I do right now?"

"Yes, I am; that is why I suffer. Most would assume that an immortal being would have infinite patience, but it is quite the opposite. I had no experience with your time until I merged with this body. You cannot comprehend my immortality, just as I could not comprehend your time. A timeless being brought down to the restriction of your time can hardly function, let alone find something to enjoy, like a hobby."

Jillian frowned. "Wait. You said the Crotgar captured your race. I thought you meant they rounded up all the Cimmerians. I feel like I missed something. The way you've been speaking, you act as if this was never your body."

"You are correct; this is not my body. Ethereal beings are likely all around us - that is, if this place is similar to where I came from. However, they have no bodies - at least, not in the sense *you* mean. The Crotgar used some type of stolen Magic device to pull our essence inward from around them in order to store it in the dead bodies of their fallen. This body is not mine; it is theirs."

The revelation was startling.

The Gor'tier - the race of giants who had brought down the Xahl'thari world - had looked just like the man standing before me?

Grey skin, black eyes, angular ears - Dreyl'vyn certainly wasn't human, but he also wasn't as alien as I might have suspected. He would fit in far better among humans than the Gnill'var, or whatever catfish-like race Boulli was. I found it fascinating that I was staring at a living, breathing Gor'tier from a legendary story I had heard.

*Well, **almost** living and breathing. For all I know, he looks more like a corpse of one.*

Jillian gasped. "But why would they do that! That's awful!" She backed up a step, attempting to get a good look at Dreyl'vyn, as he was quite tall. "So you're telling me you aren't… *you?* Your body is from a Crotgar? They were giants?"

"Yes, I am trapped within a corpse. *Giant* is a matter of perspective. There are beings in the universe far larger than a countless number of Crotgar. This vessel would go unnoticed by such a lifeform."

Jillian laughed. "Well, you're certainly a giant to me!"

"If the Odra'sti powder in my cell were less stale, I would have grown even larger. Our captors used special reagents to keep us weak, wounded, and more manageable until needed to fight again. Now freed from their effects, I will gain my full strength back eventually."

In my vision he certainly was quite giant.

Dreyl'vyn continued. "I have had a large portion of your time to reflect upon why the Crotgar bound our race. I believe they may have been driven - just as any corporeal being might be - by their desire to find immortality. They were attempting to bring their dead back to life by use of Magic, a resource neither they nor I understand how to use. But as to why they enslaved our race after finding out we were not whom they thought we would be? They simply had no choice.

"The spellwork binding us inside the corpses, when combined with our souls, had unexpected effects. To the Crotgar's surprise, we could not die. They could tear us apart, torture us, perform any number of monstrous acts, but destroy what they had created, they could not. Unable to cope with your time, we found our new existence confusing and painful, and most of our number attempted the same ourselves - to no effect, of course. Instead, we remained bewildered, led around by the Crotgar, hoping that someday we might be freed."

Jillian frowned. "Immortal slaves… I am so sorry, Dreyl'vyn." She seemed to consider something. "Now that you're free, though, can't you just travel back to your planet and find out how to revert the spell?"

Dreyl'vyn shook his head. "The Crotgar who traveled here after departing my planet are all dead; they died off in the cataclysm that befell this planet. No one has attempted to find the knowledge of what they did to us. Even if I knew how to locate my home world, it would serve me no purpose; I would remain trapped."

Filled with pity, Jillian appeared truly moved by the giant's plight. Stepping forward, she gave him a firm hug, causing pieces of their armor to clink against one another. Had Dreyl'vyn been a human, he might have been knocked backward several steps, but Jillian seemed to consider his immovable form as deserving of a more hearty gesture.

Dreyl'vyn in no way seemed to comprehend her advance, and appeared unmoved both physically and emotionally.

"I have grown too large for you to move manually," he stated. Lifting Jillian by her leather belt, he let her dangle in front of his face. "It is I who shall carry you if the need arises."

Flailing about, Jillian laughed at his lack of understanding. "No, it's a hug, ya big lug! You hug someone when you care about them, or when they're sad." She reached for his arm but missed, forcing herself into a rocking motion.

Dreyl'vyn stared at her as she swung back and forth. "I am not sad, nor do you care about me."

Jillian reached out and slapped a hand against his chest, stabilizing herself. "You're wrong on both counts, Dreyl'vyn. You've still got a lot to learn about being a corporeal being. Now put me down. I can't have a serious conversation with you while I'm swinging in the air."

Dreyl'vyn seemed confused as he placed her on the ground. "You are a being inserted into a foreign body, yet your perspective does not mirror mine. Am I incorrect in assuming another race performed a similar ritual upon you?"

While not quite correct, Dreyl'vyn is closer to the truth than he knows.

Jillian sighed and looked around before surprisingly admitting to him exactly what had happened.

"It… *is* my body, or at least it used to be, anyway. We had an accident, and the sword tried to harvest my soul. Jack managed to put me back inside my body, but he didn't have the right tools, and now my body is dead. To keep living I have to consume what I need from other people. As if that isn't bad enough, something else, something from my past, followed me back in."

She stared down at her greying flesh and sighed again. "The undead use other people's life force as fuel. It's like there's some missing link between their soul and their corpse, and because of that missing connection, they can't bridge the gap into staying alive. But there's more to me. I'm also part demon; I have a compulsion to eat Magic. For every person's life my undead body absorbs, I also can't help but consume their soul.

"Mortal souls are a source of Magic, and it-" Jillian paused and licked her lips, as if the idea really appealed to her. "It's… *irresistible* to me. I consumed a piece of Jack's soul when I wasn't in my proper state of mind, which is how it started, and then far more from my next victim. Now, I *always* think about it, as if it's an obsession. I'm slowly turning from undead to demon, and when that transformation is complete, I don't know what's going to happen to *me*." She poked the side of her head. "To what's in *here.*"

Well, it's clear she's very aware of what's happening to her. Is it wishful thinking to believe that's the first step to recovery?

Jillian stared up into Dreyl'vyn's cold, black orbs. "The practical side of me tells me I'm not going to find some Magical cure. I'm either going to die by starving myself or I'm going to transform by giving into my urges, and I don't know what's worse. I have no choice but to hope and pray that I'm wrong. But you were right about one thing: we should get moving. There's nothing left here that could benefit us. Do you know how to jog? We can head toward where we came in from."

Dreyl'vyn seemed confused by the word *jog*. "I can move my legs quickly if the need arises. How fast do you want me to move them?"

Jillian laughed. "I meant, will you run next to me? You know, to save time?

"How will we capture more of your time through movement? Do we not already have enough?"

Again, Dreyl'vyn's literal perspective caused her to smile. "Just… try to keep up, okay?"

Unexpectedly she took off running through the stadium exit and down the grand hall. Dreyl'vyn did not hesitate. I knew Jillian was fast, but he was just as quick, if not quicker, even in his armor. Gliding along next to him was like keeping pace with a rampaging behemoth. He barreled over giant boulders as his heavy feet crushed the soil, leaving a set of large compressed footprints behind him. In an instant he had caught up to her, the three of us tearing down the hallway in unison.

"How far do you intend to go?" Dreyl'vyn yelled over the booming sound of his own armored feet.

Jillian, thoroughly amused by his rumbling silhouette in the dim light, forced herself to keep from laughing at him. "I don't know, but when we get there, we won't be here!"

CHAPTER

Forty-Seven

-THE LORD AH THESE HERE LANDS-

Soon, we had reached what surely used to be a grand foyer. Pillars three times higher than the ones lining the hallways, and still mostly intact due to their immense girth, lined the long rectangular room. I would have assumed something else might have resided there at one time, but the only other object left behind had been a platform opposite the entrance archway.

The platform itself was massive, standing several feet taller than Dreyl'vyn, and three or four times as wide as it was tall. On top of it, all that remained was a massive booted foot. Whatever statue once stood there had been removed or vaporized.

Circling the platform, I found a small plaque at its base, covered in dirt and mud. Scouring the surface with a single mental push, I read what had been engraved upon it.

Lord Vael'curion Dahr'krest - Ruler of the Vaelcurian Empire

Built to commemorate the completion
of the Champion's Amphitheater

The city of Empor'Vael

✑ 21 ⚕ 203

Vael'ehn!

This statue seems to commemorate him as a hero. An entire nation ruled by a demonically-influenced man with a sinister secret; it's hard not to feel bad for them.

The building we portalled into had at one point been called the Champion's Amphitheater. More importantly, it was located in the city of Empor'Vael, inside the Vaelcurian Empire. Varek's letter had mentioned that two of the capital cities had fallen to Retrogrades; it wasn't much of a stretch to assume Empor'Vael was one of them.

I had learned not only our location but also placed us within the same rough timeframe that Jack and I had traveled through previously. I just needed to verify where our location was in relation to the tournament. But I had no further time to look around, as Jillian and Dreyl'vyn had both sprinted through the towering archway which marked the entrance to the amphitheater.

Eventually I found the two of them walking along an overgrown cobblestone road, inspecting what appeared to be rows of completely obliterated buildings. It became apparent that the colosseum had survived far better than the rest of the town had, and in its weathered state, that was certainly saying something. What I assumed from Varek's letter was a battle with the Retrogrades had truly devastated the entire city.

From the damage I saw before me, I wasn't surprised it hadn't been rebuilt, either. There wasn't anything left to rebuild upon aside from shattered foundations and crushed roadways. If the Retrogrades were that much of a threat in the area, and the town was already gone, I'd have also chosen to pack up and move on to another city or location.

Arriving at the desiccated corpse of what I knew to be a deceased Retrograde, the pair paused. Adhered to the creature's structure was a thick exoskeleton of heavily-corroded metal. Attached to the jumble were two large shattered blades and, much to my surprise, what looked to be honest-to-goodness rockets or missiles - weapons that clearly did not belong in that age.

As Jillian opened her mouth to comment on the corpse, another voice called out.

"Ahddahbe cayreful o' thayt pile ah wea-pone-ry theyre, strangahs," the voice called out in a heavy, almost indecipherable accent. To our right, a man walked out from behind a large pile of rubble. "Mighttah blow yerse'ves sky-high."

Dreyl'vyn eyed the man with overt suspicion. "State your intent." His tone indicated the words had been more of a demand than a request.

"Well hey theyre, big fellah," the man exclaimed, leaning on a precariously stacked pile of stones.

Scrawny, dirty, and *unkempt* were better adjectives than the stranger deserved. Wearing what might have once been a white shirt, but had since been stained yellow, and a pair of tattered canvas pants that looked as if he had actually soiled them, I found him absolutely repulsive. A set of crude, torn shoes, which displayed two of his toes through a large gash, and a half-burned almost bowler-esque style of hat finished his motley appearance.

"Wheyre ya headin' tah?" he asked, scratching at his matted, dirty beard, soil tumbling from it as he did so.

Jillian, trying to hide the disgust evident on her face, responded. "We're just on our way through the area... *sir.* Might you tell us what this town was called?"

The man let out a high-pitched, cackling laugh that degenerated into coughing. "*Tahn?* Ya had ah lookah ro'nd heyre, pretteh ladeh? This ain't no tahn; this heyre's ah feces pit." Seeing the pair's odd reaction, he added, "Ye'all know whaddah mean? Wheyre ex-cre-ment be pilin' up?"

A shithole?

Jillian and Dreyl'vyn continued to stare at him in silence, unsure of how to respond. I must admit, I had no idea what to say myself.

Seeing their blank expressions, the man let out another disgusting cackle.

"Nev'rmine. Anyhah, wheyre mah manners? Mah nayme's Eugene! Like thayt playnt e'ryone use tah eat!"

He wiped his nose and stuck out a grime-covered hand toward Dreyl'vyn, who stared down at it. Eyeing his massive gauntlet, Eugene immediately thought better of the gesture and put his hand back down.

Dreyl'vyn wouldn't know what a handshake is anyway.

"Ah tell ya wat. Ol' Eugene ah hep y'out. Ol' Eugene knows ah man who done learnt ah lottah 'bout e'rythang round these here parts. He's the Lord ah these here lands! He'll be tellin' ya jus' wheyre ya be. Follah ol' Eugene; he'll hep y'out."

The Lord of these lands? Is he going to lead us to Vael'ehn?

I sincerely hoped he wouldn't, but looking around, I felt like I had no choice but to follow if I wanted to find out where we were. With a curt but sloppy bow, Eugene turned and drunkenly stumbled off down a rubble-filled side street.

Jillian shrugged and looked up at Dreyl'vyn. "Well, we need to know where we are. Maybe he *does* know a person who can help."

Dreyl'vyn watched Eugene trip and fall as he tried to beckon them to follow. "Let us hope whoever he leads us to is not as impaired as *he* has become."

A few minutes later, we found ourselves being ushered by Eugene into what used to be a town square. Three equally grimy men sat around a fire, which had been built inside the remains of an old fountain. In fact, the only difference among them appeared to be that the man at the center was substantially overweight. He sat in stark contrast to the others - an effigy to gluttony in a world of poverty.

Noticing our arrival, the fat man tilted the brim of his crude hat upward with the flick of a finger and stared at us with false, welcoming eyes. "Well, well, well, Eugene, whad'jah bring us t'night?"

Eugene seemed to be quite enthralled by the man's tone. "Oh, Mistah Maul'tree. Ah fo'nd these two lookin' ait Grunk dahn tha way!"

Mister Maul'tree raised his eyebrows. "Is that rite? Ya heah that, boys? These two was just'ah lookin' at ol' Grunk dahn the way!"

The pair of men to his left and right let out a "humph" noise, but otherwise continued to prod at the fire.

"You two know wha'cha fo'nd dahn theah?" Maul'tree asked in a serious tone. "You know wut dat pile'ah bones is?"

Surprisingly, Dreyl'vyn answered the question. "It has been referred to as a Retrograde by my captors. They were brought in to fight the Champions, and I have dealt with them myself, on many occasions."

Maul'tree let out a laugh. "We'll lookie theah! The fo'tress has ah voice, nah don' it? So'nds tah me like we got ourse'ves ah fightah. You been in the ring, then, *fo'tress*? You bloodied yo' nose fo' the crowds?"

Dreyl'vyn eyed the man suspiciously. "I do not trust you. Your voice sounds false. We will be on our way," he stated dispassionately.

Maul'tree again laughed at the statement. "You heah that? The fo'tress don't take kindly tah mah voice. Wut you think ah that, Eugene? You think ah *sownd fawlse?* You think yah ol' friend Maul'tree's ah liah?"

Eugene shook his head aggressively. Bits of debris rained down on his shirt like powdered cocoa. "No sah, Mistah Maul'tree. Yain' never toe'd Eugene no lie, ays hon'st ays ahm'ah 'live!"

Maul'tree pointed toward Eugene. "You see that, fo'tress? Ah ain't *never* toe'd no lie. My maw-maw always toe'd me, the fiah's onleh fit fo' shanks an' liahs." He leaned forward, his elbows resting on his knees. "But ah tell ya wut, fo'tress. Ol' Grunk dahn the way? He ain't nah Retrah'grayde. He ain't nuthin' ah yo's. He's bein' *prah-per-tie*, an' that prah-per-tie's bein' *mine*. You undastand that, fo'tress?"

Dreyl'vyn turned toward Jillian. "They are making threats against us. I do not want the carcass, but they are insinuating we are causing trouble. We should-"

"Woah, woah, woah, woah!" interrupted Maul'tree. "Theah ya go again, fo'tress. Imposin' on mah prah-per-tie. That pretteh lil' thang's alreadeh been claimed bah ol' Maul'tree. You wou'nt beh tryin' tah snatch'er up nah, would ya?"

Dreyl'vyn turned to regard Maul'tree again. "We will be on our way now. If you try to stop us, I will tear you in half and grind the two pieces of your torso in my palms until you are nothing but paste."

From a man, that might have been an attempt at intimidation, but I suspected Dreyl'vyn had just informed Maul'tree *exactly* what he intended to do to him.

From around the square, several dozen men stepped out from the shadows in unison.

"You heah that, boys?" Maul'tree called. "This heah fo'tress gonna turn meh tah paiste!"

Several of the men laughed, but most stood silent. Maul'tree leaned back, lifted a leg, and broke wind before propping a tattered boot on his knee. He eyed the pair greedily.

"Ah tell ya wut, fo'tress. Jus' tah prove ol' Maul'tree's ah stand-up type ah mayn, Ah'm gonna invite ya tah dinnah. You come'n have ah seat roun' yon fiah heah, and we'll have ah nice ol meal." He turned his attention toward Jillian. "An' you, pretteh ladeh. How 'bout ya sit by ol' Maul'tree?" He patted the toppled column he was sitting on.

Dreyl'vyn eyed Jillian, but she returned a reassuring look.

"These boys just want some company for dinner," she said casually. "They probably haven't seen a *real* woman in a long time. We can't deny them that, can we... *fortress?*"

Dreyl'vyn's brow wrinkled at her use of the sadly accurate nickname Maul'tree had used, but he did not object as he watched her go. Dreyl'vyn might not have understood innuendo, but having certainly been manipulated over and over throughout his experience with "our time," he seemed to follow her reasoning. Rather than fight what had to be near forty men, Jillian was going to do her best to manipulate them into giving her information instead.

Gracefully Jillian sauntered toward Maul'tree, who watched her with hungry eyes. I knew the effect she had on men, and even though I was fully aware her intentions weren't genuine, I couldn't help but feel jealousy build inside me. As she slid in next to the disgusting leader, I could barely keep from lashing out toward him.

Dreyl'vyn, eyeing the men behind him, stepped slowly toward the fire. "I do not hunger, nor do I have reason to sit," he stated, stopping behind where the others were sitting down.

Maul'tree shrugged his shoulders. "Suit yo'self, fo'tress. Ah only care 'bout mah ayffair with this lil' thang o'ar heah." He turned and smiled stupidly into Jillian's eyes. Within seconds, he was snared by her gaze and unable to pull free.

"So, Mister Maul'tree, where are we right now?" Jillian asked in a false, almost Marilynn Monroe-like accent.

Maul'tree, whose jaw hung slack, began to grin like a fool, flashing a partial set of rotten, brown teeth. "Oh, yo in *mah* land. This use tah be thait Empo'vale citeh, but nah ol' Maul'tree runs it."

"My, what a man it must take to run such a large area all by himself," she exclaimed. Maul'tree's grin widened as he ate up the compliment. "Tell me, how far do you think we are from this year's tournament?"

Maul'tree's expression changed from euphoria to annoyance as the question, which had seemingly agitated him, caused her charm to dim in his eyes. "Wha ya wanna know 'bout that playce? None ah those stilted foo's pay no mind tah us. They can all buhrn with tha liah's in tha fiah fo' all ah care."

"Oh, I *know* they are," agreed Jillian, "but I bet you know *all* about it. I bet you know about *everything*. A man like you, I bet you're just *full* of smart stuff, aren't you?"

Maul'tree began to laugh. "Ya see that, boys? This one knows wut be impert'nt in ah mayn! Ye'all should been takin' notes dahn 'bout how tah trete me!" He turned back toward Jillian. "Ah tell ya wut, why don' we have us some dinnah, and ah'll tell ya ever'thin' ya be want'n tah know an' then some, hmm?"

"That sounds lovely," replied Jillian. "What are we having?"

"Oh, well see, that theah's tha thang. Onleh meat roun' heah is rotted bodehs. Ain't very oft'n we have us strangahs comin' through so close, an mah meyn, they gottah eat. That fo'tress ovah theah, he's ah lookin' mighteh tasteh right'ah 'bout nah."

In unison the group turned to stare at Dreyl'vyn, but he simply shook his head.

"If the flesh of other men is what you desire, then you will be first."

"Ah'll be furst *wut?*" replied Maul'tree, glaring at him.

"The harder life a man has dealt with, the tougher his meat becomes," replied Dreyl'vyn. "My body has seen nothing but hardship and labor."

The fat man raised his brow. "If yo' sayin' mah men don' wanna eat yo-"

Dreyl'vyn spoke over him. "Any men who remain after we leave will feast on your corpse. Your meat will be supple and full of flavor, and they will relish it. Your mouth will be silenced, and the land will finally be free to rest."

Talk about intimidating…

Maul'tree's eyes grew large but he did not respond, instead opting to prod the fire with a stick. Nor did anyone else reply, for that matter; Dreyl'vyn's grim message destroyed any conversation which might have been on their lips. Instead, the group simply stared at him, clearly trying their best to determine if he was bluffing or not. But with Dreyl'vyn there was no bluff; there was no humor; there was no compassion. He was a machine built for destruction, and if he said they'd be having fat man for dinner, you wouldn't find me doubting his words.

Maul'tree leaned back. "We'll, if ya'd be the one doin' it, ya best get tah the doin', then."

Jillian attempted to interject, still intent on prying information from Maul'tree, but Dreyl'vyn took a step forward. It was the wrong move. From behind him, a rope was thrown up and around his neck. Ten men took off running backward, pulling the colossus off his feet. As Dreyl'vyn hit the ground, the earth rippled from the impact. Time seemed to pause for the briefest of seconds before the entire area collapsed. Without warning, the fountain-fire, the toppled columns, the men, Dreyl'vyn, Jillian - the entire area disappeared into a black pit.

As I swooped down, smoke and screaming arose from the darkness around me. Making my way below, I saw that the city square had been built upon a cavern of some sort which, from years of distress and war, had finally given way. Dreyl'vyn had been the straw that broke the camel's back.

And what a straw he had been!

Searching for the pair, I quickly realized the screaming was not coming from the fallen. Most of the men were not only on their feet already but were also involved in a losing battle. Side by side, Dreyl'vyn and Jillian fought in the darkness, their vision apparently far more capable than mine.

As I prepared to illuminate the area around me, an object arose from below. A man's partial torso sailed by, his head still attached, bearing an expression of absolute dread on its dead countenance. Caught off guard, I watched it sail back into the inky black alcoves of the cave.

If I provide light to the area below, I'll only aid those awful men in their fight.

Jillian and Dreyl'vyn don't need my help to end this.

Only seconds later, the screams, shuffling, and clanging of weapons muted, proving I had been correct. Taking the opportunity to finally cast away the darkness, I illuminated Jillian just as she tore through the abdomen of one last unfortunate foe. Covered from head to toe in swaths of red, her eyes were wide and rabid. Spinning wildly, her chest heaved as she eagerly searched for the next victim to be torn apart.

Taking notice of a still form in the corner, Jillian advanced on it, only be held in place by a massive gauntlet, which loomed out from the darkness. Dreyl'vyn, coated in sticky red, stepped into full view and pulled her to him.

"Leave him for me," he commanded, stepping around her.

Picking the man up by his shoulders, he lifted the shattered body into the light. The form turned out to be Maul'tree, who had unluckily broken both his legs and one arm in the fall, likely because of his girth. Futilely he pulled at Dreyl'vyn's massive hand, attempting to release himself.

"Lemmeh go! Ya kilt all mah boys, so jus' get outtah heah alreadeh!"

Dreyl'vyn pulled Maul'tree up higher, within inches of his face. "Provide this woman with the information she desired. If you do not, I promise, you *will* be dealt a truly horrific death, far beyond that of your men."

Maul'tree spit on Dreyl'vyn's face. "If ya think ah'm scare't ah death, yah gottah 'notha thing comin'! Theah's people 'round this heah citeh, an' they won' beh takin' too kindleh tah mah mis-trete-ment. Yeh do yah wors', fo'tress! You gonna beh sorreh!"

Dreyl'vyn's eyes remained passive as the bloody saliva ran down his face. "My wrath has come and gone. I will not be your executioner on this day; *she* will."

Dreyl'vyn turned Maul'tree so he could view Jillian. Covered in blood, her skin cold and grey, her eyes wild, she looked truly terrible to behold. Unable to control herself, she lunged for him. Maul'tree screamed, his life surely flashing before his eyes. But just as Jillian would have made contact, Dreyl'vyn pulled him from danger like a matador swiping his cape from the path of a charging bull.

Again lifting Maul'tree to his face, Dreyl'vyn repeated himself. "Tell this woman what she wanted to know."

Tears in his wide eyes, Maul'tree appeared on the edge of insanity. *"Wut! Wut!* The torn-e-ment? Ah don' know! It's cleah 'cross the land! Ya mite'as well be tha farthes' from it rite nah!"

Dreyl'vyn shook Maul'tree, threatening his already fragile condition. "What direction would we head toward?" He again forced Maul'tree to face Jillian, who had begun to drool in anticipation.

Maul'tree attempted to recoil backward from the horror. "Ah'right! Ah'right! Don' let'er have meh! Ya go oh'r north er north-west like. Theah's ah road leadin' up inta the mon'tains! Ya got ah long ways ah walk, but tha's tha way, ah swear it! Nah put meh down 'n don't let er neah meh!"

Dreyl'vyn took a moment to watch Jillian while Maul'tree squirmed in his iron grip.

"You do not look well. Your condition requires correction before we can proceed."

Jillian, not at all in a proper state of mind, stared hungrily at Dreyl'vyn before leaping toward him. Leaving Maul'tree to hang from one giant gauntlet, he caught her by the neck with his other hand, ignoring her weaponized fingers, which tore at his forearm.

Bringing the two closer together, he addressed the ugly, desperate man, who was practically flailing his broken legs in macabre circles, trying to free himself.

"I was incorrect. Your men will not taste your flesh tonight; she will."

Heaving Maul'tree forward, Dreyl'vyn threw him against the cavern wall, where he slumped helplessly to the floor, before releasing Jillian. With an inhuman growl, she leapt across the room, landing on his chest. Screaming, Maul'tree attempted to break from her otherworldly grasp, but as her jaw spread, disgorging the familiar black orbs, Maul'tree's eyes widened, and he quieted.

After Jillian finished her grim task - a dry husk all that remained of Maul'tree - she stood up and stepped backward. Staring intently at her gore-drenched form, panic rolled through me in waves. I had one question which weighed upon my mind.

Is Jillian still a monster, or has she reverted to herself again?

I felt I had one surefire way to tell before she turned and potentially attacked us.

Gliding forward, I quickly touched the base of her neck.

Instantly I was transported to an unknown house. Jillian stood across the room. Her back turned toward me, she was busy feeding a bird who sat on a perch. Much older than she had been in my last vision, she still appeared younger than she had at the spelling bee.

"Frankie, Frankie, Frankie! Such a pretty birdie!" she melodiously sung as she let him peck at the crust of a sandwich she had been eating.

Upon hearing a door slam in a separate room, Frankie became startled and began to squawk.

"Ohh, it's okay, Frankie," Jillian cooed. "It's just a big mean door. You're juuust fine. Yes you are, you-"

Frankie appeared to be anything but convinced. Squawking again, he launched into the air, landing on top of a curio cabinet. There, he squawked a third time and stomped out of sight.

As repetitive, frustrated squawks continued to rain down from above, Jillian frowned. Putting her hands on her hips, she called up to the bird.

"Franklin! You come down here right now!"

Frankie did not respond.

Sighing, Jillian grumbled to herself as she walked out of the room. "Ooh, you *bad* bird. Gonna make me climb up and get you again."

Returning moments later with a chair, she positioned it in front of the cabinet. Climbing up, she reached over the cabinet's top, which was still much too high for her to peer over. Another squawk and an "ouch!" indicated the bird would not be coming down willingly.

Reaching further up and over, Jillian stood on her tiptoes and stretched.

"Where are you, you pain in- *Oh!*"

Pausing, Jillian felt around for a moment before retrieving an all-too-familiar red grimoire. As she lifted it up over the lip, a letter slipped free and fell to the floor beneath her chair. Anxiously she stepped down, recovered the letter, and opened it.

"What's this?" she muttered to herself. "It's not even written in English."

As she said the words, the letters on the page appeared to Magically shimmer. When she had first opened the letter, it appeared legible to me, as if it had been written in English, but I already knew why. For young Jillian, there was no crystal, no Oculus. Her touch, however, seemed to be the key to unlocking its secrets.

The words ceasing their shimmering, Jillian let out a gasp; it was clear the letter before her had shifted to common English. For all I knew, the transformation was the first interaction with Magic she had ever experienced - the first one she was aware of, anyway.

Staring down at the page, her eyes began to flicker back and forth as she read.

To my beloved girl,

This volume has been written for you - a Magical compendium that only you might find and understand. While you may not grasp its secrets now, in time you will. As you grow and learn, you will understand the importance of what is contained inside of it.

Not far from you lies a treasure. Its immense power and worth is beyond anything you might imagine. However, in the wrong hands its strength could take everything from those you love; it may even kill the ones you love. The only way to stop those who would do harm with its power is to capture it and bring it back to where it belongs. This is your task.

Practice the spells written inside this compendium. Learn them well. When you feel you are ready, read this letter a second time. The answers you seek will be revealed to you, and you will learn how to complete your quest and save those you love.

Be secretive, be careful, and do not trust anyone; they are not who you think they are.

With more love than I can conjure,

Your Father

Jillian scrunched up her face as she read the letter, the words clearly sailing over her head, but from the sound of it, they were meant to. When she understood what the letter said, and learned what the grimoire taught her, she would be ready for her quest.

I already knew the answer she had yet to learn: the grimoire had been sent along to recruit her for the sword's retrieval; yet another person wanted the sword for him or herself. Although, I had to admit, whoever sent her back through time had seemingly failed; Vael'ehn retrieved the sword as he had planned.

If I have the opportunity to experience another vision, perhaps the author will be revealed, but for the moment, I have to be patient.

Mouthing over some of the letter's wording again, Jillian repeated the last two words on the page. "Your Father… *daddy?*"

As she spoke, her mother walked into the room.

"What did you say, dear?" she commented absently, her attention drawn to a pile of newly delivered letters from the mail.

Jillian, who had no hope of hiding the massive grimoire from sight, glanced down at the letter again. "They are not who you think they are," she whispered to herself.

Pausing, her mother turned. "You keep whispering, silly! I can't hear you. I've gone deaf from listening to your father too much!"

Jillian swallowed. "Can… can I have this book, mom?"

As her mother's eyes trailed downward, she stared at its cover for a moment. "Oh, I had forgotten about that. It was with-" She cleared her throat, no doubt recalling it had been with Jillian when she was delivered upon their doorstep. "You, uh, find that up on the cabinet, did you? You shouldn't be climbing up on chairs without help, you know."

Jillian nodded. "I know, but Frankie's up there, and I was trying to get him down."

"I see. Well, you need to be careful. Sometimes it's okay to ask us for help, even though you know you can do it yourself, just to be safe. And if you want that book, you can have it; it's just a blank notebook. Oh, maybe you could start a journal!" Her mother put her hands on her hips and turned to stare out the window, evidently recalling her youth. "You know, I had a journal when I was your age. It's fun to go back and see what you've written years later. I think I still have mine packed up around here some- *Jill?*"

"Thanks mom!" Jillian called. She had already taken off toward the stairs leading up to her room.

Sighing, her mother stepped up onto the chair and retrieved Frankie, who chirped and nipped her fingers as she brought him down.

Addressing the bird, she shook her head. "That girl's always going a million miles an hour, Frankie. Someday she's gonna be the death of me," she said with a smile, setting the bird back on his perch.

The vision faded to reveal Jillian's cold gaze inches from my face. Startled, I launched backward through the air. I had returned to the dark cave. The abrupt contrast between day and night was almost as startling as her countenance had been. But of her face much had changed. Nearly all of the deterioration had been restored, and she once again looked as she had after consuming her first victim.

Maybe even better. In fact, I'm sure of it.

Even so, I found myself disturbed. The vision had proven Jillian was still aware of herself, but again, her hair had changed. What once could have passed for roots which hadn't been touched up was now clearly two-toned. Almost three inches had become a deep crimson red, which glistened, even in the moonlight. Worse, her dead, grey eyes had lightened, giving off a soft luminescence and adding to her inhuman gaze.

If her hair and eyes are a meter of sorts, a way to gauge her transformation, we've still got some time, but not much.

In less than a day, Jillian had consumed two people. To the best of my memory, the events with Jack had transpired over nearly eleven. While I couldn't say I'd balk at the idea of a couple dozen terrible people meeting their demise at the hands of Jillian, it didn't seem likely she would last that long. With the rate her hair was changing, I had no choice but to assume four or five more victims might trigger the end of her transformation.

After that, who knows what she will become.

"Did…" Jillian motioned toward Maul'tree's desecrated remains. "I did that, didn't I?"

"In doing so, you appear to have restored your mind and your body," Dreyl'vyn commented. His words always came across as more of a statistical analysis than actual interest.

Jillian nodded. "Yeah, I feel good. And you know what? I don't regret what I just did, either. The first time that happened, I… I'm always going to regret that. But *him-*" She waved a flippant hand toward Maul'tree. "That asshole got *exactly* what he deserved. I mean, eating people? That's-" She clamped her mouth shut, no doubt realizing the irony of what she was about to say. "Well, I bet a significant number of innocent people have shown up here for 'dinner.'"

"I believe it was the best outcome for all involved," Dreyl'vyn agreed. "They were not forthcoming with information, and their intent was to deceive. If they managed to consume my body, I would have regenerated, and they would have all become quite ill. Most of their company would have died. We did them a justice."

Jillian stared at Dreyl'vyn's cold grey skin and frowned, possibly contemplating either what he'd taste like or what might be flowing through his veins. Turning, she surveyed the carnage which had befallen the highwaymen - or whatever it was their band had called themselves.

"Unfortunately, we still don't know where the tournament is, and there's no one around to tell us," she muttered.

"The one called Maul'tree divulged that information while you were intent on consuming him. He indicated there was a path out of the city in a north by northwest direction, which leads through the mountains. He stated it would be a long journey for us to take."

Jillian smiled. "Journey for *us* to take? So you're still coming with? I guess that means you like us!" she teased.

Dreyl'vyn returned her smile with an expressionless stare. "The civilization my race attempted to forge on this planet was destroyed when we were enslaved. I do not know of other race's customs; I do not know the land; I do not know where my people went after they departed from this place. If not for you, I would have been inactive for much of your time. If I do not accompany you now, I will meander aimlessly in search of those like myself. You have a direction to head toward, and I have chosen to follow it as well. Is that a consistent decision to make, or am I a burden to you?"

Stepping up to Dreyl'vyn, Jillian patted his chest. "I knew you liked us," she said with a wink. "You're not a burden at all."

Determined to move onward, I raised the level of my illumination, allowing the rest of the cavern to be revealed. What I assumed had been a naturally created cave, however, proved to be anything but. We found ourselves standing in the remains of a very old room, crafted from dark stone. If the roof hadn't collapsed, it would have been well-preserved. From our position, three stone archways led off in different directions, two of which had been crushed by the cave-in.

"Guess that limits our options," Jillian commented as she eyed the destroyed doorways.

"I can scale this wall," Dreyl'vyn announced. "It is nothing to me."

Jillian's eyes rose, following the significant climb toward street level. "Yeah, but let's try the doorway first. I don't know about you, but it's not every day I fall into a secret chamber. I feel like exploring!"

As the pair followed me into a narrow passageway, which led on for quite some time, I wondered what it might have been used for. The stonework appeared much older than the city above it, and as far as I knew, Vael'ehn's city would have been crafted by the first Xahl'thari people to set foot in the area.

Could this be from some other race, like the Gnill'var or the Lumynar?

It wouldn't take long to have my questions replaced with even more mysteries to solve. As the narrow passage opened up into a new chamber, my illumination reflected off of something I did not expect to see: a raised altar with five familiar forms positioned upon it.

"*Oh my god,*" Jillian exclaimed, covering her mouth in both excitement and surprise.

"There is no need to call for aid from a higher power," responded Dreyl'vyn. "These creatures appear to be petrified."

Petrified was indeed a good word to describe what stood before us. In a circle stood five giant dragons, identical to those mounted in Wenton's undercroft far in the future. However, the five before us still had their bodies attached. Even more impressive, they didn't appear to be made of stone but as living, breathing beings, frozen in time.

Wenton said that the dragons sacrificed their immortality to allow lesser races to use Magic. These could be the older, complete versions of the statues he said once existed, bridging Magic across the globe.

Cautiously, Jillian moved forward. "No, I was just surprised. I've seen these before - well, just their heads, actually. In the future there were sculptures of these made from stone. Jack said they came to life and talked to him." She turned back to face Dreyl'vyn. "These - or at least some version of these - were responsible for bringing me back to my body."

Dreyl'vyn pulled his hammer out from behind him and took a step forward.

"Then they should be destroyed."

"*Woah, what!*" Jillian blurted out in astonishment. "Did you not understand? They *saved* me! If these are what I think they are, they are the reason people in this time can interact with Magic."

Dreyl'vyn paused. "These statues have bound you within a corpse. They should be destroyed before they do the same to others."

Finally comprehending Dreyl'vyn's interpretation of her comment, Jillian seemed to relax. His only perspective on the matter was one of being captured and forced into an undead vessel. He seemed to assume, as a timeless being would, that the dragons before us were some sort of a weapon or torture device.

"It's not like that, Dreyl'vyn. I understand what happened to you was something awful, but I'm still glad I was brought back, even though it didn't work quite right. Where I was before my resurrection would have been complete torture. This existence may prove to be the same, but at least I still have a chance to correct it. I think we need to learn more about these dragons instead of destroying them. Unfortunately, it looks like someone already started."

What Jillian was referring to, were two areas covered in a dusting of crushed stone where dragons matching those colors once stood. Had they all been intact, the statues would have stood in a complete circle, all seven facing toward a center point on the altar. Instead, two of them appeared to have been blown to bits and removed. What was left were only a few handfuls of purple and turquoise fragments, amounting to almost nothing.

Purple and turquoise?

I counted the dragons, including their destroyed counterparts.

Seven in total.

Based on what Wenton had once said about their future counterparts, the statues before us shared a connection with each type of Magic. As to which color might have matched which type, however, I wasn't ready to make a guess. Making matters more confusing, I had been informed there were *six* types of Magic, but in the future I had met only the five dragons still standing.

I had seen purple and turquoise Magic before. Cindee's spells had been a similar turquoise color, and the Magic channeled through my form had often been purple. Not to mention, what had been regurgitated from each of Jillian's victims were those exact same hues, lending credence to the idea that turquoise and purple might have represented life and something to do with people's souls.

Wenton had indicated that the statues were sacrificed at some point in the future - from my current perspective - during a final confrontation with Vael'ehn. But considering two had already been destroyed, and that battle had yet to happen, something seemed out of place.

The Grey dragon's words still stood out in my mind.

"It had nothing to do with the loss of Xhor'thre'vzerious and Yvehn'sssul'xahvon."

Likely, the two nearly incomprehensible names referred to the pair of destroyed dragon statues.

Five functional and two broken statues, yet only six types of Magic…

Who would have destroyed them, and why don't these numbers add up?

"You see how they're all aimed toward the center here?" Jillian observed, pointing her finger in the direction we were facing. "It's like the statues were used for summoning, or as an altar - something along those lines. At least, that's my guess. I mean, why else would they point toward the middle? To teleport someone somewhere?" She sighed. "Well, whatever they used to do in this arrangement, they don't anymore. I'd bet anything that, even if we knew their purpose, nothing would happen without those missing two."

She walked over and picked up a tiny piece of the purple statue.

"This could have been an accident, I guess, but it doesn't seem like the shattered remnants would have disappeared. It wouldn't surprise me if someone stole the pieces or got rid of them on purpose."

Gingerly setting the piece onto the floor, as if it were volatile, she walked back toward us.

"We'll have to keep this area in mind if we notice anything else relating to it, but it seems like this entire complex was forgotten and abandoned a long time ago, even further in the past than we are right now."

Her eyes traced the perimeter of the basic circular room, which didn't appear to have any other passageways leading outward from it.

"And it looks like we'll be heading back to where we came from as well."

Several minutes later, we had made our way back to the collapsed room. There, I levitated both Jillian and Dreyl'vyn out of the pit using Magic, one at a time. I had initially thought it impossible to levitate a man wearing enough armor to build a bomb shelter, but after a few moments, I had managed to convince myself otherwise.

What if, underneath all that armor, Dreyl'vyn is just full of thousands of happy thoughts?

What if he wears that gear to weigh him down so his aspirations don't rise so high, he just floats away?

It was a silly notion, one I considered keeping to myself for the rest of my days, but it worked. Both Dreyl'vyn and his happy thoughts were lifted from the pit and set on a solid section of the town square. As his feet contacted the ground, the bricks cracked under his weight. The noise, as simple as it was, elicited feelings of accomplishment inside me.

He's certainly the biggest object I've moved to date. Picking him up was quite an achievement!

And it was true. I thought back to when I had pulled down the bestiary book from inside Vael'ehn's tent. It might have been large for a book, but it was certainly nowhere near Dreyl'vyn-sized.

Upon contact with the ground, Dreyl'vyn eyed me with an expression I could have confused with respect. "You stated this person is trapped inside his form, yet he seems to have abilities far greater than our own."

Jillian, who had been impressed herself, laughed. "Dreyl'vyn, you of all people should know, being trapped is just a point of view. You may not be helpless - you may have everything someone else might want - but if you're not where *you* want to be, then you're trapped."

As Dreyl'vyn nodded in agreement, I thought about her words.

Am *I trapped?*

I was certainly trapped inside my crystal at one point, but as the journey had played out, it certainly felt less so.

Is the way to freeing myself simply to appreciate what I've become?

Jillian spun around, searching the sky for something. "Dreyl'vyn, do you know which way was is north?"

Dreyl'vyn also looked upward. "I have heard you can look to the sky on a clear night and locate Hayl'chron's star to the north of this area. Unless you are aware of that reference, it does us no good; I have never been told which star it is."

Jillian shook her head. "You're right; I have no idea who Hayl'chron is, but I bet you know which direction the sun sets." Dreyl'vyn responded by pointing out toward the darkness. "Well, the sun rises in the east and sets in the west. So that means north is probably somewhere over there, and northwest is somewhere along that direction. I can't say that's like, one hundred percent accurate, but it's *something*. When it starts to get light out again, maybe we'll be able to see where we need to go more clearly. And who knows? Maybe we'll find a sign or a road - something on our way out of town."

As we made our way out through the broken city, it was clear a sign would have been far too much to ask. The farther away from the amphitheater we moved, the worse the damage became. Even with my light to guide us, where we were heading was just an educated guess.

"How certain are you the sun was in this-" Jillian began, but the sound of a rock tumbling down from somewhere nearby caused her to pause. "*Hey!* Who's there? I saw you move! I can see pretty damn well in the dark. I swear to god, I'll eat you like I did Maul'tree! You better not be following-"

"Ahm sorreh! Don' cha eat meh! Ahm ah comin' aht!" A voice cried from the darkness.

From behind a collapsed pile of rubble, Eugene walked into view. He had apparently survived the ordeal - or at the very least avoided it - and had been following us.

"*Eugene,*" Jillian growled. Leaping forward, she grabbed him by the neck and lifted him above her head. Spinning the poor man around, she seemed prepared to throw him into the distance like a shotput.

"*Wait! Wait!*" Eugene spluttered, his windpipe mostly cut off. "Ah heard ya back theyre! Ol' Eugene kin show ya outtah heyre!"

Jillian lowered him down to eye level, his own eyes settling on her mouth. Considering his terrified expression, he must have witnessed what she did to Maul'tree.

"*You* are the reason we had to deal with Maul'tree and his crew in the first place," she growled. "You chose the wrong side. Things never end well for the snitch."

Eugene spluttered again. "Ol' Eugene don' know what's ah snatch, but ah din' mean ya no herm - well, not fro'meh, anyways! Ol' Eugene jus' had tah do wat he's toe'd. Maul'tree ain' tha type'ah guy you'anna be talkin' back ta. Ahs justah followin' orders, ah'swears! Please don' eat meh!"

Jillian set Eugene back on the ground. "Show us the way to the path that leads through the mountains, and I'll let you live." Eugene nodded. "I've watched one too many movies where a guy like you sends the heroes into a trap by leading them the wrong way. That isn't you, *is it?*"

Eugene shook his head. "Ah ain' never watched ah moo-vees. We ain' never had nothin' 'round these parts like wha'ever thayt's bein', so ol' Eugene don' even know what a moo-vees might make 'em do. Ah don' have no boss no more neither, so ah geddah do what ah want tah. Ol' Eugene kin show ya's, and theyn ah'll be'ah *long gone!*"

"On your word, then," Jillian said, extending her hand. Eugene spit on his hand and extended it, which immediately caused Jillian to lower hers. "On your word," she repeated.

Nodding vigorously, Eugene walked past her to take the lead.

"Ever seen a dragon statue around here?" Jillian whispered as he passed.

Eugene turned and started at her dumbly. "Dergin?"

Jillian shook her head. "Nothing. Go ahead and lead the way."

As Eugene headed out into the darkness, he began to describe what had transpired in relation to the once brilliant city. According to him, the fall had happened quickly, but the events leading up to it had not. The Amphitheater had once been popular - so popular in fact that the city was suffering from too many visitors and not enough food or housing to support them. In those days, the competitors never fought each other to the death; they fought as any modern combat sport did - until one of the combatants fell and could no longer continue.

Over time, however, the sport changed as it attracted larger, more brutal combatants, leading to serious problems. There was a long line of warriors interested in fighting, but almost no one wanted to risk death or injury by fighting against someone who could kill or maim them, and those at the top of the leaderboards had gained their rank for that specific reason.

The addition of Cimmerians - the only foes the champions continued to fight "to the death" - hadn't helped much, as they were always bested by the competitors.

They seemed dull, confused, and generally unable to put up a good fight. Those who *were* dangerous, like Dreyl'vyn, were kept in check by spellwork that limited their true potential. When one lost to a champion - in some cases, two or three at one time - it wasn't a surprise for anyone. Nonetheless, they were thrown in over and over.

The spectators slowly left, and the sport, which had allowed the city to accumulate great popularity, was on the verge of disappearing altogether. But out of nowhere, new combatants began to sprout up. According to the headlines, a band of rebels called "Retrogrades" had been captured - horrible, disfigured beings, bent on destruction.

The Retrogrades had been found plotting to overthrow Magical cities and take over their land. Rather than imprisoning them for their crimes, however, they were sentenced to fight in the ring until they died. That of course led to a revitalization of the sport. With the forces of evil being thrown into deadly combat against superior champions, the people couldn't wait to watch another bout.

Then one night the city was suddenly overrun by thousands of Retrogrades. No one knew where they came from, and no one saw them coming. It seemed as if they were sprouting from the ground itself. Within hours Empor'Vael had been conquered by the horrific monsters, and the residents had been massacred. Those that could, fled, but most had no warning and died. The city fell in less than a day, the damage so great it was considered better to move on and ward the other cities against further attacks than attempt to reclaim the rubble.

"An' thayt's wh'n peoples like Mistah Maul'tree show't up. They been takin' over wh'n nothin' were lef' an' tha Retrah'graydes h'd take'n off," finished Eugene.

"That's a sad story," Jillian said, "and I'm sorry you had to go through it. There's clearly nothing left for you here. If you'd like, you can come with us instead. I don't know how far we have to go, but whatever we find *has* to be better than this."

Eugene shook his head. "Ah'd love'tah go on wit you n' yer big ol' friend n' yer nifty gadget there, but ah reckon this'll be mah home fer tha rest'ah mah days, ahm thinkin'. Ol' Eugene's gonna have'tah be part'n ways with ya. Hopin' ya don' mind. This here path we been ah walkin' down, it's tha one'll get ya wheyre ye wanna be goin'. Ah were just enjoyin' talkin' ta some good folk fer once."

Jillian nodded. "I suppose *you're* the lord of these here lands now, hmm?

Eugene laughed. "Well, ya know wat? Ah reckon ah am! But ah think ol' Eugene's gon' go try'n rally some'o them others 'round heyre an' make'ah good ol' tahn instayd. Maybeh nex' time yer out 'round these heyre perts, ya'll come'n stahp on by?"

Jillian smiled. "Sounds good, Eugene. Take care of yourself."

As Eugene parted ways with us and walked back into the darkness, I couldn't help but feel both sorry and hopeful for him. He was a victim of a tragedy, but with our accidental help, it sounded as if he might make something of the ruined city. Years from now I sincerely wished, for his sake, there *would* be a "Eugenesville" on the map.

And I hope they have a school where they teach proper grammar.

CHAPTER Forty-Eight

-PRECARIOUS PASSAGE-

Throughout the night we traveled with very little spoken between the pair, Dreyl'vyn seemingly not one for small talk and the night's events no doubt weighing upon Jillian's mind. The silence, however, did not bother me. With Jack and the others, I had taken to spending most every night alone, patrolling while they slept. It seemed Jillian and Dreyl'vyn would need no sleep, and I welcomed the company.

No sleep also means I have twice as much time to catch up to Jack.

As a sliver of morning light crested over the horizon, the silhouette of a nearby mountain range revealed its outline along the sky. In the darkness I had no idea we'd been so close, but as my eyes followed the path we had been traveling as it cut up and into the mountains, I was filled with excitement.

On the other side, there might be a city of some sort. Travelers would likely need to rest afterward; what better place to do so than at a local inn and tavern?

Looking upward, Jillian gaped at the mountain. *"Oh, wow!* I could see the mountain in the distance, but I didn't realize until now that we were so close. That has to be, like-"

"Sixty-two tosses of a Kohr'ohn Lance, on Varah'then's peak, your victory dance," Dreyl'vyn interrupted.

Jillian, baffled by the odd rhyme, stopped walking. *"What?"*

Dreyl'vyn looked down at her. "It is a verse sung by Xahl'thari children. There was an annual race from the city to the peak of Mount Varah'then. I would not consider it an accurate summation; the verse is a lie."

"I would think it's a creative way of telling how far it is to the peak," Jillian considered. "Why is it a lie? How far can a Kohr'ohn Lance be thrown?"

"It is a lie because, when unimpeded, I can throw a Kohr'ohn Lance over two thousand paces, several spans greater than the Xahl'thari athletes. The mountain is one hundred and ninety thousand paces away from the city; I have heard it mentioned on many occasions. If you were to throw a Kohr'ohn Lance that far in sixty-two attempts, you would have thrown it over three thousand paces with each occurrence. The children's summation is inaccurate and should be disregarded."

"Wait, did you just calculate that in your head?" Jillian asked, surprise evident on her face as she and Dreyl'vyn continued to walk again.

"No. I have had to experience long periods of your time with no task to perform aside from thinking. It is remarkable how your time is more painful the less it is filled with; that is counterintuitive."

"How so?" Jillian asked with a wry smile. She clearly understood the statement, but for some reason seemed keen on helping Dreyl'vyn to accept his condition.

Dreyl'vyn pulled out his giant hammer and swung it for effect. It made a deep whooshing noise as it swept through the air.

"The greater the mass of a weapon, the heavier the blow, the more pain it will cause. Your time is counterintuitive. The less you fill it with, the less substance it has, but the more damage it causes you."

Jillian laughed, which garnered a raised eyebrow from Dreyl'vyn. "You said you don't function very well as a time-bound being, Dreyl, but I'll tell you what; you sure seem to understand it quite well. Having nothing but time on your hands *is* pretty painful!"

As Jillian continued to laugh, she glanced over her shoulder at the destroyed city we had left behind the night before. We must have been over twenty miles away by that point, but even so, the devastation that had befallen it was evident. The city was once quite large, but all that was left for us to see was a sweeping view of rubble with only a half-decomposed amphitheater standing in the center to identify the site as once having some sort of stature.

I wonder if the Retrogrades left it standing as a mockery of where they had once been imprisoned.

"You know, Dreyl," Jillian considered, changing the subject, "I was thinking about what Eugene said." She began to laugh again. "Sorry, that guy was almost incomprehensible!" She grabbed the sides of her head, as if she were attempting to yank out her hair. "It's like my brain began to wear out just from translating his grammar!" She sighed. "But uh, I was thinking about what he said in regard to the Retrogrades. Don't you think it's a little odd that, just as the city was losing its revenue, this *big bad threat* showed up, and the city guard just *happened* to capture them *just* in time to save the day?"

"I have fought Retrogrades on *many* occasions," Dreyl'vyn said. "I have overheard some say Retrogrades were once men - men who mutilated themselves. They are *not* men, nor have they ever been so. The corpse outside the amphitheater was from one of them, and it was typical in size and mass. I can tell you the Retrogrades were indeed ruthless and powerful, but they were also *not* a race; they were created."

"Created? How do you know? What did you see?"

"Eugene was correct. There were not many champions eager to risk death in the ring. Occasionally a Retrograde, such as Mul'bock, proved so frightening, no one would step forward. Cimmerians would be thrown into the ring instead. We would fight and be crushed over and over until the combatant was worn down. Afterward, they would be defeated by someone with higher regard than we had earned.

"You would also be correct in assuming the crowds were quite entertained to watch a group of heroes assault what they perceived as an evil force until it was vanquished. But they were deceived, at least partially. I do not know where the Retrogrades came from, but I tore them apart with my own hands. What I saw inside them was not living."

"It's referred to as technology," Jillian said. "What that Retrograde had strapped to it were called *missiles* in my time, and I find it *real* hard to believe there are missiles in this age. If you're saying those types of devices were inside their bodies, they could have been augmenting themselves with it, but as to where-"

Dreyl'vyn motioned for her to pause. "I comprehend what technology is, and I have experienced what effect it can be used for, but what I saw was not *just* internal. The organs, muscles, tissue - they were grown around, and through, and *with* the technology. If a creature is added on to, it is quite different than if it has been that way from the beginning. Whether they produced a new version of their race themselves or someone constructed them, the Retrogrades were created just as you witnessed. They were never born, they never grew, and they were never added onto."

Jillian shook her head. "Hmm… You're right; that sure sounds to me like someone stumbled upon an opportunity to create a new marketing scheme, and things got out of hand. The new attraction went wild, and no one was prepared for it, so it wiped out everything. It's like Jurassic Park."

Dreyl'vyn shook his head. "I have not been anywhere outside of the amphitheater for a significant duration of your time; I have not attended that park."

Jillian smiled. "It's… a story from my time. I wasn't thinking when I referenced it." Again turning her attention to the mountain, she changed the subject. "So, we're nearing the base of the mountain. How long do you think it'll be until we reach it?"

Dreyl'vyn squinted as he eyed the peak. "If you want an estimate, I feel we have between sixty-thousand and eighty-thousand paces left to travel."

Jillian wrinkled her brow. "Do you know what paces are in feet or miles?"

Dreyl'vyn shook his head. "I do not understand the measurement of miles, but your other term, footsteps, is similar to paces."

"Hmm…" Jillian considered. "I don't quite remember, but I think there's around five-thousand feet in a mile - something like that. If paces are similar to feet, then we're talking twelve to sixteen miles-ish. That's not bad. Maybe four or five hours on flat ground at the rate we're traveling. We should be to the top in no time, and then it's all downhill from there!"

Jillian's summation appeared correct, and we covered the distance to the base of the mountain with no incidents. The path, which had been compact and level, stopped abruptly at the remains of a small building, which might have been used for resting before or after the difficult trek over the mountain. The building had long since disintegrated, and the trail, too, seemed to have been neglected for just as long.

Before much progress had been made, the hike became less of a hike and more of a rock climbing session. In large areas the mountain had collapsed - either from a landslide or some other event - and the path had been entirely wiped away. In its place were countless boulders and heaps of rock. Dreyl'vyn had taken it upon himself to toss or push them down the hill, but climbing up and over proved more time-effective.

At first I had begun to hoist the pair upward, my efforts proving to make them quite light on their feet as they leaped from boulder to boulder, but soon I tired mentally. As much as I hated to admit it, I still had my limits, and my limits were not very high.

Excruciating hours ticked by until, eventually, we progressed past the collapsed areas of the path. Unfortunately, we found ourselves face to face with a new opposition: cold. Slowly but surely, as we made our way up the side of the mountain, snow began to blanket the ground. Flecks turned into a dusting, a dusting turned into a coating, a coating turned into a blanket, and a blanket turned into a *wall*.

Worse, the cold seemed to have a noticeable effect on Jillian and Dreyl'vyn. Immortal, vampiric, regenerative, ghoulish - whatever they were, whatever Magic coursed through their bodies, it seemed to be slowed by cold. Before long, triumphant strides diminished into trudging, and trudging degenerated into stumbling.

As the sun slowly dipped behind the mountains, clouds condensed and the wind increased; a blizzard on Mount Varah'then could appear in minutes, without any warning, or so it seemed. The snow around us was whipped into the air, and our vision was reduced to inches. Try as I might, already weakened by my prior efforts, I could not hold the adverse weather at bay. Battered by what felt like hurricane-force winds, I was relegated to hiding behind Dreyl'vyn's towering form just to stay in place.

Slogging through snow passing her waist, which had already been plowed through by Dreyl'vyn's tree trunk-sized legs, Jillian finally halted her progress before collapsing. Falling face first, her form dropped into the white, leaving a humanoid indentation in the frozen precipitation. Pausing, Dreyl'vyn turned toward the site of her descent. Reaching down, he removed Jillian from the icy tomb and laid her out on top of it, her prone form preventing her from sinking very far.

"It would seem these forms *do* have a weakness: that of cold," Dreyl'vyn boomed over the deafening wind. "I expected opposition, but this is different. I have not experienced this level of impediment before. I suspect if we continue onward at this pace, we will not arrive at the other side before solidifying entirely." And it was true; the snow rising to his knees, he, too, had slowed to a crawl.

Jillian did not respond. Her skin paling to a soft blue hue, she had passed out entirely. Grimly, I moved forward, intent on checking whether or not she could still summon a vision. Inches from her face, her eyes popped open, startling me. I drifted backward as she attempted to sit up, the action causing her to sink back into the snow.

"Dreyl, we... I... it's..."

Dreyl'vyn regarded her, seeming to consider their predicament. At last, he reached back and removed the colossal battle hammer; it likely weighed a few dozen pounds more than Jillian did.

"I do not have the ability to carry you both," he announced to the weapon. "May you someday reveal yourself to a new warrior worthy of your protection."

He heaved it out into the distance, watching it sail into the white until its dark form had disappeared from view.

Dreyl'vyn once again lifted Jillian from the snow. Draping her over his shoulder, he began to barrel forward, his massive legs plowing through the snow as he forged ahead. His movement caused a wave of powder to deflect upward from his chest and over his head, likely obscuring his already limited view in the storm.

Quickly I swept down behind the small of his back where his wake left an undisturbed, snow-free pocket to ride within.

Unexpectedly, a hidden rock caused Dreyl'vyn to stumble. The momentary lapse in his forward movement forced me to collide with his armor. To my surprise, touching the cold metal plate pulled me away from the snow-covered mountain to a land somewhere far away.

My mind taking a moment to adjust from the blinding white of the mountainside, I found myself hovering in a lush green forest, surrounded by armored and robed men whom I had never met before. Kneeling, a battered and bloody soldier regarded a tall, greying commander in ornate red and black armor, not dissimilar from Dreyl'vyn's set.

"Please, Ty'berus, don't do this. I have a family," the man pleaded.

"Surely you know why we *must* do this," Ty'berus replied. "Do you think I take joy in your suffering? Your eyes tell me that your mind has returned, but moments ago you tried to pull the very soul from Lord Tor'vish." He pointed to a pale, sickly man leaning against a tree. "Thar'ceron, what happened to you can not be corrected. You are as one of the Dghem'oni horde now. If not in this moment, then surely in another."

Thar'ceron began to cry. Looking down at the tears blotting his blood-stained hands, he took notice of their darkened tinge. "*Why!* Why did they do this to me!"

"Do you not see? They did this on purpose to destroy our Order from the inside. If you are to continue on, you will lose your mind completely and usher in the destruction they bring with them. The tainted must *all* be put to rest before the darkness spreads."

Thar'ceron's eyes widened in realization that it was not just he who they had been after. Looking up, he found himself snared in Ty'berus' sorrowful gaze. "Surely you can not mean you would harm my family? They are innocent people! They had nothing to do with what happened to me!"

"It matters not the intent. What is done, is done. If left to their own devices, any who are tainted will consume Magic until they no longer remember their convictions, and the Dghem'oni horde finds their way through to Xahl."

Tainted tears continued to stream from Thar'ceron's eyes. "My... my oldest son was born before I was corrupted. Surely you can save *him?* Raise him as your own, I beg of you. Teach him the ways of the Order. Allow him to destroy what defeated me."

Ty'berus frowned but nodded. "I will see that your oldest son does not suffer the same fate as your family."

Thar'ceron managed a weak smile, knowing that at least a small part of his lineage would carry on. "Before you end my life, would you... perform one more action in my name, Ty'berus?"

Ty'berus nodded. "What would you ask of me?"

Trembling, Thar'ceron stood to his feet and extended his hands. "Bind my soul to this armor so that it becomes an Object of Power to protect my son when he is old enough to wear it."

Ty'berus seemed surprised by the request. "I understand your intent, Thar'ceron, but no one would agree to partner with you and perform such an act. An Object of Power with only one contributor would be as nothing against a Dghem'on. It would-"

"No," Thar'ceron interjected. "My *entire* soul. You know you have to wipe me from existence so that I can never be brought back by the Dghem'oni, should they learn the proper spells. Bind me entirely to the armor instead. I will not remember who I am for I will not be who I once was, but I will be led by my convictions."

Removing his armored gauntlets, Ty'berus tossed them to the ground and wiped sweat from his forehead with a cloth. Looking around at his men, he shook his head. "Do you have any idea what you ask, Thar'ceron? That type of spellwork has not been performed for a very long time. No one would volunteer to bind their entire soul to an object. It is-"

"It is my only chance to fight for revenge! My only chance to crush those who have destroyed my family! Please, I beg of you, do this for me."

Letting out a long sigh, Ty'berus nodded. "You have been a faithful soldier all your years, Thar'ceron. I will try my best to honor your request."

Turning to the others, he discussed the ritual he intended to perform. Several in attendance protested but eventually acquiesced due to Ty'berus' persistence.

"P-please hurry," Thar'ceron stuttered. He had begun to shake and sweat, his eyes glowing with a hunger that would soon pull him away from his conscious mind.

Surrounding Thar'ceron, Ty'berus and a group of six men laid hands upon his armor. Summoning an ancient tome, Ty'berus paged through it and began to read a series of spells intended to pull from one's soul, implanting that power into the intended object.

Before long, Thar'ceron's armor began to glow with the power harvested from his soul. When the time came for the closing incantations to be read, Ty'berus instead continued on, repeating the spells over and over again.

Thar'ceron, falling to his knees, closed his eyes and steadied himself as tears spattered the ground before him. After the spellwork had made several repetitions, his posture drooped, and his expression went slack. Thar'ceron's body, although seemingly alive, had been completely scoured of its soul.

Finally, Ty'berus read the closing incantations and the six motioned, in unison, toward the unconscious body. Thar'ceron's skin turned grey; seconds later it crumbled to dust. The enchanted armor fell to the ground among the ashes, but glowed brilliantly with the power it had attained.

"And now unto you, artifact," Ty'berus announced, "I bestow the name of Loh'Mach, the Unrelenting, for you are one who has forgotten his name but will never forsake his purpose. Come forth, Loh'Mach, your master calls you."

Rising from the ground, the armor was filled by a shadowy, swirling visage, which hinted at the shape of a man. Taking no action, it stood silently, waiting for further commands.

Ty'berus eyed the apparition as one might an old friend. "I hope you find the revenge you seek," he whispered. "For all our sakes."

Dissipating, the spirit faded away, allowing the pieces of armor to come to a rest upon the ground.

Turning, Ty'berus regarded his men. "Dorr'rel, load Loh'Mach into a traveling chest. Everyone else prepare to teleport; we are heading to Thar'ceron's home."

I arrived from the vision to find the blizzard still in full force, Dreyl'vyn weakly plowing his way through an increasingly deep wash of snow. The chances of either he or Jillian making it off the mountain without freezing seemed low, and I felt there was nothing within my Magical abilities to change that fact.

Turning my attention toward Dreyl'vyn's armor - a set which had once belonged to Vael'ehn's father - I considered the vision I had just experienced. Somehow I had interacted with it, somehow it had managed to tell me its tale, indicating it had retained a consciousness. Thar'ceron's soul still resided somewhere within its metal plates.

Drifting forward, I touched it again, but received no response.

I know who you are, Loh'Mach. You were once Thar'ceron, who gave his soul to protect his son, Vael'curion. After your death, your son was manipulated by demons, just as you were. I am on a mission to rescue him so he can aid us in ridding the world of their taint.

If you allow these warriors to freeze on this mountain, your son will die. He will be consumed by the demonic corruption growing inside him, and this planet's Magic will be offered up to create a portal for Roth'Roh'Kah to travel through.

I call upon you now, Thar'ceron! Remember your name. Remember your purpose. Remember your vow.

Slowing down, Dreyl'vyn began to teeter back and forth. The upper layers of his exposed skin had turned black, and several areas had fractured after having been frozen solid. Laying Jillian down on the snow, he called out: "Come forth, Loh'Mach, your master calls you!"

The armor phased out of reality and drifted off of him, coalescing into the form it had taken inside my vision.

Dreyl'vyn regarded the armored wraith as if it were a fellow warrior. "I cannot go on with you, my old friend. May you someday reveal yourself-"

But Loh'Mach did not wait for him to finish. Turning toward the direction we had been heading, the armor began to glow. From within it a sphere of blazing fire formed, which grew until it was larger than even Dreyl'vyn himself. The snow around us erupted into giant billows of steam as it melted, causing rivers to run down the surface of the mountain. Sprinting forward, Loh'Mach began to blaze its way through the storm, carving a path not only through snow but also boulders and outcroppings of earth.

Picking up Jillian, Dreyl'vyn sprinted forward in an effort to keep up with the disembodied man. Together they ran on for what seemed like hours.

Dreyl'vyn stopped abruptly as Loh'Mach's spellwork fizzled away. The two stood in a quickly filling, ice-lined caldera, formed by the blazing globe of Magic. Collapsing to its knees, Loh'Mach faded in and out of existence as its armor began to rust and decay, as if it were experiencing hundreds of years' worth of wear in an instant.

Seeing that his old ally had given everything to allow us a fighting chance, Dreyl'vyn reached out and placed a hand upon its pauldron, which crumbled under his touch. "Loh'Mach, your master releases you," he stated, his voice almost lost upon the howling wind. As he withdrew his hand, the remains of the armor disintegrated before being swept up in the storm.

Eyeing the mountain peak with his hardened, dark gaze, Dreyl'vyn again hoisted Jillian in his arms, this time plowing headfirst into the deep frozen wasteland ahead of him. Awash in waves of ice, I closed in behind the giant in an attempt to shield myself. I couldn't help but feel foolish as I watched him continue onward, completely nude and faced with still hours of trudging through deep snow. There I was, invulnerable, able to fly up to the mountain peak in an instant, yet I had to count on a naked dead man and a spirit to save Jillian from dying.

I have to pull myself together. I cannot count on others to save the day.

My world blotted out by white on one side, Dreyl'vyn's back on the other, we continued on throughout the day. I spent the entire voyage attempting to warm both the giant and Jillian with my Magic, but I knew it was a losing battle. The wind pushed harder, the snow became deeper, and I still had my limits. The more I felt the strain of my spellwork, the more desperate I became, and the less effective my spells were.

If she dies, you're to blame. Everyone else did their part.

Suddenly, Dreyl'vyn came to a halt, the shower of snow dispersing from around him. My view clearing, I was able to see that not only had the storm ceased but he had nearly plowed his way to the top of the mountain. For miles around, the landscape sloped down around us. To the southeast I could still make out the broken form of the city and, further south from its location, an incredible sprawling wall, likely constructed to stem the Retrograde threat. To the west lay some sort of transitional pine-covered forest and, farther out, what could have passed for farmland. To the north rose yet more mountains, and possibly a glacier.

Dreyl'vyn, large portions of his body frozen solid from exposure, had not stopped to admire the view, nor had he paused to plot a new course. Teetering back and forth, he toppled forward, crashing face first onto the ice. The earth around us shook violently, followed shortly after by a loud cracking noise. Within seconds, both he and Jillian disappeared from view into a chasm below.

Panicking, I swooped down after them, intent on pulling the pair from the fissure before they hit the bottom. However, as I made my way inside, I spotted their bodies ahead of me. The two had fallen into a lengthy cavern, its walls lined entirely in pure blue ice. Along its floor, a stream of water flowed, its path likely carving out the room over many years. Jillian and Dreyl'vyn lay face down in the water, limply sliding along the channel together.

Gliding down, I pulled them out of the stream and onto a flat depression. Ignoring Dreyl'vyn for the moment, I drifted over to inspect Jillian's much smaller form. Cold and still, she lay unconscious on the ice, her skin severely frostbitten and purple. Fearing the worst, I moved closer and touched her forehead.

As my vision constricted, I was transported to Jillian's familiar bedroom. Appearing similar to how it had in prior visions, it must have been near the time of the spelling bee or the first incident with the demon. Whether the timeframe was before or after those incidents, I could not tell.

Before me, Jillian sat on the floor, the grimoire and letter in her lap. Frowning, she stared down at the page. "I've performed Magic from almost every section of this book, and nothing seems confusing to me anymore. When are you going to show me something different!" she demanded of the letter.

In response the page shimmered and rippled, the letters rearranging themselves into dozens of rows, columns, and shapes. In seconds they had drawn a crude depiction of a map.

"Hey, that's our house!" she exclaimed, appearing to recognize the area. "And that mark… that's… right down the street!"

Leaping to her feet, Jillian hastily slid the book under her bed before racing toward a flight of stairs. As I followed behind, she descended the steps two at a time while yelling across the house: "I'm going outside to play!"

Her mother attempted a response of some sort, but the door had slammed, and we had left, before her first words were complete.

Racing down the sidewalk at a full sprint, Jillian studied the map as best she could while shaking violently. At last, she came to a halt in front of a small house.

"This is it," she mouthed in between puffs of air.

As if she were imagining herself as being invisible - and perhaps she was - she began to slink up the driveway, her eyes twitching back and forth with every small sound she heard. As she reached the rear fence, a noise from the road caused her to turn. Seeing nothing, she returned to the direction she had been heading, only to find a young boy staring back at her instead.

"Hello," the boy called. "I'm Jack!"

Startled by his sudden appearance, Jillian jumped. "You're not on the map!" she exclaimed, the odd statement no doubt formed by the unexpected interaction.

Jack wrinkled his nose and laughed at the silly comment. "How would I be on a map? I move around a lot!"

Jillian, regaining her composure, also laughed, her cheeks darkening. "Is… is this *your* backyard?" she asked, eyeing the plot of land behind him.

"It's my dad's. Or my grandpa's, or somethin'. I'm Jack," he repeated. "What's your name?"

Jillian again peered over his shoulder at the backyard, no doubt wondering if the object she sought lay where the map had indicated. Finally, she gave him her full attention.

"I'm Jill. Have you lived here a long time?"

The vision fading, the icy cold of the cave swept back in, causing me to shudder from the extreme temperature change. Finding myself able to experience the temperature while remaining largely unaffected by it, the response was more of a trained reaction than a necessity.

You're not cold. Stop acting like it.

Jillian and Dreyl'vyn still lay before me, unconscious and frostbitten. I had proven Jillian remained inside her inhuman body, but I needed to verify the same of Dreyl'vyn. Gliding over, I touched his bare cheek. Met by no response, I felt ashamed to find he was completely devoid of life.

Both he and Thar'ceron have given all of themselves to get us this far.

But how can Dreyl'vyn die? I'm supposed to see him in Wenton's secret room; I was told so by my vision!

Dreyl'vyn had accompanied the rest of the group, not only undamaged by frost and larger than life, but adorned in armor that had just given itself for our safety. Yet there he lay before me, frozen, dead, and nude, his armor long gone.

A horrible thought occurred to me, filling me with disappointment.

I was supposed to keep him alive! I needed to protect him from the storm and I haven't;

I huddled behind him like a coward, and now he is gone!

You are such a failure! You've relied on others to do your job for you, and because of your incompetence, you've ruined everything!

Disgusted with myself, I looked around at the bleak, frozen cave. Finding nothing at all but water and ice, my focus settled upon Jillian.

The least you can do is prevent yourself from making the same mistake twice.

Regarding Dreyl'vyn's corpse, I made a grim conclusion.

We've fallen into a room made of frozen water, on top of a snow-covered, barren mountain, and I need to create a fire to save Jillian.

I'm sorry, Dreyl'vyn, but your body is the only fuel I have.

Pausing a moment longer, I studied the giant's passive, stone-like face, as if it had been evaluating my decision.

You know you'd do the same - make a decision with no emotion, just because it was "correct." That's how you viewed the world, and this is how it has to be.

Besides, you never liked your body anyway.

Reassuring myself that what I was about to do was for the greater good, I focused on Dreyl'vyn's corpse and imagined the spark of a match. Instantly his body ignited into flames, his massive bulk burning like no natural fire could have. Grimly I watched his flesh as it was consumed by the blaze.

Thank you for getting us as far as you did. At least my mistake has released you from your bondage once and for all. If you're still alive, up there hovering somewhere, I wish you all the best.

After dragging Jillian's body closer to the fire, I had hoped she would soon regain consciousness. Sadly, I was wrong; hours passed by, the corpse barely aflame, Jillian's body lying cold and motionless.

How can I do this poorly with what I've been given? I should have all the answers, but I constantly find myself with none!

For all I know, in the prior version of events, before I arrived and changed everything, Jillian had met Dreyl'vyn, and they both made it past the mountain, somehow unhindered.

Perhaps, without my assistance, they simply turned around or chose a different route.

I assumed that, with all I had learned, I'd have had a positive effect on what took place - some sort of direction to guide us toward or some omnipotent advice to bestow upon those in my company. But I had nothing to show for my trouble. Everyone around me had either died or was about to, and this time I had no sword to blame my troubles on.

What now, you fool?

Dreyl'vyn's corpse - which had continued to smolder long after the wild flames had gone out - popped, causing an ember to float up and land upon me. I watched it lay there, an orange spot blotting out part of my vision until it depleted its energy and glided away.

Will I, too, fizzle out with no purpose, all of my energy depleted on something unattainable?

Turning back toward Jillian, I watched her body, somehow hoping against hope that she might awaken or, at the very least, move.

Are you even alive, or have you also left me?

Cold, alone, and without any notion of what I should do next, I drifted forward to touch her. I had finally come to terms with the idea that no vision would envelop me. Failure had been achieved yet a second time thanks to my ineptitude, and all that was left was for me to receive confirmation.

As I made contact with Jillian's icy skin, I was shocked to find myself whisked away from my surroundings, a new vision exploding to life before my eyes. I had left the barren cavern a second time, inserted instead into a conversation at a dinner table.

Before me sat Jillian and her parents, Theodore and Susan. As before, she had aged since last I saw her. Time had gone far beyond that of the spelling bee, and her taste for the macabre had begun to take over in regard to her stylistic choices.

"I just don't understand why you can't dress like your girlfriends," Susan queried. "When you were younger, you ran around in little dresses."

Jillian seemed displeased with a conversation that had clearly taken place on multiple occasions. "They're not my *girlfriends*. And do you seriously want me dancing around in a little flower dress, mom? You *really* think that'd fit me. That'd just make you *so* happy, wouldn't it?"

Theodore chuckled at the sarcastic reply, but Susan gave him a look which said far more than words could have. Clamping his mouth shut, his attention returned to his potatoes; for some reason they had suddenly become quite fascinating.

"Well, maybe not flower dresses, but people talk, you know?" Susan continued. "When you dress like that, with black all over, like you're going to a funeral every day, people think there's something wrong with you. We don't think so, of course, but they don't know you like we do."

Jillian raised her eyebrows. "I seriously doubt you have *any* clue what I'm *really* like. And before you ask, no, I'm not going to bother explaining my life to you. Didn't you guys do anything strange when you were kids? You didn't do *anything* someone might think was weird?"

The pair shrugged in unison, frustrating Jillian, who threw her arms in the air.

"Oh come on! You're *nothing* like me. It's like I'm adopted! You guys don't-"

Pausing, Jillian noticed her parent's expressions. On the word *adopted*, they had both turned pale. Attempting to act natural afterward could in no way hide what Jillian had already picked up on.

"Are you serious?" Her eyes darted back and forth between her parents, searching for anything which might betray the reaction as a joke. "I'm almost an adult and you *still* haven't told me! When were you going to? *Were* you going to!"

"Well, we uh, we were talking about it…" Susan began.

Jillian's eyes grew wide. "They are not who you think they are," she whispered to herself.

"Now what is that supposed to mean?" Theodore demanded, finally attempting to participate in the conversation.

But Jillian had already stood up and rushed from the table. I chased after, frantic not to be left behind. Running into her bedroom, she slammed the door moments after I passed through it.

Her room had changed significantly since I had last seen it. Painted red and black, its walls had been covered in posters of menacing bands, and her window had been blocked to reduce incoming light.

Digging under the bed, Jillian growled to herself. "Where are you? Where did I put you?" Reaching nearly to the back, she retrieved a dust-coated old sweatshirt enshrouding a book she had seemingly forgotten about. "*There* you are!"

Tossing the sweatshirt to the side, she flipped open the book's cover and unfolded the sheet of paper, which had reverted to letter-form again. Scanning it quickly, she arrived at the end.

"Be secretive, be careful, and do not trust anyone. They are not who you think they are. With more love than I can conjure, your Father," she read aloud.

Filled with emotion, she gripped the page, attempting to come to terms with the information she had acquired. "Who are *they?* Who were *you?* I need answers *now*," she yelled, shaking the letter in her hands.

She began to flip through the book, clearly aware of the section she searched for. As the pages fluttered by, they paused for a moment - almost intentionally - on the mantra she had once read when seeking aid on her homework. A charred page with a hole in its center slid out from the section and drifted to the ground.

Surprised, Jillian picked up the page and read the top line. "Scrump scrud…" She looked back down at the book and read the last line of the mantra. "May my soul be bound to you, until the task is done."

The words seemed to jog something in her memory. Walking over to her desk drawer, Jillian withdrew a pencil. Placing the burned and stained page on the table, she made short work of the simple math equations - what was left of them anyway. Flipping the page back over, she erased "Scrump scrud" and replaced it with "Jillian Winters."

Digging through the desk drawer, she withdrew one of what I could see were many half-burned candles. Lighting it, she then set it on the table.

Holding the page out at chest height, Jillian called out: "The task is done; I am no longer bound to you. Now, tell me who I am and why I have been lied to for so long."

Certain the words would do nothing, I was stunned when the burned hole in the page wreathed itself in green flames and darkness. From within, a familiar, dark voice ushered forth.

"Hello, little one. My, how you have grown."

"My task is done," repeated Jillian. "I am no longer bound to you. Tell me who I am and why I have been lied to."

The voice cackled from within the void. "*Your* task may be done, but that is not how the bargain was struck. You asked me long ago if I had arrived to do your bidding. That was your mistake; your juvenile spellwork did not specify the task at hand, and you did not command me to do so. Instead you accepted my statement as fact when you were informed you would do mine. The task at hand has *not* been completed, as I have not yet made my way into your time. Accept your destiny, and aid my cause. When I have arrived, you will be released from your bond."

Jillian stood still, terror filling her eyes. Somehow she managed the courage to hang onto the enchanted page, but her hands trembled.

"Answer my two questions, and I will help you, whoever you are."

Silence followed her proposed bargain - silence which stretched on until, at last, she opened her mouth to speak again, but the voice returned.

"You are Vael'ora, granddaughter of Thar'ceron, daughter of Vael'ehn. Thar'ceron, the seed. Vael'ehn, the tree. Vael'ora, the fruit. *I* have come for the harvest."

Jillian shook her head. "You're speaking in riddles. I don't know any of those names. I think you might be mistaken-"

"I've mistaken *nothing!*" the voice boomed. "It is your destiny to serve Roth'Roh'Kah, the Devourer!"

Jillian screamed as the mark on her arm flared to life. Green smoke rose from the design and began to envelope her. Crying in agony, she collapsed to her knees.

As they once had years ago, feet pounded against the stairs. Seconds later the door to her room was thrown open by her parents. Wide-eyed, they gasped at the sight before them. Unaware of Magic's existence, they seemed unable to comprehend what was happening to their daughter.

Her eyes filling with an unholy hunger, Jillian turned toward the pair. *"Run!"* she growled.

Rather than heed her warning, Jillian's parents stepped into the room, intent on rescuing her from whatever ailment she was suffering. It was the wrong decision.

Jillian leapt on Theodore, pushing him to the floor. There, she began to pull glowing orbs from his mouth, consuming them with vigor. Screaming, her mother shoved her off. Speaking in a foreign tongue, Jillian rose to her feet and launched toward her mother, knocking her backward. Unable to regain her balance, Susan stumbled several paces before falling off the top step of the stairs, head first. A series of loud, horrific breaking noises echoed from below as she disappeared from view. Turning, Jillian climbed back on top of Theodore to finish her grim work.

Gasping for breath, gasping for life, Theodore looked up at her with ever-dimming eyes. With one last exhale, he whispered, "But we loved you-" before passing away.

Jillian paused, the words somehow managing to reignite her conscious mind. As if awakening in a fog which had obscured her surroundings, she peered around in a daze, blinking her eyes repeatedly. At last, she took notice of the page, which still hovered in mid-air before her. From within, glowing green orbs regarded the young teen with immense satisfaction.

"Yesss," hissed the voice. "Fulfill your destiny, young one."

Crawling forward, Jillian grasped the pages in her hands.

"Not… today," she rumbled in an inhuman voice.

Pulling in opposite directions, she tore the page in half. With a *whoomp*, the candle snuffed out, and the flaming void held within the page vanished from view. Jillian let the halves flutter to the ground. Crawling up onto her bed, she leaned against the wall of her room. Staring down at her hands, she attempted to cry but could not.

"What have I done?" she quietly murmured.

Forcefully I was thrown backward into the frigid, barren cave of ice. Horrified by what I had just learned, I stared down at Jillian's body.

*Jillian is Vael'ehn's daughter… **Vael'ehn's own daughter!***

But that… that means Varek is her estranged brother…

And she doesn't even know!

I shook from the impact the words had made in my own mind.

Vael'ehn's daughter… Vael'ehn's daughter…

His own daughter was sent into the future.

I backed away from her, terrified by who she really was. But a strange thought occurred to me - one which stood in opposition to the monster I had just witnessed.

Why didn't she retrieve the sword? She must have had plenty of opportunities to do so.

The reason why Jillian had not strolled down to Jack's house, dug up the sword in the middle of the night, and fulfilled her destiny by returning it to her true father, was completely lost to me.

She knew an object was there, she said so in a prior vision - so why keep it buried?

The answer was simple: she was ignorant to her heritage. She had no idea who Vael'ehn was, and she had no reason to care about him. But she *did* appear to have a solid moral compass - one that would cause her to rise up against what she believed was true evil.

Could it be, she rebelled against Roth'Roh'Kah, took it upon herself to make sure his plans would not come to fruition?

I wanted to believe that had been true. I wanted to believe the tearing of that page had been the first step toward a lifetime of denying the demon lord what he wanted. I wanted to believe Jillian was really who I wished she was, who I yearned for her to be, who I *needed* her to be.

But why do you need her to be anything?

The thought was one I hadn't expected to have, and its answer was one I didn't want to admit, one that made me feel selfish and foolish.

Whoever she is, whoever she has become… I just… need her. I love her.

Staring down at Jillian's body, I knew I could never tell her the truth of what I had learned that day, lest she be tempted to return to her demented father's fold. But none of that would matter if I let her die alone and cold in a cave. Dreyl'vyn was gone, and it was up to me to succeed or fail. Whether or not she had done the right thing, whether or not she represented all that was good or evil in the world, I had regained my resolve through a fragile emotional state boosted by love.

Swooping down, I levitated Jillian's body above me, determined to begin my descent down the other side of the mountain. However, as I made my way toward the entrance, a scratching, crackling sound from behind drew my attention back inside. Focusing toward the rear of the cave, what I saw nearly caused me to drop my precious cargo. From the blackened indention in the ice, Dreyl'vyn's charred and crumbling corpse had begun to drag itself forward.

Setting Jillian out in the sunlight, optimistic it could only improve her condition, I drifted back to meet what was left of the man, terrified at what I had done to him. As I neared, a trembling arm reached upward, attempting to grab me. Overwhelmed by what I had caused, I let him do so.

Surprisingly, I was met with nothing but cold, dead remnants of skin and bone. I had assumed Dreyl'vyn would react to my touch like a human; since he hadn't, I had concluded he was dead.

Dreyl'vyn doesn't exist as we do. His soul is different from ours.

The realization was appalling.

What have I done? I've burnt him alive!

Pulling against me, the corpse lifted itself off the ground and onto its knees. There it sat for several minutes, its movement kept to a minimum. I couldn't take my eyes off of it, unable to imagine what it might have been like to be burned alive for hours on end, never able to accept death.

I have to make up for this. I have to help him.

Not at all confident in what I was doing, I reached out mentally to Dreyl'vyn's body, intent on offering him some part of my own life force or health - anything I could. Focusing, I pushed against him.

Take it. Take anything you need. Absorb my power. Let it heal you.

As I pressed against him, the charred remains of Dreyl'vyn's flesh crumbled away. Beneath it lay raw, soot-covered musculature and tendons, which pulled and tensed in a disturbing mechanical dance. Shaking the rest of the dead flesh loose, Dreyl'vyn unsteadily rose to his feet. As he did so, his body continued to rebuild itself.

The quivering form revealed underneath the charred exterior had once been completely consumed by fire. When it had finally gone out, Dreyl'vyn seemed to have begun some sort of restoration process. As much as I wished it wasn't the case, I knew my mental offering hadn't done anything for him. He was immortal, and nothing could destroy his body forever.

After a time, Dreyl'vyn had regained what someone might have mistaken for skin, had they squinted hard enough. Altogether he looked terrible, but seeing how far he had come in such a short period of time was awe-inspiring. Thankfully, when he opened his familiar black orbs, he seemed to display no malice toward my mistake whatsoever.

If someone had done that to me, I can't say I'd have been happy to see them again.

My mind awash with guilt, I began an attempt at a written apology but stopped soon after; anything I might have written seemed inadequate for what I had done to the man. My lack of concentration apparent, three purple words hung in the air like crude, writhing glow worms. I hadn't even emblazoned them upon the icy floor like I intended.

I'm sorry, I

Parting thin, almost translucent lips, Dreyl'vyn began to speak in a voice barely audible to me despite hovering only feet away from him.

"Do not… feel shame for what… you did. My body could… no longer cope with the… cold. Pain is all… I have known in your time, and I have suffered… far worse. This is not the first instance… I have been burned… until I was nothing. Your actions… may have been unthinkable to some, but I… would not have regained my movement… if my temperature had been left… so low."

"Your actions may have been unthinkable to some."

The words replayed in my head. It had been a terrible decision to make. Even so, I couldn't help but agree with Dreyl'vyn; had I not jumpstarted his body temperature, he would have remained frozen. I couldn't claim that I had done it on purpose - the whole event had been painful, regrettable, and terrifying - but it seemed like I had actually done something good for him.

Taking notice of Jillian's body resting against the side of the cave entrance, Dreyl'vyn considered her state. "She has not awoken. Does she still live?"

Wiping the purple words away - words I had stupidly let hang in the air as a reminder of my poor choices - I replaced them with a new set, which also floated in the air. What I had created by mistake was likely a better choice than communicating on a surface that could be trampled upon.

Yes. She is still alive.

Dreyl'vyn nodded, proving he understood my words. Thankfully, whatever translational spells existed in that time were not thwarted by the Magic animating my crystal. I had once considered my inability to speak as a way to prevent me from sharing information. Luckily for me, that did not appear to be the case.

Walking forward on legs which had already grown taller and thicker, Dreyl'vyn called back to me. "We need to move her from this place. Our descent from the mountain must be swift. Should another storm arise, I suspect you will be left without aid and forced to proceed on your journey alone."

Unclothed and barely covered in what passed for skin, Dreyl'vyn bent down and hefted Jillian over his shoulder again. Already reaching and surpassing his prior height, he again towered over typical humans, as he had in my vision.

Dreyl'vyn mentioned his captors had used something to keep his people smaller, something to keep them in line. Watching him grow so fast, I couldn't help but conclude that the chemicals binding his body had finally been burned away. He was now stronger and healthier, in his own way, than he ever had been in captivity.

You lucked out. Any other person and you'd have murdered them.

You have to be more careful with your choices from now on.

CHAPTER
forty-Nine

-FATAL FOREIGNERS-

Seemingly revitalized, the naked giant lunged down the side of the mountain, taking vast, sweeping strides through the snow. With each step, he seemed to grow, his muscles pushing harder and faster. Seeing him in that light - his new vitality, not his lack of clothes - he had clearly been far more impaired than I thought. I had once marveled at his mass and strength, but now knew the true strength he possessed.

What had taken the entire previous day in an uphill slog over boulders and through snow, only took mere hours when aided by gravity. We found ourselves down the mountain and into an unfamiliar tree line before I considered where we might have been heading. Whether it had ended or we had lost it, the trail was curiously missing after reaching the peak. It very well might have been beneath our feet at one point, but if that were the case, the snow had hidden it long enough for us to lose our way.

As we headed deeper and deeper into the shade of the towering trees, I began to consider whether or not we were irreversibly lost.

None of us have been here before, and now that we're in a forest, it seems unlikely we will have any indicators as to where we are.

We may burn all the extra time I have accumulated simply by looking for the next town.

But all thoughts of finding our way were erased by a distant chopping sound. Dreyl'vyn took notice as well, and headed toward it, his sense of direction appearing far keener than mine.

Minutes later, Dreyl'vyn was carefully creeping along through the forest. He had reduced his ground-shaking pace to a surprisingly quiet gait. Despite his size, he seemed intent on finding the source of the noise before it found us.

Whoever we find, we can't assume they are friendly.

Through a copse of trees ahead, we spotted three men who were hard at work felling trees. Using tools similar to modern axes, and animals which could be mistaken for distorted oxen, the group were doing an excellent job of making their lives far more difficult by ignoring the opportunity to use Magic. Unsurprisingly, Dreyl'vyn's massive form moving through the trees caught their attention within seconds.

As they began to confer with each other, two of the men gestured toward the giant. Their expressions conveyed the conversation quite well; Dreyl'vyn's size was clearly of surprise to them. Throughout our journey I had yet to see many people who varied drastically in height, but I thought it reasonable to surmise beings as tall as Dreyl'vyn were not at all common.

Given his imposing nature, I would have expected the men to either run or take a stand against Dreyl'vyn, but their response was unexpected.

"Come forward, traveler! You're none too difficult to spot up there. Would you be descending from the ruins of Empor'Vael?" one of the men inquired.

After listening to their greeting, Dreyl'vyn turned toward me, seeming to expect my opinion or guidance on the matter. Quickly, I traced four words in the air.

Be nice. Make friends.

It was an absurd thing to write, but I suspected his form might make people nervous, and the three standing before us could provide a rare chance to verify our location.

Nodding, Dreyl'vyn moved forward, leaning on a nearby tree for support as he stepped down from a large escarpment. Poorly anchored in the soil, it nearly toppled over, pausing at a forty-five degree angle in the direction of the men.

Seeing his effect on the massive plant, the man who had first addressed us laughed. "We could use someone like you around here more often! Each push of your arm would save us hours of labor!" He shook his head. "But your people have become a rarity, I'd say. We haven't seen any of your kind through these parts for well over a year, maybe more. Thought you'd all moved on."

The comment seemed to confuse Dreyl'vyn. "You have seen more Cimmerians traveling over this mountain?" he inquired, his booming voice echoing down the hillside.

"If that's what your kind are called, indeed we have," responded a second man. "Not enough of them to warrant a count I'd say, but one or two, here or there, over a quantity of months. Not very talkative, but polite. Every single one asked if any others had moved through the area before they had. I told them all the same, except for the first, of course, who asked for directions to the nearest town. Sent him to Mor'shor. It's about ten thousand paces from here - well, probably fewer of *your* paces." He laughed, his eyes turning down toward Dreyl'vyn's massive feet.

Eyeing the giant up and down, the third man leaned on his axe. "You look like you've had a rough time, Cimmerian." Risking a glance toward Dreyl'vyn's unmentionables, he too laughed. "And unless you want to make all the men of Mor'shor jealous, you could use some clothing. And who is that over your shoulder?" he quickly added, taking notice that Jillian was not a traveling sack.

Dreyl'vyn, not at all embarrassed by being naked, turned his head toward Jillian's slumped form. "She is called Jill. She is also a traveler from Empor'Vael. She is alive, but not well. I am Dreyl'vyn Glaas of the Cimmerians. This is…" he began to motion toward me, but thought better of it. "This is… the path to the tournament?" he finished, turning his sentence into an awkward question.

The third man raised his brow in surprise. "The Tournament of the Five Nations? Long legs or not, you are a *far* way from there, my newly found friend. If that is your destination, you need to locate a mage, and quick. I don't recall from memory the exact date, but I know it starts soon - far sooner than it'd take for you to walk there, I know that."

Dreyl'vyn motioned toward the man. "Then we are in need of a mage. Where can we locate one?"

The man chuckled. "Not here, that's for certain!" he replied, slapping the man next to him on the shoulder. "My name is Ch'ern. This here is For'shen, and that is Fuer'ehn. Why don't you come back to our village with us? Your friend seems to have seen better days. Let us give you some food and supplies. Perhaps we can have a drink and laugh while the women attempt to craft pants large enough for you to wear."

Dreyl'vyn began to explain that neither of them needed to eat food but, seeing confusion in their eyes, thought better of it. "I am in your debt for this hospitality," he finally replied. "I will follow if you will lead the way."

As the men led us through the labyrinthine forest, they attempted to make small talk regarding the bouts they had heard spoken of inside the amphitheater. However, after repeated attempts to expand upon the often one-word answers provided by Dreyl'vyn, they quieted, seeming to acknowledge he was not one well-acclimated to long conversations.

Eventually the painful silence was broken as the forest opened up onto a long, gently sloping plain. Not far in the distance stood a diminutive farming community; less than a dozen small houses indicated it was a meager existence.

"Welcome to the land of the Bortari," Ch'ern announced enthusiastically. "We don't have much, but that which we do have is earned by the sweat of our brows."

The Bortari... These are the lands of Matteus' people.

Somewhere across the countryside lay Matteus' own village. He had certainly come a long way from a meager existence to compete at the tournament. Even as we proceeded toward the Bortari village before us, he walked away from his own, unaware that in just a handful of days, he would meet his fate.

Jack and I had both been saddened that Matteus - someone who was completely innocent and showed much promise - had been killed by inadvertently coming into contact with Mor'dresh. After finding his people, it was not lost upon me that I might be able to influence such an event.

Is it possible for me to correct his death?

I could easily pass that information on to these people, explain that his life is about to end.

The answer, of course, was more far complicated than that. I could have announced that Matteus was in danger, but Ch'ern himself had stated that there were no mages anywhere near their village. Worse, if someone *did* manage to rescue Matteus, I had no idea what effect that action might have on Jack's future.

If Jack changed his course, even one tiny bit, we could arrive where he wasn't, with no clue of where he had gone. That was also assuming the people escorting us chose to believe me. They could just as easily assume it wasn't a coincidence that we had arrived with such knowledge, and detain us under suspicion of foul play, which was something I couldn't risk.

As nice as it would feel to save Matteus, my hands are tied; he will remain an unfortunate victim of circumstance.

I had to remain focused; after all, I was dealing with demons and Shadow Magic. If I became too distracted by every unfortunate event that had happened, I could lose my way or cause another disaster by my own good intentions. Matteus, like Renault, was simply one of several casualties caused by the actions of Vael'ehn, Roth'Roh'Kah, and the sword - one of several which would be cemented in place to give us a fighting chance.

"Welcome to Duff!" Ch'ern exclaimed as he opened the mediocre front gate to his small town.

Duff? What a terrible name for a village.

Inside, dozens of potato-shaped pig creatures ran this way and that, frantically trying to escape the confines of the town. Ch'ern firmly shoved one away from the door with his boot.

"Get back, Gr'oon! Yer not gettin' out this time!"

A small child ran up and tackled Gr'oon.

"I got em, papa!" she squealed as Gr'oon made fart-like noises and tried his best to wiggle free.

But Ch'ern's daughter was not the only person to greet us at the gate. Within seconds of our arrival, the entire town - which only consisted of a couple dozen men, women, and children - had gathered in front of us. They had surely seen Dreyl'vyn's towering form approaching from afar; he had continued to grow since the incident at the ice cavern, and stood ten or eleven feet high by that time.

As For'shen and Fuer'ehn took their places next to who I assumed were their wives, Ch'ern addressed the villagers.

"This is Dreyl'vyn and Jill from the Vaelcurian Empire. They're fleeing the city of Empor'Vael, like the other Cimmerians have, and they're heading to the tournament."

"They're more than a few shakes away from there!" an old rat-like man commented, causing laughter among the others.

Another Gnill'var! If I didn't know any better, I'd say he is Wenton's twin!

But as I studied the Gnill'var elder, my first impression seemed inaccurate. He appeared much older than Wenton, and certainly accustomed to a far more basic lifestyle.

Quality robes and castles, this Gnill'var does not have.

Ch'ern nodded. "Yes, they are, Wesson. But as you can see, they're in need of our help. If we can get them going in the right direction, they still have time to hire a mage to send them off. The female Cimmerian, Jill, is in no shape to travel. And Dreyl'vyn, *well…*" He motioned toward Dreyl'vyn's curious lack of clothing. The crowd again laughed, but Dreyl'vyn didn't seem to take notice.

Clapping his hands, Ch'ern stepped toward the crowd. "Alright. Der'ehssa, please see if you all can craft something resembling clothing for this mountain of a man. Wesson, please come with me to tend to Jill's needs."

As everyone ran to attend to various tasks, Ch'ern turned toward Dreyl'vyn. "Alright, Cimmerian, you can hand Jill off to me. We will see that she gets the care she needs. You can go get fitted for some clothing."

Dreyl'vyn glanced toward me before stooping down to pass Jillian into Ch'ern's arms. "This gemstone will accompany you," he announced. "It is hers, and it travels where she does. I know little of Xahl'thari bobbles." Dreyl'vyn watched me intently, likely looking for affirmation, but as I drifted toward Ch'ern, he seemed content he had made the right decision.

"Yes, most of the Xahl'thari carry around something at least similar to that," Ch'ern replied. "My son had one. He insisted on picking it up from the Capital despite not receiving one at his birth. We have no use for those around here, but do not worry yourself; it will be in honest hands. No one in this city is a thief, I can assure you of that!"

As Dreyl'vyn was surrounded by a group of women with measuring devices, we were lead away toward a small house.

Laying Jillian out on a crude, fur-covered bed, Ch'ern stepped back.

"Wesson, see if you can use your gifts to do anything for this poor soul. I didn't want to upset Dreyl'vyn, as he seems well-intentioned, but this *Jill* he's been carrying appears to have been dead for quite some time."

I, of course, knew better; the visons had continued, which meant Jillian's essence was still trapped inside her damaged body. Visually, Jillian had deteriorated further, and more than a few spots appeared to have been ruined by frostbite, but bodily harm was something I had paid little consideration to. Both Jillian and Dreyl'vyn were quite capable of a complete physical restoration under the proper circumstances.

I just hope "the proper circumstances" don't need to happen in this village.

Wesson stepped forward, placing one furry hand on Jillian's forehead and one on her stomach. Closing his eyes, he began to improvise a disturbing song.

"Mmm, mmm, mmm, mmm, this girl, she is not dead.
Mmm, mmm, mmm, mmm, inside she lies awake.
Mmm, mmm, mmm, mmm, she will rise again.
Mmm, mmm, mmm, mmm, a soul she needs to take."

Opening his dim eyes again, Wesson found Ch'ern eyeing him suspiciously.

"A soul she needs to take? What does that mean?"

Wesson scratched his temple with a dull claw. "Is that what I said? You know how this works, Ch'ern. They're just glimpses of emotions - a little of this and that. Likely, it was something that rhymes with soul. My hearing's not what it used to be." He continued to prattle off random words to himself. "Fruit, hat, deep, cure... Oh, *take a cure*, maybe! That must be it."

In their language, those words must all rhyme with **soul***. But then, if his song rhymed correctly through the translation, why didn't those?*

Could it be possible, when choosing certain words, the translational spell takes into account the importance of rhyme and rhythm as well?

Or, once translated, do they cease to rhyme at all, but the spell is brainwashing me into believing they do?

If so, that's... wow.

I was distracted by Ch'ern, who began to fiddle with the miniature talons still attached to Jillian's fingers as he listened to the old Gnill'var mumble to himself.

He might be easily convinced otherwise, but I knew the truth. Wesson's musical attempt to delve into Jillian's psyche has been surprisingly accurate, and it told me what I needed to know: she would be required to feed to revive herself.

But even if she wasn't in some sort of coma, who could we find among these people?

Surely we can't start massacring innocents in the name of justice.

Silently I prayed for circumstances to change, for Jillian to awaken and still be healthy enough to run far away from the village. Though, deep inside I couldn't help but wonder if the loss would be justified, if a few innocent lives were worth losing for the greater good.

After all, the alternative is the destruction of the entire planet.

Seeing Wesson was likely to continue his nonsensical banter, Ch'ern impatiently rapped his knuckles against the side of his leg. "It doesn't matter. Let me know if her condition changes. I must go collect some supplies for our travelers and draw a map for them to follow on their way to Mor'shor. Thank you, my old friend," he called as he stepped out from the small building.

Wesson didn't respond, instead continuing on with his looney word suggestions. "Nut, shake, leap, scald…" But the second Ch'ern stepped away, the old rat turned, his unsteady, clouded gaze falling upon me.

"I have spent many years on this planet, and I have never sensed one such as you. An enigma traveling with a Cimmerian and a Dghem'oni-afflicted Xahl'thari. I wonder what might lead you three to these parts?" He continued to eye me steadily. "I can feel your uncertainty toward my words. I ask you now, do you intend to harm this village?"

This Gnill'var can sense far more than he lets on. His brain isn't addled at all. If he's even half as talented as Wenton, I have no chance of lying to him.

"Wenton, hmm?" he said, a small smile creeping into his features.

How did he...

Seeing my guise had been broken in the presence of a true clairvoyant, I decided to show my hand. Slowly I wrote four words for the old rat, which hung in the air before him.

No harm. Hunting Vael'ehn.

His unkempt, wispy eyebrows raised. "*Vael'ehn*, you say? You are on *quite* the quest, then, aren't you? It's been some time since I've heard that name mentioned in this land."

He stepped toward the doorway and peered out at the townsfolk bustling around.

"Ch'ern is a good man. He looks out for others, keeps them safe, aids weary travelers. But he isn't too keen on Magic. Poor man can't seem to find the confidence to use it."

Wesson walked back toward Jillian and watched her still form for a moment.

"No, if he knew half the capabilities I *really* had, he'd send me on my way. I think he has his suspicions, but he knows he would struggle if this 'crazy old Gnill'var' wasn't around to treat his people's maladies." He shook his head. "I'm surprised he's agreed to help you on your way to the tournament. Probably better in his mind to send you far away than keep you near. While here, you're a threat to his way of life, you know. When his son announced he'd be heading off to the tournament himself-"

His son went to the tournament, too? Is Ch'ern Matteus' father?

Wesson's eyes crinkled at the corner as he turned his gaze back upon me. "That's quite the response! Do you have some sort of history with his son?"

Grimacing, I wrote his name in the air.

Matteus

Wesson nodded. "Yes, I gathered that. I sense dark emotions from you surrounding that name. You are aware of something that has befallen... *no*, something that has yet to happen to young Matteus." He sighed. "Something you're determined *not* to correct, hmm?"

He knows everything I think. I can't let him change the past. It would ruin everything. I need to make sure Jack follows the same timeline. He can't tell Ch'ern.

Wesson studied me as if he were attempting to read very small print on a poster.

"You needn't worry; I wouldn't dare tell Ch'ern of his son's fate. He is incapable of using Magic, and the knowledge of being unable to help would cause him too much pain. The two argued with each other before Matteus left. I suspect Ch'ern assumes he will never see his son again. That, I believe, is for the best."

Wesson placed his hand on Jillian's forehead and closed his eyes. "The future is clouded for her. I sense a battle for good and evil - one which rages inside of her as we speak. Her fate, *our* fates, have not yet been written." He frowned. "But if she is allowed to die here, in this town, I am certain they will be."

Turning his gaze back toward me, his face had become gravely pale. His eyes grew wide and blank, as if he had seen a ghost.

"When the moment arrives, you will feel its coming. Do not tarry in what you know needs to be done," he warned in a monotone, cold voice.

Wesson's brow knitting together, he seemed to snap back to reality.

"I... I have work to do within this woman's mind before she is capable of consciousness. I will experience events and I will reveal information, knowledge that is not for your ears, words that may change your course. You should leave here for the night. Tomorrow morning, when the sun crests the mountains, you shall come back, and she will be ready to travel again."

As Wesson turned back toward Jillian, seemingly uninterested in any reply I might have had, I couldn't help but wonder what he meant.

Should I stay here? Spy on him to see what-

"No, you should not," Wesson called over his shoulder. "Be on your way."

Stunned that anything I might have thought appeared to be on display for the old rat, I drifted out into the village and toward Dreyl'vyn, who was busy laying giant, carved tree trunks down in front of a fire pit to use as seating for everyone. His waist wrapped with a temporary covering - no doubt more for the villager's sake than for his - he seemed content to aid in whatever labor they requested of him.

He's spent so long in captivity, that's all he knows.

Then again, making his home inside a village like this could be good for him. Small, personable, far from Magic - it would probably go a long way toward teaching him the enjoyable aspects of life.

Later that night, a fire had been built, and the entire town gathered in front of it to hear a story recited by Ch'ern.

"This is the tale of Bor'ton and the seed," Ch'ern began, withdrawing a small book from his vest pocket. "I believe it illustrates the principles we live by quite well."

As he opened the little tome, everyone rocked backward in unison, as if a strong wind had pushed against them. I was no exception. Not quite a vision, but certainly far more than imagination, the scene unfolded before us as Ch'ern began to read from the enchanted book.

"It was the season of planting on Xahl, the world we called home long before our ancestors traveled the skies and arrived on this planet. As was the custom, the local people had gathered in the town of Nam'has for the planting festival. Among many friendly competitions, the Nissen Bean Race pitted the people against each other in a test to see who could most effectively grow a Nissen Bean stalk.

"On the judging table stood many stalks, but three had grown much larger than the other's had. Behind those three stalks stood three people whom you all should know: Bor'ton, Vael'curion, and Demel'sa." On the word *Bor'ton*, everyone cheered, and on the word *Vael'curion*, everyone booed. "Ah, but this was long before they met their destinies on the planet we now reside," Ch'ern announced, raising a hand. "They were young, and the world around them was still very new and mysterious.

"Inspecting each plant for leaf color, stalk height, and bean weight - the three criteria which would determine the winner - the judges slowly moved down the line. Everyone held their breath, but it was clear only three were truly capable of winning. Soon, the judges had picked a winner, and it was Bor'ton who had won!" Everyone sitting around the fire cheered for their hero. "Bor'ton's plant was nearly two full inches taller than the others, and its leaves were wide and red. But his beans, they were the most impressive of all; his were well over *twice* as plump as the others!

"After the judges had awarded Bor'ton and moved along, Demel'sa stepped over to speak. 'So what did you two use to aid your Nissen stalks?' she asked of Bor'ton and Vael'curion. 'I created a bubble where time passed by more quickly, giving mine a longer growing duration. But I let it advance for longer than I should have, and it passed its most fertile period before I could slow it down!'

"Vael'curion laughed. 'That was smart, Demel'sa. I projected light around mine, and it was able to grow through the night without going into its dormancy period. But my light was too intense, and the beans had almost been cooked by the time I noticed! What had you chosen to aid yours, Bor'ton?'

"Bor'ton smiled at them both. 'I did not use Magic,' he responded, to both their surprise. 'I went to the local farmers and asked them each for their special growing secrets. One told me how to grow tall stalks, another told me how to grow wide leaves, and the third told me how to grow plump beans. Using all three techniques, I gathered the proper soil, gave the plant the nutrition it needed, and only allowed it to have the proper amount of heat and light.'

"Well, I need not tell you the result, for surely you have already guessed; the pair were stunned," Ch'ern announced. "Their Magic had been bested by Bor'ton's knowledge of growing. He knew Magic wasn't required to achieve the outcome he wanted, so he hadn't used it at all!"

Oddly enough, as I imagined the story being told, every instance someone used the word *Bor'ton*, their lips hadn't kept in sync. Rather, it was as if they had mentioned another name - one starting with an *R*. No one else seemed to notice, however; they clapped excitedly.

The story was clearly a parable illustrating the virtues of living in a Magic-free existence. While everything may or may not have gone the way Ch'ern had described it, his words were certainly an effective piece of propaganda for a society who proclaimed to do just that.

As Ch'ern continued to prattle on about his ideals, I couldn't help but notice that the setting for his story had remained forefront in my mind, like a morning dream I hadn't quite roused from. Turning my focus upon the young Vael'curion and Demel'sa, I saw that, despite Ch'ern failing to narrate their conversation, the pair had continued to carry on even after Bor'ton - or whoever it was - had walked away.

If I could just listen in on what they're saying…

To my surprise, sounds sprung forth from their lips.

"…does not matter if he won. He spent most of his waking hours tending to his plant. We almost beat him with no effort on our part. My spell took but a few moments to complete, and I know yours could not have taken much longer. I feel as if it is we who have won, title or not," Vael'curion proclaimed.

Demel'sa laughed. "Always looking for an angle to play, are you not, Vael?"

Vael'curion grinned. "If I did not do so, you would not recognize who I am! If I may ask, what might you intend to fill your time with tonight?"

"Oh, I do not have anywhere I need to be," Demel'sa responded, shrugging.

Vael'curion perked up at her response. "Would you be so kind as to escort me to the Loa'han falls?" he queried, extending a hand.

Demel'sa giggled. "I would be honored to. Thank you for asking me."

As the two strolled away into the distance, the book's spell seemed to fade, allowing me to return to the campfire with the others. Ch'ern had since stopped talking, and the villagers had moved on to other topics. It seemed my abilities had allowed the book to play on like a deleted scene from a movie, despite the inattention of the others. I was glad it had done so - the forgotten conversation had been informative - but with it had come countless other questions.

When would this have taken place?

By Vael'curion's appearance, it very well could have been after he wiped out the Forgotten Order. Varek's story had said Vael'curion appeared to be in his twenties, and although the enchanted tale hadn't been as vivid as Ch'ern's, I had imagined him as having been the same. For all I knew, Vael'curion might not have even known how old he was when he woke up from the spell Roth'Roh'Kah had put him under. He could have assumed he was around the same age as the other two simply because he looked similar.

I wonder if he stayed in contact with Bor'ton and Demel'sa for all the years leading up to when his race chose him to wield one of the Weapons of Legend.

Had he and Demel'sa continued on in their relationship?

A surprising thought occurred to me.

Demel'sa could have grown up and become one of the Xahl'thari heroes as well. After all, the company she kept certainly had. If so, they both would have traveled to Earth.

Could Demel'sa be Jillian's mother?

I supposed anything was possible, but what troubled me most was the hidden identity of the person Ch'ern had mislabeled as Bor'ton. The tales I had been told stated that Vael'curion had killed Bor'ton, assassinated him from behind with Kaldre'shen.

Would Vael'curion kill his own friend?

To me it appeared he may not have killed Bor'ton, but an unnamed hero instead.

I have to find out.

Ignoring the fact that no one but Wesson knew of my sentience, I drifted over to Ch'ern. His back to everyone, he silently stared up at the night sky, his mind clearly far away from the small settlement. There, I created a series of words in front of him where no one else could see.

That wasn't Bor'ton. Who was it?

As the words shimmered to life before him, Ch'ern flinched, but mostly kept his composure. Eyeing the question suspiciously, he looked around until he caught sight of my presence.

"So you are not a Coadjutor, as I assumed?" he asked, waving his hand through the floating words, causing them to swirl about like oil on water.

Quickly, I cast them away and began again.

No, but I am a friend - a friend without a mouth, who does not tell secrets.

Reading the statement, Ch'ern turned his attention back toward the sky and sighed. After a few moments, he seemed to come to a decision within his mind.

"I'm not sure how you learned about that detail, but the answer is far more mundane than you might think. You are correct; Bor'ton was not present at the Nissen Bean Race. In fact, what I have learned of Bor'ton tells me he was an avid, aggressive user of offensive Magic, and an exceptional, level-headed warrior."

Ch'ern turned his attention toward me, his expression sullen. "But that doesn't play well for a group of farmers who, despite being his descendants, have grown up without an education in Magic, does it? I can't use Magic, nor can most of the people behind me. My son, he…" Ch'ern sighed. "He moved on. There was no place for him in this village. I don't… I don't blame him. He will do great things; I am certain of it."

On the verge of tears, Ch'ern took a moment to steady himself.

"The identity of the person in the story you heard is Ridd'en, not Bor'ton. Ridd'en was the one who loved plants. Absurdly enough, he also loved Magic and used it quite often while cultivating his greenery. It seems there is very little justification for a people devoid of Magic on this planet."

As Ch'ern turned back toward the night sky, I found myself surprised by the revelation. He had simply wanted to inspire his people, encourage pride in the rough existence they endured in the middle of nowhere. I had found yet another person disgruntled by their place in a Magic-filled world. He seemed to believe he and his village were misfits, yet where I was from, they would have fit in perfectly.

As everyone continued to talk late into the night, I drifted around the perimeter of the gathering, my mind alight with possibilities of what could have happened to Vael'ehn and Demel'sa in the time between the story and the trip to Earth, what their potential relationship might have meant, and how someone afflicted by a demon could have lived unaware of that fact for so many years.

After a time, I took notice that everyone had gone back to their homes; it was only Dreyl'vyn and I who still attended the fire. As if he were an android someone had shut down for the night, he silently stared off into the distance. I, too, turned my attention toward where he gazed, but found nothing of consequence to focus upon.

Clearly, the years of isolation had given Dreyl'vyn far more patience than any other man on earth, and he had become content with absolutely nothing for long periods of time. For all I knew, simply being away from his torture chamber was more excitement than he could handle. If it had been me in his place, I'd have gone mad long, long ago.

CHAPTER

-THE DEMON WITHIN-

The sun finally gleaming over the distant mountains, I headed back to the center of town, toward Wesson's hut. Inside, he stood by Jillian's body, grasping her head with his fur-covered hands. Electricity crackled along his fingers, down to the sides of her temples. Surprisingly, Jillian's eyes popped open. With an inhuman growl, she grabbed his head and pulled it toward her. Wesson did not resist. Steadying himself for what he knew was sure to come, he closed his eyes.

"Do what you must to save us all," he whispered.

Jillian did not respond. Pulling him even closer, she began the grim, familiar work necessary to rejuvenate her body and taint her mind.

As Wesson's shriveled, fur-covered corpse fell to the ground, Jillian sat upright on the table. Rapidly, her eyes searched the small room for others, but seeing no one, she leapt onto the floor in a crouching position. At that very moment, Ch'ern walked through the door.

"Wesson, I need-" His eyes grew large as he spotted Wesson's crumpled remains on the floor. "By Bor'ton's hammer... what have you done!" he exclaimed, noticing Jillian's form peering over the table.

Jillian did not respond. Seeming altogether not herself, she leaped toward Ch'ern, who was either unprepared or unable to defend himself. Grasping him by the neck, she lifted him into the air and pulled him deeper into the room. As he struggled, the blades adorning her fingers released, biting into his neck and spilling blood down his chest and her arm. Turning, she threw him onto the table. He, too, fell victim to her dark abilities.

Silently I watched, uncertain if I should aid the man. Not only was I doubtful that I could overpower Jillian in such a ravenous state, but I found myself terrified of what hidden abilities she might unleash upon me.

Watching Ch'ern's eyes close, my thoughts turned to Wesson's last words.

"Do what you must to save us all."

The sentiment was strange, and likely hadn't been meant for my ears, but whatever Wesson had found inside her, it had convinced him to sacrifice his life. I hadn't much knowledge of who Wesson was, but considering he was able to sense even my own emotions, I had to assume he was powerful indeed. To consider himself expendable said volumes for his decision.

Who am I to make his sacrifice worth nothing?

As Jillian turned from yet another victim, I saw that her skin had repaired itself completely. Not only had the signs of frostbite and decay left her, so too had the effects of death. Before me stood a woman who was far more radiant than she had been in life. She was still the same person, of course, but her skin seemed to glow. Her eyes, no longer grey, had begun to shift toward a vibrant greenish hue. Her hair, which had further transformed in color, gleamed like spun glass.

I've never seen anyone so beautiful in all my life.

What I wouldn't give to touch you just once.

As if she had heard me, Jillian took notice of my presence. Stalking forward, she inspected my form with curiosity, as if she had never seen me before. Reaching out, she tapped me with a knife-tipped finger, making a clinking noise. Expecting a gentle, inquisitive touch, I was instead pulled from my reverie as I took notice of her hand.

That's not a knife; that's a talon!

Several of Jillian's armaments had fallen off in the struggle. What was once a woman's hand had instead been transformed into a blackened, demonic claw. Worse, when she had touched me, no vision ushered forth.

People share visions with me; demons… don't.

Unsure of what the interaction meant, I backed away. I had expected Jillian's transformation to be slower - I thought she'd remain herself until her hair had completed its color change - but I couldn't deny what I had just witnessed. Not only had she begun to physically transform, but it appeared as if she wasn't aware of who she was.

Should I have stopped her from consuming Ch'ern?

Should she have been forced to degrade before feeding again?

She doesn't even know who I am!

What have I done!

Laughter from outside pulled Jillian's attention toward the doorway. Creeping quietly forward, she disappeared through the entrance before I could consider stopping her.

On the other side, I found her intently watching Dreyl'vyn, a group of children laughing as they ran around his legs as if they were trees. The women of the village had indeed been able to fashion clothing for him, and not just the makeshift variety either. Although obviously patched from multiple pieces of fabric, he had been adorned in relatively handsome garb befitting someone of culture.

Noticing our arrival, Dreyl'vyn bent down toward Jillian. "I see you are conscious again. The women have completed their task. They say I am lovely. We are now free to-"

Jillian had no interest in conversation. Leaping into the air, she extended her talons, ready to fell the giant. Dreyl'vyn, seemingly incapable of being caught off guard, grabbed her by the head before she stood any chance of reaching him, his massive hand completely enveloping her face. Pivoting on his heel, he spun around, hurtling her through the air.

Screaming in anger, Jillian landed nearly thirty feet away in a cloud of dirt. Rolling several times, she came to rest on her feet in a crouching position. Without pause, she charged back toward Dreyl'vyn, who prepared himself for a second attack. Before the two could collide, however, For'shen stepped between the pair.

"Wait!" he exclaimed, raising his arms.

Whatever he had intended, his timing couldn't have been worse. Sliding to a halt in front of the poor man, Jillian grabbed the sides of his head with her claws. For'shen's skull swelled with dark energy before exploding, showering those nearby with blood. As the cries of his friends and family filled the air, thousands of tiny particles spun outward from For'shen's neck in a swirl of shadows, which Jillian gobbled up greedily.

In an instant she appeared both more radiant *and* terrible. Her eyes, which had appeared a light shade of green moments before, flushed considerably with color, glowing despite the morning light. Her skin, although flawless, had further been marred with virus-like tendrils of black, which crept upward along her forearms from her talons. Worst of all, she had become far less animalistic and began to speak. Calling out to those around her, she taunted the townsfolk in the guttural, incomprehensible language of the demons.

This has to stop. I have to do something.

As Jillian once again charged toward Dreyl'vyn, I rushed forward, imagining a giant hand reaching out before me. As its humongous Magical fingers coalesced into being, they seized Jillian's body with a crushing force. Lifting her up from the ground, my creation denied her any movement whatsoever.

Growling and gnashing her teeth in defiance of my efforts, Jillian eyed me with intelligent, hate-filled eyes. Her expression filled me with terror and pain, but I held fast. Under her breath she had begun to curse me in her new, strange tongue. Whether the words held power or were just filled with spite, I could not say, but she seemed incapable of breaking free from my hold as long as I remained focused.

Belatedly I realized silence had washed over the town. Peering around, I saw that the villagers had all fled. Where once the entire populace of Duff had stood, only Dreyl'vyn towered over an empty path. Everyone had hidden themselves from the battle, and with good reason.

Perfect. We don't need more casualties.

I turned my attention back toward Jillian's beautiful, terrible face. It had become clear Wesson had known I would be the one to end her life; he simply hadn't suspected it would be minutes after his own death. If I had considered my actions more carefully and restrained her earlier, Ch'ern and For'shen wouldn't have died, and Jillian might have retained her humanity - whatever little was left of it. But I had not done so, and I had cost us our future. All that was left before me was a woman more closely resembling a demon than anything she had once been.

This is the time Wesson had spoken of.

"When the moment arrives, you will feel its coming. Do not tarry in what you know needs to be done."

Sadness overtook me as I realized the woman I cared about more than anything was about to die by my own hand, long before she ever had a chance to learn who I was.

I am so sorry, Jillian. I have failed you, and it is all my fault.

I have failed you, and I hate myself for it!

Forcing the thoughts away, I focused on what I needed to do, knowing full well that if I paused, my conviction would continue to fade. Jillian, her body compressing inward, let out a horrific, inhuman yell as I forced my summoned fist to squeeze even harder. Again she spit strange words in my direction, hatred continuing to build in her sinister, pupilless green eyes.

"Halt," Dreyl'vyn called in his typical, emotionless tone. "There may be one last option we can attempt before she perishes."

Relief washed over me, and I lessened my grip. I had in no way expected a reprieve from my mistakes, but Dreyl'vyn had offered me one; I wasn't about to decline. Staring up into his dark orbs, I couldn't be certain, but I had an idea of what he might be thinking. Dreyl'vyn's body had shown me nothing when I had touched him; it was a sure bet it didn't respond the way a human body did. Even so, I couldn't say for sure what the results might be if Jillian was allowed to feed off of him.

Will Dreyl'vyn's life force or soul be more or less potent than a human's? Will it even be compatible at all?

Will he poison her, as he had indicated his body would have done if Maul'tree and his men had consumed his flesh?

*And what will happen to him if she **does** consume him? Will he finally receive the death he has been searching for?*

Is that the real reason he's about to suggest what I think he will?

Kneeling down, Dreyl'vyn regarded me. "She has lost her way. That is unacceptable. She is more important to the resolution of your objectives than I am. My body is not that of a living being; it is a corpse. I am not tied to it as the Xahl'thari are. It has nothing of what she seeks. I am not certain what will happen, but all I see before me are victims to empower her, and a partner who has decided to destroy her. I believe this is worth trying."

Being careful not to relinquish my hold on Jillian, I wrote three words in the air.

You may die.

Dreyl'vyn nodded. "You are correct. I have considered such a fate already. If my death were to allow you to further your objectives, it would be a victory in my eyes. I have longed for such an opportunity for much of your time."

Laying down on his back, Dreyl'vyn closed his eyes in preparation for what was to come. "I believe it is customary to pass luck on to you before you start. I do not know how, but take as much as you need, and then release her upon me."

I didn't need luck. I felt as if Dreyl'vyn had blessed me with the greatest gift a man could ever have been given: the option to avoid killing someone I longed to be with.

Without hesitation I drew Jillian over to him and released her upon his broad chest. Snarling, she turned a suspicious eye toward me. Her intense hunger was terrifying, but the intelligence contained within her burning eyes truly shook me. Even in her demonic state, she could comprehend how unlikely an action we were taking. Thankfully, her hesitation only lasted for a moment, her appetite winning out over suspicion.

Grabbing the sides of Dreyl'vyn's head, Jillian's fingers began to crackle with dark energy. Sickening Magic rippled along Dreyl'vyn's skull, tearing into his skin and causing wisps of smoke to rise into the air. Even so, he remained still, as if it were nothing; his capacity to tolerate pain was unlike anything I had ever seen. Any normal person would have cried out in agony. Then again, any normal person would have lost their life within seconds. As to the familiar floating orbs, however, there were none; Dreyl'vyn refused to produce anything for her.

Again, Jillian spoke in the odd language. For once I could ascertain another emotion besides hatred: a sense of confusion. Concentrating, she pushed with all her might, the force of her efforts causing her hands to swell from the amount of Magic being sent into Dreyl'vyn. His skin nearly burned away, large portions of his skull began to show, along with tendons and other bits of gristle. And yet, still, he appeared unable to give her what she desired.

Roaring in frustration, Jillian pushed even harder. Corrupted blood vessels popped in her face and arms like tiny dots of black ink. Her body shook from the over-expenditure of energy. Black blood trickled from her nose and ears, matching almost equally black tears running down her cheeks.

And then, in an instant, her spellwork stopped. Jillian began to sway back and forth until, her power expended, she collapsed onto his chest, unconscious.

But just as I was about to lift her up, Jillian rose again, her eyes dull, expression blank, and jaw slackened. Opening her mouth wider, black orbs spewed forth, bathing Dreyl'vyn in shadowy Magic. Surprisingly, he refrained from coughing; the particles had no effect on him whatsoever.

Likely, he too only uses air to speak.

I moved forward, intent on interrupting her fruitless ritual, but Dreyl'vyn blocked my way with a massive hand. Intentionally breathing in the horrible orbs, he vacuumed them up just as fast as she produced them. Then, with one violent lurch, he stilled.

Glowing orange particles began to flow from his mouth. Their obvious color aside, they appeared quite different from those flowing from other victims. Almost humming with radiant power, they in no way seemed fragile or wispy. Nor, for that matter, were they accompanied by purple or turquoise particles.

Whatever those are, let us hope they don't have the same effect as a person's soul.

Jillian rampantly gobbled the orange spheres up by the dozens. As she did so, Dreyl'vyn's body began to shrivel. Faster and faster, she absorbed them, causing the poor man to decrease in mass, as if he were rapidly dehydrating. Soon, Dreyl'vyn had once again become the scabrous corpse we found at Empor'Vael, but on a much larger scale. Jillian, however, was undergoing a new transformation. Her body shaking and twitching, the black demonic taint stretching up her arms began to retreat backward, and her eyes returned to a disconcerting but intelligent dull glow.

Teetering back and forth, she fell off of Dreyl'vyn and collapsed to the ground. Slowly writhing around, as if poisoned, she scraped long troughs into the earth with her talon-like fingers. Coughing and growling, she looked around with a chaotic expression, repeatedly shaking her head. In between demonic cries, human-like utterances could be heard as the two sides of her fought a violent internal struggle for control.

At last, Jillian stilled, and her body relaxed. Her hands had not entirely healed, and her hair had stayed the same - both were indications we hadn't removed the demonic taint - but her condition appeared to have been treated and restrained.

The demonic forces at work within Jillian seemed to have exhausted themselves after her immense efforts, allowing the necromantic Magic animating her body to take over. Bolstered by whatever immortal life force Dreyl'vyn had blessed Jillian with, it clearly rallied enough to fight against the demonic taint - fight and claim a sound victory.

She might still be closer to a demon than she was before, but at the very least, she is herself again. I hope.

Knowing full well what would prove to me that she had regained her humanity, I glided forward and touched Jillian's arm.

The town of Duff spun wildly as I was transported to a porch - the same one I had seen long ago when a young Jack and his grandfather discussed stories together. Jillian, who was not much older than the last vision, lay out on a chair in a swimsuit, tanning herself. Sporting a few tattoos - tattoos she might have been a little too young to have received legally - she seemed quite content.

"Hey, you could go do that out in the yard," Jack commented as he walked out of the house and handed her a drink. "Get outta the shadow of this house or whatever, you know? I always like bein' right out in the middle, myself. Feels *just* right."

Jillian stared out at the backyard and grimaced. "Nah, there's um, too many bugs in the grass, and bug spray screws up my tan. I like it up here." She smiled reassuringly.

Jack shrugged. "Suit yerself. Shit, I forgot my own damn drink. My dad says I'd forget my head if it wasn't glued to my neck." Laughing, he walked back inside.

As Jack disappeared through the door, Jillian quickly turned toward the backyard.

"Feels *just* right, hmm?" she muttered to herself. "You're not calling to him *that* easily." Waving her hand, a tiny ward appeared above a benign grassy area - a location I knew all too well. The ward, which resembled a withered tree with disembodied, floating branches, hovered just inches from the grass. "Wearing down my wards again, are you?"

With a snap of her fingers, the ward illuminated from a dull blue-grey to a vivid neon blue. The change elicited new growth from the tiny trunk, and it expanded, reconnecting with the branches hovering above it. Seemingly unsatisfied, Jillian snapped twice more, creating two more identical copies of the same ward. All three began to rotate around each other before vanishing.

"Let's see you get through *that*," she taunted with a smirk.

"Whad ya say?" Jack asked as he arrived with another drink in his hand.

"Ah, nothing. Just squashed a pest that keeps bothering me," Jillian said innocently. "Now you're safe again!"

Jack laughed and made a mock shiver. "Ooh, good. I was gettin' scared of my own backyard there for a second."

Jillian turned her gaze toward the grassy area again. "You *should* be..." she replied quietly.

As the vision faded, I arrived back in front of Jillian, who was struggling to remain coherent after the battle waged within her body. The vision, however, had proven she was both alive and healthy. Its content couldn't have been more timely *or* uplifting.

Jillian, you stayed!

You stayed and protected Jack from the sword instead of retrieving it yourself!

I may have been missing a large section of history between certain visions, but it had shown me everything I needed to know. I had once suspected Jillian of foul play, and rightfully so. The book she had used as a Magical teaching aid had been given to her through the influence of a demon, but after accidentally consuming her father and sending her mother to her demise, she had seemingly risen up to oppose the evil lurking inside her.

Had she been living alone all that time - just a teenager in her parent's house?

I supposed it was possible, given her talents. Since the day her parents had been killed, she would have been required to forge their signatures, pay their bills, submit their taxes, send herself to school, fight a demonic taint that had taken root inside her - it was almost mind-boggling that she had pulled it all off. There was no telling what she had done, what sort of spellwork she had used to negate any problems that had arisen. But if I had to point my finger at one child who could have done so, it certainly would have been her.

And all that time, while she was already dealing with so much, she must have kept the secret of whatever was buried in Jack's yard to herself, carried that burden in secrecy for years.

She is truly brilliant, one of a kind.

Ironically, Jillian was unaware that Jack's family watched over the sword's resting place, that she had inadvertently allied with them in their efforts to prevent it from being uncovered. If I were human, I'd have laughed out loud. The sword was in the care of a man who, although he was aware of its danger, had decided to abstain from teaching his son that information. Yet a young, demonically-influenced girl - the biggest threat to Thaddeus' descendants - chose instead to ward the area with spells to keep it hidden.

That's just bad luck on Roth'Roh'Kah's part!

But even bad luck can run out. Jack must have been mowing the lawn exactly when the wards weakened just enough for him to hear the sword's call. Jillian must have forgotten, or fallen asleep, or become distracted - anything could have happened. By the time she realized what was taking place, there was nothing left for her to do. The timing wouldn't have been a coincidence either; the sword would have been waiting, watching for just the right moment to pounce.

And pounce it did. What a horrible tragedy.

Sitting up, Jillian frowned at the shriveled corpse of Dreyl'vyn, which was mostly obscured by a set of clothes far too big for it. Its skull largely barren and its eyes burned from its sockets, it appeared to be the victim of a lightning strike or fire, which had then been mummified shortly afterward. In truth there was little left to identify it as once having been Dreyl'vyn, aside from its size.

"Where are we?" Jillian asked, noticing me hovering behind her. "Are we off the mountain? Why do I feel so sick?"

I wanted no part in hurting Jillian's feelings or adding to her already considerable guilt, but I saw no benefit in confusing her further by denying her the truth. Hating myself for every word I wrote, I laid the events out in glowing letters before her, the sheet of text rippling like a flag in the wind.

```
             You passed out from cold.
       Dreyl'vyn carried you to this town.
                Your body failed you.
      Wesson (another Gnill'var) revived you.
         You ate him, but it was necessary.
             He wanted you to do so.
        You ate two other people by accident.
            It was my fault, not yours.
           You nearly turned into a demon.
               You ate Dreyl'vyn.
            He suggested you do so.
           His life force was powerful.
      Your demonic side lost to your undead side.
          You woke up. You are you again.
```

You are you again. What a stupid thing to write.

Jillian gasped and covered her mouth with her hands. *"I killed innocent people again!"* Angry black tears welled up in her furious eyes. "You should have just killed me! Why am I even here!"

Quickly, I continued to write in the air.

```
        You're important.
     You need to find Jack.
Stopping Roth'Roh'Kah justifies all costs.
   You are the key to everything.
        Wesson knew that.
       Dreyl'vyn knew that.
         And I need you.
```

But as I scrawled the last sentence, Jillian was distracted by Fuer'ehn, who walked out of a nearby building, a pack in hand. Hastily I wiped the words away, embarrassed I had even written them in the first place.

Seeing For'shen's and Dreyl'vyn's bodies on the ground, Fuer'ehn swallowed nervously. His body trembled so violently I thought he might pass out.

Just wait until you find Wesson and Ch'ern in the building next to us.

Unsteadily Fuer'ehn opened the pack and handed a hastily-drawn map to Jillian.

"I don't know what you are, but you can't be here," he said, tears running down his cheeks. "What you just did to these men is… is…" He stifled a panicked breath. "W-we lack the skills to fight you, so please have mercy on us and leave instead. We've made this map to guide you to Mor'shor. I'm not sure it was the right decision - I'm not sure they deserve the plague you bring - but I can't see any other way to convince you to move on from our lands. Here are some supplies. Please go before you kill other innocent people. *Please.*"

Jillian, who had continued to cry as he spoke, took the map but declined the pack of supplies. "You've seen what I need to eat," she muttered, breaking down into even more tears. Black, inky blotches dripped down from her cheeks and stained the page.

As Fuer'ehn turned and walked back into a nearby building, no doubt to take cover again, Jillian stared down at her blackened fingers, which still mostly resembled talons.

"Never again," she whispered, determination in her voice. Looking up toward me, she pointed in my direction. "If I need to take another innocent life to live, kill me right then and there. Move on without me. Do you understand? *Kill me!*"

Yes.

I wrote the word in the air, but it was a lie; next time she needed to feed, I would provide another temporary cure for her. It had been my mistake in letting her feed too much, too fast. If she permanently lost her mind in the process sometime in the future, so be it, but I wouldn't allow her to die as I knew her. Not with her consciousness still attached to a corrupted body.

Standing, Jillian studied the map for a while before taking note of where the mountains were.

"I guess we should go in that direction," she stated while pointing out across a great valley.

Movement behind us caused her to turn. Dreyl'vyn's corpse, shaking violently, rose to its feet. With only rudimentary muscular regrowth, and next to no skin, he reminded me of some ridiculous *He-man* villain. Attempting to speak, all that ushered forth was a series of hissing breaths; he had neither a tongue nor the muscles to move his jaw properly. Jillian's spellwork had depleted him far more than even my campfire had, but somehow he had managed to survive it. Thankfully, without the prior restrictions of his captors, he appeared to be making a quick recovery.

Jillian flung herself into the macabre man's arms, nearly knocking him over in his weakened state. "I didn't kill you! *I didn't kill you!* Thank god you're alive! Oh my god, Dreyl'vyn, you're okay! Thank you so much for living!" She repeatedly kissed and squeezed him.

Dreyl'vyn, whose mostly-regenerated eyes had grown wide from being jostled around, didn't bother to attempt another incomprehensible response. Instead, he grabbed Jillian by the shoulders and pointed in the direction she had indicated.

Taking a moment to partially disrobe, Dreyl'vyn left only his shirt draped across his emaciated body. It hung about him like a billowing gown. Rolling up his massive pants and other accessories for later use, he slung them over his shoulder, as one would with a bed roll, and indicated he was ready.

We then set out toward our destiny, praying the people of Mor'shor wouldn't suffer the same fate as the residents of Duff.

CHAPTER
Fifty-One
-CONCEALED CONSPIRACY-

Over the next several hours, we wordlessly traveled in a straight line toward the direction Jillian had pointed. Dreyl'vyn, slowly restoring his appearance, looked less and less like a walking amalgamation of beef jerky, but otherwise said nothing. Eventually, while pausing to put his clothes back on - clothes which still hung off him like curtains - he opened his mouth to speak.

"If the need arises, we will repeat this transaction," he announced in a rough whisper. Jillian, stunned by the statement, broke into tears and began to protest, but he held up a hand to quiet her. "I thought my form might have a negative impact on your demonic attributes, and I was correct in that assumption."

"That doesn't mean it's *okay*, Dreyl'vyn!"

"Such considerations toward morality serve no purpose. I can provide you exactly what you need, for as long as you need it. I do not possess knowledge of the Magic which animates your body, but you have explained that it is in a continual state of collapse. It is capable of regeneration, but not without allowing your demonic sickness to advance, as the sickness is also attempting its own type of conversion through consumption of an alternate accompanying resource."

And somehow Dreyl'vyn makes the act of eating a person sound like a scientific process.

"This body contained the strength to restore you, but I am not bound to it like the living are. There is a gap between my true form and what you see before you. It seems demons cannot consume what they cannot reach. Absorbing the strength contained within this body denies any further demonic transformation to take place inside you. I am immortal; this body will always be restored as long as I am held within it. We will repeat this transaction when necessary, as many times as necessary."

Jillian wiped her eyes. She in no way seemed comfortable with what had happened, even after Dreyl'vyn's clarification as to why it had been both fundamental and prudent to continue. "But, won't you get weaker? Like, every time I take some of your strength, aren't you dying a little bit by replenishing it?"

"No."

"Why not? I mean, I'm very glad to hear that, but why *don't* you get weaker?"

"You have asked me to explain a concept I am incapable of explaining."

Jillian motioned toward him. "Well, what makes you different than us, then? Why is it that your soul constantly regenerates and ours doesn't?"

"What you call *your soul* does not diminish; your flesh does. My people do not live within flesh."

Jillian appeared to have happened upon a new concept. "Are… you saying when we die, we carry on to the dimension where your people live?"

Dreyl'vyn shook his head. "What happens after your death is beyond my knowledge, but you do not join my people." He paused for a moment to consider his words. "You are meant to live within flesh; I am not. Without a body, I remain; without a body, you do not. As I stand before you, I am complete, but trapped. As you stand before me, you are incomplete and in need of repair."

"So then you're saying, when humans lose our bodies, we are gone forever?"

"If that is what death is. I have not experienced such a state of being, so I am incapable of answering your question."

"If that is what death is…" Jillian repeated to herself. Seeing that Dreyl'vyn had no further knowledge to impart, she changed the subject. "Does it hurt? I mean, when I take some of your strength."

Dreyl'vyn regarded her with his passive gaze. "You could say the simple act of being bound inside this body causes me pain."

"It hurts just to stand there?"

"In a way. You are aware of yourself. You comprehend your own existence, at least to a point, and can tell yourself such ideas without opening your mouth. Is that correct to assume?" Jillian nodded. "Beings who exist beyond you, those who are more than you, are aware of each other in similar ways."

"More than us…" Jillian said, considering what Dreyl'vyn meant. "You mean, humans are self-aware, and they can speak to themselves inside their mind, but you're saying you can hear the thoughts of other Cimmerians too. And you can't while in that body?"

"In a way. You refer to your race as *self-aware*. With those who are more than you, there is also more than self-awareness; there is… *mutual*-awareness. A state where one's self is not as much a self… as it is… not… a self."

Dreyl'vyn appeared to have reached an end to what his words could accomplish.

Jillian, seeing his difficulty, permitted herself a small smile. "You're saying you have a community - a *thought* community - where you co-exist and both are and are not one with each of your race, and it hurts you to be away from that."

"I believe that may be as close as your race can come to comprehension of my true existence, but it matters not. I have experienced this pain for such a long duration, it is like breathing once was to you - it is a part of me now. Do not think about my physical discomfort; it is nothing compared to my inner isolation. Focus on your objective. The fluid which runs down your face indicates guilt, which you should not burden yourself with. If you complete your task successfully, then anything required to reach your goal will be justified."

Dreyl'vyn had a way of making the worst actions sound completely benign. If someone were to remove emotions from everything, all they'd be left with would be an analysis of cause and effect, and that described his thought process to a tee. Even so, I had to agree with his assessment. The entire world was about to be wiped out, and some people might be required to suffer or perish while we attempted to save it.

If it is a certainty that everyone is going to die, wouldn't saving a portion of them justify the extinction of the rest?

Or am I, too, becoming a monster, and that is an inhumane ideal to consider?

Jillian stared down at her fingers again, the tips of which still remained talon-like and blackened by demonic taint. "I hope you're right, Dreyl'vyn; I really do. At this point, though, it's going to take a lot of good to make me forget what I just did, even if I don't remember doing it. To me that's no excuse. Innocent people's lives should never be taken lightly."

As we continued to walk, Jillian asked Dreyl'vyn to summarize what had happened before she woke up. He, of course, knew little of what I had done, and to be fair, I had done little myself. But he was still able to provide a fair amount of detail overall. None of what he said, however, had any positive effect on Jillian. She continued to blame herself for the entire situation despite having had no control over her body whatsoever.

The two also discussed at great length why cold seemed to affect them, but they eventually settled on the idea that the cold was simply *cold*. Everything becomes slower, stiffer, and eventually shuts down when chilled, and their bodies, although powered by dark Magic, were not immune to such tendencies. Warmth may very well have brought them back, but had their circumstances been different, they might have remained frozen on the side of the mountain forever.

The conversation came to an end as we happened upon a small cottage. It was decided in short order that while we did have a map, verifying our exact position on it would be most useful. Until that point we had only garnered a general idea of where we were based on large landmarks with quite a distance in between each one.

Surely, someone is inside or nearby. They can help us pinpoint where we are.

Upon entering, the cottage was found to be clean and tidy, but otherwise seemed to have been abandoned for quite some time. Small, bordering on cramped, it wasn't much larger than Thaddeus' secret room had been.

To sleep here for a night would be painful, let alone living here for any period of time.

Dreyl'vyn, who was tall enough to brush the rafters with his head, dipped through the entrance, his shoulders askew and one hand on the ground. Once inside, he hunched over awkwardly. Running a giant finger across the table, it left a clean streak behind.

"There has been no tenant here for a long while," he concluded.

Sighing, Jillian nodded. "Then there's no reason to wait for someone to show up. Let's get out of here and keep going."

Turning toward the entrance, she paused. Darkening the doorway stood none other than the tree-portal-traveling time-wizard from my visions. Clad in black trimmed with gold, a hood pulled over his head, he was every bit the gaunt, cold man I had kept in my memories.

Varek!

Of all moments, this might be the most opportune time to talk to him.

I have so many questions!

It was then I realized Varek might not be there to talk; he could have arrived to "set things straight" by removing us from the timeline. Unfortunately, my concern was not immediately diffused.

"Might I be so bold as to keep you three here a while longer?" Varek inquired, his voice smooth and sharp.

Poised as a request, his expression indicated otherwise. I thought back to how he had conversed with Renault, and concluded he had spoken very much the same way to his victim.

Jillian wrinkled her nose. To her, he was a stranger; she had no idea she was related to him, or even that it was *he* who had written the book we read in the ruins of Empor'Vael, detailing their father's descent into madness.

I wrote one word in the air, which illuminated us all in dim purple light.

Varek'ehn

Varek smiled. "Indeed I am, Laurence. How astute of you," he commented in his fluidic, unnerving voice. "I did not expect to track you down in this land after sensing your presence in, well…" He smiled again, a curious expression crossing his features.

"Who's Laurence?" Jillian inquired, her body language informing me she in no way trusted the man before her.

"I recognize this man," Dreyl'vyn announced from above, his booming voice echoing off the rafters. "He is the descendant of my captor, and the one who awarded me with my armor, Loh'Mach. Do you consider him friend or foe? I cannot tell by either of your reactions."

"I'm having that problem, too," Jillian growled. Tensing her muscles, she appeared ready to lunge at Varek. I could only conclude that would be a mistake, given the man's considerable powers.

Varek laughed darkly. "Dangerous you both might be, but no match for me, I'm afraid." Extending a hand before Dreyl'vyn, he summoned a massive chair, which took up a full third of the small cottage. "Have a seat, Cimmerian," he said, using an unseen force to push the giant into a seated positon. "I, too, remember well your accomplishments. You were quite effective in the ring. Shame to see you've lost your armor. It was… one of a kind. I often wondered if they'd honor you as one of the champions based on your many successes, but I suppose that would have gone against my father's agenda, hmm?"

Seeing Jillian continue to bare her teeth, Varek sighed. "*All* of you, please sit," he repeated, staring directly at Jillian. She, too, was pushed backward into a chair that had not existed a moment ago.

"I am here as a friend, but I understand your concern," he admitted. "I will first tell you a tale, and then you can decide for yourself whether or not you'd enjoy my company. And to answer your question, Jillian, Laurence is the name of the man made of stone, your crystalline companion."

Eyeing me hesitantly, Jillian leaned an elbow on the table before extending a flippant hand toward Varek, motioning that he begin his tale. Smiling, Varek closed the door behind him and summoned a pair of floating candles, which provided a dim, flickering illumination to the interior of the cottage. Having a seat himself on a quaint stool, he began his tale.

"Unbeknownst to my father, Vael'ehn, I met Thaddeus once at a local tavern." Seeing Jillian's confused expression, Varek added, "Jack's ancestor, whom you have not met." The clarification only further served to confuse her, but Varek moved on anyway. "The tavern was quiet, and I happened to overhear a group of men who were on the lookout for someone carrying a very powerful artifact. Apparently there was a substantial reward of some sort involved.

"Thaddeus, whom I hadn't been introduced to by that time, seemed rather uncomfortable upon hearing the news himself. He immediately stood and left the tavern. On his way out, he happened to notice my presence, which caused him further displeasure. The expression felt suspicious to me, and I decided to follow him. After all, I only had my father's bidding to attend to on that day - nothing of import, in my humble opinion.

"I followed him until he arrived at a Telestone, which he had hidden behind a brick, set within the wall of a building. Upon touching it, he vanished. Surprised by the revelation, I waited to see if he returned. Minutes later, he did exactly that, and I, being the curious person I am, decided to confront him.

"As I approached, Thaddeus took notice of me. He attempted to flee, but I called out, informing him I meant no harm. That, of course, was a partial truth; I saw no reason to harm him, but I had no objections to the contrary. I had decided to let him prove his worth to me first.

"Letting out a sigh, he walked toward me and extended a hand in greeting. As I took it, a spell was cast over me despite my many wards which might prevent such an interaction. Looking up into my eyes, Thaddeus uttered the following words, which I will never forget:

"'My name is Thaddeus, and I met your father once. You have both his power and his curse inside you. If there is ever a point where you doubt what he has told you, the stone behind me will become your tool to undo him. Until that day, it will be useless to you, as will attempting to follow me.'

"An odd statement from someone you've just met, don't you think?"

Jillian shrugged, causing Varek to smile.

He continued. "Upon completing his introduction, Thaddeus vanished. And I do not use those words as one who had just seen someone teleport away. I consider myself a man of considerable skill, and I was not able to ascertain where he went. Vanishing before *my* eyes is an act which will immediately garner both my respect and intrigue. So it was, that I never forgot the interaction I had with him.

"Some time later, my father received a portent from his *Temploscope*." Varek sighed. "The vast number of hours that man has prattled on about the brilliance of his invention, I will never understand." He shook his head. "He insisted he had learned of his demise due to the failed return of his sword, which should have been transported back to him by a man named Jack. Mind you, at that time I did not know who Jack was, nor did I connect my father's sword with the object those men at the tavern were hunting.

"My father asked - no, *demanded* - that I head to a future age, set billions of years from now, to kill whoever was to heal a woman named Jillian. That would be you." He motioned toward Jillian, who shrugged. "You can imagine my surprise. *Billions* of years! What a ridiculous distance. Such a task is one *no* man would accept lightly, and one very few have ever taken upon themselves to complete. Nonetheless, he *insisted* your death was necessary as, without it, his sword would prove unable to manipulate Jack properly, and therefore remain hidden until it faded away.

So not only does Varek have no idea who Jillian really is, but neither does Vael'ehn?

"Needless to say, I found myself suspicious that he would send his son, of all people, and when I found myself unsure of his decision, Thaddeus' spell finally took full effect. His words came rolling back into my mind as if he had just whispered them into my ear:

"'If there is ever a point where you doubt what he has told you, the stone behind me will become your tool to undo him.'

"Those words aided in my suspicion, and when my father was absent, I decided to use the Temploscope myself to learn what he had seen. Unfortunately, my father had felt it necessary to avoid teaching me how to use his infernal contraption - an omission I suspect was on purpose. You might assume it would have been accompanied by a set of instructions or labels, but it was not, and an instrument such as that - being half Magic and half machine - is nearly impossible to operate with skill unless you have been instructed on how to do so by its creator.

"With that in mind, I assumed I would fail, but I was not deterred. I immediately began the arduous process of deciphering the Temploscope's use by commanding it to function. However, my initial words, 'Show me what my father has hidden,' did not reveal anything of value to my eyes; it retrieved some vague references to books and objects I had no interest in. Foolishly I began to fiddle with the abundance of knobs and dials instead, which did little good for my cause.

"Out of frustration, I uttered the words, 'I require this damned contraption to show me what my father has experienced,' or something similar; I don't quite remember. To my surprise, the Temploscope dug *far* into his past, uncovering something I'm certain neither he nor anyone else knows about: the events I documented in the notebook you found. It took many attempts to collect the entire story - the machine tended to waver in and out of various timelines, likely due to my inexperience - but I did eventually see it all." Varek shook his head. "To depict such a series of happenings, it would appear his device is far more powerful than even *he* is aware.

"Upon uncovering the truth of his past, I realized my father was not in control of his own faculties. What he has done, his choices leading up to this point and beyond, are not of his choosing. What he does now, he does not do for the betterment of our race, even if he *is* convinced that is his intention. What I witnessed could not be ignored. I had no choice but to undo what my father had started.

"Again I attempted to use the Temploscope with several failed settings and commands until a random adjustment, combined with the words, 'show me what my father has seen of the future,' brought about a second series of visions. They were similar to what he had spoken of but also varied in many important details. You see, the future changed because I had decided to be directly involved in its undoing; meddling with the Temploscope had altered my own intent and, therefore, the future.

"I continued to view the Temploscope with the same settings, each time attempting to devise a plan which would adjust events to serve me better. With each repeated viewing, the future changed, my knowledge and involvement adjusting what might come to pass. I saw that preventing your transformation, Jillian, would indeed keep Jack from traveling into the past. If that were all that was required to stop my father, however, I could have simply traveled to a point when you were younger and dispatched you both before you laid eyes on the sword. As you might imagine, it was not that simple."

"*Gee*, thanks," Jillian commented.

Varek smiled at the sarcastic remark. "The truth is, you are not the only casualty; many will fair far worse than you have. The future is much more complicated than you are aware, but informing you of all its secrets will only allow time to become less predictable. I have to keep some to myself; my plans have already become too muddled.

"What I *can* tell you is this: my father's obsession over the Temploscope was brought on by a desire to verify the fruition of his goals. However, after learning of his death, and how he might correct it, he failed to view what would happen directly afterward.

"What he does not know, is that he *always* dies in the visions, sword or not. He is incapable of fighting against the entire combined might of the world, and everything falls down around him despite his convictions. He does not expect how willing people will be to sacrifice *everything* they hold dear for no reason other than to eliminate him. The only difference in regard to him regaining his sword is the casualties he causes in the process, both physical and Magical.

So… the other version of myself didn't stop him? Everyone else does, whether he gains the sword or not?

It's as if everything I've done hasn't mattered at all!

"There is even a version of the future where you all remain safe, and the sword is kept hidden. It is never given a chance to be purified *or* fully corrupted, and it weakens until it is no more. But within that timeline, a greater tragedy still comes to pass.

"Roth'Roh'Kah's plans do not require my father to live in order to succeed. When my father dies, he continues to manipulate others to do his bidding. He is always a threat, and eventually he finds a way through, no matter what his opposition tries. Our true mission is *his* destruction. In order to accomplish that, we need to change the sword back to what it once was.

"And that is not an impossible task. We *do* have an opportunity to reform the sword and use it against a force that will destroy us all. However, if we allow my father to corrupt it, he will push it past the point where it can be reclaimed. It will be hidden away after his death, where it withers away and dies in secret.

"It *was* within Wenton's abilities to heal you, Jillian, but I required the conviction your transformation would bring. It was *my* decision to refrain from writing you out of danger. It was *I* who labeled you as the first casualty of my plan, who allowed you to be taken by the sword. If the story of your conversion requires a villain, then I have played that part. Mor'dresh, however, is not to blame for this; in truth it is trying its best to correct itself-"

Jillian burst out laughing. "You had me until then, you really did. But you are *not* going to convince me that the thing which almost *killed* me did so out of the goodness in its heart!"

Varek smiled mirthlessly. "Consider my words carefully. Mor'dresh was taken by Thaddeus, taken directly from Vael'ehn's possession. A Weapon of Legend would only allow such a thing if it desired that to happen; otherwise it would fight tooth and nail for its master. It could have crushed Thaddeus, torn his soul directly from his body. Mor'dresh is simply *not* an artifact a person can walk up and take."

He leaned forward toward Jillian. "Why would it consume your soul so slowly? Why would it give Jack such an obvious opening for your soul to be pulled from its grasp and planted back in your body? Why would it allow circumstances to be put in play which grant you dark powers that fight *against* the demonic transformation taking place inside you? Surely you are aware it knows far more than you do. It is capable of seeing things you don't, remembering things you can't. What you have gotten away with is not an oversight on its part, I assure you."

Jillian's cocky, unconvinced demeanor had changed drastically as Varek explained further. Hesitantly, she looked first toward me and then up to Dreyl'vyn. Neither of us had answers to provide her with, nor was I about to refute what Varek had just said, given my own experiences with the sword.

She finally opened her mouth to respond, but Varek held up a hand.

"I *do* understand how brutal its actions have been. Mor'dresh cannot change what Vael'ehn has done to it on its own. You have to understand, up until now its only choice was to use the dark power it had been imbued with to manipulate events into *causing* Vael'ehn's failure. There *is* such a thing as using an element against itself, and that is exactly what Mor'dresh is attempting to do."

"Fighting fire with fire..." Jillian muttered.

Varek motioned toward her. "Indeed. But remaining in the middle of all that fire is not always pleasant, as you have experienced."

Then, Mor'dresh allowed itself to be corrupted, allowed Jack to be killed.

It can see things I can't. It knows what is to come, at least in part.

"That being said, my attempts at altering the future always ended with Vael'ehn exercising enough of his power over the sword to fully corrupt it, which destroys our most important tool forever. What I really needed was someone removed from the process entirely, someone unaffected by time. It was the only way to influence Jack directly and keep him on course until the sword could stand against the corruption on its own. But that idea did not even enter my mind, and I did not stumble upon it, until I changed my strategy entirely.

"Frustrated by my apparent failures, and unable to remove Thaddeus' words from my mind, I traveled back to where I had once found him, and uncovered his Telestone. Touching it transported me to a curious, hidden room. To my surprise, I found two pieces of parchment - one addressed to Thaddeus' future heir and one addressed to *me*. Upon them rested a Coadjutor, one in a unique hue.

"The letter explained that the artifact was a *two*-part creation which had once been a pair of Coadjutors, supplemented with Magic from Obli'tahrs. He referred to his invention as a *Coadju'tahr* - a memorable if not meaningless name. The piece of the Coadju'tahr left for me was programmed to absorb a sliver of the soul from the first person who touched it - an action which I had inadvertently performed in order to retrieve the letters. It would then combine with the entire soul of the second person to touch it.

My crystal has a name!

Coadju'tahr... *I like that.*

"Once the process was complete, the entire spell matrix would transfer itself to the second piece of the Coadju'tahr. Not only did it hold the captured soul, as an Obli'tahr would, but it could also be controlled by that soul rather than being confined by it. It is, in essence, an Object of Power with the entire soul of a man." He motioned toward Dreyl'vyn. "Your armor was similar, Cimmerian.

"Objects of Power, as you know, are typically created by a great many people who have given up part of their souls. That is where the object draws its strength and state of semi-awareness from. His invention, however, is unique in that it is open-ended. His Coadju'tahr was created weak and vulnerable, but it is capable of drawing from the souls of those it touches, therefore gaining its full power as the user interacts with sympathetic people in their environment.

I've been gaining power from people I've touched along the way?

"The letter went on to explain that Thaddeus had imbued the Coadju'tahr with a complex series of wards which, to put it plainly, kept someone from harming themselves or their own bloodline. By touching the artifact, I caused it to become impenetrable to my spells, to my *father's* spells. As far as Vael'ehn is concerned, the Coadju'tahr *is* invincible, as long as it is he who is controlling the Magic being used against it.

"Due to its basis on the design of a Coadjutor - an object only partially bound by time - I was warned that the person residing within might experience visions, memories, or other strange disturbances when making contact with the souls of those they touch." Varek eyed me with a sense of admiration. "That may have been quite disorienting for you to cope with, Laurence. I can only imagine as I have no experience with how those effects might manifest."

Quickly, I responded.

> It was confusing, but fascinating.
> I figured it out, and now it aids me.
> I have full control of my abilities.

Taking the opportunity to interject, Jillian stepped into the conversation. "Wait. I followed *very* little of what you just explained. Is this important?" Her eyes narrowed. "Or are you making this *intentionally* complicated to confuse me?"

Varek grinned; he was in no way troubled by her doubt. "It is not important for *you*, Jillian, but Laurence deserved to learn what happened to him. I do not think you can begin to imagine the journey he has been on, and being held in ignorance would have only caused him further distress. Beside that point, it proves to him the value and purpose he represents on this mission."

And it was true. The information Varek had provided, while technical and hard to understand in some ways, told me a great deal of why my body had been created and what purpose it had. But Varek wasn't done explaining.

"Thaddeus packaged up his spellwork with other minor wards, translational spells, and safeguards, and completed the Coadju'tahr. How he was able to combine so much into such a minor Object of Power, I cannot fathom, but my respect for him has only continued to grow. He then laid it in a chest next to Mor'dresh before traveling to the future to hide and protect it. If someone were ever to unearth the sword, they would also find the Coadju'tahr nearby. Mor'dresh would inevitably open a portal to the past using the Coadju'tahr to do so.

"You see, in our time Coadjutors are the easiest, most reliable way to open a portal, and are preferred to using one's own memory, which can have undesired effects. Mor'dresh would be fully aware of that knowledge and incapable of counting on someone, such as Wenton, to open a portal to where it was being drawn. It would rely on the only object from the past it had - one that also carried a strength of its own," Varek beamed. "It's rather brilliant actually.

"Thaddeus had his suspicions that Mor'dresh allowed him to take it in an effort to correct itself, but there was - and still is - a tumultuous battle being waged inside it. He couldn't allow it to have free range, allow it the chance to appear too close to Vael'ehn. He wanted to make sure that, when it traveled through time, it would arrive at a location that gave us a clear advantage.

"He left me one last minor spell with which to impart my own destination of choice into the Coadju'tahr - a location only I would know. I chose the fallen library at Empor'Vael, an abandoned location far from anywhere my father might be. I also decided to leave the journal there for Jack to read, so he would understand what he truly dealt with. He and you, Laurence, would be the only two, aside from myself, to have such valuable information.

"Thaddeus' letter finished by informing me that in order to assist in correcting the sword's corruption, I should enlist someone willing to sacrifice their body for the cause, someone I trusted completely. That might be a simple request for some, but not for me. My life, being what it is, has surrounded me with disloyal, dishonest thieves. There is no one on this planet I would even call a friend.

"To find a possible candidate, I waited until I could use the Temploscope without my father's knowledge. By requesting that it show me those in the future who were attuned to Magic - a request that yielded almost *no* results - I was able to pick through a small number of prospects. Out of those who might be of use, very few were uninformed of Magic and able to be guided by my hand. An experienced mage would have introduced thousands of other variables into my plan, and I had no time to account for those complexities. The person I chose needed to be easily led, easily influenced.

"At last, Laurence, I came upon you. Young, bright, not yet manipulated or tainted by your world - you would be the perfect candidate for me to guide and, regrettably, the second victim of this plan. After finding you, I headed to the future under the guise of pursuing my father's task. I did not, however, travel to the time he had indicated. Slowly, meticulously, I wound my way further and further through time, adjusting relevant details, one by one. It was an arduous task, I assure you.

"You may remember a series of odd events throughout your life; perhaps you do not. They were all caused by myself in order to prepare you for your destiny. It was even I who placed the first piece of the Coadju'tahr there at the Green Dragon Emporium for you to find. I wish you could have seen your face when you spotted it." Varek laughed to himself. "It is not often someone who knows nothing of Magic is led to find it in such a peculiar way.

"I then made my way to Wenton's hidden locale and gravely injured Renault. I led him to believe he was protecting a tome Wenton would use to restore you, Jillian. In actuality, I stole *both* tomes he would need. They reside within my father's tent for now. He is unaware they have even been added to his collection."

He glanced down toward Jillian's arm. "I endured a small amount of guilt when conceptualizing that deception. I was, after all, cementing your fate as something other than human. But seeing you now, I no longer do. Sooner or later, you would have given in to your hunger, and life as you know it would have been far shorter."

Jillian sighed and stared down at her hands. Tiny black tendrils had crept up her knuckles, growing ever so slightly with whatever bit of power still remained from the souls she had devoured. It wasn't much of a change, but it was an indication that the taint was ever present, always pushing to gain a further hold on her.

Varek offered at least some consolation, however grim it might have been. "I do not know when you first had dealings with demons, but it illustrates the point that Roth'Roh'Kah has interacted with *many* beings in *many* times. My father is quite powerful, but he is only one of countless pawns the demon lord has manipulated in a bid for this planet. Know that your suffering is for the good of a great many people, both in the past and the future. You will all lose your lives, as will I, but this cause justifies our losses, no matter how great."

I couldn't help but focus on Varek's portent of our future destinies.

Lose our lives? All of us? What has he seen?

He also said I was a victim of his plan, someone who would sacrifice my body to enter the Coadju'tahr. Does that mean my body is gone for good?

Varek continued. "After my task was complete, I returned to my time. Making one final journey to Thaddeus' secret room, I left a note for you, Laurence. I kept it vague enough so as not to be traced back to me, but competent enough to keep you focused on your task without influencing the future more than intended.

"The timeline manipulated, the journal in place, Thaddeus alive and well in the future, my plan had been set in motion. But of my father, there was no sign. I found that suspicious, as he hadn't informed me he would be leaving prior to my departure, nor had he indicated he was aware of the location at which Jack would arrive.

"I decided it best to track him down in order to gain an idea of what his plans might have been, but the destination of his teleportation spell had faded and only gave me a vague area to work with. I knew the Long Road to the tournament was far closer to that location, so I chose to attend while I searched for him.

"The tournament was an event he had forbidden me from taking part in, despite receiving multiple invites. It would likely anger him greatly, but it would also provide a convincing alibi, as I have often gone against his advice throughout my life. So, leaving a letter of intent in my father's secret study, I set off on my journey in a grand, official manner.

That's where Vael'ehn trapped me, then - his secret study.

"As I suspected it would be, my progress was slow going but uneventful. I cannot convey my surprise when, on the fourth day of my journey, I managed to locate my father. Of all places, he had somehow arrived within viewing distance of my company and had created a camp with none other than Jack and you, Laurence.

"That was no coincidence; he had found my letter. I knew in an instant, either my spellwork had failed and Jack had not made it to the library, or my father had figured out my plan and intercepted him at Empor'Vael. I suspected the former, however, as I'd have been murdered had he learned of my duplicity.

"My escorts also noticed his nearby disturbance but were not keen enough to detect who or what had caused it. While they investigated your hidden camp, I kept quiet, so as not to rouse suspicion, but began to consider a different plan to aid Jack. Considering he was in league with my father, I knew he would be manipulated into following along with whatever it was my father had contrived. Since they were camping next to the long road, that left little speculation as to what he intended.

"Assuming my father would manipulate Jack into attending the tournament with the sword - an event he had no invite or Coadjutor to enter with - I concluded I would aid Jack and allow myself more freedom in one simple act. Setting a faster pace, I moved out ahead of them. Near a rock formation, I murdered my escorts. I feel no shame in doing so; they were not to be trusted.

"The task done, I left my invite and my Coadjutor behind. Imbuing it with a series of spells my father had taught me, I knew it would function for Jack and cause him to adopt my royal outfit as well. I hoped my action would not only lead my father to assume Jack had killed me but also appear suspicious in Jack's eyes, as my father would have been furious with me for deserting the kingdom.

"I could not be sure if Jack knew my father's true identity or not, but sooner or later the truth would reveal itself: he and I are related. Any open threats my father might have made toward me by then would have sowed mistrust in Jack. It was the perfect set of circumstances to tear down what was likely a near-infallible strategy, without my father becoming aware of my participation beforehand.

And this entire time Jack and I had both assumed Vael'ehn killed his own son. Apparently he wasn't lying about everything.

That means Jack could have used Varek's Coadjutor without risk. What a mess. I destroyed the entire registration tent for nothing.

Varek continued. "Free to travel unhindered after faking my own death, I made my way back to Empor'Vael to learn why my spellwork had unraveled. It seemed strange that something should go wrong considering the meticulous planning of both Thaddeus and myself. Upon my arrival I was startled to find that you, Laurence, had indeed shown up at that location several days prior, but with Jillian instead. Complicating matters, I had *also* sensed you with Jack and my father near the Long Road; I was sure of it.

When he's done, I should explain why a version of me was at both locations.

"Unable to ascertain what had happened, I tracked your movements through your spellwork." Varek laughed darkly. "You three have left, well, let us just say you have left some *unhappy* people and a series of strange corpses in your wake. And here I now sit, face to face with you three, not at all certain what has happened. Despite my careful planning, *something* has gone wrong, of which I have no knowledge. Time is not kind and does not forgive those who meddle in its mysteries," he muttered.

Jillian sighed. "That's a detailed story, but I can't verify *any* of it, Varek'ehn. You might be telling the truth, or you might be setting us up for something awful. I've been told your father is *quite* the liar. With that much information, it's impossible for me to tell where a lie might be hidden."

Varek laughed, his hoarse chuckle clearly of little use in the Vaelcurian Empire. "Oh, come now. Give me at least *some* credit. It was a significant effort to contrive such a complex story with which to fool you!"

Jillian, not at all pleased with Varek's sarcasm, pursed her lips. "I'm just saying it was hard to follow."

Varek waved the comment away. "Nonsense. My storytelling is superb. Why, if I turned everything I had accomplished into a novel, I dare say it would be quite the success."

Jillian cocked an eyebrow. "You think people want to read page after page of you blathering on and on about what you did in the shadows, practically spoon-feeding them all the answers without allowing them to solve the mystery for themselves?"

Varek leaned forward, giving Jillian a conspiratorial smile. "I *did* say I kept some details to myself, did I not?" He winked, causing Jillian to frown.

Dreyl'vyn shook his head. "I feel he is being truthful. I have watched many of your race lie to each other throughout my existence on this planet. There are telltale signs when one of you is not being truthful. I have yet to observe any of them while watching him."

"And here you are, Cimmerian, coming to my aid after all those years of captivity. I should say, I would think you'd have built up some sort of aggression toward my family by now."

"I do not believe you were directly involved in my capture and imprisonment," Dreyl'vyn replied, staring down at Varek. "Even if I were to draw those conclusions, my persecution has already passed, and I have been freed. Revenge does not serve a purpose to my existence. Whether or not you have arrived to aid us is another matter. From the events you informed us of, I have concluded you are here to correct a future tragedy."

"I don't enjoy being in a position like this, but I have to ignore what you've both said," Jillian interjected. "You may be telling the truth, but following you also exposes us to a big risk. Vael'ehn is your father, and familial bonds can be quite strong when push comes to shove." She leaned forward. "*Especially* demonic ones." The statement caused Varek to display the slightest hint of a frown, but Jillian didn't push him. "We need to continue on with our plan alone, as if we'd never met you. And speaking of that-"

Interrupting Jillian, I swooped down to the center of the table. She was correct; she couldn't verify anything Varek had said, but I could. Every word he had spoken lined up in one way or another with each event I had gone through so far. He could have been hiding a few lies in between his truthful information, but I doubted it. He had volunteered many details he had no reason to share in order to appear just as convincing.

An overly detailed explanation can reveal a lie far more easily than a vague one.

At last, I had my answers from the time-wizard, and I was ready to provide him with some of my own. Creating a flurry of purple letters, I filled most of the small room with enchanted, hovering writing, which undulated in large sweeping waves.

```
              Varek is not lying.
         Everything he has said is true.
             He needs answers, too.

           There are two versions of me.
           I am from an alternate timeline.
         Varek, your portal spell almost worked.
          I might not have been strong enough
                to make sure it succeeded.

    The sword created one portal, your spell another.
     The two spells fought back and forth inside me.
      I went through one portal, following after Jack.
        Jillian went through the other portal alone.
      I do not know what happened to her the first time.
```

```
Jack met Vael'ehn inside the Kaap'vaal Mountains.
Vael'ehn lied to us. Claimed to be Thaddeus.
Jack took on the role of "Prince Varek."
He had an accident and killed people.
He was crowned as a winner of the tournament.

We traveled to the Citadel of the Shattered Moon.
We fought against Vael'ehn's Retrograde army.
Vael'ehn killed everyone and captured Jack.
Vael'ehn tricked him into murdering innocents.
Mor'dresh killed and absorbed Jack.
Mor'dresh was corrupted and Vael'ehn claimed it.

We lost.

I traveled back to the future -
to before we went through the portal.
I took the other portal with Jillian.
We arrived at Empor'Vael and read your book.

There is still a version of me with Jack.
We are traveling to the tournament to meet him.
With our powers combined, we can win.

Can we show Vael'ehn what we have seen?
Will he change his ways if he knows his past?
Without his influence, the sword can change.
We can use him to help fight Roth'Roh'Kah.
```

As Varek read the words, his face displayed a myriad of emotions ranging from amusement upon learning that I had traveled backward and reset everything, to fury upon learning that his father had killed Jack and won despite his careful planning. Scanning over my last questions, he leaned backward, rubbing his chin.

Seeming to reach a conclusion within his mind, Varek motioned toward the giant rippling sheets of words. "I enjoy your sky writing very much. I did not realize you would be unable to communicate within the Coadju'tahr. What an interesting way of circumventing such an infuriating disability. I am both surprised and impressed that you have done so much, Laurence."

He shook a finger at Jillian. "*See*, this is why we needed a person like him." Fully aware she had no say in the matter, she simply shrugged. Turning back to me, Varek smiled. "I did not expect such a monumental effort. It would seem my choice in recruiting you was well-founded despite my doubts. It may not feel as such, but you have saved us all."

I don't think he will ever know how much those compliments mean to me.

Varek's expression slowly faded. "Despite your knowledge of the future, however, there are still many threats awaiting us. I assume by your questions that you have faith my father will change his ways if his heritage is made known to him. I would think not. His genes have been manipulated by Roth'Roh'Kah; he is not a rational man. It is not a matter of what *he* wants. Attempting to reason with him has never been a rewarding action for anyone, and providing him with knowledge of our existence will only worsen matters.

"It is interesting that you described a Retrograde army under his command. The Retrogrades do not follow logic. They cannot be led. They are a blight upon the land, destroying everything they come in contact with. My father would have been capable of leading them against the Citadel for one reason alone: he not only had something they wanted, but he also gave it to them. He has no idea I am aware of his dealings with the Retrogrades, but I know what he has offered as payment.

"You are not from this time period, so you may not have heard a common story about our history. Suffice it to say, the Xahl'thari sailed to this continent on immense seafaring vessels long after the planet was ravaged by a great tragedy. Most were disassembled over time to be repurposed as buildings or devices, but there is one that was not. Those who descended from Ridd'en - one of the Xahl'thari heroes - landed somewhere off the coast of the Shai'nah Crater, far to the west. It is, I believe, the location you referenced arriving within.

"The great trek the Riddari made through the mountains before arriving in the land they claimed as their own, is a widely known story. The location they first landed upon was flat, barren, and served little use; that is why they made the trek in the first place. The ship was left behind to be reclaimed by nature. The Riddari viewed the transport or disassembly of a giant, cobbled-together ship as a great undertaking for little benefit to their culture.

"But there is one race who desire nothing more than technology: the Retrogrades. The components stored within that ancient vessel are not the same as what those savages currently wield. They are very powerful, even in their ancient state. The Retrogrades hunted tirelessly until they gained knowledge of the ship's whereabouts, but they were never successful in crossing the continent.

"Vael'ehn promised them safe passage if they would spare the Vaelcurian Empire and ally with him to conquer the planet by his side. The deal was struck but not yet completed. In the meantime the Retrogrades have been left to pillage our abandoned cities while we move on, both to satisfy their lust for resources and to avoid rousing suspicion from the other nations. Better to hide his plans for conquest under the guise of a war-torn land."

I think I know where that ship is. I've seen it!

The hill Jack and I portalled onto had been revealed to contain a mass of metal underneath it. Thinking back upon the crater with the knowledge I had just gained, it certainly *did* resemble the bow of an impossibly large boat. We had quite literally been standing on it. Mostly-sunken, covered in dirt and grass, it had rested upon an ancient beach for thousands of years.

Vael'ehn's giant golem uncovered his secret, and I finally know what it is going to be used for. This is the advantage I've needed to make a true difference!

Varek continued. "It would appear Vael'ehn has chosen to finalize those plans. Before he calls upon his army, we need to arrive *first* and open up negotiations with them. Words, however, mean nothing to the Retrogrades. In order to convince them to side with us instead, we will be required to show them the exact spot where it is buried, if not take them directly to it. They *will* honor their word, but only if they feel we can benefit their race."

"But what about Jack?" Jillian queried. "We can't just leave him behind."

Her words asked permission, but her tone said otherwise; she wasn't about to allow Varek to undermine her agenda. Whether or not he agreed to aid her, she was clearly still intent on heading off to find Jack, and I wasn't about to let her out of my sight again.

Varek studied her face. "Your eyes do not hide your emotions well enough. You would not come with me now, even if I demanded it of you."

Jillian crossed her arms. "It's *not* going to happen without Jack. I can't risk letting him die again. While we're off digging up a boat, Vael'ehn might take notice and change his tactics. He could still gain control of the sword. We *do* have an advantage though; Laurence knows exactly what will happen and, therefore, where everyone will be. We can use that to make sure we rescue Jack and still have enough time to stop Vael'ehn afterward."

Surprisingly, Varek seemed to consider her words carefully. "By now Jack and Vael'ehn would have discovered my 'body.' The details of their discovery don't matter since Laurence has confirmed Jack makes it to the tournament under some semblance of my guise." Varek turned to regard me. "Laurence, does Jack continue to lie about his identity, or does he attract the attention of Wenton?"

Wenton finds out the truth and aids us.
He is on our side, along with many others.
But after he finds out, we don't have much time.

"If Wenton knows the truth, we will find no enemies inside the tournament," Varek said. "That is a very good thing, as I believe it would be the safest time to excise Jack from Vael'ehn's influence. Without allowing Jack to lose his mind and transfer the sword, Vael'ehn will not stand a chance against the combined might of Wenton's army and the Retrogrades. Even better, if we can manage to use the sword against him, that might be a turning point in correcting its corruption."

You can't access the tournament without a Coadjutor.
We left yours behind. I can show you where.

Varek scoffed. "You left it behind? Odd choice. That must have made your lives far more... *difficult*." He considered the idea further. "It certainly would have appeared more believable to my father if he found it lying there though; perhaps it was for the best.

"You are correct, however; no one can break through the barrier which protects the tournament. From what I've heard, it pales in comparison to the spellwork the Xahl'thari heroes used long ago to protect Arkken'Arak from being destroyed by the raging planet, but it is still incredible.

"Complicating matters even more, if I were to retrieve my Coadjutor from where it was left - that is, if my father didn't take it - he would still sense me nearby. He is far more powerful than I am, and I would not be able to shield you from him. We cannot risk the revelation that I am still alive; it is my only advantage over him. If he senses me, his behavior will change, and everything Laurence believes will happen may not."

Jillian let out a defeated sigh, surely assuming the tournament was impossible to access, but Varek shot her a devious smile. "I feel it would be remiss of me if I did not mention, there *is* one object powerful enough to allow us to bypass that shield, but it can only be retrieved by... less than honest means. In the capital city of Toriash'ahn lies a massive vault full of artifacts too powerful to risk being exposed to the public. Amongst those items is a Weapon of Legend: Ahso'lar, Touch of the Unknown, the wand carried by Esmer'ee.

"Ahso'lar is the most powerful Arcane artifact *ever* forged. It can create a portal so precise, it can pierce the barrier surrounding the tournament as if it were nothing. Even better, if we transport directly onto the tournament grounds, Vael'ehn will not be made aware of our existence at all. I would encourage you to consider stealing the wand with me. It might be our only course-"

Jillian stood abruptly, knocking her chair over in the process. "Then *that's* where we're heading!" she exclaimed, pounding a fist on the table. Its aged wooden surface fractured under the force.

Varek grinned at her response. "I am invigorated by your enthusiasm, but it will not be easy to procure. You may not be well acquainted with Toriash'ahn, but it is the largest city in all the land, and the vault we are attempting to break into is the most guarded. Innocent people could very well die."

Jillian leaned forward on the table, allowing her blackened fingers to be exposed again. Only a few inches from his own hands, Varek eyed them with more apprehension than his typical boastful attitude let on. "Dealing death seems to be the only talent I have left nowadays," she replied grimly.

"Our cause *will* justify our losses," Dreyl'vyn reminded her.

Varek nodded, staring up at the giant. "Indeed. Succeeding in this cause will certainly justify each and every loss the denizens of this planet take. For if we lose, the alternative is unthinkable."

Despite Jillian's insistence that we should leave at that very second, Varek was resolute in his decision that he get some rest first. The events he described had happened in quick succession, and he hadn't slept for several days. I, too, felt it was for the best. Not only were we moving more quickly than my alternate version had, but Varek was also far more adept at Magic than I. Sneaking into Toriash'ahn would be no small task. We needed his abilities to be as strong as possible.

As Varek summoned a bed, we made our way outside. The immense size of Dreyl'vyn combined with the cramped cottage provided little room for us to sit and talk while he attempted to sleep.

Determined to use the time wisely, I knew precisely the conversation I wanted to have with Jillian. Drifting over to her, I began to write.

```
            I have visions when I touch people.
    I have seen Jack's past, and I have seen yours.
                  I saw you as a baby.
            I know your history with demons.
        I know how your adopted parents died.
                I know you tried your best
          to protect the sword from being found.
```

Jillian gaped at me, terror filling her eyes, but I continued.

```
        You don't know Jack's history.
       Thaddeus didn't just bury the sword.
    Thaddeus had descendants for multiple generations.
     They all watched over it up until Jack's father.


        His father never told Jack the truth.
        He wanted a normal life for his son.
              You were their ally.
             You were all protectors.
         You helped keep it safe together.
```

Jillian's eyes began to well up. "Do you know how badly I've wanted to tell him all these years, tell him everything I've done? It's been horrible. And this is all *my* fault; I forgot to refresh my wards. It took *one* mistake! That sword broke through and called to him once. *Once,* Laurence! That's all it took! Years of protection gone in an instant.

"I didn't even know what I had been watching over until Jack opened the chest. The letter told me it was an object, but I didn't know it was a sword, and I didn't know it would hurt us! I thought I was stopping the demon from getting his hands on it. I thought it was enchanted to convince people like Jack to reveal its location. I thought that, as long as it remained hidden in his backyard, we would be fine.

"At first I tried to convince Jack to leave it buried, but I knew he wouldn't listen; he's just too bull-headed. But then I realized I could use the situation as an opportunity to tell him the truth. I thought I'd be able to convince him to put it back once we saw what it was and he learned what I had been through." Tears continued to stream down her face. "But everything happened so fast!"

```
             It's not your fault.
    It would have escaped far sooner if not for you.
          It almost escaped with his father, too.
       You were just a child with a confusing past,
           trying your best to prevent a tragedy.
```

The sword needed to be freed to defeat Roth,
but it could have released itself too early
and found Jack's ancestors to be lacking.

Think about it.
It was the proper time.
You made that possible for us!

We simply need to purify it now.
It will help us win this war.

We will save Jack.
We will cure you.
Everything is going to be okay.

Jillian smiled humorlessly at me. "I can see why Jack trusted you; you're the best of us all. Hopefully we *will* save Jack, but you can't save me. You heard Varek's words; I'm turning into a demon, Laurence. My life is at an end. You don't know the terrible thoughts that go on inside my mind now. I'm just trying to make up for what I am before it's my time to die.

No, I *do* know you.
You are a victim; you are *not* terrible.

I've been with you for
far longer then you know.

Staring into her striking, inhuman eyes, I couldn't hold back any longer.

This may be my only chance to tell you this.

Whether you save Jack or not,
whether we have a future or not,
whether you ever find out who I am...
I love you.

As Jillian read the words, her expression fell, and tears continued to roll down her cheeks. "No, Laurence, you don't. I'm sure you *think* you do, but I'm a succubus. Everyone who sees me, wants me. That's what the demonic spellwork inside me does; it traps people so I can consume them.

"You remember when we were first out getting food for Jack, right? Everyone just stared at me like an idiot because they were being brainwashed. You're just another one of my victims. You may still be alive because of your hardened exterior, but inside, your emotions have already been consumed by me.

"I don't know you well, but it seems like you're heroic, you're sensitive, and you care deeply for those around you. When I was a human, I belonged to Jack, and I'm determined not to hurt him or anyone else who matters to me, but I am no longer a human. I will be alone until I die, and seeing how quickly I've been degrading, that won't take long. Do yourself a favor, and try your best to forget about me. It will make it easier when I finally transform, and either you or Dreyl'vyn has to put me down; I know Jack won't be able to do it himself."

Staring compassionately toward me, Jillian gave me another humorless smile. "I do not love you, Laurence, nor do you love me. It is for the best."

Jillian had attempted to let me down gracefully, and for the most part she had done so, but inside me a great pain swelled. It was pain which I had never experienced before, pain which felt as if she had reached out and shattered me with her demonic claws, leaving my insides to bleed out upon the soil.

Silently, I drifted away into the darkness, cold and alone, forcing myself to stare into the void without focusing on what I was leaving behind.

CHAPTER
Fifty-Two

-SHROUDED SHAFT-

I spent the night, nearly inconsolable, drifting aimlessly through the darkness. Stupidly, as the light disappeared, I found myself unable to see. In my emotional distress I was also incapable of summoning any type of spell which might illuminate my surroundings. Silently I cursed both my lack of focus and knowledge.

If I knew even a single damn spell, I wouldn't be blind right now!

Finding the rage far easier to cope with than my fragile mental state, I let it consume me. Wandering aimlessly for hours, I filled my head with dramatic thoughts and imagined interactions between Jillian and I. Most of the night had come and gone before my raw emotions burned themselves down to smoldering coals. Even so, the darkness continued to blind me. Not to say I would have returned to the cottage had my situation improved; embarrassment weighed heavily in the forefront of my mind.

Light had crested the distant mountains before I finally built up the courage to return. Whether it had been the hours of internal reflection or the time spent away from Jillian's succubus-like powers, I couldn't say, but I found myself feeling more mentally capable despite the ever-present emotional pain. Upon seeing her standing outside the cottage, however, twinges of distress flared back to life, igniting my insides. Nevertheless, I pushed them down, refusing to acknowledge their existence ever again.

"Laurence seems to believe-" Jillian paused her conversation, noticing my presence.

"Speak of a man and he shall appear," interjected Varek, motioning toward me with a hand.

Jillian shot me a remorseful look but chose not to dwell on the past, instead continuing what she had been about to say.

"Laurence seems to believe everything you've said, Varek, but now you've got us retrieving a powerful Magic wand for you. I did a lot of thinking about that last night. Your father has made it his life's goal to reacquire one of these Weapons of Legend, and you've convinced us to do the same thing for you. Do you seriously think we should accept that as a coincidence?"

That's *what you were thinking about last night?*

Varek smiled. "The irony is not lost upon me, I assure you, but I am not looking to *re*-acquire something I lost. I would rather you view our circumstances as more of a necessity than a bid for power, but I *do* understand your mistrust. I also do not expect to gain that trust throughout this endeavor, nor would it serve any purpose in my life."

He turned toward Dreyl'vyn, who was again staring into the distance like a robot who had powered down. "And the same applies to you, Cimmerian. You have every right to despise my family and my nation, and you can continue to do so after this mission is complete. It does not bother me in the least. To be honest, I was surprised you didn't attempt to kill me when you first laid eyes upon me. I *was* prepared for a fight."

The statement, which mirrored one he had made before, seemed odd and combative. If I didn't know better, I'd say Varek was making an attempt to hide his dissatisfaction toward being mistrusted by calling out everyone around him in an effort to prove they felt the way he suspected they might.

He's clearly a product of a traumatic upbringing.

Dreyl'vyn remained where he was, motionless and emotionless. "I have no use for revenge. I have no understanding of hatred. Your nation *did* capture my people and put them to work; so did the Crotgar before you. *You* did not do that. You have been trapped inside your circumstances just as I have. I can tell it is so; its burden is carried within your voice.

"It does not matter where a man lives or who he is descended from. It is what he has decided to do with the years he has been given, that makes him who he is. Should I deem you worthy of death by your actions in the future, you will have died before you take notice of my decision. But today is not that day."

"That's about as close as Dreyl'vyn gets to telling you he likes you," Jillian added after watching Varek frown. "But he's right; it would suck to be in your position, and it seems like you're trying to do the right thing. Don't fuck us over though. You'd be making a big mistake." She poked Varek in the chest, failing to take into consideration how dangerous he could be.

Varek stared down at her blackened finger, his frown deepening. "Yes, I'm sure it would be indeed. Let us hope sneaking into the Grand Magus' vault is also not a mistake. Now that Laurence has returned, we should be on our way. Everyone gather closely around me." Turning his gaze up toward Dreyl'vyn, who towered over us all, he sighed. "*Very* close. It will take a monumental effort to teleport your gargantuan bulk, Cimmerian."

Dreyl'vyn squatted and bent over, so that his head was less than a foot above us, while Varek extended a hand toward the center of our group.

Jillian, who seemed perplexed by what he was about to attempt, eyed it. "What are you-"

We were not standing in the same spot we had been moments ago; Varek had transported us to a different location entirely. Judging by the climate, which had dipped substantially in temperature, we had also traveled a great distance.

As Jillian turned around, she witnessed what I, too, had just taken note of: we had been teleported to a region much closer to the Kaap'vaal Mountain range. At our present location, the dagger-like mountains stood out to the west, whereas last time I had seen them with Jack and Vael'ehn, we appeared to have been farther south.

"Where are we?" she inquired. "Those mountains are amazing!"

Varek, who appeared sickly, took a moment to steady himself. "We have traveled far across the continent. I have done so as stealthily as possible. Roughly one day has passed; I hope that was slow enough to avoid suspicion. I did not have the strength in me to stretch the spell any longer."

Jillian seemed confused, but Varek only offered a basic response. "I am avoiding Seekers - people who are tasked with tracking down unusual Magical activity. We have teleported from far in the east to far in the west. By your measurements, we are a few miles north of Toriash'ahn, to be specific."

Squatting down, Varek poked at the dirt with his finger and began to draw a surprisingly detailed layout of a city. Oddly, for every line he drew, several others were carved in unrelated areas, allowing him to finish in minutes what would have taken a normal person far longer.

"We are *here*, and Toriash'ahn is *here*. The artifact room floats high above the city at the top of the tower. It is in the middle of the Grand Magus' complex, which is *here* at the center of the capital district. Most do not even know it is a vault; they think it an enormous decorative gem of some sort.

"Around the Magus' tower is an immense field of Magic which prevents all from entering it unless they are attuned. It is very much like the one protecting the tournament. We cannot walk in; even with invisibility wards, we would be detected.

"There is, however, an abandoned series of tunnels near *here*. Dug by the Gnill'var, they wind their way under Toriash'ahn, and were completed long before it was ever settled. Those in the city do not know of their existence, and we can use one to make our way directly under the tower."

"Then how do *you* know it exists?" Jillian inquired.

Varek prodded absently at the dirt with his finger. "It won't make me appear any more trustworthy, but my father planned to overthrow Toriash'ahn with the Retrogrades by using the tunnels. He would gain control over those in power *very* quickly if he were to do so. While the city was under siege, and the guards involved in battle, I was to head through a separate tunnel, make my way up, and steal everything I could from the vault."

"I thought you said you weren't attempting to gain an artifact like your father," Jillian commented, suspicion evident in her eyes.

Varek smiled. "That is the irony of what I'm doing. We're using my father's ideas against him, step by step. If I had told you this plan before you agreed to help me, I would have risked looking *too* suspicious. Informing you of it after you agreed but before we traveled would have been just as pointless. Telling you now, after traversing such a distance, gave me the best chance of success."

"And you don't look suspicious now?" Jillian countered, crossing her arms.

"Do I?" Varek inquired, attempting an innocent expression.

"Yes, Varek," Jillian replied, deliberately nodding her head. "Very much so. Is there anything else you'd like to tell us that you haven't brought to our attention yet?"

Varek grinned. "I would certainly hope not. Any additional complications will no doubt cause me to appear even worse in *your* eyes." Jillian sighed but let Varek continue. "When we arrive at the proper position under the tower, we will open the earth above us and head up. Once inside, we should be relatively isolated. Not many people are allowed within its walls, and those that are have little reason to linger in that specific spot."

Varek rubbed the dirt from his fingers. "After we climb the tower, that's the risky part. I have to teleport us into the artifact room, which will be floating in the air above us. There are no stairs, nor is there a way to mask my spell. When we arrive, we need to grab the wand and disappear. If we do not, we will be seized by the magus' counter-spells.

"And speaking of being elusive…" Varek eyed Dreyl'vyn. "Your size will not suit this mission well, Cimmerian."

Dreyl'vyn, removing his shirt, seemed to understand what he had in mind. "Do what you are required to. I am accustomed to it."

Snapping his fingers, Varek summoned an odd vial full of red powder. "You're a free man now, Cimmerian. Would you like the honors of restricting yourself? You needn't worry; it has been adjusted to retain your strength."

Dreyl'vyn eyed the bottle for a moment, but surprisingly accepted it. Deftly uncorking it with his massive fingers, he emptied it upon himself and began to rub it into his skin. As if we were watching a time-lapse video of a piece of fruit drying up, he appeared to both dehydrate and shrink in size until he was no longer much taller than a typical man. Withered and rough, he was nearly as terrible looking as he had been after Jillian assaulted him. His eyes, however, were alert and pain-free, and his movements were crisp and precise.

"It is done," he announced to everyone.

"Well, not quite," Varek corrected, smiling at Dreyl'vyn's absurd set of massive pants, which had fallen around his ankles.

Extending a hand, the clothing was replaced by a dust-colored ensemble which covered Dreyl'vyn's features from head to toe; only his eyes peered out from a hooded mask.

"Now you will appear more forgettable if you are spotted." Turning, Varek motioned toward a protuberance of rocks rising up from the flat earth in the distance. "Time to head in that direction."

As we began to move, Jillian strode up next to him. "Hey, these people you keep mentioning - Esmer'ee, Ridd'en - who are they? Are they around here?"

Varek shook his head. "No, they are not. I don't know how much you have been told, but I suspect you know very little." He then proceeded to fill Jillian in on the missing details regarding the history between the Xahl'thari and the Gor'tier.

Varek's synopsis was briefer than the prior versions I had heard, but concise and filled with all the necessary information.

"Lori'adier, Bor'ton, Ridd'en, Esmer'ee, Demel'sa - they have all died," he finished. "The only one who remains alive is my father - ancient, angry, and tainted by demons."

Demel'sa. So she did grow up to become one of the heroes.

But was she Varek and Jillian's mother?

Jillian frowned. "Well, how come he's still around, and the others aren't?"

Varek laughed darkly. "No one else has proven evil and clever enough to both deem the absorption of another's life force as necessary and continue on without being destroyed. Augmenting another's life into your own is just one step from consuming Magic and turning into a demon. Since this ordeal began, I am sure you've become all too familiar with both sides of that coin," he teased.

In return, Jillian's expression turned into a snarl, but Varek held up a hand before revising his statement. "I did not mean to say I think you are evil. I will not mince words; you are certainly heading in that direction. But you're still battling those forces inside you, whereas Vael'ehn is not. The only reason he hasn't been encouraged to become a demon is because it does not suit Roth'Roh'Kah's surreptitious agenda."

Jillian nodded, but the painful observation had clearly ended their conversation. She remained silent for the next few minutes until we reached the rear of the rock formation we had been traveling toward.

Peering around the series of large stones, Varek finally seemed to settle on one. Extending his hand, he touched it, causing part of the rock face to vanish. In its place, a hidden passage was revealed - a passage that had been so cleverly disguised, there was no way of knowing it lay inside the massive boulder.

Summoning a floating candle over his shoulder, Varek ventured inward.

The moment we had all made our way into the shaft, the stone reappeared behind us, sealing us in.

Turning, Varek eyed the boulder with approval. "Good. I do not want anyone following us in," he stated resolutely.

"And just who might be following you?" called a voice from the darkness.

Betraying his typically impassive facade, Varek leapt in surprise and spun to meet the stranger, energy crackling along his fingertips. Stepping forward into the candlelight, a short, rotund Gnill'var appeared before us.

Seeing that the voice belonged to someone far less threatening than he imagined, Varek appeared to relax. "There should be no one inside these tunnels. How did you make your way in here?"

"Why should I be somewhere else?" the Gnill'var asked. "*You're* the one who's entered *our* home."

Varek shook his head. "How can you claim this is your home? These tunnels were abandoned long ago."

The Gnill'var raised a tufted eyebrow. "You sure do ask a large number of questions for a stranger who is trespassing and has not identified himself." He seemed to consider something. "Then again, I suppose that might be typical of someone who doesn't know very much."

Frowning, Varek appeared to consider the position he had found himself in. Sighing, he ignored the Gnill'var's taunt and gave him the information he sought.

"My name is Varek. Our intent is to travel through these tunnels as quickly and covertly as possible. We will cause you no trouble."

The Gnill'var shook his head. "Your name isn't familiar; I don't think you've been cleared for access. My name is Weaton, and I am guard of this entrance. Despite what you were led to believe, these tunnels are not abandoned, nor have they ever been. I cannot permit you passage - it is not my appointment to do so - but I can show you the way to one who might. He is our leader, Weston. Although, I must say, he is not fond of newcomers. He may turn you away, and it will be my duty at that point to force you to leave."

Turning to face away from the rodent, Varek regarded the three of us. He said nothing, but his expression gave him away; he was considering whether to play along with the rat man or wipe him from the face of the earth.

Considering Weaton had indicated there might be a large number of people in the tunnels, I certainly did not want to risk making enemies when the passage before us seemed to be our only option for stealthy travel. Quickly, I replied to Varek's unspoken query.

**We should not make enemies here.
It will not take long to meet his leader.
We can request peaceful passage and be on our way.**

Varek studied me for a moment, my crystalline form reflecting his candlelight back upon his face. At last, he pursed his lips and nodded before turning back to Weaton.

"Alright, Gnill'var, I concede. I was misinformed of your tunnels, and considering your occupation of them, I will follow you to your leader."

Weaton nodded and began to waddle down the dark corridor, his keen eyes requiring little light to see the way. Watching him, I couldn't help but conclude he was an odd choice for a guard. With no weapon and no physical prowess, he must have had something up his sleeve, so to speak. And in a land where much was not as it seemed, whatever secret Weaton had, it could have been potent indeed.

After passing a myriad of seemingly random corridors, the sound of bustling feet became louder and louder until we entered an immense chamber filled with reed buildings, carts full of supplies, and many, many rat folk. Smoke rose from several braziers to condense in a heady cloud at the top of the chamber, while the smell of hop-infused bread assaulted my senses. Somewhere far in the distance, a musician played a simple melodious tune on some sort of woodwind instrument, giving the otherwise dim and smoky area a dose of geniality.

Upon noticing our intrusion, however, the entire group of inhabitants went silent, our foreign presence causing great distress on several of their faces. Dozens, if not hundreds, of furry faces turned to meet our gaze.

"It is quite alright everyone! These strangers are here on official business," Weaton announced.

Surprisingly, Weaton's voice carried incredible weight with his people; the crowd appeared to believe him. Losing interest entirely, they went back to their shuffling, talking, and trading. Their concern over the threat we might represent had been defused by someone they trusted, and beyond that matter they seemed to have no interest in whom we might have been.

Wading through the sea of rat folk, we were led into one of the larger reed buildings, which extended far deeper into the rock than I had expected. Opening up into a grand room built from polished stone, an old Gnill'var sat on a throne carved from a large tree stump. Around him sat a dozen small children, enraptured by whatever tale he might have been telling them.

"And that is why you are the most important generation of them all," he concluded. "After *you* grow, there will be no more, but do not let that cause you distress; each of you will have an opportunity to study and correct our mistakes as you age, and I have faith in you all to solve our problem if we cannot."

The plague that wiped out his race must have recently begun. What a shame. They aren't aware their efforts will be futile.

The old rat, seemingly pulled from his discussion by some unheard interruption, paused in the middle of a sentence. Looking up, his eyes flickered toward me, his mouth turning into a small frown. The expression, likely unnoticed by everyone else, gave me the distinct impression he had heard my thoughts.

This must be Weston.

I have to be more careful about what I think. I'm from the future, after all.

Weaton motioned toward the younglings, who scuttled away, before waving a furred claw, indicating we should proceed forward.

"Wenton and Wesson," the old rat exclaimed as we approached. "You have an air of both their lives *and* their deaths about you. But as for Wenton, I know without a shadow of doubt he still lives." He eyed me suspiciously for a moment. "These are curious times I live in, it would seem. State your piece, strangers. I do not like to waste my time, as it is becoming a much rarer commodity."

Varek stepped forward. "I had no knowledge of your residence within these caves prior to our arrival, and I apologize for the intrusion, Lord Weston, leader of the Gnill'var. My name is Varek, and my information was poor. I thought this was an old abandoned tunnel, created long before Toriash'ahn. We mean you all no harm. We are simply looking for passage through, and then you will never see us again."

Weston smiled. "Your thoughts betray you despite your attempt to mask them. You are a powerful man, and very guarded, but I have already searched your mind. You were truthful, and it is a good thing you were. I do not doubt you could erase us from existence with just one spell, but had you done so, these tunnels would have become your labyrinthine prison. They were built using ancient Magic no man can understand."

I wonder if the Magic used to build the security features into Castle Ahr'bor'ahk were created by Wenton using the same Gnill'var techniques.

"You are close to correct," Weston replied, answering my unspoken question.

Motioning toward the entrance to his throne chamber, he addressed Varek again.

"The information given to you by your father was indeed poor… or dishonest. These tunnels were constructed long before Toriash'ahn was built, it is true, but they have never been abandoned. They are, and always will be, our home. This is one of just a few Gnill'var settlements still remaining in this world. Our numbers are dwindling, but that is no concern of the Xahl'thari."

Weston let out a slow breath as he studied Varek before speaking again.

"You do not like that I am aware of your identity, hmm? I can feel your uncertainty in regard to my upcoming decision. You wish to attain a powerful Xahl'thari artifact from Toriash'ahn far above, but you are not sure if you should divulge such secrets to me." The old rat managed a feeble smile, clearly aware he had put Varek in a tough spot.

Varek, who had likely believed politics and grandstanding would come into play, seemed unsure of what to say next. At last, he threw his hands in the air and shook his head. "I cannot keep anything from you, it would seem. I wasn't aware that clairvoyants with such strong abilities as yours still lived."

Weston nodded. "Indeed, there are few of us remaining." Glancing toward Jillian, he frowned. "And still fewer by the minute."

Changing the subject, he looked up to the roof of the chamber, as if he could see something we could not. "Those who guard Ahso'lar's resting place will certainly object to your theft. Even so, I can sense your quest is well-intentioned, but I cannot decide whether or not its purpose pertains to *this* time…" His eyes trailed over toward me. "…or another. However, I must admit, I find myself more than curious as to what decisions you will make when you enter that chamber high above."

"Are you looking to procure something yourself?" Varek queried, confused by the rat leader's curiosity. "Since we'll be making our way through, we could-"

Weston shook his head. "I have no use for baubles and trinkets. But what you find there might be different from what you expect." Varek tried to inquire further, but Weston stopped him. "You have my permission for safe passage. Do not allow those above to find our location down below; it has been shielded from their eyes.

That is all that I require in return. We have kept this secret for a long time. Today will be no different."

Nodding, Varek walked back toward us.

"He's playing games with us," he whispered to Jillian. "He knows something, but I'm no match for his mind. He's not going to give us more information under any circumstances. I think it best to leave while remaining within his good graces."

Giving one last glance toward Weston, I watched him smile as we headed out. His eyes flitting toward me, he winked before motioning for the Gnill'var younglings to come back into the room.

After meeting Wenton, Wesson, and Weston, I felt it was safe to assume Gnill'var were trustworthy and wise folk. That being said, they always seemed to know far more than they were willing to let on, despite being prone to idle conversation.

What isn't he telling us?

Walking out of the building, we found ourselves in the bustling masses of rat folk, who still appeared far too busy with their day-to-day lives to pay us any mind. Looking around, Varek eyed the myriad of passageways branching off from the main chamber and sighed; there was no real way of knowing which one to choose. Eventually, his meandering gaze met Weaton, who had perched his considerable bulk on a nearby barrel. Reaching out a pudgy, furred claw, the round Gnill'var pointed toward a far tunnel, indicating it was the direction we should head toward.

Perhaps Weaton was chosen as the guard because he is the only one who can remember where all these caverns go.

As we traversed the darkened, expertly carved corridors, lit only by candlelight, Varek shook his head. "I don't like this," he muttered. "My father never told me about Gnill'var down here. It could have just been his prerogative, but Weston also withheld information from us. He knows we're going to find something unexpected in that room. The question is what that might be. A person, a trap - I don't know what to expect, and I don't like it."

Watching Varek's frustration toward another person's potential dishonesty, I found myself caught off guard. When I had first considered who he might be, I had doubted his truthfulness, but it seemed honesty was all he could count on. He may have had a dark side, and he was clearly willing to do whatever it took to get the job done, but overall he didn't appear to be an evil person at all. At least, not from what I could see, anyway.

How can someone so corrupted raise someone capable of denying that heritage?

"So you *do* think it could be a trap, then?" Jillian asked. "You think he's not trying to help; he's leading us to our death by allowing us to pass?"

Varek shrugged. "Clairvoyants are horrible creatures to speak with no matter the race. They live beyond time for they can see everything, feel everything, hear everything. If they're powerful enough, that is. You tell me: would you inform everyone of what they were about to encounter if you knew the outcome of every single event? You'd be changing time with every word you uttered."

"I see. So he just wants to make sure he hasn't said so much that we change our destiny."

Again, Varek shrugged. "That is why they're so hard to deal with. They can read you, but you can't read them. And if you try, they'll shut you down. I'm not on Weston's level; if I reached into his mind, he'd crush my consciousness before I blinked." He shook his head. "He clearly knows what's waiting for us, but we won't find out if its delight or death until we're in the thick of it. I find that particularly irritating because we're already here, and we don't have any other options but to play along."

"Kind of ironic, don't you think?" Jillian teased, indicating the situation we had found ourselves in with Varek.

Varek rolled his eyes and continued on into the darkness.

We spent the next several hours listening to Varek grunt and shuffle his way through the chamber. As we ventured further and further from the Gnill'var settlement, the tunnel became smaller and less refined. What had started out as a series of grand chambers, large enough for Dreyl'vyn to move through in his full-sized form, had reduced to passages similar in size to Wenton's dungeon stairs. While they might not have included steps, they were still awkward to walk through for anyone aside from a Gnill'var.

At last, Varek paused. Sweat matted his wavy black hair, and he rubbed his lower back, which was clearly sore from bending over. Of the four of us, he was the only one who I'd have considered "alive," and as such, the trek had taken its toll on him in particular. Turning, he growled as his elbow collided with a rocky protrusion.

"We are at long last where we need to be, and not soon enough. I'd like nothing more than to demolish this damned cave for the pain its put me through!"

Dreyl'vyn peered around. "There is nothing here aside from ourselves."

Having been completely silent for the entire journey, everyone jumped as his booming voice echoed down the corridor; he seemed incapable of whispering.

Varek, grimacing from the sudden outburst, motioned upward. "Last time I was in Toriash'ahn, I created a small ward just beyond the Grand Magus' tower. I've been counting our paces since I felt its emanations above us. If my measurements are correct, we should be below the tower. The ward feels weaker than I expected, which means we've also descended quite a distance."

"So, do you teleport us up?" Jillian inquired.

"No, they'll sense a teleportation spell the second I begin to cast it. That reason is why I created *this*."

Varek withdrew a large flask from a fold in his robe that couldn't have held such a voluminous item without spellwork of its own. The flask itself appeared to be filled with mud.

"Wet soil," Dreyl'vyn concluded.

Varek smiled. "Yes, Cimmerian, but this is *enchanted* wet soil," he corrected, wiggling his fingers. "It has been manipulated to change earthen elements into precisely what *it* is. That is to say, change stone and hard dirt into sopping mud. The effect, however, will only be temporary. In a few seconds it will revert to its former state."

Unstoppering the vial, Varek smeared a little on the ceiling and stepped back. Surprisingly, the ceiling turned from cold grey stone to sloppy brown earth before drooping and plopping onto the ground. It continued to do so until nearly half the chamber's height had been filled. Soon after each drip hit the ground, the mud hardened and changed back into stone, leaving a giant rocky heap in our midst. Climbing up onto the stone platform he had created, Varek encouraged everyone to do the same. He then smeared more on the roof, which sagged and began to drip down around us.

"If it touches you, immediately shake it off," he cautioned. "Once it hardens, you're not going to be happy."

Using some minor spellwork of my own, I managed to not only keep the mud from touching everyone before it hardened but also create a funneling barrier of sorts. Utilizing the spell to pour in one spot, climb up, and then pour where we had been, we created a series of back and forth steps, hastening our ascent through the rock above.

Hours passed by with Varek repeatedly smearing, mud pouring, rock hardening, and the group shuffling back and forth in the makeshift void. I couldn't help but feel it might have been the least practical solution Varek could have come up with, but it was quiet, isolated, and most importantly, I felt it held up our end of the bargain with Weston.

No one will have a clue where we started our tunnel; there isn't one to find. The Gnill'var are safe.

Still more hours had passed, our surroundings providing no indicator of where we were. Varek smeared the last of the drops from his vial. The ceiling sagged, the once-hard stone dripped, and near our feet, it hardened.

Staring up at even more stone, Varek frowned. "I made *far* more than I expected I'd need. I did not realize how deep within the earth we had traveled. I fear we will have to risk-"

A muffled noise from above caused him to go silent. Soon, the mumbling was accompanied by three footsteps, which echoed through the stone above us.

Conspiratorially, Varek dropped to his knees, dismissing his enchanted candle.

"We are *right* beneath the tower floor!" he whispered.

Moments later, a door slammed, creating a near-deafening noise in our tiny chamber.

"Alright, Cimmerian. Push up on the stone above us. See if it will budge. I do not want to use any Magic here."

Again seeing it was up to me to provide a solution for illumination, I summoned some of my own. Taking inspiration from Varek, a candle, complete with an eerie purple flame, exploded to life, startling the group.

Varek froze, no doubt expecting guards to burst in, but none did. Breathing a sigh of relief, he inspected the candle which floated inches from his eyes. "I very much wish I could have spent time with Thaddeus; his techniques continue to astound me. Whatever Magic you use, Laurence, it seems to produce almost no emanations. At least none that *I* can sense."

As Dreyl'vyn moved into position, I thought back to what Vael'ehn had said.

"I am surprised your friend's little light stunt was so efficient. If you or I had done that, we would have been captured by now. Or dead, for that matter."

Vael'ehn, too, had taken notice. My Coadju'tahr seemed to manipulate Magic outside the rules of what most considered normal, as if I had an easier time tapping into it than humans did.

*Humans. Even **I** am starting to refer to others as if I'm not one of them.*

Standing on the pile of stone we had just created, Dreyl'vyn pushed his back and shoulders up against the ceiling and began to shudder. In his odd, prune-like form, I would have expected his strength to have waned, but it seemed Varek had been truthful; Dreyl'vyn was just as strong as ever. The edges of our chamber crumbling, he grunted as the stone ceiling above us was hoisted into the air. I thought light might spill down into our small hole, but none issued forth; the room beyond was just as black as our tunnel had once been.

As Dreyl'vyn continued to carefully make his way out of the hole, the stone carefully poised upon his mighty shoulders, we could see that he had separated a giant, hexagonal floor tile from the base of the room. Upon it sat a bench and a small tree, which looked quite comical balancing above him.

After we had made our exit, he expertly set the tile back in place, careful not to make any noise or tip the furniture over in the process. Once in its original position again, it was impossible to tell that the floor had ever been moved.

*If anyone **does** decide to replace it in the future, all they'll find is a small pit underneath.*

Peering around the room, which had been cast in rippling purple light from my candle, it was clear we had at least entered into an area where we could proceed upward. The structure, made of stone and completely round, had no roof I could make out. A spiral staircase jutted outward from the stones themselves and wound in corkscrew fashion as it ascended into the blackness far above.

Varek grinned to himself. "Might you have *any* clue where we've managed to enter?" Dreyl'vyn opened his mouth to respond, but Varek answered for him before his booming voice poured forth. "We've managed to make our way into the *center* of the Magus' tower. These stairs lead directly up to the top where we can teleport into the artifact vault!" He shook his head in disbelief. "Luck is clearly on our side today. I could not have asked for a better re-"

The door, which we had heard close just minutes prior, opened as a guard in gleaming sliver armor stepped through. His eyes widening in surprise, our four forms were the last thing he saw before he perished. Wasting no time, Varek reached out with a gruesome spell, crushing the man until he appeared to be nothing more than a bleeding ball of aluminum foil. Lifting the tree from its pot, he deposited the man's remains inside. From under the tree I could hear muffled noises as the remains continued to crumple in on themselves.

"I fear that was not the brightest course of action on my part," Varek commented as he rapidly searched the room. "In my haste I have just given our position away."

Wedging the bench against the door, he cast some sort of spell upon it before sprinting toward the stairs. "We need to move, *now!*"

Without hesitating, Jillian and Dreyl'vyn bolted after him while I floated up the middle of the tower, illuminating the spiral staircase with my candlelight as they went.

Below us a loud explosion could be heard as guards blasted their way into the room, sending the bench and the door to their demise. Our group, however, had already made it to the top. Bursting through a second door, we were met by a pair of sentinels, who stood silhouetted in front of an early morning sky. A blustering wind caused their red and gold capes to rapidly billow around them.

High above, a monumental red sphere hung in mid-air, our six small forms depicted flawlessly on its mirror-like exterior. Below the massive tower, an endless gleaming city stretched out in all directions.

Absently I took notice of a few predominant buildings I had seen before.

I recognize some of these. Somewhere in this city is Thaddeus' secret room - the room where my body was crafted.

As the first sentinel drew his sword, he began to slowly advance toward us.

"You have entered a restricted sp-" he began, but Jillian leapt toward him, shoving the unfortunate man backward off the small platform.

As the second guard moved to intercept her, Dreyl'vyn stepped between the pair, punching him in the face with impossible force. The devastating blow destroyed the man's skull, Dreyl'vyn's fist disappearing into a mass of metal, gore, and brains. He, too, fell from view, dead before his feet left the tower.

"Don't move!" Varek yelled over the wind.

Instantaneously our surroundings vanished, replaced instead by the most remarkable sight I'd ever seen. We had arrived in a cramped, spherical chamber filled from floor to ceiling with rows and columns of neatly-packed, catalogued Magical artifacts. In several areas, large cases had been erected, displaying unusual weapons and jewelry. One could only guess as to their purpose or power. I needed no introduction; we had just broken into the most valuable room on the entire planet.

Walking briskly across the densely packed area, Varek eyed the many prizes; each one held untold abilities and infinite secrets. A thief could likely retire by plucking just one item from the room, and there were hundreds, if not thousands, to choose from. But Varek knew precisely where he was heading: a small chest set upon a dais in the center of the room. Grinning, he stepped up to the container and opened its lid.

His grin vanished. "W-what? It's… *gone!*"

As Dreyl'vyn and Jillian motioned to head in his direction, two pillars of blue light descended from above, enveloping the pair. Finding themselves frozen in place, a booming voice echoed through the room.

"You have been caught intruding upon the artifact chamber of Grand Magus Tol'shen Faa'shaan. In doing so, you have given up any right to trial and have been sentenced to imprisonment with the possibility of execution. Any attempt to resist will result in your immediate deaths."

"Don't. Move," Varek growled through gritted teeth. A third pillar, which had attempted to descend over him as well, was being held at bay by a quickly failing shield spell he had cast. Turning his head, he spotted me several feet away. "You're their only chance of escape, Laurence."

And with that, he vanished.

The blue beam collided with the floor where Varek had stood and, finding no target, disappeared. Around the dais, three wizards appeared in gold robes trimmed in red. Searching the room, they quickly spotted Dreyl'vyn and Jillian. Still frozen in the neon blue beams of light, they were hard to miss.

As two of the wizards made their way toward their prisoners, the third took note of the open chest on the dais. "They've attempted to steal an artifact," he muttered to himself. Glancing around, his eyes settled on me. *"Ah!"*

Stepping forward, the wizard plucked me from the air and set me in the chest. "There we go. No harm done." Snapping the lid closed over me, he called out to the others. "Take them to the containment room for interrogation."

A loud crackling was heard, followed by silence - an indication that everyone had disappeared. Opening the lid to the chest, I drifted out, stunned by how poorly everything had gone for our group. Instead of sadness or guilt, however, I found myself filled with renewed determination.

What a fool! That wizard had me in his grasp. He just let his greatest foe slip through his fingers and left me alone in a room full of powerful weapons!

*He's lucky he was wearing gloves or I might have walked away with a few of **his** secrets too.*

Laughing to myself, I stared down at the small empty chest where Ahso'lar had been kept. The wizard, although uneducated as to what belonged inside, clearly believed it should not have been vacant.

Is that what Weston had known? Had he suspected we'd not only be caught but miss out on what we were looking for?

Had he already taken the wand for himself? Is that why he found our quest so interesting?

The chest, however, was not entirely devoid of contents. Ahso'lar was nowhere to be seen, but in its stead was a tiny scroll - a scroll which I had flattened after being placed upon it.

Carefully I unrolled the piece of parchment to see what it said. Fully expecting it to be a letter from the thief, gloating about his or her triumph over the Grand Magus, I found something much more mysterious.

Ahso'lar, ah, so long.
I could have sold it for a song.
But alas, I kept it safe,
hidden away inside a cave.

Ahso'lar, an explorer's dream.
It can lead to secrets unseen.
But only one can earn this purse,
one who proves to me their worth.

Where to look, of course I'll tell,
if you study each riddle well.
So now my wisdom I'll bestow:
Delve due West on, a journey far below.

The riddle, although surely troublesome to those unaware, couldn't have been clearer given where we had just come from. The west wasn't a direction; it was a living being. Weston, the leader of the Gnill'var, lived far below. Even better, the misplaced comma only served to bolster such an idea. That being said, had we not just spoken with him, I wouldn't have had a chance of deciphering it myself.

Maybe Weston will be able to help me now, seeing as I've already solved the riddle.

Turning my attention toward the immense horde of Magical artifacts, I considered taking some of them with me - perhaps even all of them - but immediately thought better of it.

If I begin to use Magic inside this room, I can't be sure what will happen, and my best advantage at the moment is subtlety.

Drifting around the cramped space, I began to search for an exit. Seeing no doors, I tried to calm my nerves for what I knew was the one way in or out of the strange vault: teleportation.

You have no choice but to teleport. You might as well head back to Weston's location before searching for where the others are being held.

Relax. Imagine exactly what it looks like. You'll arrive right where you had been.

My surroundings vanished. Startled by the sudden change, I found I had reappeared in the brisk morning air. Instead of arriving to meet with Weston, I had teleported myself in front of the stone which marked the entrance to the Gnill'var's underground colony.

This is in no way what I was imagining. Have they blocked others from teleporting directly into their colony?

Considering their efforts had stopped anyone from potentially following my spell directly *to* the Gnill'var, it was probably for the best; I still needed to enlist their aid, and I didn't want to upset Weston. Even so, I found myself frustrated by the setback.

I'm going to have to speak with Weaton and explain everything just to be allowed back in.

I spent nearly an hour attempting to manipulate the rock leading to the subterranean Gnill'var city before finally accepting defeat. Either Weston didn't want any other visitors, or I was missing something Varek hadn't informed us of. Unfortunately, that left only one course of action: heading back toward Toriash'ahn.

If no one will help me, then I'll free Jillian and Dreyl'vyn by myself!

CHAPTER
Fifty-Three

-MAN IN THE MIRROR-

Without the others to slow me down, I made short work of the distance between the Gnill'var colony and Toriash'ahn's red- and gold-gilded front gates. The sun still high in the sky, I rolled right on through the busy entryway, my sights set on the grand tower at the center of the city.

As I drifted down the spacious roads and claustrophobic alleyways, I found making progress toward my goal was incredibly difficult. No one stopped me, no one seemed to notice my presence; the inhabitants of the city were too busy to care. Nor was the city easy to get lost in, as all major roads seemed to point directly toward the tower. Rather, every building I passed was one I'd have died to stop for a moment and browse through, and I found each missed opportunity to be quite painful.

But Jillian was far more important to me than Magical artifacts, and before long I found myself outside the massive building framing the high-reaching tower in the middle. Nearing the front doors, I imagined myself invisible as I glided closer and closer to a pair of soldiers identical to those who had been killed far above.

Good, they don't see me. But how do I get through these doors? If I open them, they'll surely know someone is sneaking through!

Instead of risking exposure, I decided to be patient and wait until a door was opened for me. Unfortunately, that time never came. The guards stood motionless with no end to their shift in sight.

Nearly an hour later, or so I guessed, one of them finally spoke up.

"Have you heard of the scandal involving the new prisoners?" he whispered.

The second guard seemed surprised. "We shouldn't be talking, Moore. They say we're not supposed to talk out here. People could be listening."

Moore shrugged. "We'll be standing here all day. What, do you suspect they have eyes and ears on us at all times? And besides, the new prisoners have their *full* attention; I can guarantee you that."

The second guard seemed intrigued. "*Why?* I didn't hear. What did they do?"

Moore laughed. "They managed to get into the Magus' tower, that's what! Made it *all the way* to the top *and* inside, they did. Killed three guards too. One appeared as if his head had gone inside out."

The second guard looked as if he was going to be sick from fear.

"Oh, relax, Pont, they've already been caught. We've arrived here after all the fun. All we get to do is sit."

"They don't want us to sit either, Moore," Pont corrected.

Moore threw his hands in the air. "Oh, for the love of Magic… *yes,* I know that, Pont. I was…"

Their voices quieted as I drifted away from them. It was clear the two guards weren't going to be leaving their post anytime soon considering the commotion we had caused in the tower. Seeing how fast word was spreading, I also felt it wouldn't be in Jillian and Dreyl'vyn's best interests to wait all day long until the guards were swapped for new ones.

Gliding along the edge of the building, I searched for another door, window, or some other entrance which might allow a being smaller than a person to enter. Arriving at what appeared to be a drain or vent pipe, I paused. It was certainly large enough to accommodate me, but where it went, I couldn't be sure. Looking around, I decided I'd find no better; the Grand Magus would clearly have implemented excellent security measures.

The pipe, it turned out, was a vent for a sort of indoor plumbing system, but the novelty that someone had invented plumbing billions of years ago had worn off shortly after I entered the labyrinthine sewer. Instead, the reality that I might have gotten lost gradually rose to the forefront of my mind after finding no way out for quite some time.

You do not need skin to feel disgusting when covered in shit. Why don't they use spells to dispose of this!

I need to get out of here!

Finally emerging from what I assumed to be a toilet - although it didn't look much like one - I was thankful to have finished my "adventure." The Coadju'tahr had gifted me with human-like senses, which included something similar to touch and smell. Luckily, it neglected to include taste. While something I might miss in time, I was thankful to be rid of it at that precise moment.

Using a small stack of strange, cloth-like swatches to wipe myself off as best I could, I found they not only cleaned far better than a rag might but also reappeared in a neat stack after use, instantly laundered and fresh again. Toilets seemed to be an unavoidable necessity, but the people of Toriash'ahn had certainly improved upon the intricacies of using one.

I drifted out from the alcove into a larger part of what was clearly a bathroom. As I made my way across the space, a simple wooden door opened, and a woman walked in. Panicking, I made myself invisible. As she made her way toward me, however, I noticed a large, highly-reflective mirror behind her.

I wonder if I can see myself in the mirror…

It was the wrong thought to have and the wrong time to have it. The inadvertent idea had distracted me from my true task at hand. I reappeared directly in front of the woman, who cried out and stumbled backward. As she attempted to run, I again panicked, reaching out to try and stop her.

Shh! You need to be quiet!

But my overreaction had come with a price. As I reached out mentally to prevent her from yelling and moving, I squeezed too tightly. As if she had been strangled to death - and maybe she had - the woman stumbled forward and fell. Seeing her limp form hit the floor, my world spun.

Did I just kill her!

Oh my god.

*I think I **killed** her…*

What do I do? What do I do!

Please don't be dead. Move. Please.

There was no avoiding it. My enchanted vision told me what my mind refused to accept: in a state of desperation, I had murdered an innocent woman.

"Mar'trice? Was that you? Are you-"

A slender young woman walked through the door. At the sight of my Coadju'tahr hovering over her dead friend, her eyes grew wide, and she stopped in her tracks. Turning on her heels, she attempted to run.

Slamming the door shut in front of her, I grabbed ahold of her clothing and pulled her backward into the room. The woman struggled, trying to pull free of her outer robe, but I held her fast.

She can't alert the guards.. I need to tell her what happened!

Reaching outward mentally, I imagined how I had interacted with the verification cell at the tournament, how I might dive into this woman's mind and convince her to stop. In truth, I didn't know if I was capable of such an action, but I had no other ideas.

Please. You have to listen to me! I need you to be quiet and stop moving!

Suddenly my perspective changed, my vision narrowing down to humanoid eyesight. A swirl of confusing senses poured through me, overwhelming my mind with perceptions I had been alienated from for far too long.

The transition caused me to falter.

Am I… Is this a vision?

Reverting back to my prior viewpoint, the woman was released from my hold. As I drifted away, completely stunned by what had happened to me, she launched forward and screamed, throwing the door open to leave. I reached out and slammed it, grabbing ahold of her consciousness a second time.

You have to do exactly what I say! ***Everything*** *I say!*

As before, my vision jumped, the change shocking me almost as much as it had just seconds ago. But this time I realized what had taken place. I was viewing the world through the eyes of the woman before me. All her senses, everything she used to interact with her environment, were mine to control.

Turning my gaze toward the mirror, I was met not by the image of a Coadju'tahr but with that of the woman I had ensnared. Awestruck, I stepped backward, almost losing my mastery over her again.

"Nuuuuuuhhhh," she slurred, her mouth going slack.

Quickly I pushed the woman's mental faculties back down, infatuated by what I saw in the mirror.

"You!" I spoke out loud. "Laurence, you are *her* now!"

I laughed, the sensation of breathing, of lips moving, bringing me endless joy and fascination. I stared down at her body and hands.

"I'm... *human* again!"

I laughed a second time, spinning on the heels of my feet.

An odd thought occurring to me, I turned to see my Coadju'tahr abandoned on the floor. Frowning, I walked over and picked it up. It felt warm, powerful - far more than when I first found it resting inside Frank's shop amongst a pile of rubbish. Somewhere in the back of my mind, I felt something call out, a familiar draw I knew all too well.

It's experiencing a vision due to her touch...

For a moment I wondered whether or not I should withdraw from the woman's mind, but ultimately decided against it. What I was experiencing was far more than anything a vision of a stranger could tell me, and I couldn't risk allowing her to flee while I was distracted.

Instead I slid the Coadju'tahr into the woman's dress pocket. Patting the heavy hidden form, I smiled to myself. "Can't toss you away just yet."

"Mah'rhena?" A voice called from behind.

Turning, I was confronted by three more women.

Pel'omia! Bell'ohmie! Help me! I've been taken-

The words, *the thoughts*, were not mine. Feeling dizzy, I took several steps backward until I regained my footing. Attempting to calm myself, I forced the presence back down; it was clear what would happen if I wasn't careful.

I'm controlling this woman just like Vael'ehn had discussed with Jack, but one lazy thought and I'll lose control.

What... why have you done this!

Ignoring the voice, I looked up at the women, trying my best to appear composed, but not *too* composed.

"Pel'omia, Bell'ohmie... I'm so sorry, it was I who screamed. I just found Mar'trice. I think she has died!"

I pointed toward the corpse lying on the floor behind me. As the trio of women rushed over to see if they could aid their fallen friend, I slipped out the door.

"I'll go get help!" I yelled over my shoulder.

Hopefully they can revive her, but if not... well, I still have to keep moving.

As I walked down a myriad of foreign hallways, the voice returned in the back of my mind.

What do you want? Who are you? Let me go!

I will let you go when I find my friends in prison. If you want to help me, tell me where they are, and you will get your body back.

You're with those two who killed the guards!

Yes I am, and we're here to save all of you. Those guards we killed would have stopped our quest, and this planet would have been destroyed. Their loss was justified. Now tell me where we are heading, so I can move on with the next step of our plan.

Never. You'll never know! I'll never aid a murderer and a liar!

My mind was filled with absurd images of horses leaving their droppings on the ground. Feeling frustration and rage building inside me, I immediately dismissed them.

You want your body, Mah'rhena? You want it back? I can stay in here as long as I want, impersonate you as long as I want! I can force you to be a passenger for the rest of your days! I'm pretty comfortable. I enjoy being a human. I like your body far more than my crystal.

Do you want that?

Emotions of incredible distress bubbled up from the back of my mind. Feelings of immense sorrow began to wash over me again and again, filling me with guilt.

No… Please, don't.

The response was unbearably hopeless and caused me to falter in my conviction. Sighing out loud, I stepped into a side room. Removing the Coadju'tahr from my pocket, I held it out in front of me. Again, a strange sensation, a missed vision.

Do you see this? This is called a Coadju'tahr. It has been my prison for what feels like a lifetime. I was put in here for a very specific purpose: to save the world. You may not understand now, but as you come along with me, you will. I am sorry I became angry with you, and I'm sorry I kidnapped you, but I am dealing with a lot of stress right now. It is not my intent to harm you.

*If your friend died, it was an honest accident, as was capturing you. I just wanted to stop you from revealing my presence. But now that I have you, I'm going to use your body to provide me cover while I investigate this place. If you help me, if you aid me in the freeing of my people, I promise I **will** let you go. I will return to my Coadju'tahr when we're done.*

What followed was silence for twenty or thirty seconds before she finally replied.

The door you need to go through is at the end of the hall on your right.

Good. Thank you. I'm glad we have an understanding.

Stepping out from the side room, I ran down the length of the hall and opened the door she had indicated. Inside, five guards sat around a table, eating bowls of food.

"Oh, hello, Mah'rhena!" one of them exclaimed. "We're taking a break. Would you like to-"

"Not right now, hon," I answered, cutting the man off. Quickly I shut the door again.

*Do you think that's funny? You thought you'd lead me to a bunch of guards? Let me remind you this is **your** body, not mine. If I was as dangerous as you think I am, I could have killed them all, and their blood would be on **your** hands! You'd be convicted for the crime, and I'd simply vanish.*

Would you rather I do that?

No... please... I am sorry.

Then let's try again, hmm? What direction should I go to find where my people are being held?

Head back down the hall. It will be the third door on your left.

If this is a trick I'll have to resort to more drastic measures, Mah'rhena. I am trying my best to be calm and reasonable. Should I become the terrible person you believe I am?

An evil person would probably force you to punch yourself, maybe cut your arm a few times. They might throw you down the stairs. All I'm asking is for directions to-

Enough! You've proven your point, you horrible thing! Just do your dirty work so you can leave my body!

*The faster we get there, the faster I will do so. Think what you may, but I **am** doing this for you, in a way.*

Opening the door Mah'rhena had indicated revealed a series of stairs spiraling downward.

When you get to the bottom, turn right. Go through the second door on your left. You'll find more stairs.

As I wound my way lower and lower through the building, Mah'rhena continually gave me directions, seemingly cooperating with me in an unsteady truce, until I came to one last door.

On the other side are two guards. I bring them food every day and talk to them. They won't suspect a thing by my presence. We can bring them something to drink. Perhaps you can drug them or cast a spell so they fall asleep-

I had no time to be subtle; Seekers with who knew what type of terrible spells would be onto my trail after investigating the murder of Mar'trice. Pushing the door open, I raised my hands.

"Oh, greetings, Mah-" the first guard began, but his voice was cut off, along with his head, which toppled from his shoulders.

Whoops.

It was an embarrassing thought to have, but I was genuinely surprised by my own action. Controlling Magic within Mah'rhena's body was far different than inside the Coadju'tahr, and what had started as a spell to knock the guard unconscious had instead turned out deadly.

What in the name of fate have you done!

"I… I didn't mean…" I began.

The second guard leapt to his feet, drawing a sword. Sadly, he met much the same fate. Showing more restraint, my second spell was still far too potent, breaking his neck instead.

"No, I…"

You monster!

I shook from the impact of the actions I had just taken.

I didn't want to. I didn't mean that.

Those were good people!

I'm so sorry. I didn't mean to kill them. This is... I'm doing this for a good reason, I swear! I'm so, so sorry but I have to continue on.

In truth, as I apologized, the psychological weight of the murders had already begun to dull. I found channeling Magic not only less restricting when inhabiting Mah'rhena's body but also far more visceral. Each time I used it, the act was followed by an adrenaline rush and a jump in my heart rate, which I found invigorating, almost intoxicating. The body was that of a waifish young lady, but there was something inside her that hinted at more. Far more.

You said you weren't dangerous!

I said I wasn't evil. I'm not going to harm you, and I didn't mean to harm them. At least not that much. But I don't have time to discuss morals with you. You have to accept this task for what it is. In the end, what we lose will be justified by our success.

The words of a tyrant...

Turning my attention to the far end of the room, my eyes were met by those of Jillian and Dreyl'vyn, who stood in a seemingly empty room with no bars.

"Let's go!" I yelled. "We don't have much time before they track me down!" Seeing Jillian's odd expression, I added, "This is Laurence speaking."

See, even she doesn't trust you.

She didn't know who I was! Please be quiet.

Why don't you make me? You seem all too familiar with silencing people.

Don't force me to-

"*Laurence?*" Jillian mouthed, her quiet voice pulling me to attention, as if she had demanded it from me. "If that *is* you, then don't step over here. It doesn't look like there's anything preventing us from leaving, but there's a spell of some sort keeping us from crossing that line." She pointed down toward a row of discolored bricks, which appeared to have been burned.

How do I free them?

You don't. It doesn't work by lock and key. That spell needs a counter spell to release them. No one will teach it to you. Your plans have been ruined.

No, that's not how this works. I just need to believe.

Focusing on where the Magical wall stood, I put up my hands. "I command you to disappear!"

The wall began to electrify as my spellwork collided with it. Encouraged, I focused harder after seeing where it stood.

"I command you to disappear!" I yelled louder. "You *do not* exist!"

The wall began to shake and darken, causing debris to rain down from the ceiling. Stones along the edge of the barrier fractured and crumbled under the stress of my spellwork. Tendrils of electricity arced out from it, crackling along the walls and scorching objects they contacted. Nearby, a stool caught on fire, forcing me to step backward.

You don't understand, it absorbs Magic! It will take us and them along with it if you keep pushing! You need to stop!

Accepting that Mah'rhena might be right, I ceased my efforts against the wall. Immediately the crackling lightshow died out, and the wall vanished from existence. Behind it, Jillian and Dreyl'vyn had backed up as far as they could. Jillian stared in my direction, concern evident on her face.

Looking around the room, an idea occurred to me. Focusing on where the pair stood, I imagined teleporting inside to rescue them.

Don't do-

With a pop, I instantly arrived on the other side.

Now you've done it! How do you think they were put in here? You've imprisoned us, too!

And Mah'rhena was correct. The second I had arrived on the other side, I intended to vanish with the pair, but could not. My attempt had been met with failure.

It's just a matter of time before they pull you from my mind. You have chosen the worst people to declare war against.

"What are you waiting for?" Jillian exclaimed. "Let's get out of here!"

"I can't. I just tried multiple times," I replied. "You can teleport into this cell, but you can't get back out. I've just made a mistake, and I've trapped myself, too." Embarrassingly, Mah'rhena's soft voice managed to amplify the distress I was experiencing.

You'd think someone with such power would be smarter.

Look who's in whose body and rethink that comment. You're the failure.

Laugher filled my mind.

What a sorry being you are, picking on poor, defenseless women.

Enough! I can tell you're not defenseless. Your body responds all too well to Magic. If anything, your strength is the reason those guards are dead.

Tired of the mental battle, I shoved Mah'rhena back down into my subconscious.

"There has to be a way to get through here," I surmised. "I'm just not trying hard enough. With absolute faith in my own abilities, I can teleport *anywhere* I want to!"

"Then why are we looking for that wand?" Jillian countered. "If you can go anywhere, why can't you get into the tournament?"

Frowning, I realized the stupidity of my comment. She was correct; there *were* limits to what my abilities could do, even if I didn't want to admit it.

The only person who could seemingly pop in and out of any location he wanted was-

Wenton's comment came rushing back to my mind.

"Soh'rovians inherit those instinctual abilities from birth. If they decide they want to attend an event, you simply cannot keep them away."

"Doug-Bug!" I yelled.

Jillian eyed me as if I had gone mad. *"What...?"*

"It's a man... er, a *being* I met at the tournament with Jack. Wenton said he couldn't keep him away because his race can teleport anywhere they want to." Spinning around, I yelled again. "Doug-Bug! Where are you? We need bugs *right now!*"

From nowhere at all, Doug-Bug unfolded like a piece of origami paper until he stood in our cell next to us. Grinning, he extended his many arms.

"Any insect breed, Doug-Bug's got whatcha need! What can I do for you fine folks today? We're having a special on wart-tossers!"

I shook my head. "No, Doug, we need you to teleport us out of here."

Doug-Bug frowned, appearing uneasy as he considered the request.

"I'm... I'm not supposed to do that. Mister Wenton says I should just... just sell bugs."

"Oh, I know," I responded, attempting to sooth his insecurities. "You *will* be selling bugs. *All* of your bugs, in fact. We're going to buy *every* bug you have, but first you have to let us out. *Then* we can pay you for them."

Doug-Bug gave me a suspicious glare. "I happen to have an *awful lot* of bugs."

Glancing at the door, expecting dozens of guards to pour through at any second, I nodded frantically. "Yes, Doug, as many as you have!"

"But why do you want so many bugs-" he began.

"It doesn't matter, Doug! We need them now! Will you or will you not teleport us out so we can buy your bugs?"

"*All* of my bugs, *and* as many bugs as I can find in a week," he countered.

"Fine! All your bugs and as many as you can find in a *year!*" I yelled. "I don't care! Whatever you want. Get us out!"

"Deal!" Doug replied, sticking out two hands which shook both of mine.

Motioning for the three of us to gather round him, he grabbed onto us with as many appendages as he could.

"And a one, and a two, and a-"

From inside I felt a sickening feeling, as if my organs were folding in on themselves.

*No, they **are** folding in on themselves!*

What have you done to us!

Staring down at my feet, I began to fold up, smaller and smaller, until I completely collapsed into myself. The moment it finished, the effect then reversed its progress until we all stood on the opposite side of the barrier. Disoriented, I lost control of Mah'rhena, who began to vomit repeatedly on the ground.

Drifting out from her pocket, I narrowly avoided Doug, who did not seem at all concerned for Mah'rhena's well-being. Bending over by her face, he made repeated demands for a payment he would not receive. From nowhere, jars of bugs began to appear by the dozens.

"I need forty-thousand Rhou'deens for my bugs!" He poked Mah'rhena on the back of the head. *"Forty-thousand!"*

She responded by vomiting on his foot.

In front of us, six wizards materialized. Without pause they raised their staves high and let loose with a torrent of Magic. Deflecting their assault with a barrier of my own, the blast instead tore into the wall to our right, melting the smooth stones.

The spell took far more effort than I expected. Uncertain if I could dispatch six highly trained practitioners of offensive Magic, I did the first thing that came to mind. Imagining us teleporting as slowly as possible - a trick I had seen both Vael'ehn and Varek use - I picked the one area no one would *dare* follow us to.

As one reality blurred into another, I found myself surrounded by Dark, gnarled Archaeus trees. The sky had turned from light to dark, and the ancient plants tilted toward the moon, absorbing its reflected light. Jillian, Dreyl'vyn, and Mah'rhena lay on the ground. Luckily, a disgruntled Doug-Bug was nowhere to be found.

I hope the wizards treat him fairly.

Sitting up, Jillian stared wide-eyed at the forest. "Where are-"

Mah'rhena's screaming cut her off as I attempted to take control of her mind. Leaping to her feet, she stumbled drunkenly through the forest. *"Help! Help! Someone stop him! He's stealing my body! Help!"*

As fast as I could, I raced after her, managing to recapture Mah'rhena's mind just as she reached for a low tree branch to climb. As I pushed her consciousness down into the depths of my mind, her frantic screaming reduced in volume until it became mindless drivel. Soon after, it ceased altogether. Slipping my Coadju'tahr into her dress pocket again, I turned toward the others and smiled.

You shouldn't go running away. You almost killed yourself by touching that tree.

You promised you'd free me if I helped you escape!

I will free you as promised. I just require your aid a little longer.

You're a liar.

The truth was, I didn't require Mah'rhena's body; I had *never* required it. She hadn't been the only way I could sneak around unnoticed. If subtlety was what I desired, I could have turned invisible. Rather, possessing her body had been invigorating, her human senses filling my mind with sensations I had long taken for granted. After Doug-Bug had performed his duties, I found myself thrust into a cold shell I no longer wanted to be confined to, and my thoughts were filled with longing for a human form again.

"Who are you?" Jillian said, stepping up to me, assuming incorrectly that she was still addressing Mah'rhena.

"It's Laurence," I answered. "But you can call me Mah'rhena in front of others if you like." I gave her a reassuring smile which she didn't return.

"You're *inside* someone's body? Like, you mind-controlled them?" Her expression indicated she thought it distasteful.

"I didn't do it on purpose, but I've found I am far more powerful when inside it! Trust me, her body will be quite useful for the rest of our journey."

It was a lie.

Jillian seemed uncertain. "What happens to her when we're done? Do you just let her go?"

I nodded. "Of course. No need to keep what's not mine. She's just having trouble comprehending that I mean her no harm. I'm working on it."

"These are Archaeus trees," Dreyl'vyn commented, thankfully interrupting a conversation which circled a topic I didn't want to discuss. "I have not seen one for a long time. I was not aware they grew on this planet as well."

Jillian refrained from turning toward Dreyl'vyn, choosing instead to continue staring at me, uncertainty evident in her eyes.

I took the opportunity to address Dreyl'vyn instead. "Yes, I heard these are the last of their kind... on this planet, at least. No one seems keen on keeping them around, as they're dangerous. I wouldn't touch one; they'll eat you."

Jillian raised her eyebrows. "*Eat* us?"

"Yes, well, in a way. You'll be converted into a tree and then absorbed into them as food." I considered telling her about Jack's plight, but thought better of it. "I chose this location because everyone knows it's dangerous and wouldn't think to look here. I transported us as slowly as possible. At least, I *think* I did. Hopefully they won't be able to trace my spell."

Who is Jack?

It's nobody. Stay quiet.

No, that's not right. He's important somehow. He's... he's... her lover! And you don't like that, do you? No, you don't! You're jealous of-

Shut up! You don't know anything about me. Stop trying to root around in my memories, or I'll keep your body forever!

Why do I feel like you'll be doing that anyway? I might as well spend my time figuring out what has made you so horrible.

I said, leave my memories alone or I'll-

"So what do we do now?" Jillian asked, pulling me from the terrible inner monologue.

Sighing, I found myself enraptured by her eyes. Mah'rhena of course was correct; whether it had been caused by demonic influence or not, I was both incredibly jealous of Jack and infatuated with Jillian.

"Well, when I was up in that vault, I found a riddle," I responded, attempting to ignore my feelings. "I'd recite it for you, but I don't remember the exact words. Someone was there before us, and they stole the wand. The riddle said it could be ours if we follow the clues."

"What clues did the riddle offer us?" Dreyl'vyn inquired.

"The thief referred to Weston as being the person who could give us our next clue, but I already tried to teleport into their settlement after you two were captured. I was redirected to outside the entrance, but wasn't able to get through the boulder. Whatever Varek did, I wasn't able to repeat it, so we need to find him and-"

"Ask and ye shall receive," came Varek's smooth voice from behind me.

Turning, I saw that not only had he somehow followed us, he was also completely unscathed and grinning from ear to ear.

Who is that? I don't trust him.

*That must be saying something if you're telling **me** that. Haven't you been digging through my memories? Shouldn't you already know?*

Well, I was trying to be polite. But since you gave me permission...

Ignoring Mah'rhena, I questioned Varek instead. "And just where did *you* go?" I asked, distrust thick upon my voice.

"I'm sorry, who are you?" Varek asked, ignoring the question I had posed.

I didn't feel like I owed him an explanation. "The name's Mah'rhena. I'm in charge of-"

"It's Laurence," Jillian divulged, destroying my attempt at subterfuge. "He's hijacked an innocent person's body for his own perverse pleasure." She eyed me with open contempt, the expression not only surprising me but also causing me a great deal of pain.

See. You're not going to win her over by doing horrible deeds like this.

You don't know what she and I have been through together. We have a deeper bond than that.

Seems to me she thinks you love her because she's a Dghem'on. For someone who's honest and innocent, you certainly keep strange company. She's more dangerous than you are. Even if she remembers you for now, she won't for long.

And what would you know of demons?

More than you, apparently.

Stop digging through my mind!

You just told me I could!

"*Laurence!* My, my, my! I must admit, I didn't think you had *that* in you," Varek exclaimed, his grin widening. "Dark deeds for a dark time, hmm? But then again, being locked in that Coadju'tahr for so long, I bet you just couldn't *wait* to stretch your arms and legs again." He looked down at Mah'rhena's body and laughed. "Well, couldn't wait to *have* arms and legs again, anyway."

"It's not like that!" I lied. "And who are you two to judge me? You crushed that poor guard into pulp, and Jillian, you've eaten what, *five* people now? You've even eaten Dreyl'vyn! I've done the least wrong of us all, yet you're all pointing fingers!"

"I have dealt with worse," Dreyl'vyn commented, seemingly immune to any displeasure one might have felt over being eaten.

"That's not my point!" I yelled, anger building inside me. "I happen to borrow someone's body for a time, and you two stand against me, faultless in your own eyes. You should-"

"It's not like I can control what I've done when I'm not self-aware!" Jillian cried, her face a mixture of rage and pain. My comment insinuated she had done so on purpose, which was of course false; I had simply lashed out at them after feeling put upon.

Varek burst into laughter, causing us both to whirl toward him.

"What!" we yelled in unison.

"Oh, it's just ironic, don't you think?" he responded while continuing to laugh. "The lot of us, a group of murderers, all heading out on a quest to save the planet. Every turn we take, someone else pays for the 'good' we are doing. If we are this world's best and brightest, may those in the spirit realms have pity on us."

"You're the only one of us walking around killing people on purpose," Jillian countered accusatorily.

Is that what she thinks? If only she knew the truth of where she's going.

*Don't you dare start on **her** ethics.*

"*Oh, of course*," Varek responded sarcastically. "Those two guards lying at the bottom of the Magus' tower might like a word with you. If they were still alive, that is."

"That was in self-defense!" Jillian growled, her eyes narrowing. "They were about to attack us, and *you* told us we only had seconds to teleport into that room and leave before being caught."

Varek better watch it. She looks as if she's considering her next meal.

That's not funny. And if she is, you should stop this right now before something horrible happens.

Again, Mah'rhena was correct; I needed to end what I had inadvertently started before it went too far. The pair seemed as if they were about to exchange blows, or worse.

Changing the subject, I repeated my question. "Where did you go when we were caught, Varek?"

Varek displayed a dark grin, his eyes snapping from Jillian to me. "From the sound of your tone, you'd rather I had been sent to the same cell you three had, hmm?" He eyed me presumptuously. "I felt the spellwork form before it descended upon me. I had no time to save you three. I left because I was the only one who could do so. But bravo on the rescue, Laurence. I sensed you all leaving the cell just as I made my way in."

"How convenient," Jillian growled. "I'm sure you were *just* about to rescue us too."

Varek laughed at the accusation. "Of course I was. You think I'd abandon the only chance I have of achieving my goals, even if those goals are nefarious, as you suspect? I arrived to find six very confused mages nearly drowning in an inconceivable horde of insects while a Soh'rovian demanded payment for their delivery." He laughed again.

"And you probably killed them all," Jillian added.

"I did," Varek responded, his face becoming cold in an instant. "Whisked them all right up into space." He made a choking expression, which did not amuse Jillian in the least.

"You killed Doug-Bug?" I asked, feeling guilty for having misled the poor creature.

That was too much for Varek. "It has a moniker!" He burst out into a fit of laughter. "Wait, wait. That was *you* who called upon him, *you* who demanded delivery of those insects? Oh, this is too…" Waving his hand as he attempted to catch his breath, he finally calmed himself enough to answer. "No, no, the Soh'rovian left upon seeing who I was." He chuckled again. "*Ohhh*, you have no idea how many insects there were."

"Oh, how generous. You let one out of seven live," Jillian said, infuriated by how casually Varek handled the lives of others.

Seeing the argument wasn't about to end, I tried to change the topic again. "Well, you missed a clue, Varek. We need your help to get back to Weston. Someone stole the wand and left a riddle telling us where to find it. Its solution pointed to him."

Varek raised an eyebrow, becoming suddenly serious. "So *that's* what the old creature was hiding, then. He knew we'd arrive to find an empty case and a riddle. He didn't want us to become aware of its existence prior, lest we skip a step in his little ruse. For all we know, *he* took it."

I shook my head. "The riddle didn't sound like him, but I agree with everything else you said. I *do* think he's involved; I just don't think he wanted to share that information with us until *after* we proved we could retrieve it. But I wasn't able to access the cave by myself to find out what he knows."

"No, I suppose you wouldn't have. The cave entrance needs to be touched. You uh…" He smiled, wiggling his fingers around. "Let us say, being disembodied did not help your cause, for once."

Frowning, I extended my arms. "Well I've fixed that now, *haven't I?*"

Yeah, you seem to have done that quite well. I'm surprised you're even bothering to search for this wand. Its only purpose is to allow you to meet up with Jack again. Wouldn't you rather just let him die, keep Jillian all to yourself? Or are you just looking to buy more time with her, perhaps even win her over before confronting him again?

Just because I have feelings for someone doesn't mean I want other people to die.

Jack is a good man. He's just...

In the way?

I didn't say that!

You didn't have to.

"So, shall we head back?" Varek inquired.

"It is the next step in the riddle," replied Dreyl'vyn. "To head elsewhere would not be productive."

Varek laughed and extended a hand. "The Cimmerian has a point."

Instantly we were teleported back to the rock formation outside the entrance to the Gnill'var colony.

"Slow teleport?" I asked, noticing the sun was again suspended in the sky.

Varek, who was sweating profusely from the effort his spell had cost him, nodded. "Just ten hours or so. No one is looking for us at the Broken Peninsula right now, but I did not want to be too careless."

Touching the rock, he closed his eyes, causing it to disappear. After I had witnessed his success, he shot me a wink.

As we made our way inside, as before, we were greeted by Weaton.

"Come to see Weston again, have you?" he inquired. Varek nodded, causing the short round rat to turn. "Follow me, then," he called over his shoulder, heading into the myriad of passageways.

Upon reentry to Weston's chamber, he seemed already apprised of our arrival. "And here stand the heroes once again, triumphant from their quest. Have you found what you sought?"

I shook my head. "Not quite. What do you know about riddles? *Delve due West on a journey far below* ring a bell?"

Weston eyed me for a moment before responding.

"Interesting choice," he whispered to himself. "You have indeed solved it correctly. No doubt your prior journey down here was of some aid in reducing its difficulty. Coincidence or intention, I wonder." His eyes continued to linger upon me for a moment.

Varek stepped forward. "So now that we've found you, and the wand is still missing, what is the next step? Did *you* take it?"

Weston smiled. "Oh, I've no use for such trifles. If there had been some cheese stashed up in that chamber, however…" He smile widened, as if he were imagining a giant wheel of the stuff sitting in his lap.

I would have thought that accusing a Gnill'var of having a penchant for cheese might be the most insulting comment someone could make, but it seemed Weston was more than willing to make light of the comparison.

Perhaps they're closer to rats than most of their race are willing to let on.

What do you mean by that word? Are you insulting them?

*No… I meant **Rats**. You know, tiny cousins to the Gnill'var? And shouldn't you already* *know what they are from digging through my personal thoughts?*

Well there certainly seems to be a lot of thoughts! You talk to yourself quite often!

That wasn't a problem until now.

I'd say that is your fault more than mine.

I couldn't argue; she had me on that point.

Fine. So, there aren't any rats in this time? Did that not translate? Rodent, mouse - do either of those work?

Oh. Your prior word was blurry, as if you had said several words at once. It almost sounded as if you had accused him of betrayal.

*That... **does** work, in a different context. In my time that word is thrown around in quite a few ways, and I suppose most of them are negative.*

It is a wonder anyone can communicate in your society with words like that.

I couldn't argue with that conclusion either.

"So you want something in return, then," Varek surmised by Weston's humor. "For helping us, that is."

Weston waved his hand back and forth in a flippant gesture. "Oh, nothing of the sort. I'm just taking an opportunity to entertain myself." He smiled. "The wand you seek was indeed stolen, but not for nefarious purposes. I was entrusted with the second clue should anyone ever solve the first. I should say, considering my age, I was not the best choice for *that* duty."

Weston withdrew a small scroll which he tossed to Varek. Unrolling the tiny piece of parchment, Varek began to read.

Long, long ago, a ship from the sky
was brought down by a giant, fury in his eyes.
And as it began its fiery descent,
a grin split his lips; he would have his revenge.

The damage he caused was both far and wide.
And he hurt countless people; most of them died.
The only thing capable of helping them mend,
was a Magical staff, which had just met its end.

On a quest for a wand, which has prior been found,
you've gained your next clue from under the ground.
Now travel to islands, both desolate and brown,
and look for a ship that is meant to be drowned.

Varek scrunched up his nose as he looked up from the page. "In the first paragraph, the author is referring to Galgot-Dreth, leader of the Gor'tier. He pulled *Arkken'Arak*, the great ship, down upon my ancestors. He then refers to the destruction of Khalla'sall in the second." He motioned toward Weston. "I don't understand. What does this hunt have to do with that part of our history?"

Weston shrugged. "It is a mystery to me; even I have my limits. I have done as I have been instructed to do, and now I am free from that burden."

"Burden?" Varek repeated, seeming confused. "Who wrote this riddle?"

Weston shook his head. "I cannot say."

"Cannot or *will* not," Varek questioned, again appearing skeptical of Weston.

"Cannot," Weston surprisingly replied. "I am bound by Magic and incapable of repeating the name; it was a condition of my participation. But I suspect you'll figure it out considering the help you have brought along with you." He eyed me again.

He's referring to me.

So what is the answer?

And I should simply help you? Help you find an artifact that'll make you far more powerful than you already are?

There's only one way out of this for you: by helping me.

You keep saying that. Do you think I'm that stupid? You want me to believe that if I keep helping you, you'll eventually release me, but in the end, you won't. You'll find a way to remove me from my own body so you can take my place.

Oh, I know! You'll trap me in that purple device we're carrying around, won't you? You just haven't figured out how to do so yet.

That's not what I had in mind.

No, I suspect if you did, I'd already have found out.

You're right; you would have. And if you know what I'm thinking, then you know I'm being honest. I'll release you, but not yet.

What if I promise to help only if you allow me to do so while in control of my own body?

I paused for a moment, considering her proposition. Mah'rhena was offering to aid us, to become a part of our team, for no reason other than to regain the use of her body. It was an offer born from desperation. I had lost my own body and in turn taken hers; the irony was not lost upon me.

Mah'rhena, I have been without my body for a very long time. If I were to add up the days, it would only amount to a couple of weeks, but for me it has felt like far longer. I… miss my body very much. I'll be honest; I didn't miss it until today, but having yours has been, well… it has been amazing. It is far more than I ever expected it to be. I don't mean you harm, but I'm not ready to leave. Please let me stay for just a while longer.

Mah'rhena did not reply at first, my question receiving only silence instead.

You're asking me for permission to stay inside my body?

Yes. I fear I am becoming a person I very much do not wish to be, and I would like to ask your permission to show my intent, if nothing else.

You… you cannot have me forever, Laurence. Do you understand that?

Yes, I do.

Then you can have me for now. I will aid you, but so help me, if this is a trap, if you kill me or force me into that crystal, I hope you get what you deserve in the end.

I've no doubt I'll get what I deserve in the end, no matter what I do. I've suspected for quite some time this story does not end well for me, and others have told me just as much. But this is not a trap for you. Please, just aid us for now. Allow me the use of your body to preserve my sanity. I will prove to you I'm not as horrible as you've come to believe.

Silence again met my request. At last, after an audible sigh, she replied.

In the last two sentences, the person who wrote the riddle is talking about the Deserted Islands of Lorn.

How do you know?

Unlike you, I live here, Laurence. Do they not have maps where you are from?

They do, but there has to be more than one set of brown islands surrounding this continent.

Not like the islands of Lorn; there is nothing on them. A horrible tragedy removed all life from their surface, and nothing will grow, no animals will stay. If someone asked me to point out a series of deserted, brown islands, there's only one location I'd point to. There's only one location *anyone* **would point to.**

Are the islands small or large? Will we see what we're looking for when we arrive?

Two of them are, the third one is small. Why?

If I was going to tell someone to head to a series of islands, and two of them were too large to search effectively, I'd assume they'd try the third first. Wouldn't you? At the very least it would be easy to mark off the list.

That does make sense.

"Laurence? Or... Mah'rhena? Are you alright? Who is with us now?" Jillian queried, as if she had been participating in a séance.

The unusual question pulling me from my conversation, I realized I must have been dumbly staring forward for quite some time.

"Yes," I responded. "I mean, uh, I'm sorry; it's Laurence. I was talking to Mah'rhena."

Jillian cocked an eyebrow. "In... *your head?*"

"Yes, she's still in there with me. We've uh, arrived at a compromise. She says the islands the riddle is referring to are the Deserted Islands of Lorn. We would like to try the small one first."

"Hmm..." considered Varek. "Yes, I can see why she would think that - the old story of the destruction that took place there and whatnot. Very well, then." He extended a hand toward the group. "To the islands of Lorn!"

CHAPTER *fifty-four*

—PERPLEXING POLTERGEISTS, CONFOUNDING CRAFT—

"We have not moved," commented Dreyl'vyn after a few moments. He was correct; Varek had stood there, his hand outstretched for some time, seeming to have expected something to happen.

"Very astute of you, Cimmerian," Varek replied sarcastically. "I haven't been there before. I assumed the imagery I had seen throughout my life would have been sufficient, but it would seem I do not have a clear enough mental picture to perform the act." He glowered to himself, his cheeks darkening. "I have the power to make the journey, of course, but I will require assistance with the location."

"I haven't been there either," replied Jillian. "Laurence, Dreyl'vyn - have either of you?"

Dreyl'vyn shook his head, as did I.

I've been there before. Not to the small island, but to a larger one. I don't know how to teleport us though.

Do you have a Coadjutor?

Of course, but its back in my quarters. They don't follow people around like you do inside your device. You didn't exactly give me time to consider what traveling supplies I'd bring before abducting me.

I know, I didn't. If you had it with you, that would have made everything much easier.

Can you show me what you've seen? Think back upon the time when you arrived there.

Immediately my mind filled with a flood of imagery - a sea voyage of some sort, which must have ended on the coast of a deserted beach.

We didn't intend to go there. We were hunting Trill'ok off the coast - they're a type of sea fish - but our ship began to take on water. We had to pull it up on the shore to repair its hull before heading back to the mainland. I couldn't point out the specific location on a map; I just know those islands were where we ended up.

The images, while correct, didn't precisely correspond with how she described them. I gained a sense that she was departing rather than arriving, but I attributed it to the idea that she might have been anxious to repair her ship and leave, given the fact that the island was the scene of a tragedy.

No, that's exactly what I needed to see. Thank you, Mah'rhena.

Are you going to teleport us all there?

Yes, I-

I paused, realizing full well what might be required of me.

Is teleporting somewhere you've imagined different from somewhere you've been?

Yes, it is.

Oh, I wasn't... I wasn't asking you, per say, just considering to myself.

As often you do.

Yes... and I can see that habit is going to come back to haunt me now.

I could see why it would be difficult to teleport there, even if I could picture it vividly. It simply wasn't quite real, like a dream hovering just beyond my grasp.

Even Varek had encountered trouble attempting that very same action. Rather, I suspected we would be required to open a portal to Lorn. If something went wrong, an incorrect portal would at least refrain from instantly killing us or alienating our group on some foreign land. We would be able to see what awaited us before heading through.

However, only Mah'rhena and I had access to a viable image, and creating a portal would require the Coadju'tahr. That meant leaving her body behind. Mah'rhena wasn't stupid; quite the opposite if I was being honest in my appraisal of her. Whatever servitude appointment she had been given at the tower, it was *far* beneath her abilities. I may have been new to manipulating Magic through a human body, but it was hard to believe she would have been so keyed to its usage without prior knowledge of advanced spellwork.

And that intelligence will cause her to run the moment I leave.

No, I won't run. I made you a promise. I've seen who you are and what you've been through. While I don't agree with all of your choices, especially in regard to Jillian, I feel you're trying to make the best of a situation you have been forced to participate in. I am scared for you, for the person you're becoming; but I promise, I will not run.

It was a nice sentiment, but I knew if it were me in her position, I'd take off the moment my captor was distracted. And once I had opened the portal, I wouldn't be able to chase after.

"Mah'rhena has been there. She has shared the location with me," I announced to the others. "Before I make the change, Varek, are you able to open a portal with a Coadjutor?"

Varek snorted. *"Isn't everyone?"*

Jillian rolled her eyes at him.

I ignored his pompous response. "Alright, well get ready."

Gently pushing backward from Mah'rhena's mind, I released my hold on it. As I backed away, her consciousness flooded into the void I left behind, and her breath caught in her chest. Feeling disoriented, my vision swelled as my perspective changed from that of the group to the inside of a pocket.

Disappointment filled me as my surroundings were tainted by the sterile crystalline shell. What I had eventually accepted as my fate, even enjoyed for a time, had once again become my prison.

Slowly I drifted out of Mah'rhena's pocket and up to meet her eyes.

"It's alright," she said, giving me a warm smile. "See, I am still here."

I haven't given you your opportunity to run yet.

I floated to the middle of the room, where Varek extended a hand toward me. His spellwork pinning me in place, I did not resist, instead imagining the desolate coastline Mah'rhena had shown to me. Beneath my form, the familiar edges of the portal descended downward until they met the floor. From the center of the doorframe, reality was pulled backward, distorting until it at last tore open.

Within was revealed the exact spot I had pictured in my mind. The sound of the ocean, the crashing of waves, the calls of birds - they all ushered forth from inside the Magical doorway. A large wave rolled in from beyond the portal, causing water to spill out from around its edges and onto Weston's floor.

Weston clapped wildly. "Oh, how exciting this is, isn't it?"

Varek laughed. "Would you like to come along since you find this so amusing?"

Weston shook his head. "No, I am afraid adventures are no longer appropriate for one as addled as I, but should you return in a timely manner, I would greatly enjoy a retelling of your adventure." He shook a clawed, trembling finger at Varek. "But mind yourself while near the borders of Lorn. The ruins at its center are no place for a group so small. Now head off, all of you. Find that which you seek!"

Nodding, Varek walked through the portal and onto the beach, followed by Dreyl'vyn, and then Jillian, who paused halfway through. Staring back at Mah'rhena, she pursed her lips.

"Now is your chance to run," she called. "He can't shut the portal without cutting me in half."

What Jillian said was true - we had watched that exact thing happen to Wenton in his library - but the idea that she felt it necessary to resort to such measures, that she disapproved of my methods so strongly, hurt me deep inside.

If she had been in this shell like I have, experienced the world like I have, seen visions like I have, she'd agree with my decisions.

Taking one unsteady step forward, Mah'rhena shook her head. "No, I made him a promise. We're learning to trust each other. If I run now, what will that teach him? He'll fall further into darkness. If I left, there would be other victims after me. What I do will be a good example for him to follow in the future."

He'll fall further into darkness…

The words rang out inside my mind over and over. Mah'rhena had seen my memories and felt my emotions, and the conclusion she made was that I had begun to fall into darkness. I shook from embarrassment and pain, causing the portal to shimmer and ripple. Noticing the phenomena, the pair quickly hurried through, Mah'rhena glancing toward me as she did so. Her face was not one of resentment but one filled with pity.

Is she right? Have I fallen? Have the events I've been through begun to ruin me?

Watching the pair travel safely to the other side, I took one last look at Weston, who winked at me. Steadying myself, I tumbled through.

On the other side, the portal flailed around before exploding into a shower of particles. My surroundings changing from the dim subterranean building to that of a bright sunlit beach, I found myself astounded at the spellwork. Out of everything I had cast, portals still had to be the most magnificent to experience.

Around us lay a sparkling, sand-blanketed coastline bordering a calm, teal ocean, which lapped gently at the shore. Far in the distance I could just barely make out the mainland coast, shrouded in haze. The island itself, surreal and silent, seemed to cast a disconcerting shadow over the otherwise peaceful scene, as if it were viewing the world with a disapproving gaze.

Focusing inland, I saw that, while the isle seemed to have no trees or plant life, it certainly *did* have something on it: a desolate, destroyed castle complex built upon a towering upheaval of rocks. Its ruins lay tossed about, as if a giant wave had obliterated it in a single instant.

Whatever happened at this location must have been sudden and violent.

Turning away from the ruins, I glided forward toward the group, only to notice Mah'rhena staring at me.

"Well, you did it. We made it through, and I'm still here," she said, flapping her arms at her sides nervously. "I made you a promise, so go ahead and take me again."

Gliding closer to her, I paused, inspecting her face. Taking Mah'rhena's body from her *had* been a truly horrible thing to do. The moment it happened I should have released her and let her be. I could have handled the situation much better than I had chosen to. Controlling everyone was a task much better suited for someone corrupt, like Vael'ehn.

I can't allow myself to fall to his level.

What I had seen in the past, in the future, made me a unique participant in this quest, and if I fell victim to dark desires, we would *all* fall. Staring deep into Mah'rhena's uncertain, searching eyes, I made my decision. Reverting back to my purple floating alphabet - a choice which I found most painful after regaining the ability to speak - I began to write in the air.

```
                    Not this time.
            You are right; I have fallen.

        I need to remain better than those
                I'm fighting against.

            Thank you for showing me that,
            but I will remain on my own.

            If you want to stay, you can.
```

Reading the letters, Mah'rhena smiled. "You made the right choice, but you should be rewarded for doing so. I would like to stay, but I feel we *do* make a good team. I invite you, take me again. We will work together. And from now on, you can call me Rhen. Most everyone else already does."

If I had been in control of a possessed body, what she had said would have made me cry. It was not every day someone concluded I had fallen into darkness, only to see redemptive qualities inside me instead. Her words meant the world to me, and I had to agree; it did seem like we were becoming a very good team.

Gently I reached forward and touched her consciousness. Pushing my way inward as respectfully as I could, I felt no resistance, only warmth and welcome. My vision becoming hers, I watched as the Coadju'tahr hit the sand, my attention no longer set on manipulating it. As I bent down and picked it up, I stared into its purple facets as I once had in Frank's shop.

I wonder why you don't experience visions when you touch it with my body.

If I wanted to, I certainly could experience a vision and learn something about you. Every time I touch it, I can feel it pulling at my mind. Even as we speak, a new scenario is playing out as it absorbs a small part of your soul to enhance its power.

A wave of anxiety washed through Rhen.

It's eating me!

No, no, nothing like that. It's an Object of Power, and it gains strength when it touches people. A while ago, I might have thought that would weaken a person, but I no longer believe that's the case, based on what I've seen and learned. Demons might consume our souls, but my Coadju'tahr doesn't work like that.

And you don't want to learn what secrets it's showing you?

Not about you. I think I've violated enough of your privacy already.

In response I felt a sort of relief, as if Rhen had been truly scared I might learn something she wished to remain hidden. I ignored the feeling and moved on, knowing full well I had no right to investigate.

Thank you for what you're doing. You could have left our group, and I wouldn't have thought ill of you.

I know, but I must admit, I was a little harsh on you. I mean, I had good reason to be; no one should have their body taken from them. Even so, it wasn't your intention to do that at first. I'm starting to realize, even though you have more power than I've seen in a long time, you're also new to it. You're scared and desperate, and the emotions you're experiencing are often raw and confusing. I think you've learned the lesson I was trying to teach you.

The statement was embarrassing, but it was also completely true.

And to be fair, this adventure is far more enticing than what I would have been doing back at the castle. The prospect of working together with you is very entertaining. As long as we can cooperate and respect each other, I think this will be fun.

And what would you have been doing back at the castle?

I'd probably be cleaning the lavatories.

Don't they allow you to use spells for that? I've been curious about why you all have toilets with pipes and some sort of sewer system, yet you have rags that clean themselves after people use them.

Well, of course we use spells, but someone has to cast them. Continual dissolution spells within each of the tiny basins were used at one point - I know, I researched it. But there were far too many mishaps with people dropping objects, only to have them vanish forever. One unlucky soul even had his hand vanish after attempting to reach for whatever he had dropped. It was just too much of a liability.

Portals were also used for a while, but they require concentration to keep open. No one wants to stand there, listening to, well, you know. And allowing everyone to manually teleport their own leavings proved too unpleasant. You'd be surprised how lazy or inconsiderate people can be with their spellwork! And of those that do clean up after themselves, not all are able to… aim properly. Then you have the people who can't use Magic, and they just leave their makings behind.

No, it all goes to one place where it piles up, and we take turns making it vanish. Let me tell you, a large amount of people use those lavatories, and banishing that much mire silt to the corners of the universe is-

I felt an almost physical shudder.

Mire silt?

Yes, what do you… oh, you call it poo.

Have you ever had to clean up poo?

Yes, yes I have. And I suppose you're right; I would much rather be on an adventure than clean up… mire silt.

"Are you two going to come along and help us decipher this mess, or should we give you some additional time to be alone with each other?" Varek called, interrupting our colorful conversation.

"Yes, sorry," I answered, feeling embarrassed.

Jogging up to meet the group, I couldn't help but smile - not because of our secret conversation, but because of the sand. The act of running on a beach - even in a dress, of all things - felt fantastic. But it wasn't until that particular moment that our series of events had calmed down enough for me to consider the implications of *being* a woman.

Don't you dare, Laurence!

What? No! I wouldn't think of it. I was just admiring your dress. I've never worn one before, you know, and I, uh-

No, that's not at all what you thought, and you know it! And those ideas better stay put. If I catch you rooting around under my garments, we're going to have trouble!

The comment caused me to laugh out loud, which in turn encouraged Jillian to raise an eyebrow. "What's so funny?"

"Nothing, just something Rhen said."

Jillian's brows drew together. "*Rhen?*"

"Mah'rhena," I clarified. "She said I could call her Rhen."

"So you're getting along, then?" Jillian surmised, crossing her arms. Clearly, she was still suspicious of my intent.

"Yes, she's made me realize I was being a selfish ass," I admitted. "We're a team now, her and I. You have nothing to worry about. It's with her permission that I'm in here."

"It's quite lovely that you two are playing homemaker in her brain, but we *really* should be on our way," interrupted Varek. "We do not want to dally around here until dark. These islands may be deserted, but they are not devoid of *everything*.

What still remains on this land, I have been told, is not pleasant."

He's referring to the Withered. They're just a phenomena, really. The dangerous tales people tell each other are for effect. They're certainly nothing anyone needs to investigate or fear.

"I've heard the dangers posed by the Withered are just tall tales," I responded, taking the opportunity to sound informed.

"*Tales?*" Varek countered. "Did you not hear Weston? He told us to avoid the ruins with such a small group. There are plenty of tales from plenty of fools, but this is not one of them."

"What are the Withered?" Jillian whispered to Dreyl'vyn.

"I have not encountered such beings," Dreyl'vyn responded loudly, the idea of a covert conversation also seemingly lost on him.

"*The Withered,*" responded Varek, "are lost and confused souls who wander these islands, trapped within a realm they were not supposed to access. They were separated from their bodies after a powerful spell was cast incorrectly. The entire city of Lorn was blown apart, leaving only ruins behind. They say the souls are eager to find new bodies; that people who venture here lose their way and are condemned to swap places with the Withered; that when they leave, it is the Withered who have escaped their bonds."

That's not true. No one is looking to steal anyone's body.

"Rhen was here before," I interrupted. "She didn't have her body stolen by some evil being." I clamped my mouth shut, realizing I had opened the way for another of Varek's pompous remarks, but it was too late.

Varek grinned, taking the opportunity to make me feel stupid. "She might not have had her body stolen *here...*" he countered, his smile somehow widening. Turning, he pointed toward the ruined buildings. "Mah'rhena did not venture up into the ruins, and she certainly did not stay until dark."

"Look, it doesn't matter either way," Jillian interjected. "There's plenty of light left in the day. We can find the ship and be on our way long before night falls."

"Yes, on our way to find a ship that's *meant to be drowned*," Varek said. "Why would a ship that was destined to sink be on an island?"

Jillian shook her head. "I don't think the riddle was referring to a ship that was built just for someone to sink it. I believe it's referring to a submarine. I mean, what else would a ship that's meant to be drowned be?"

"I am not familiar with a ship of that designation," Varek commented. "The translational spells are not interpreting your words correctly. What you said sounds similar to *under the sea*."

"That's close to what it means," I offered. "It's a vessel that's sealed off from the water on all sides. It doesn't have an open top, so water can't pour in. It's meant to go under the water, which is what its name is derived from. It can go all the way to the bottom of the ocean and then come back up."

You have ships like that where you come from?

*Yes we do, but not all our ships are like that; most aren't, in fact. Not to mention, submarines are **very** expensive. But I bet Magic can do a better job of reaching the bottom of the ocean if you use it correctly.*

Well, no one I know uses Magic to do that.

"Hmm…" Varek considered. "I have not seen a ship of that description anywhere. You say it's a ship with a hull all around?" Jillian and I nodded. "Very well."

Varek extended his hand, causing a spinning blue geometric orb to appear. It raced down the beach twenty or so yards and stopped.

"This construct will lead us toward the nearest object which matches that description."

Without waiting for a reply, he began to walk down the beach toward his creation.

After heading along the beach for some time, Jillian and Varek began to argue back and forth over whether or not someone, once they had been exposed to demonic genes, could return to being a human, free of taint.

Jillian surmised that since demons were essentially a being who had fed on Magic, demonhood would be similar to a virus and might have a cure. She assumed she had been exposed to it before feeding, and it had spread inside her. Therefore she believed it could also be killed off.

Varek, on the other hand, was not as optimistic. He insisted that, once exposed, it changed you into something else entirely. Even though you might look, think, and act like the person you once were, at least for a time, you were in fact not a person at all.

I understood the value in both arguments, but seeing as no one had mentioned a cure in a land where Magic could do anything, I had to conclude that the answer, whatever it was, would be both very complicated and far beyond what we could comprehend. Worse, Jillian hadn't been exposed; it had always been part of her, buried deep inside since birth.

The conversation was cut short by Varek's enchanted device, which stopped to hover over a large mound. Nearly the size of a modest dwelling, my heart leapt as I set eyes upon it.

*It may be covered in dirt and sand, but Varek's orb stopped above it. It **has** to be what we were looking for!*

We'll find out soon enough!

Raising his hands, Varek forcibly levitated all of the dirt, sand, and debris from the object and threw it farther out onto the beach. What remained behind was revealed to be a giant turtle shell, complete with an intact skeleton protruding from its orifices. Dwarfing most automobiles, it was far larger than any turtle I had ever known to have existed.

"Well, that is certainly *not* your ship," Varek concluded. "I suppose it has a hull all around, and it travels to the bottom of the ocean, but it is still incorrect."

Jillian looked up, her eyes traveling along the beach, which stretched onward for quite some distance before curving out of sight.

"Why not just create another one of those light balls?" she offered.

Varek scoffed. "My *light ball* is referred to as a Demmi'dant. And I am not summoning another because I have nothing further to reference. It would refuse to depart from this location, as I have never seen what you speak of."

What's that in the Scallok's mouth?

Scallok?

The dead creature there.

Unexpectedly, Rhen had spotted something I hadn't, despite inhabiting the same body. There in the turtle's mouth lay a small pot. Walking over, I pulled it out from between the open jaws, carefully avoiding its disturbingly large teeth. The pot, having no visible opening, appeared to be completely sealed from the elements.

"What is *that?*" Jillian inquired as she walked over to where we stood.

I shrugged. "Your guess is as good as mine."

Tapping the pot several times on the edge of the turtle's massive shell, I managed to crack it open. Inside had been placed a third small scroll, identical to the other two we had found.

"*Bingo!*" Jillian exclaimed.

Varek seemed irritated by our discovery. "But that's not a ship! If this is what the riddle was referring to, then that is a poor choice of words."

Jillian threw a hand up in the air. "We find a scroll by accident, and you're going to complain about the clue? Why don't we just read it and move on?"

"Accident or not, we could have missed it," Varek countered, still appearing disgruntled. "The author was clearly not as well-versed in the creation of riddles as we initially assumed. If I had written it, this never would have occurred."

"There are plenty of ways to achieve the same result, Varek."

"Not from my perspective," Varek muttered under his breath.

Ignoring the two of them, I unrolled the scroll and read it aloud.

You've made your trek to find a ship.
Instead, you've uncovered some bones.
Do not fret; you haven't wasted a trip.
Keep searching; do not head home.

Not far from here, a small island lies.
On it your terminus calls.
Keep moving to beat the darkening skies.
The dead will crawl out from the walls.

"Oh good…" Jillian muttered with a sneer. "More talk of creatures coming to kill us. How fun."

"Indeed," Varek agreed. "As you can see, it's not just a tale. Let us keep moving. I'd rather not be around for that."

We traveled along the coast far longer than I expected to. Several hours passed by until, at last, we spotted a small island out in the water. To my disappointment, the sun was beginning to set by that time. Behind us a noise caused the group to pause in unison. Far up on the hills, near the shattered walls of the city, *something* moved.

"That is *not* what I wanted to see," Varek growled, wrinkling his lip. "We need to leave."

Turning, he motioned toward the water. The giant turtle carcass we had found earlier appeared from thin air. Rotating upside down, the shell split in half, and the belly-portion was discarded. Gently, Varek sat it down in the water against a pair of large rocks along the shoreline. What remained was an impromptu boat, large enough to hold far more than our group of four.

As we piled into the shell, we watched abstract, shadowy forms drift around some of the collapsed city stones. I had expected them to charge out toward the boat, but they hadn't. Instead, the odd shapes meandered aimlessly, without purpose or direction, as if they were lost.

They're so sad and confused. They don't know where they are.

You think so?

Yes. They wish for nothing more than to be freed. I imagine.

Well, if we make it back from this journey, you and I should find a way to set them free.

You'd do that, Laurence?

Of course. Why wouldn't I?

It would seem I made the right decision in partnering with you after all.

"And we make our escape," called Varek, who pushed us off from the coast using an unseen force. "Just in time to avoid losing our bodies to those wretches, too!"

"They don't seem like they're hunting us," Jillian countered, watching the shadows bob up and down along the rocks.

Varek rolled his eyes; clearly, he thought she was being naïve.

Staring down at the inside of the shell, the remnants of the giant turtle's spine protruding upward inside of it, I found myself curious as to its purpose in Varek's spellwork.

"Varek, why did you summon this turtle shell? Why not just teleport us over to that island? Or summon a boat, for that matter?"

"I can't see the island very well, for one," he responded. "I could have dumped us out in the water or impaled our bodies on those trees. With the Withered looming up over those rocks, I did not feel comfortable taking the chance. The turtle shell, as you call it, was still prominent in my mind; the clue aggravated me because it was poorly written. I knew my idea would work without complication." Turning, he pointed a finger toward me. "Always choose the simplest solution when using Magic, and use whatever you can to your advantage, no matter what that might be. Even if it is a poorly written clue held within a carcass."

I nodded, seeing the logic in his comment. I had considered it an odd choice, but after hearing his reasoning, I thought it quite brilliant. He had used what he believed would be simple and worry-free. We might be riding on a boat built from a turtle, but it was a boat nonetheless, and we were heading toward our destination without incident. I couldn't argue with his results.

Soon, we arrived on the small island, the turtle shell burying itself into the sand deeply enough to allow us our departure without jumping into the water. Looking around at the small parcel of land, the vegetation surprised me. When Varek had mentioned seeing trees, it hadn't occurred to me there shouldn't have been any.

"Why are there trees here?" I asked.

Varek shrugged. "Ask your companion; I've never been here before. Perhaps this island was far enough away from the calamity to spare it from destruction. Does it really matter?"

"Well, yeah," I replied. "It might mean something. I'm just making an observation."

He is correct; it *was* **far enough away.**

"Why don't you two observe *that,* then," Jillian called excitedly.

She pointed toward another form, which I had absently mistaken for a large rock. Upon closer inspection, it appeared to be an honest-to-goodness submarine covered in rust, barnacles, and driftwood. However, large, it certainly was not. At around three feet tall and five or six feet long, it was almost comical in proportion.

"*That* is your ship?" questioned Varek. "It is no larger than a beacon!"

I couldn't help but agree. "You're right - I thought it would be bigger myself, but I didn't know for sure. In our time they can vary from being the size of a small animal to massive machines, used to carry hundreds of people. There was really no way of knowing where it would fall on that scale."

Varek extended a hand, causing the ship to tear in half. Its rusted exterior made a horrific groaning noise as the rivets holding it together pulled free.

"What if we were supposed to use that!" Jillian exclaimed.

"*I* certainly wouldn't head to the bottom of the ocean in that mediocre vessel," Varek replied. "There are also four of us. Am I to infer you would have been content to wedge yourself in there with the Cimmerian? He's still larger than any two of us. If we need to, I will summon a barrier around our group to aid in our descent into the depths."

Jillian's perturbed expression remained unchanged, but she kept silent, walking over to the sub instead. Inside, wrapped in an old cloth, sat another clay pot, cradled between a series of levers, pedals, and cranks. Picking it up, she cracked it on the edge of the ship like an egg. A fourth small scroll rested inside.

Turning around, she smiled. "Would *you* like to read it, Dreyl'vyn?"

"What advantage would that bring us?" Dreyl'vyn asked.

Jillian shrugged. "Was just trying to be fair."

"She thinks it a game," Varek interjected mockingly. "She's trying to give you a turn."

Rolling her eyes, Jillian extended the scroll and read its words aloud.

The bottom of the sea, where they've spent their days.
The remnants incomplete, it was never remade.
But what could not be fixed, was finally used.
To craft something new, the pieces were fused.

But dangerous work should never be done.
Certain skills are required, obtained by just one.
Using his tools, he slaved over years -
the banging of hammers, the turning of gears.

In a city of gold, gilded in red,
resides such a man, begging for bread.
Whisper the words he's been longing to hear,
otherwise you've lost; he'll just disappear.

"Every riddle we find has less and less to do with Ahso'lar and more and more to do with this person's mad quest to fix something," Varek concluded. "Even more absurd, I believe he's trying to infer that he's not only found remnants of Khalla'sall but used them to craft something else, which is rubbish."

"Why is it rubbish?" asked Jillian. "It sounds reasonable to me."

Varek sighed, indicating he hadn't intended to explain further, but continued anyway. "Khalla'sall was crushed by *Arkken'Arak*, which *obliterated* it. Then, when Galgot-Dreth ruined this planet, everyone piled inside the ruins of the ship and used it as a home for many generations. You'd best believe they worked their way through the hull to see if they could discover any pieces underneath."

You know they must have found something.

"Well, what did they dig up?" I asked, finding the story fascinating.

"From what I've read, little bits, nothing which held any hint of its former power. The impact could have launched pieces of the staff in all directions for vast distances. Even if this unknown author *had* found a few, it wouldn't amount to much. The writer of these riddles isn't sending us on a journey to find the wand; he's telling us his own story to add some sort of significance to his life. From the looks of it, I don't feel like we're going to uncover anything but nonsense here. We have a deadline, and we're burning a resource we have very little of. This quest has lost its value to me; its purpose is gone. We are going to try a different route."

I think we should keep going. The riddle is referencing Toriash'ahn, the city of red and gold. They have an extensive, abandoned forge there, which sounds like a good place to start.

I agree with you. I've spent my whole life wanting to go on an adventure, and maybe I'm being selfish, but I'd like to see this through. If we quit now, I'll wonder what might have been waiting for us. Whether or not we find the wand at the end of it, will be another matter entirely.

"I think we should continue on with this, Varek," I stated. "I agree; the author *does* seem to have another agenda or story to tell, but he also promised to give us what we were looking for if we followed his clues. Perhaps hearing his story or following in his footsteps is simply the cost of our admission."

Varek shook his head. "Out of the four of us, I am the only one with intimate knowledge of the information contained within these riddles. It would be unwise to continue onward if even *I* fail to see the point."

"Rhen showed us the islands," Jillian countered.

"*Everyone* is aware of these islands," Varek retorted. "I have studied *thousands* of tomes referencing the history of the Xahl'thari. I would argue there are few still alive who know the old stories as well as I. Perhaps not even my father, in regard to some accounts. If I say this author, whoever he might be, is wasting our time, then you will listen! We have just days before a war begins, which will clearly lead to the eventual summoning of demons, and you would rather frolic along, solving your little enigmas, playing your little game, until this world is destroyed and you are turned to dust!"

Jillian eyed Varek, her demeanor changing. "I say we're going to follow this riddle," she stated resolutely. "If you don't like it, leave. You can do whatever you want as long as you don't contact Jack without us."

Varek met her evenly, stepping forward to stand just feet from her face. "We *must* regain the sword; that is why I have carried on with this ludicrous task for even *this* long. With or without you, inside or outside the tournament, I *will* pay him a visit."

Jillian bristled at Varek. "You're going to stay away from him unless I'm there. And our group is *following* this riddle." Her gaze intensifying as she spoke, she made a clear attempt to tap into the succubus-like powers she had been imbued with.

Surprisingly, Varek laughed. "How foolish. You have no power over me; you will heed *my* decision. We are no longer following that drivel, *demon.*"

Jillian's eyes widened and her brow tightened. Clenching her jaw, she growled at Varek. "*What did you just call me?*"

Varek stepped even closer. "The fate of the world rests in *my* hands, not yours. Demons will take this planet for their own; I am certain of it. Either you are at my side or you are at *theirs*." He looked her up and down. "I appear to have been quite foolish myself for seeing you as you are and assuming the former.

"I have no further need of you, demon. Laurence will aid me in my task. You have become a hindrance to our progress, and I am convinced you will only cause me that much more trouble if left to your own devices."

Varek's eyes flashed with power as he lifted his hands from his sides.

Jillian stepped backward, unsure whether she should defend herself or lash out toward the man, but Dreyl'vyn launched between the two, making the decision for her. Faster than I would have given him credit for, he swung his fist upward, colliding with Varek's chest and crushing his ribcage.

Spurting a trail of blood from his mouth, Varek crumpled in on himself as he was sent hurdling far out to sea. With a loud slapping noise his limp form contacted the ocean, no doubt compounding the internal trauma he had already suffered. From deep below the surface, a shadowy form emerged, yanking his body down into the depths.

Stunned, Jillian stared up at Dreyl'vyn, wide-eyed. "You... you... you just killed Varek! *Oh my god, Dreyl'vyn!*" She looked around, shaken by how rapidly our circumstances had changed.

My jaw slack, I too could barely comprehend what Dreyl'vyn had done.

Varek is... dead?

I... think so.

Dreyl'vyn watched the myriad of expressions wash over Jillian's face with his dark cold orbs, his face free of emotion. "Varek put this mission at risk. I watched him carefully and evaluated his actions. He was careless, he was unnecessarily violent when other paths could have been taken, and he would not listen to reason. If it were those matters alone, I would have allowed him to live, but he concluded you would stand against him at the side of demons. His body language told me he was about to harm you. I was willing to allow him to manipulate my power due to his mistrust, but I would-"

"*Manipulate your power?*" I interrupted. "What are you talking about?"

Dreyl'vyn pulled his clothing upward, revealing his withered chest. "I have not yet recovered. The mixture he gave me to reduce my form included something he did not disclose. Its effects should have begun to wane long before now. I believe he may have hindered my regenerative qualities permanently, but he underestimated the strength I possess."

Greatly underestimated, I'd say.

Jillian eyed Dreyl'vyn's chest in horror. "Dreyl'vyn, I'm... I'm so sorry. Are you going to be okay?"

"There is no need for concern. His choices were suspicious. He repeatedly made mention that he was surprised I harbored him no ill will. I suspect this was his way of making sure. That, too, would not have concerned me, but his choice may have hampered my ability to heal you if you need to feed again.

"He searched us out because his plans had not gone as intended. With one such as him, there are no mistakes. He has plotted his course down to the smallest of details. When he realized we were incapable of being controlled, he changed his demeanor. We could not trust him. We are better off with him dead."

And yet Varek didn't see this coming.

Sometimes people can't see what's right in front of them.

"He's right, Jillian," I said, stepping up to the pair. "I don't want to sound cold, and please hear me out, Rhen, but he was about to get out of hand. I was willing to put up with his cocky attitude while he was playing along, but Dreyl'vyn made the right decision; I could see he was ready, or at least tempted, to hurt you.

"Varek was *not* the type of person you could just ask to leave. He may laugh and seem benign, but do something to upset him and he'll immediately become dangerous. As far as I'm concerned, it was him or you, and Dreyl'vyn chose correctly. It's what I would have done had I the time to react. We should be thankful he's so quick." Turning toward Dreyl'vyn, I motioned in his direction. "Thank you, Dreyl'vyn. We are in your debt."

"I do not collect debts."

I smiled. "I know, but I appreciate what you did for us. That statement means we will always be grateful for what you did, and we do not know how to show you just how much it means to us."

Dreyl'vyn silently stared in my direction, seemingly unable to accept our gratitude. He had seen what he considered to be a situation that had gotten out of hand, and he had dealt with it the best way he knew how. For him the case was closed.

I've never seen a man die like that...

I'm sorry you had to see it at all.

It's not your fault. I know you all have been through far worse than that. I don't mean to sound childish. I've witnessed unpleasant events, people being killed in a myriad of means, but to be crushed in such a way, it's so...

Visceral.

Yes.

I don't think that of you. I don't expect you to deal with violence like we have. I wouldn't say becoming cold to such an event is a positive attribute. Perhaps its best if-

No, we're sticking together. It just startled me. I could see that Varek was about to do something, as much as I don't want to admit it. Dreyl'vyn made sure we didn't have any repercussions. If we had given Varek a chance, Jillian might be

dead instead of him, and we might have been forced to do whatever he told us to. Dreyl'vyn just chose…

The most effective path, even if it was a brutal one.

I suppose it was. To kill her brother like that-

So you've uncovered that memory. Keep in mind Jillian doesn't know he was her brother; she can never know. You can obviously see the damage he and Vael'ehn can cause. If she were to find out her true heritage, it-

I understand. I don't want to cause her any more pain than she's already going through. I agree, its best she doesn't learn. At least not now.

"Well, for what it's worth, his outburst at least made me that much more determined to find what we're looking for," Jillian admitted. "Our mission is incredibly important, and we can't fail." Staring out into the ocean where Varek had disappeared beneath the waves, she shook her head. "What do we do now? Does anyone know what the riddle was referring to?"

"Yes, Rhen does," I responded. "The city is Toriash'ahn, where you and Dreyl'vyn were held, which *does* make things awkward. She said it has a great forge in it, and that's where we should look first. I can teleport us. I'm well-versed in what it looks like, having been there before. But that's the easy part. The guards are going to be on the lookout for us. As far as they're concerned, we failed in the acquisition of what we came for. If I were in charge of the city, after hearing the thieves broke out of prison and killed several more people, I'd be leery of them making a return trip."

"Alright, then what do we do to hide ourselves?"

Backing up a few paces to inspect the pair before me, I studied them for a moment.

"We improvise."

CHAPTER
fifty-five

-THE FORGEMASTER AND THE SPELLSMITH-

"Are you sure this will work?" asked Jillian, who no longer appeared to resemble herself.

Before passing through the city gates, I had done my best to modify all three of our appearances. Imagining a series of flawless, living masks, a new set of identities had been laid over our skin. Much to my satisfaction, the disguises were indistinguishable from any other person; we all appeared nondescript and ordinary.

"Yes," I responded, as if the idea had been something I was even remotely confident would work. "Even I can't tell who you are. Unless someone is able to see through my Magic by some means other than their own eyes, I believe we are safe."

Dreyl'vyn stared down at hands which were no longer wrinkled and prune-like and nodded. "I believe it would be effective to wear this disguise permanently. I would no longer attract attention in public."

"Well, I don't know how long a spell like this lasts," I said, "but once we leave this city, it won't be an issue either way."

Beyond us lay a vast capital city, the gleam of its red and gold buildings muted in the moonlight. Most of the crowds had left, leaving the roads and passages easier to traverse but harder to blend into while on the move. As we traveled down the main street, I couldn't help but glance back and forth along each intersection, Rhen's limited human vision increasing my paranoia.

Go down that road to our right. Do you see where it opens up?

Yes.

That's where the forge is. It's no longer active, but it still remains in place.

Following Rhen's instructions, we made our way out into a vast industrial area, which appeared to have been shut down for years. Most of the real estate, once filled with who knew what types of Magically-enhanced equipment, had been converted to a town square, and small vendor carts lined the perimeter instead. All appeared to have closed at some point earlier in the day, but in the distance, one still called out for our attention.

"Welcome to the city, travelers!" a strangely lanky, sharply-dressed man called from our left. "Care to check out any of my wares? I was just about to shut down for the night, but I'll stay open if you like."

Determined to avoid suspicion, I stepped up to his cart, immediately noticing several unusual globes, which still managed to sparkle in the darkness.

"Ah, miss, I see you've an appreciation for my selection of At'gornia. I'll let them go for a low price. It's almost a complete set, only missing the fourth."

Bending down, I eyed the globes. "What do they do?"

"A full set of At'gornia can sooth your entire body. It's missing the one you'd use for your mind, which is typical - headaches and such - but for people who use their hands or stand on their feet, they're a must-have. I've used them myself a few times! Gotta get through those busy days somehow, eh?" He chuckled.

Smiling, I straightened. "They're intriguing, but I'm afraid we must be on our way."

Frowning, the man eyed my face. "Are… are you feeling well?"

Confused by the comment, I turned toward Jillian and Dreyl'vyn. Their faces had begun to sag; mine must have as well. While studying the other-worldly trinkets, I had temporarily been distracted from my insecurities regarding the masks' effectiveness. Quickly I corrected the mistake before the man was allowed to take notice of the others.

Does my spellwork need to be maintained with my mind?

It looks like it, Laurence. We can't afford any distractions. You have to pay more attention to our disguises!

Our faces straightened, I turned back toward the man and smiled. "Of course. I am just tired. It has been a long day."

Rubbing his eyes, he stared at me a while longer. "Yes, I think it's been a long day for both of us. Looks like I could use an At'gornian mind treatment myself." He laughed. "Have a good evening, miss."

Walking behind his cart, the man shook his head again before beginning his nightly routine of stowing merchandise and collapsing shelving units.

My heart raced from the close call.

We can't afford to do that again. Rhen, I think I need you to control your body while I focus on this disguise. I'm not acclimated to splitting my attention between multiple people and interactions.

I understand. I'll do my best to help.

Backing away from her mind, I found myself in her pocket again. Drifting upward, I hovered over her shoulder, my attention directed mainly toward keeping our disguises intact.

"What just happened?" Jillian whispered, noticing my departure from the pocket.

"Laurence needs to devote more attention toward our disguises. When interacting with the man, they began to... *melt*."

Jillian's brow raised, but she nodded in comprehension.

As we continued on, I took notice of the massive forge, which towered over the vendor carts. Unlike a modern construct, it was circular and seemed to spin on a giant pivot mounted deep into the ground. If I were to guess, it appeared almost gyroscopic in design. Its inner workings, however, were far beyond my understanding.

On the steps leading up to its center sat a broken old man, his arms trembling uncontrollably. Stepping up to the stranger, Rhen eyed him. Slowly he, too, raised his gaze to meet hers.

"Would you be so kind as to share some bread with a useless old man?" the stranger croaked.

Glancing upward at the towering forge behind him, Rhen appeared to consider the situation. The riddle had not only indicated we would find a man but had also predicted what he would say. In addition, it had warned that if we did not supply him with the words he wanted to hear, he would vanish.

I wonder if his disappearance is literal or figurative.

I better remain ready to track down any teleportation spell he uses.

Rhen turned her attention toward the man's trembling hands; well-muscled, thick-fingered, and calloused, they had clearly been involved with manual labor for many years. "You used to work with this forge," she said, a smile crossing her lips.

The man paused, attempting to read her eyes. "I am the Forgemaster. Well, at least I used to be. It was a long time ago, when this city was first being built."

"Then why call yourself a useless old man, Forgemaster? From my perspective, this city would not exist without you. They should owe you everything, yet here you sit."

Brightening, the man's chest seemed to inflate, and a dim twinkle returned to his eyes. "Everyone has forgotten what this land looked like before we began our work on the city. It was cold and uninviting, and predators crept in from all sides."

Rhen seemed to consider something else. "Not everyone has forgotten what you have done. Someone came to you for one last project, something which could only be completed with your unique talents."

His eyes widening, the man seemed to recognize who he was talking to. "You found the riddle," he whispered.

"Yes, we did, and it led us to you. What would you have us do next, Forgemaster?"

The old man smiled. "You have shown an old man the respect all others have taken away by remembering the sweat and labor this city was founded upon. I never wanted pity; your words are what I've longed to hear these many years. Thusly, you shall have your answer.

"A strange man came to me with an even stranger request. He had with him a broken mount for a stone of some sort. He asked of me to forge it into a wand with a setting, and even gave me a rough sketch with the dimensions. When it was completed I asked only that he provide the owner with the name of the man who had crafted it: Forgemaster Bel'don.

"He agreed to the exchange with one of his own terms: that I keep a riddle for one who might seek it. The riddle was lost long ago, as was I, but it pointed toward a dear friend of mine: a Spellsmith by the name of No'ahn. You will find her not far from here."

"Admiring the old forge?" a voice called out from behind us, pulling our group from the conversation. It was the salesman who had offered to sell the orbs to us. "Hasn't been used in a long time, but I've been told it was quite the sight to see when it was operational. But anyway, it's late. You all have a lovely night."

As Rhen brought her attention back to the old man, he was nowhere to be found.

"Bel'don?" she called, but she found no response.

I, of course, knew the truth: Bel'don had vanished. Whether he held more power than he let on or he had been something other than a man, I couldn't say, but I suspected no one would see Bel'don again.

Spinning, Rhen called out to the merchant, who had begun to walk away. "Do you know where we can find a woman by the name of No'ahn?"

Pausing, the man turned. "The Spellsmith, No'ahn? She operates from that establishment over there. Nice old lady, she is."

He pointed to a storefront across the way. Small and cottage-like, I would have assumed the dwelling to be anything but a business, had a small sign not been hung beneath the overhang of its roof. Barely visible, the weathered letters read, "Professional Spells and Enchantments - Crafted while you wait - Accurate results guaranteed!"

As we walked over to the storefront, we were met with a locked door and darkness from within.

"We will be required to come back tomorrow, I think," Rhen concluded, but as she turned to walk away, the door shuddered and clacked before being opened.

A small wrinkled woman poked her face out from behind it. "I'm sorry, travelers, but I'm closed for the night," she politely informed us.

Rhen smiled. "I'm sorry to disturb you. My name is Rhen. We will come back tomorrow. Bel'don told us to come find you, so we were checking to see if you were still here."

The old woman's eyes grew several sizes larger. "*Bel'don* told you to seek me out?"

Rhen nodded. "Come, come! Come inside, all of you. I was not aware you were sent by Bel'don. Please, might I fetch you all something to drink?" she asked with a sense of urgency.

Walking inside, we found ourselves in what appeared to be a small home, proving my initial impression to be quite accurate. Tiny crystals, doodads, and other Magically-related items lay strewn about in small, disorganized heaps. The majority of the room was taken up by a small kitchen, a table, and a set of stairs leading upward to a cramped second floor.

"Whichever one of you has applied that concealment charm, you needn't use it in here," the woman said with a knowing smile. "I can see right through them."

Well, those were of little use.

As if expelling a breath I had been holding inside for far too long, I let go of the spell. The faux masks fell from the group's faces and landed upon the floor with a puff, evaporating into nothingness. I hadn't wanted to admit it, but the complex disguises had been far more taxing than I expected, and after teleporting to the city, I already felt weak.

Perhaps I made a mistake by imagining living masks. It felt almost as if they were feeding vicariously off of my life force. Next time I should just imagine removable, animated faces.

Rhen, her face revealed, smiled at the old woman. Noticing tea of some sort steeping on the stove, she motioned toward it. "I'll certainly take a cup of whatever you're brewing if you're offering. The air was beginning to give me a chill. Something warm *would* be nice."

The woman returned the smile and bowed politely. Turning toward Jillian and Dreyl'vyn, she opened her mouth to inquire whether they would also like something but, seeing their complexions, thought better of it. Her expression told me she was well aware of what they represented, but not overly concerned by it.

I wonder how much experience she's had with zombies, demons, and dead Gor'tier…

Handing Rhen a steamy cup, the woman turned to regard the group. "If you haven't guessed by the sign, my name is No'ahn. And you three... *four*," she corrected, noticing my presence, "are on a journey involving a series of riddles, are you not?" Rhen nodded, causing No'ahn to smile. "Good! I'd have very much wished to have seen Bel'don. Such a shame. I stood outside my store not one hour ago before heading inside, and now here you are."

"Could you tell us more about Bel'don?" Jillian inquired. "He seemed to have teleported away after speaking to us."

No'ahn's smile broadened. "That he vanished *after* you spoke with him is a good thing. Bel'don was my friend, and as you must know by now, he was the Forgemaster for Toriash'ahn long ago. What you interacted with was a reflection, a small part of a man who died years before your arrival. On his death bed, he made me swear that I would take the last of him and enchant the forge. He knew he had lost his purpose in this world, and he was insistent that he would not fail at the last task he had been given - a task to pass along a riddle.

"The Bel'don who sits at the forge only appears for those who seek what history has forgotten, and he only stays if you tell him what he wants to hear: that he was a dedicated member of society who contributed much to what you see around you. If you give him the respect he sought in life, he will reward you with the riddle you seek. Provided the person *is* seeking it, of course." She winked.

"We did not receive our reward," Dreyl'vyn stated bluntly, his voice easily overwhelming the small residence. "Bel'don did not remember the riddle's text but instead indicated you were its answer."

"You are correct," responded No'ahn. "He certainly wouldn't have; there was not much left of his mind when I performed the ritual. But the riddle was not lost, as he may have indicated. *I* still have it. Would you like to read it?"

Rhen nodded. "Very much so!" she exclaimed, excitement evident in her voice. It was clear this was the first time she had ever gotten involved in an adventure of this type.

Turning, No'ahn opened a small drawer under a desk and withdrew two scrolls, one of which she handed to Rhen.

"The first to read and the second as your reward when you solve it," she announced with another wink.

Giggling, Rhen opened the first scroll and read its contents aloud.

The shaft forged, the setting done,
my work has only just begun.
The shattered remnants of its stones
must be repaired before they'll glow.

Useless rocks, the state they lay.
They cannot perform as they had that day.
But power remains inside them still.
It can be saved by one with skill.

Not far from where you found the forge,
resides a shop, largely ignored.
Inside, a woman works and dwells
and spends her days crafting spells.

Looking up, Rhen scanned the room in mock confusion. "Does that sound like anyone we've met recently? Anyone at all? *Ooh*, I have no idea; this is so hard…"

Grinning, No'ahn put her arm up. "Oh, I think I know. Is it… *me?*"

"It is clear the riddle points to you," Dreyl'vyn responded, not at all picking up on the idea that the two were being facetious with one another.

"Your friend is not much for play," No'ahn concluded, winking at him. "But yes, I am the one the riddle refers to. The man who wrote it sought me out for a specific purpose. He believed I could build a spell which would temporarily remove the power bound inside an Object until a new vessel could be made for it."

"So, you can transfer power to and from Objects, then?" Jillian inquired.

I suspected she was curious - as was I - if the ability could somehow be applied toward correcting Mor'dresh's condition.

No'ahn raised her hands in an uncertain gesture. "Not quite. It had never been attempted before I tried. To remove power from an Object, it must first be broken. And if you had seen the condition of what he brought to me, you'd agree, it certainly was. But it must not be so broken that it has lost everything that made it what it once was, which is rare."

"What did this man bring you?" Jillian asked.

"He showed me a series of shattered turquoise crystals. Whatever they had come from, it was once very powerful, but in their current state, most would have assumed they were nothing but rocks. The shards wouldn't have shown *any* indication of power. It wasn't until I began to thoroughly probe them with my own proprietary spellwork that I concluded otherwise. How or where he found them, I haven't any idea."

Turquoise is the color which appears to represent life.

Those must have been pieces from Khalla'sall. Or, at the very least, the stranger believed they were.

No'ahn continued. "The longer I worked, the more power I was able to coax out of them. They had lost most of what they once were, but in the end, I'd say it was worth the endeavor. He of course offered to pay for my efforts, but I declined. The spells he encouraged me to create were unique, and the ability to keep them for myself was more than payment.

"Even though I fashioned a containment vessel for him, he insisted that he also take the original crystal shards, stating they were of further use to him, which was strange. When I inquired as to why, he instead left me with this riddle." She handed the second scroll to Rhen. "He said it was important, and when he finished his work, it would tell the tale of what he sought to achieve. So I've kept it all these years, waiting to see what would come of it. And here you all are on my doorstep."

"Yes we are," Rhen agreed with a smile as she unrolled the second riddle.

The power remains, as I hoped it would.
But keeping it contained won't do any good.
From whence it came will soon be remade.
Those with the skill are unwilling to trade.

The ones who lived long before we arrived,
under the ocean, where they laugh and dive,
have a number of secrets which no other knows,
so travel to a bay, where the ocean water flows.

When you arrive, ask not what you seek.
Offer a task you'll perform without fee.
When they see your hearts are empty of greed,
the last piece of your puzzle, from their grasp will be freed.

As Rhen finished reading, Jillian sighed and shook her head. "That means absolutely nothing to me. These riddles always refer to details from *this* time."

"It's okay," Rhen reassured her. "The only bay which ocean water flows into that *also* harbors a race of ancient beings is Herien Bay. The bay is named after the sea folk themselves. The riddle was being polite when it said the Herien are unwilling to trade. They don't see any reason to interact with anyone at all, and they don't enjoy newcomers."

"We will announce our intentions to do labor from afar," Dreyl'vyn said. "I will call out to them, and they will be well informed by the time we arrive."

Laughing at Dreyl'vyn, No'ahn shook her head. "I'm not so sure that will work. Herien Bay is a dangerous place indeed. Herien are known for pulling ships onto the rocks with their spellwork before asking questions, as they do not trust outsiders. If you're all determined to go there, and I assume you are, you will need a spell to bring you directly *to* them. If you meet face to face instead of using a ship, perhaps you'll have a few moments to inform them of your intentions. Otherwise-"

"There will be no otherwise," Dreyl'vyn stated, cutting off No'ahn's sentiment. "They will listen. We are not weak fishermen who are willing to perish under the waves before voicing our intent."

"I can see you are not weak, but when you arrive, do not mistake their fragile appearances for weakness. They have potent Magic, spells which the Xahl'thari have yet to learn. They can be nasty."

"We will be careful, of course," Rhen replied, "but we have nothing to offer you, aside from our tale, once we return. Would you be so generous to provide us with such a spell, No'ahn?"

No'ahn smiled. "Of course, child. Your group has fulfilled an old woman's wish. I had wondered if I'd ever see the day when someone would come searching for this riddle. As of today, I have."

Rummaging through the small cottage, No'ahn collected a smooth white stone, a detailed map of the continent, and a needle. Carrying all three back to where we stood, she laid them out on a table.

Reaching for Rhen's finger, No'ahn pricked it and, after studying the map for a moment, blotted a tiny island with a speckle of blood. Placing the stone upon the spot, she spun it. As the stone rotated, rather than slowing, it increased in speed, slowly changing from chalky white to a rich crimson. It came to a gradual stop, its color as red as the blood from Rhen's finger.

"You will all be able to travel to their island now," No'ahn announced. "That is, as long as you are with Rhen, and as long as you all touch the stone. What you will find there, I cannot say."

Rhen stepped closer and gave the old woman a hug. "Thank you, No'ahn. We might have been at great risk had you not aided us."

"I would do it again and again until my heart ceased its beating," No'ahn replied with a smile. "In a world such as this, we have very few adventures left."

If that's how you feel, you should see the stale crouton of a planet Jillian and I harken from.

No'ahn looked into Rhen's eyes. "You are exhausted. Before you leave, child, you really need to rest first. You should stay here for the night, lest your strength fail you when you require it most."

Turning, Rhen looked toward Jillian. "Do we have time?"

Jillian extended a hand, transferring the final say over to me. "*Do we?*"

I wasn't sure exactly how much time we had left before the irreparable events that took place with Jack unfolded, but we had been moving far faster than my prior group, as they had taken time each night to rest. Now that Rhen was with us, our pace would slow, but as far as I could tell, we were still ahead.

I left my response hanging in the air, which greatly amused No'ahn.

Yes, get some rest.

As Rhen followed the old woman up the stairs, Jillian and Dreyl'vyn sat down at the table.

The next series of hours will no doubt be dull, quiet, and awkward.

I was not wrong in my assumption. Quite some time passed in silence with no one finding it necessary to communicate. Dreyl'vyn, seemingly content to stare forward in his typical "offline android" pose, was of no use. Jillian, her eyes fixed upon the table before her, seemed disinclined to even look in my direction. Rounding out the group was myself - the player with the omnipotent speech impediment. We did not make for the best table conversation.

Focusing downward, I saw that Jillian had not simply been staring at the table in a mindless effort to pass the time. Instead, she was twiddling her fingers around a small stone - one similar to but smaller than the rock No'ahn had transformed. It was at that moment I realized something peculiar: since meeting Jillian, I had yet to see her use Magic. I assumed she had - in several of my visions I had watched her use spellwork - but over the course of our journey she hadn't even tried.

Has the guilt of what she dealt with in her past caused her to give up on using it?

Deciding to see if I could unearth something else from her past, I drifted forward and touched her hand.

The cramped cottage interior faded slowly, only to be replaced by another small room: Jillian's bedroom inside her parent's house. In silence she sat on her bed, staring out the window toward the direction of Jack's house. Appearing near the age I had last seen her, at least some time had passed, as she had added to her tattoo collection. Despite the likelihood that she had free range of the empty house, she still chose to stay in her own room.

Sighing, she let the black drapes close. "I wish I knew more about who I really am and how I got here," she commented in a yearning voice, addressing the ancient red grimoire, which lay closed in her lap. "Can you show me that?"

The book offered no response.

"Show me why I am here!" she demanded of the heavy tome.

Again, it refused to give up any secrets. Growling in disappointment, Jillian tossed it onto her comforter, the careless action causing it to slide off and hit the floor with a thump.

"Time to take a shower," she muttered, ignoring the accident.

Watching her leave, I had to admit, I was tempted to follow, but a sound from below drew my attention downward. The grimoire, which still lay upon the floor, seemed to be emitting noises from within. Cautiously I crept toward it, fully aware that I was experiencing a vision but still finding myself leery of interacting with such a dangerous book.

As I neared, its cover was flung open, the pages flipping until they reached a blank sheet of parchment, which appeared to hum with Magic. I watched intently as a series of letters crawled onto the page, scurrying about in rapid succession. Shrinking in size and accumulating together in clumps, they soon formed a crude image. Rising up to better view what was being depicted, I realized they had formed a video clip of sorts - a video depicting the interior of a grand tent.

Vael'ehn's tent.

As I watched the enchanted page, it continued to refine its detail until it was indistinguishable from reality itself and had become a viewing portal to another time. Changing its perspective, the depiction rose until it displayed Vael'ehn, who had fallen asleep in his chair. Both he and the chair appeared much younger, and both had suffered far less weathering to their exteriors.

Vael'ehn's breath catching in his chest, his typical, rhythmic breathing was cut off. His eyes popping open, they were tinted a familiar vibrant green for the briefest of moments before returning to normal.

"My grimoire," Vael'ehn muttered to himself in a monotone voice - one similar to a person who might have been sleepwalking. "I must retrieve my grimoire."

Sliding out of his chair, his body slumped, as if he had been suspended on wires. Slinking down the stairs using long, irregular strides, he almost toppled off of them several times, only to be pulled back into line by some unseen force.

"My grimoire," he repeated as his feet clamored across the floor, causing his body to sway this way and that.

Vael'ehn's arm swung out wildly as his body abruptly turned toward the second set of stairs, knocking a row of Magical tools and knickknacks from a shelf. One of them, an ancient lantern, brought back bad memories of my first interactions with the man. Stumbling wildly, a second swing almost sent him careening off the steps, but he again avoided death or injury by being tugged backward against gravity. Finding his way through the alchemy level, which was devoid of the typical bubbling beakers and flasks, he eventually arrived at the ground floor.

"My grimoire," he repeated a third time while clumsily plodding across the room.

Stopping in front of a seemingly random shelf, Vael'ehn withdrew a familiar red book - *Magic: Manipulation & Mastery* - and touched its cover. The book shifted to a shade of green before returning to its prior hue. Stowing it under his arm, he turned toward the entrance to the tent.

"Vael'ehn, the tree. Vael'ora, the fruit," he muttered as his uneven gate continued to carry him along.

The vision snapping to an alternate location, Vael'ehn shambled through the entrance to a darkened, extravagant bedroom. On the bed lay a woman and, nearby, a pair of cribs with two sleeping children inside. Moving toward the nearest crib, Vael'ehn picked up the child who, still asleep, only made a few small noises in return.

"Vael'ehn, the tree. Vael'ora, the fruit," he repeated out loud.

The sentence was enough to wake the woman. Sitting up in bed, she rubbed her eyes. Although many years had passed, I knew in an instant who she was; time had been very kind to her face. Before me lay Demel'sa, a person I had learned was not only a love interest of Vael'curion but one of the Xahl'thari Heroes who had passed away long ago.

Startled by Vael'ehn's presence, she let out a quiet yelp. "Vael, why are you awake at this hour?"

Turning, Vael'ehn's half-slumped form regarded her. "Vael'ehn, the tree. Vael'ora, the fruit," he repeated emotionlessly, as if that would make any sense to her.

Demel'sa's face contorted, as if she thought him strange. "Who is Vael'ehn? Are you feeling well?"

Vael'ehn bent down by the cribs and lifted a basket into view - the basket Jillian had arrived inside. Into it he placed both the child and the book. Turning back toward Demel'sa, he grinned drunkenly. "Demel'sa, he has come for the harvest."

Demel'sa, picking up on the fact that something was wrong with Vael'ehn, smoothly slid out of bed. "Yes, he has," she replied, as if she understood. "What do we need to do for him now that he is here?"

"The fruit is going to the harvest," Vael'ehn replied, his disturbing grin widening. "Our daughter is ready for him!"

Demel'sa dove toward a stack of vestments kept by her bed. In one motion, she grabbed a fantastical, gleaming bow from the stack, rolled, spun, and stood again. She might have been a beautiful woman wearing a nightgown, but she was also a well-practiced warrior. Pulling the drawstring backward, a gleaming, translucent arrow formed on its rest.

"Put our child down, Vael'curion. You are ill," she demanded of him.

Vael'ehn stared at the bow, seemingly undisturbed by the threat of death. "She has come of age. It is time for her arrival. Our daughter is ready for him."

Lifting the basket into the air, he left it to hover on its own. Raising his hands, Vael'ehn closed his eyes.

Demel'sa did not wait to find out what he intended. Releasing the enchanted arrow, it screamed toward her mate. Piercing through his shoulder, a shower of sparks and blood peppered the wall behind him. Both his clothing and the skin surrounding the wound crinkled and dried, as if they had grown incredibly old. Seemingly oblivious to traumatic injury, Vael'ehn only smiled and opened his eyes.

Seeing her mate wouldn't be brought down by a lesser injury, Demel'sa created another arrow, took aim, and fired. The moment the arrow had been loosed, Vael'ehn snapped his fingers, causing the projectile to flash with a sickly green light. Altering its course, it missed his face by inches, impacting the basket instead. Glowing brightly, the arrow shimmered out of existence, taking the basket with it.

"See! She has fulfilled her destiny!" Vael'ehn exclaimed.

Her mouth gaping, tears swelled in Demel'sa's eyes. "Where did you just send our daughter!" she yelled, desperation evident in her voice.

"She has been sent to the future," Vael'ehn replied calmly. "She has gone to be collected on the day of the harvest."

"*Where* in the future!" Demel'sa demanded.

Pulling back the drawstring, a third arrow appeared, which she removed from the bow. Holding it up to her neck, she seemed ready to stab herself with it. Considering what had happened to the basket, however, I suspected her intent was something completely different.

"Tell me where! I'm going after her!"

Vael'ehn cocked his head. "But that is not your destiny."

"What would you have me do!" pleaded Demel'sa. "You would force me to stay here while our daughter has been sent off to some unknown time and place!"

Vael'ehn shook his head. "No, your destiny is to be wiped clean."

Motioning toward Demel'sa, he created a wave of shadowy Magic. Her clothes, skin, and flesh were wiped from her bones, as if they had never existed. What remained of Demel'sa landed in a heap, the enchanted bow clattering down on top of her remains.

"Varek'ehn, the disease," Vael'ehn growled, turning toward the cribs.

Strangely, he stumbled forward, the green illumination within his eyes dimming somewhat. Walking over to the second crib, he stared down into its depths. From inside I could barely make out the sounds of the second child mewling in fear. Motioning toward the wall, Vael'ehn created a portal - one without a green tinge. Within its depths stood the interior of his tent. Through the portal, he pushed the crib. Seconds later it snapped shut.

"May you... correct what I have done... in a time when I can... no longer fight... against it," he whispered.

Turning toward the crib, he summoned another child - one identical to the first - before taking a step backward. The new baby made no noise, nor did it move.

A decoy?

The vibrant green roaring back to life in his eyes, Vael'ehn leapt toward the crib. Grabbing the infant, he lifted it into the air and incinerated it with a burst of green fire.

"The disease... eradicated."

The horrific task complete, Vael'ehn shook violently before collapsing upon the floor, unconscious.

I arrived back inside No'ahn's cottage to the sound of a tapping noise. The sound in question was being made by Jillian's hand. Still touching her, I had begun to shake, causing her to tap the stone against the table.

"What's wrong with you?" she asked. Her eyes widening, she seemed to remember my prior words. "Wait, did you just have a vision?"

Backing away, I stared at her for quite some time.

My god, it's worse than I thought! Vael'curion was once a loving father.

Roth'Roh'Kah forced him to destroy his life, murder his family...

It took me nearly a minute to come to terms with the imagery of Demel'sa's body being wiped away. At last, I brought my attention back down to the stone Jillian had attempted to spin - a task she had not yet completed. Using her action as a reprieve from what I had seen, I decided to ask her about it instead of responding to her question.

Can you use Magic, or are you choosing not to?

The question was blunt, but it was the quickest way to get to the bottom of what I wanted to investigate.

Reading the words caused Jillian to frown. "No, I can't use it anymore," she replied coldly. "It seems that whatever I've become keeps me from accessing Magic. Well, the types of Magic I *want* to access, anyway."

**Perhaps it is what happened in your past
that's causing you to lose focus.**

Jillian's frown deepened. "No, I can tell. I've probably used Magic longer than you have. Although, I have to say, most of the stuff you do is far more impressive. I didn't feel like telling anyone, considering how many people we've been around who have copious amounts of power. I guess it hasn't really mattered."

You matter to me.

Jillian scoffed. "Don't start that again. This is just another reminder of what I am: a demon." She laughed darkly. "And I'm not *just* turning into a demon either.

Lucky me, I can't even do that right. I'm some sort of ruined, zombie-demon hybrid, only keeping myself alive long enough to makes matters worse!

"I *think* if I had continued on with my life without being attacked by Mor'dresh, I could have managed to ignore it. I could have continued to use Magic. When Roth-whatever his name was first stirred up those instincts inside me, I went after my parents, but seeing what I had done, it brought my self-awareness back. After that I forced it down over and over again; it creeped me out and caused me feelings of guilt. Ironically, that kept it in check.

"But after Jack brought me back, *wow*. I must have been pushed too far. I can't stop thinking about eating people now." She motioned as if her head was about to explode. "The part of me that's bound up by dark Magic is constantly in a state of falling apart, constantly needing *more*. And it's not like that feeling compels me to mindlessly eat people all the time - I'm not going to run upstairs and chow down on No'ahn or Rhen right now - but as my body starts to reach its limits, it *will* take over, and I won't come back until its finished."

Her lip quivered, but she maintained her composure. "That's the scary part. When I feed, it forces the demon part to progress further. You can see my hair. Dreyl'vyn's sacrifice helped lessen what happened, but I don't have much time left. You know the length of my hair color is probably a countdown timer of sorts, right? It has to be.

Good thing you haven't seen your new eyes.

"Last time I fed… I'm so thankful I don't remember. If I did, I don't think I'd be able to cope with it." She looked up at me. "I'm not even certain I'm important to this mission anymore. Maybe Dreyl'vyn *should* have let Varek kill me. Maybe he should kill me right now."

"I see no reason to do so," Dreyl'vyn responded loudly, startling us both.

He of course had been witness to the entire conversation, but his quiet and motionless demeanor often caused him to be regarded as more of a statue than a person.

"Why not?" Jillian inquired. "I'm dangerous to everyone around me!"

Dreyl'vyn shook his head. "You are not dangerous to me *or* him. You have proven that you cannot kill me, and you have not even attempted to feed off of Laurence. We are the only three who are necessary to this mission."

Jillian threw her hands in the air. "Your immunity might be gone considering what Varek did to you. Your body isn't the same as it was. What if I kill you next time, huh? And how am I necessary?"

"You will interact with Jack. Xahl'thari decisions are often convoluted and entangled within their emotional state. He will not listen to Laurence and I if we arrive alone. He may hear what we say, but it will not take root in his mind unless you speak the words yourself. If you tell him what is required of him, he will follow, not only because of what you intend but because of what you have become."

Dreyl'vyn was of course referencing Jillian's ability to compel people due to her demonic powers. The comment was not lost on her, as she nearly broke into tears.

"I can't even be with my boyfriend anymore!" she exclaimed. "Not that I've even been *allowed* to think of things like that since coming back. My mind is focused on *one* thing now, and it's *not* affection! Oh, I'm sure you're right, Dreyl'vyn; Jack *will* follow me to the ends of the earth, but for all the *wrong* reasons! There's no way I get out of this with my humanity intact. This has already ruined my future, and I'm in danger of ruining everyone else's future too. Why don't you just end this nightmare for me right now!"

I couldn't listen to Jillian feed into her sorrow.

> This might have ruined your future.
> It might have ruined all our futures.
> But this situation has gone far beyond us.
>
> This is about the entire world now.
> This world and many others will be destroyed.
> If Roth'Roh'Kah is allowed to proceed,
> he'll ruin everything for everyone.

```
         His actions are also tied to
     why we don't have Magic in the future.
   Other tragedies happen between now and then
    which destroy this wonderful civilization,
       and I want to try and prevent them.
```

Jillian frowned while reading my words, but appeared to comprehend the importance of our task. "Speaking of the future," she said at last, "if I had a little guidance, I might have actually turned out normal. Handing a child a dangerous spellbook wasn't exactly a good idea. Why, of *all* people on this planet, was *I* born with those incredibly rare abilities, only to be adopted by two people who had no comprehension of Magic?" She waved a flippant hand. "And don't make a stupid joke about me being *the chosen one*."

She's skirting around the truth, information she's going to find out sooner or later.

It might as well come from me.

I paused for a moment, considering just how much Jillian had forgotten from the events of her youth. For me the visions of her past had just happened, but as a child, she had experienced them long ago.

At last, I wrote the words that had burned themselves into my mind.

```
         Thar'ceron, the seed.
          Vael'ehn, the tree.
         Vael'ora, the fruit.
       I have come for the harvest.
```

It took only a second for Jillian to read the quote. Recognition dawning in her enchanted eyes, she dropped the stone on the table and stood up. Backing away, she shook her head.

"No… I had forgotten that. How did you know what he said to me!"

> You asked if I had a vision.
> I have visions every time I touch you.
> I have seen your past. I know everything.

Jillian, recognizing her given name, took on the full realization of what her history meant. "It's not true! It can't be!"

Breaking down, she slumped against a cabinet and began to sob.

Time passed by in silence until, at last, Jillian was able to steady herself again. Looking up at me, confusion and anger flashed across her features.

"So what? I'm Vael'ora, Vael'ehn's estranged child? Is this where I'm from - the time we're in now? Did he just toss me through a portal onto my adopted parent's porch?"

Her question was sarcastic, but sadly, it was the truth, more or less. I of course had access to far more details than I felt it necessary to share; traumatizing her was not on my list of things to do that evening. Even so, seeing the confusion in her eyes, I felt I needed to give her something which would allow her to learn the truth.

> Thar'ceron was infected by Roth'Roh'Kah.
> That infection was passed to Vael'ehn.
> He passed it on to you.
>
> He did send you to the future,
> but it wasn't his choice;
> it was another attempt by Roth'Roh'Kah
> to gain control over the sword.
>
> You and Vael'ehn are both victims.
> He isn't aware of what has happened to him.
> He has forgotten his past.
> Deep inside, he isn't really an evil person.
> But he *is* dangerous, and he *is* being controlled.

It was brave of you to oppose Roth'Roh'Kah.
You should be very proud of
how hard you've fought against him,
how hard you're *still* fighting against him.

I was rewarded with a small, humorless smile. It wasn't much, but it was far better than oily black tears. Standing up, Jillian walked around the room, casually looking through stacks of papers and inside small drawers and cabinets. I suspected she wasn't searching for anything in particular; the action simply drew some attention away from the pain inside her.

"It's not every day an orphan finds out they're from a faraway Magical land, I guess," she muttered. "I just wish I didn't have to learn of my ancestry like this. And I wish *he* wasn't my-"

Jillian's dropped a small coin she had picked up, her face becoming paler than it already was. Turning toward me, her shock didn't diminish.

"Varek… Varek was my… brother… "

And there it is…

Whether or not Varek uncovered that information for himself, I guess we'll never know.

"You were related to Varek?" Dreyl'vyn asked. Jillian simply shrugged. "I have learned relationships are important to the Xahl'thari race. I have done you a great disservice by destroying him. I will-"

Jillian held up a hand, silencing the withered giant. "*Don't*. Before you start in on whatever it is you're about to say, I *in no way* care about Varek. My brother or not, we were separated by a *lot* of time. I didn't know him, I don't want to know him, and I am certainly *not* mourning his loss now. And don't forget, he was going to kill me. He didn't know who I was, either, and he got what he deserved." Grimly, she shook her head. "Looks like I'm just following the old family tradition: demons and dark Magic."

The rest of the night was filled with a thousand questions from Jillian regarding her history and her mother. None of them received a detailed answer from me, as I did not have many answers to provide on those topics, but she did take heart that her mother had at least been a hero and a lovely person.

In the end, however, Jillian could not help but theorize as to what life might have been like for her had she stayed with her actual parents. Her line of reasoning eventually came to the same conclusion mine had: that being sent away from Vael'ehn had been a far preferable childhood than growing up under the threat of demons and destruction would have been.

Unfortunately, she may not have escaped either of them.

CHAPTER Fifty-Six

-MARITIME METROPOLIS-

As the morning sun rose through the windows of the small house, so too did Rhen and No'ahn, who descended the stairs together. After a brief, quiet breakfast, we said our goodbyes and surrounded Rhen, who held out the stone she had been given the night prior. Reaching forward, Jillian and Dreyl'vyn touched it, followed by myself.

"What command do we give it to-"

No'ahn and her home had vanished.

Looking around, we found ourselves within a copse of trees on the outskirts of an ancient civilization. When Rhen had mentioned "sea folk" after reading the riddle, I had assumed it was a reference to the idea that they made their livelihood off of the sea, whatever race they were. Instead, what she had meant was that they were *from* the sea. Bipedal they may have been, but with webbed feet and hands, scales, and large spines reaching up their back and over their heads, they were anything but human.

Crouching down, Rhen shuddered. "We're right in the middle of their town!" she whispered, fear evident in her voice. "These beings are *very* dangerous! I don't think I want to be here." Looking up at me, her eyes appeared desperate. "Laurence, take control of me. I can't do this myself!"

Drifting forward, I paused. Jillian, seeing my hesitation, seemed to interpret why I had done so.

"It's okay if she's *asking* you to do it, Laurence; she's given you her permission."

Staring down at Rhen, I thought of a way I might make her feel a bit more prepared. Focusing on her ragged and stained dress, I changed it to a near-duplicate of the leather, buckle-laden combat gear Modera had worn at the tournament. There was one modification of course: a loop of leather on the rear of her belt for my Coadju'tahr to be stowed inside.

Looking down, Rhen appeared stunned by the transformation. "You've... I... this feels *great!* Thank you. But if you could still-"

She found herself unable to complete the sentence, as I had already merged with her mind.

Hello again, Rhen.

Hello. I'm sorry I couldn't continue. I just don't know anything about combat. If it comes to such a thing, I mean. I'm too scared.

Well, I'm not complaining.

I took a deep breath and admired her body, which I found far preferable to the Coadju'tahr.

Rhen is right; this leather gear does feel great!

See, I told you.

"Are you two good to go?" Jillian asked.

"Yes, but I don't think we'll accomplish anything by sneaking around. If they catch us, that isn't going to build trust. That big building out there in front - I say we just walk in. They'll probably try to capture us, but I'm not going to let that happen. Just don't make any moves toward them, and I'll keep us safe from any spells or weapons they might use. We'll have enough time to tell them why we're here before anything gets violent."

"Alright. Do you understand, Dreyl'vyn? We're not squashing anyone here, okay? At least not yet."

Dreyl'vyn nodded but thankfully refrained from opening his mouth.

Stepping out from the safety of the foliage we had hidden behind, we hadn't taken two steps before being spotted.

"Intruder!" a Herien male gushed in a wet accent.

Immediately, over a dozen sea folk descended on our location, but they were unable to make contact with us. Several feet away, they were kept at bay by a Magical barrier I had summoned, which I prayed would hold.

"You have pow-ar-ful Ma-gic," a Herien female bubbled, her fish-like mouth seeming to struggle with speech. "We sum-on Sy-ren. They bring for-en-ers to knees!"

Syren?

"That won't be necessary," Jillian said to the female. "The shield is for our own safety because we have heard how powerful *your* race is. We wanted to talk to you before being captured. We're not here to cause you any harm; we're here to work for you." Seeing the female's odd expression, she added, "Free of charge, of course."

The Herien looked back and forth between each other. "Why we trust you, Xahl-thar-i? You can-not ex-tend hand in peace when it be-hind wall."

"We were told you don't like visitors," Jillian responded.

The female gurgled with amusement, the sound reminiscent of someone blowing bubbles in milk. "You were told cor-ect-ly."

From behind, a group of three Herien stepped forward. Clad in odd armor, encrusted with glowing jewels, they looked anything but glad to see us. Putting their hands on my shield, they opened their mouths and turned their attention toward the Herien who had been speaking to us.

"You low-er shield be-fore they force you," the female burbled. "If you ah-temt no-thing, you brought be-fore lead-er un-harmed. You have our word."

I was curious whether or not their spellwork would have had any effect on me, seeing as I wasn't human, but considering the form I was inhabiting, I decided not to take any chances. Lowering the shield, I waited for the sea folk to grab us or bind us, but they made no motions to do so.

Pausing for a moment to see if we would attempt something brash, the female finally nodded. "In-tell-ah-gent de-ci-shun," she bubbled. "Foll-oh us."

Parting, the crowd tracked along with our group as we were led toward the large building we had already decided ourselves to breach. As the heavy, carved, pearl-laden doors opened, the inside was revealed to be quite ornate, and had been adorned with thousands of decorations.

Most of the items in here look like they were plucked from shipwrecks.

I bet that's exactly where they came from.

In the center, on a throne made of coral, sat a young female, who held a magnificent, jewel-encrusted trident. She beckoned the group forward, eyeing us suspiciously.

"These in-tru-ders found way on-to eye-land with-out our know-ledge," the first female bubbled. "They have pow-ar-ful Ma-gic, yet in-sist they come here to lay-bor with-out com-pen-say-shun."

The leader gurgled, a small smile crossing her features. "Why do you insist on using their primitive tongue, Cora'loon? Can you not see the trinket the female wears?" As Cora'loon turned away, embarrassment upon her face, the leader addressed us. "Strong Magic and free labor do not arrive hand in hand," she burbled. "Why have you come here, strangers? You have my attention. Now, what do you seek?"

How am I able to understand her? Xahl'thari translational spells don't work on Herien speech.

I can only assume it's an effect from my Coadju'tahr. Considering the leader's reaction to Jillian's Oculus, I'm going to assume they've met Wenton, or have at least encountered his creations before. Dreyl'vyn, on the other hand, might be struggling; I'm not sure.

"We offer you a task," I responded. "We will perform it for you and ask no compensation. If you wish for us to leave afterward, we will do so."

The female studied me for a moment. "You will, won't you? You've come here despite having knowledge of the risks, and you *are* willing perform a task, free of compensation. Whatever I ask of you, as well; I can see it in your eyes." She flapped a webbed foot on the ground as she considered what that might mean.

At last, she leaned forward, putting weight on the trident. "I am not senseless, stranger. You *do* want something, but you are willing to prove your integrity before you ask it. If you want to complete a task for me, I will not stop you, but do not expect anything in return. Whether or not you do as I have asked, I will likely turn you away."

"That's fine," I replied. "Whatever you ask of us."

Secretly I hoped that was not the case, but I wasn't about to argue. I had to trust that we had been informed correctly, that after completing our chore, she'd rethink her opinion of us.

Drumming her webbed fingers along the edge of her coral throne, the leader seemed to consider what she would ask. Eventually settling on an idea, she smiled deviously; it was clear she did not have an easy task in mind.

"Not far from here is a lake: Lake Dorren. In its depths grows a rare type of plant.

I believe your sailors call it Fish's Fin. It used to grow throughout the area, but the Retrogrades have polluted our waters; it has all died. Lake Dorren is the last natural habitat where it grows. Bring me some of it and consider your task complete."

I've been to Lake Dorren. Fish's fin grows everywhere on the bottom and becomes tangled in the fisherman's lines and nets. We won't have any issues finding it for them.

"Very well," I replied. "We will bring you more than you know what to do with." Turning, I motioned to leave the building.

"No request for aid?"

Looking back, I shook my head. "It wouldn't be a task for us to complete if you completed it for us," I replied, hoping the response would sound truly selfless. Secretly I knew she was asking because something wasn't as it seemed.

That sounds ominous.

You're not kidding.

Walking out from the building under the watchful gaze of dozens of fish folk, we headed toward the area we had first teleported into. Again surrounded by foliage, we discussed our plans.

Once more sharing her memories of the area, Rhen was able to provide me with far more than I expected to have at my disposal, but there was just one problem: I had no one to assist me with a portal, and I wasn't about to ask the sea folk for help.

"Rhen has shown me where Dorren is, but I don't have Varek to create another portal. Does anyone object to an attempt to teleport us there instead? I should mention, I've never tried teleporting somewhere I haven't personally been to before."

Jillian shook her head. "It doesn't seem any more risky than anything else we've tried before."

"It is the one choice we have before us," responded Dreyl'vyn. "We will take it no matter the risk."

I have faith in you. You'll be able to do it.

Thank you, but I have to make sure I have the same faith in myself first.

I closed my eyes, intent on calming myself before initiating the spellwork.

When I opened them again, ready to proceed, we had already been brought to a different location, my intent alone proving potent enough to make the transition. Buffeted by the intense panoramic vision of my crystalline body, I jostled up and down against Rhen's belt as she repeatedly vomited on the grass.

I, too, felt weak, the task requiring far more of my power than I expected. Re-entering Rhen's mind, I was immediately overcome by the feeling of nausea, a state of being I did not miss experiencing. Unable to control the sensation, we continued to vomit together until her body began to cooperate again.

I'm sorry, I didn't realize your body would have such a reaction. Next time I will leave your mind before I attempt such a teleportation.

Don't apologize. I need to get used to this. It is like riding a ship out on the ocean for the first time. If you shelter yourself, you will never learn the benefits, nor will you become immune to its effects.

"We did it!" Jillian exclaimed. "Good job! Sorry it made you sick though." She bent over and patted us on the back. "Wait, this *is* the proper lake, *right?*"

Cautiously, I looked around. The picture I had imagined - a bench where Rhen had sat with an older man - was exactly where it should have been. Beyond the bench lay a beautiful, serene lake, far away from any sort of civilization. Surrounding it stood a dusting of trees with long, vine-like, orange branches, which hung like willows.

"Yes, the teleportation was just a little much for Rhen's body. We made it to the right place though." Taking note of the water's edge, I didn't see any plants that reminded me of a fish's fin. "But it looks like we need to head to the bottom of this lake to get what we've come for."

Reaching forward, I made a parting motion with my hands and pushed outward, the edges of the lake rising like the tide as I did so. Between the two walls of water lay a muddy channel filled with rocks, branches and, farther out, a plentiful supply of a silver plant. Amusingly, its leaves looked very much like small fish fins.

Trudging out into the muck, Jillian frowned as her boots sunk in deep. Every footstep was accompanied by a sucking noise and a wet plop. Dreyl'vyn, however, did not seem to notice; his feet left behind large cisterns, which Jillian tried her best to place her feet within.

As we made our way farther out into the lake, I could see that my reach, which had been greatly weakened by the teleportation, only extended so far. Soon the path which had led us out onto the lake floor was swallowed up from behind, leaving us to stand in an elongated lakebed, similar to a reverse swimming pool. Staring into the wall of water surrounding us, I found myself entertained by the many types of fish, which darted back and forth just out of reach.

I've never seen the lake from this perspective! I'm glad you thought of this, Laurence. It's beautiful and fascinating!

Yes, I must admit, it's-

My amusement was cut off by a massive fish, which rivaled Dreyl'vyn's unhindered form in size. Slowly looming out from the darkness and gliding along the artificial wall, I felt it appeared far more interested in us than it should have. Eyeing our group with large, reflective yellow eyes, it circled the oval of mud several times before swimming out of sight again.

"That did *not* look like a friendly fish," Jillian concluded after watching it depart. "We should grab some of this stuff and leave before you get tired, Laurence. If you begin to lose your hold on this water, that thing'll definitely come after us."

Stooping down, she and Dreyl'vyn began to tear up large clumps of Fish's Fin from the lake floor.

After a few minutes, Jillian turned from a large barren spot, her arms full of slick silver plants. "Alright, that's probably-" she began, but paused, her enchanted eyes narrowing as she spotted movement out in the murky depths. "Sorry, I thought I saw that damn fish again. This is all I can carry. I'm gonna-"

Charging at the watery wall, the fish exploded through my barrier, catching us by surprise. Its gaping mouth spread wide and full of teeth, it was in every way capable of swallowing Jillian whole.

Leaping from behind, Dreyl'vyn collided with the fish, the two of them crashing back into the water. As it attempted to right itself in familiar territory, Dreyl'vyn anchored his boots into the muddy, sucking soil and leaned backward. Pulling the massive predator away from the waves, he lifted it over his head, struggling to gain purchase on its slippery, muscular flesh. At last, his hand met with its gill, and he brought it down upon his knee with tremendous force.

The fish's spine broke with a horrible popping noise, yet somehow it managed to survive, continuing to snap at Dreyl'vyn as he held onto his perilous foe. Wrapping his arms around it as best he could, he squeezed harder and harder. The fish's eyes popped from their sockets as blood and the contents of its stomach were expelled down his back and onto the mud below.

Triumphantly he threw the dead fish back into the water, the group watching as its body was assaulted by a myriad of smaller creatures. I couldn't help but imagine their feeding frenzy was brought on by a lifetime of living in fear.

Turning, Dreyl'vyn regarded Jillian, who sat in the mud staring up at him, wide-eyed. "It is safe to continue harvesting," he concluded, as if wrestling a massive fish had not been anything to balk at.

"My hero!" she exclaimed, flashing him a genuinely grateful smile.

Clamoring to her feet, Jillian turned toward the pile of plants she had dropped in the fray. Frowning, she saw it had been covered by gore the fish had discharged. To her astonishment, however, something unusual lay within the mess. Reaching down, she pulled a slime-encrusted object from the filth. Brushing it off with a muddy finger, a brilliant sapphire-blue briolette, nearly the size of a baseball, lay revealed on her palm.

"Would you look at that," she whispered, awe evident in her voice.

That cannot possibly be a coincidence.

Finding a priceless gem in a fish?

Exactly. How likely is it to head out on a quest into a lake, intent on harvesting a common plant, but instead battle a massive fish and attain a priceless jewel?

I'm almost certain the Herien leader knew we'd deal with that fish. I bet she didn't think we'd be coming back, either. The question remains: did she know about the gem?

I think we're going to find out.

"Are you thinking what I'm thinking?" Jillian said, her unsettling eyes twinkling as she looked up at me.

"We both are," I responded. "We weren't sent here to retrieve some weeds. She knew we'd find this fish and, likely, this gem too."

"But we could have just taken it," Jillian considered. "Not that I have any use for a gemstone in this age."

"It could have a very real, not to mention powerful, Magical enchantment," I surmised. "For all we know, it will hurt us if we choose to steal it. That could be its entire purpose - to test people's honesty."

"The Herien leader could see we took a considerable risk in regard to our own safety by arriving on their island and lowering our shield," Dreyl'vyn stated. "She may have responded in kind, based on who she believes we are."

"Even so, she doesn't *know* who we are," Jillian countered. "I say we return it to prove our honesty. This may be exactly what we need in order to retrieve more information about the riddle. And who knows, maybe the author of the riddles knew about this thing. Let's head back and show it to her."

Sloshing out of the mud, I collapsed onto dry ground, allowing the water to wash back into the area we had ventured out into. I was grateful Dreyl'vyn had leapt to Jillian's aid. In my weakened state, I wouldn't have been able to hold the water at bay *and* fight the fish at the same time. We might have had to fend it off in its territory, which could have meant swimming for our lives.

Releasing Rhen from my mental hold, I took some time to relax and recover before recouping enough strength to attempt another teleport. Still unnerved by the unexpected battle, everyone seemed content to do the same.

Teleporting to a location I had already visited was, thankfully, far less strenuous than teleporting somewhere I imagined we had visited. Minutes after our arrival, we stood before the Herien leader, soaking wet and covered in mud.

Stepping forward, Dreyl'vyn threw a humongous bundle of Fish's Fin down before her feet. The size of a large cow, it would surely last them a long time.

That is, if they needed it at all.

You know they didn't need it. I thought it was common before, and now I'm sure they feel the same.

"Your Fish's Fin, as requested," I stated proudly.

The Herien leader seemed surprised. "And... that was of no burden to you?" she murmured, suspicion evident in her tone.

"Not at all," Jillian exclaimed. Turning away from the leader, as if she were about to leave, she paused. "Oh, I almost forgot. We also found *this*." Spinning around, she revealed the beautiful gem in her palm.

The Herien's face lit up. *"Salguine's Eye!* You defeated the monster!"

Jillian casually tossed it to the Herien leader, who fumbled the beautiful gem in her webbed fingers before finally grasping it. "We're not stupid. You sent us there knowing full well we'd encounter that fish. Dreyl'vyn here just about squished it to bits though. Lucky us."

Smiling, the leader walked over to a dry fountain, where she positioned the gem high above it. The stone floated in place, spinning slowly as it hovered. From below, a gush of water rose to meet it before splashing downward, filling a pool beneath the fountain.

Turning, she regarded us. "Many ages ago, our race lived under the great sea that covers this planet. We sought to head out onto the land, but the Herien can only hold their breath for so long. While attempting to craft a spell to allow us breath without water, a void filled with unfamiliar Magic was accidentally created. Through it that stone arrived, accompanied by a voice. It offered us a partnership: if we were to allow it entrance into our world, it would provide unto the Herien the ability to breath on land. To prove its claim, the voice allowed us to drink from water the stone had touched. Doing so forever transformed those of us who had tasted its power into beings who could live above *and* below the water.

"Suspicious of the voice's intentions, we declined its invitation despite the amazing results the stone had bestowed upon us. In response the voice summoned a great fish from the depths, who swallowed the stone. The voice told us we would live with the knowledge that what we sought would always swim in the same water we inhabited, but we would never be able to attain it unless we allowed the voice admittance into our world.

"The great fish had been enchanted to forever swim away from us. Over time we directed it into what is now Lake Dorren, sealing the land up behind it, but it seemed the voice had thought of everything. When we searched for the fish in the lake, it did not seem to exist! At least, not while *we* were present. We suspected it was there, that it was able to fool us somehow, but we could not tell for sure.

"Over the course of time, we considered informing others of its existence, but we did not do so for fear they would steal the stone for themselves and lord it over us. Nor did we dare to summon the voice into our world again, despite having the knowledge to do so. We had learned that it came from Magic that should not exist, and we believe it seeks to consume us.

"Upon your arrival, I felt something dark *and* redeeming about your group, as if you had been touched by the very Magic we found, yet fought against it. My decision was a great risk for our people, sending you to the lake. The weeds, of course, meant nothing, but should I have been correct about your intentions, I felt it would change our society forever." The leader motioned toward the gem. "Now, my many brothers and sisters will also gain the ability to venture forth from the great sea after they, too, drink from the waters of Salguine's Eye."

Is it safe, considering where it came from?

I guess it must be, if they've already tried it and haven't felt any adverse effects after all these years. It sounds as if Roth'Roh'Kah was using it as a bargaining chip, and they finally found a clever way to gain what they wanted without agreeing to his terms.

Leaning forward, the Herien leader eyed us with newfound respect. "My name is Sieriana, daughter of the waves, leader of the Herien. You have earned the knowledge of my name. In our culture, earning one's name through a task completed selflessly comes with the right to compel its bearer for aid. Tell me that which you seek, and it shall be yours."

Rather than ask for a riddle, we deemed it appropriate that Sieriana be apprised of everything that had happened so far, considering how much she had entrusted to our care. The voice in the void almost certainly belonged to Roth'Roh'Kah, and I suspected it had been another attempt by him to gain entrance into our world. Luckily for us, it had been a failed attempt. Even so, I felt it was in the Herien's best interest to learn of whom they had dealt with - a being they may have to fight against in the world they were about to venture forth onto.

Upon completion of our tale, Sieriana sighed - a kind of spluttering noise. "I believe the words you speak, and should you need an ally, the Herien will come to your aid, but of riddles, I know nothing. There was a small man once who sought us out, asking to complete a task as you have. Seeing his stature, I did not force him to hunt the great fish." She smiled. "When finished, he asked for the repair of a gemstone he had acquired. All of the pieces he provided us with were too damaged to be reassembled, but we were able to re-cut one into a usable form. What he did with it, I am not aware, but I feel I can be of at least *some* assistance to you."

Reaching up, Sieriana took a necklace from around her neck and handed it to Jillian. "This seashell is enchanted. Whisper what you truly want, and it will bring you to its location." She raised her finger. "Be honest with what you say, for the shell can read your heart. And make your choice count; it will only work once before returning to me."

"Thank you," Jillian replied as she graciously accepted the gift. "I know you have no love for our race, but you will find as you occupy more of the land, not everyone out there is bad. There will always be those you can't trust - be careful - but there will also be those who are like us."

Smiling, Sieriana bowed her head. "Thank you, Jillian, daughter of the future. May you and your group find that which you seek."

As we walked out from Sieriana's throne room, Jillian eyed the seashell in her hand. "I'd best not be the one to use this. I feel like it will attempt to take us to Jack's location. And if it fails, and we haven't located the wand beforehand, I'll have screwed us over badly."

She handed it to me without questioning whether or not I felt the same.

I wonder if she's right. Could this shell house enough power to send us through the tournament barrier?

It may, but I agree; we can't count on it to do so. We've come so far. Let's keep going in the direction we have. Besides, I know Jack is not who you truly want to be close to.

Realizing she was correct, I paused for a moment. Out of everything, I wanted to be close to Jillian. Sieriana had indicated we simply needed to whisper our choice to the shell, but I was not at all willing to risk a spell we only had one opportunity to use. For all I knew, it could teleport me a few feet in Jillian's direction.

Rhen, you need to use this shell. Jillian, myself - we have too many mental burdens, and god only knows what might be running through Dreyl'vyn's mind.

What if the location of the next clue isn't where I want to go most?

Where would you go, if you could?

Back in time to correct a great tragedy.

I could sense pain lacing Rhen's words, so I didn't press further.

I don't believe the shell works through time, based on what I know. Aside from that, what do you want most?

For a while it would have been to return from this ordeal, but since these events have taken place, I would very much like to see it through to its end. I would forever live in regret for having failed to solve these riddles.

That's what I was hoping to hear. I'm going to leave you for a moment. Send us where we need to go.

Without waiting for a response, I backed out of Rhen's mind, allowing the Coadju'tahr to pull me in again.

Raising the shell in the air, Rhen smiled at me. "Everyone, please touch the shell." Waiting until the group had all touched it, she leaned forward and whispered the words the shell needed to hear. "Bring us to the location the author of our riddles wants us to find."

It was a good command and one I may not have chosen off the top of my head. Most importantly, it worked. In an instant, we were transported away from the Herien city and onto a tiny island without any visual or auditory phenomenon to indicate a spell had come into play. True to Sieriana's words, the shell had disappeared from Rhen's fingers.

Judging by the change in climate, which felt far more tropical, we had clearly traveled far away from our prior location. Aiding in my theory, I could see that we were surrounded by a boundless ocean stretching out in every direction. Aside from a pair of dead trees, all that remained on the tiny plot of land was a small cave, just shallow enough that I could see something sitting toward the rear of it.

"This is it, then," Jillian concluded, her expression indicating she was both nervous and excited. "I believed we'd make it, but… this is just so surreal."

Moving forward, the four of us ventured forth into the small cavern. Inside, a flattened stone sat at the back, half buried in the sand. Upon it had been placed a small chest, identical in size to the empty one in the Grand Magus' tower.

Stooping down, Jillian eyed the small chest. "Which one of us should open it?" Seeming to consider an idea, she frowned. "Wait, it should be Rhen. It could have some sort of security measures on it preventing people with dark Magic from accessing it."

Rhen appeared terrified. "I'm… I'm not familiar with strange chests; I don't want to ruin anything. Laurence, come back and open it with my hands."

Gently, I pressed into Rhen's mind and caused her body to lean forward. Pausing just inches from the chest, I swallowed. Jillian's prediction of potential booby-traps had all but caused them to appear, at least in my mind.

Hoping for the best, fingers trembling, I finally built the courage to delicately lift the lid. Inside, on a bed of cerulean velvet, lay another tiny scroll.

You can't be serious!

If someone else stole this wand, I'm going to make them eat this chest!

Laughter filled my head. The sound unexpected, I found myself set on edge by what it might mean.

Did Rhen have something to do with the disappearance of the wand?

Oh, don't be silly. I was laughing at what you said. Now read the letter! It's probably another clue.

"Where's the wand?" Jillian asked, her tone also indicating disappointment.

Instead of responding to a question I was incapable of answering, I unrolled the scroll and read what had been written upon it.

Greetings adventurer(s)!

You have finally made it. By luck, by skill, or by fate, you have deciphered my clues, met a wonderful series of people, and learned an odd tale. But what have I crafted, you might ask? Well, now that you've proven yourself worthy, you shall be rewarded with that knowledge.

I stole Ahso'lar for the purpose of aiding in my travels. There were quite a few locations I could not access on my own, and I needed both help and secrecy if I was to find what I sought. And let me tell you, what I sought was precious indeed!

You see, after the war with the Gor'tier, the Xahl'thari created a new home in the fallen vessel, *Arkken'Arak*. Fully aware it had crushed Lori'adier and Khalla'sall, they worked their way through the structure, descending until they reached the earth beneath it. There, they found what they were looking for. Well, some of it, anyway.

Khalla'sall, the great staff, was verified to have been destroyed for good, but only a few fragments were located under the ruined ship. I had a suspicion there might be some glimmer of power left in a few of the pieces they had not found, pieces which had likely been blown far away from the initial impact. My gut told me any number of fragments could have been left in the dark depths of the ocean.

Finding those pieces would be the first step; it might have even proven the easiest step. I knew my mission would be long and arduous with many perils. Completing it, however, was worth the risk. What I sought to create would allow me to save one I loved from the crippled life she was destined to lead. So, following my heart, I made my daring theft and set out on my excursion.

With the aid of the wand, some inventions of my own tinkering, and the brilliance of those I came in contact with, I was able to achieve the impossible. Far under the ocean, where the Xahl'thari never thought to search, I found remnants of the great staff and pieces of the gem it once held.

I had the staff remnant reforged by Bel'don into a base and setting, and asked No'ahn to strip the remaining power from the gemstone shards. The Herien recut the largest of the empty shards into a useable Magic gemstone, which I then mounted into the setting. Lastly, I introduced the power No'ahn had removed back into the completed artifact.

Shockingly, my attempt worked! I had created a new Object of Power, a wand crafted from a staff lost to all for ages upon ages. I called it Khalla'lar, the Touch of Life. It is every bit as wonderful as I had imagined. I have healed that which afflicted my beloved, and now we are free to experience this vast and rich world together again.

You will not find Khalla'lar in this chest; it has been given to one who holds my heart. However, if you have completed each of my clues yourself and read this letter, *word for word*, to completion, you will be rewarded with what you have been searching for: Ahso'lar, Touch of the Unknown.

I wish you the best, whomever you may be, and I hope this journey has enhanced your life, just as it did mine.

One step into the unknown is an adventure not soon forgotten,

Aurthur G. Ma'lorean

As I completed the letter, I absently noticed Jillian's frantic exclamations as she watched Ahso'lar appear before her in the small chest. Aurthur had apparently kept his word, but my mind was far from the tiny cave.

Ma'lorean.

Have you met Aurthur before?

No, never, but that's Cindee's last name, and she has amazing healing powers.

Aurthur left Khalla'lar with the one who held his heart...

He left it with his daughter, Cindee.

CHAPTER Fifty-Seven

-DARK DESTINY-

"This is it!" Jillian exclaimed, reaching for the wand. "Now we can meet up with Jack! We can finally fix this whole nightmare!"

I stared into her excited, desperate, unsettling eyes. She had every reason to be thrilled. With Ahso'lar found, we could move on to the next step in our plan: that of enlisting the aid of Jack and the others. At long last we could stop Vael'ehn from bringing about a war which further corrupted the sword and advanced Roth'Roh'Kah's agenda.

Those eyes will never be healed though. They'll continue on, dead and cold, until she finally turns into a demon and forces us to destroy her, and I have no idea how to correct that.

But there's one person who might be able to help me before I sentence her to that fate.

Laurence… are you planning what I think you are?

Leaping forward, I snatched Ahso'lar from Jillian's anxious reach.

"I'm sorry, I have something to do first! I'll be back in a moment," I announced.

Waving the wand in front of me, unaware if I was accomplishing what I sought to perform, I vanished from the cave.

With a loud clap of thunder, I appeared in front of a campfire flanked by two simple tents. Vael'ehn sat on a piece of wood, a book in one hand, a warm beverage in the other. Unconcerned by my sudden and no doubt unexpected appearance, his eyes flickered upward in my direction for the briefest of moments. Closing the book, which vanished from his hand, he adjusted his legs, crossing the opposite knee.

"And whom might you proclaim to be?" he asked casually, as if a stranger appearing in front of him hadn't surprised him in the least.

I had been unsure of what I might find after making the decision to teleport to Vael'ehn's camp overlooking the long road. I had expected he would be slow to react - he always appeared unimpressed by those around him - but the simple fact that he sat in front of me, performing the exact action I had pictured, stunned me into inaction.

How good can my luck get?

Laurence, who is that?

You know who it is; it's Vael'ehn.

No... You didn't... Laurence, we have to leave!

He isn't going to hurt us, I promise. I've got this handled.

"I am a time traveler," I answered after a moment of deliberation.

"Oh?" Vael'ehn replied with mock surprise. "A traveler of time, you say? There appears to be a large quantity of those roaming around these days. And what has occurred through the time you have traversed that I should be graced by your sudden appearance within my camp?"

The response was smooth, effective, and immediately stripped me of any prestige I had attempted to build. His question, too, was meant to both belittle me and give him the upper hand - something I couldn't allow him to attain. Trying to remain calm, I sat down upon a piece of wood once used by Jack.

"You speak slowly and at length. For someone with such destructive power, I imagine that is a rare quality," I said, hoping the compliment would appease Vael'ehn while also alerting him to the fact that I knew who he truly was.

"Words are what set us apart from beasts," he replied. "Beware the man who refuses to sit and speak; he has gained little knowledge, and his choices will always reflect his ignorance."

"I, too, have gained much knowledge through the... *conversations* I have had," I replied, attempting to sound both wise and knowledgeable.

"You do not say," Vael'ehn countered while appearing to study my face. "I can not read your thoughts, time traveler," he concluded after a brief pause. "It is as though your body is an empty vessel with nothing inside it. I would wager even *I* could not guard my mind against others as you have."

Eyeing Ahso'lar, which I still held in my hand, Vael'ehn watched its two small blue gems orbit each other slowly as they levitated near its tip. After a moment, he smiled.

"I have not set my eyes upon that wand in quite some time. I knew Esmer'ee when she commanded its power. She fell while maintaining the great dome, as she was the most burdened by the task. It would seem you are a talented individual to have gained access to such a limitless Weapon, but you are not her, and you are not its owner. It appears to follow through with your commands, otherwise your intrusion would have proved impossible, but it has not bound itself to you. I question why that is."

It was a thought I hadn't even considered, but I chose to ignore its potential repercussions. Sliding the wand into my belt, I shook my head. "Who I am and what I have done before arriving here are not important questions. What I have seen is why I have come to speak with you before I continue on with my journey."

"Then *do* share," replied Vael'ehn, appearing bored with my equivocation. He continued to study me intently, no doubt trying to break through the spellwork which held his dark talents at bay.

He's going to find out who I am!

No, he's not. He's already admitted that he has no idea who we are, and he isn't lying. The spell my Coadju'tahr was created with is protecting us from being read. It was made with part of Varek's soul; his father has no power over me.

"I've come to discuss with you the reason your daughter was sent to the future."

Vael'ehn dropped his mug on the ground, causing it to shatter. The moment it impacted, it vanished, reappearing in his hand. The entire act happened so quickly, I couldn't help but wonder if it had occurred at all.

"*My daughter*," he whispered. "And what would *you* know of my daughter, *time traveler?*" His voice indicated suspicion, but something in his eyes told me another story - one of desperation. In an instant his probing had become more aggressive, turning into a palpable poking sensation as he frantically searched for answers.

*…He thinks there is a chance I may **be** her! But he isn't going to admit that to me, at least not yet.*

His daughter? Please don't act like you're Jillian. If he finds out, he'll murder us.

He's far too desperate to do that. He wants nothing more than to have her back in his arms.

"Her name is Vael'ora," I responded, much to Vael'ehn's surprise, "and she arrived far in the future - in *my* time - with a curious book at her side. It was entitled *Magic: Manipulation & Mastery,* and it once belonged to you. It even included a letter written *by* you. She was adopted by two innocent people who have lost their lives due to the meddling of a demon lord. His name is-"

"Roth'Roh'Kah," Vael'ehn whispered to himself, almost instinctually.

"Yes," I agreed. "The same Roth'Roh'Kah who destroyed the Forgotten Order."

The statement managed to further unhinge Vael'ehn's demeanor. Mouth wordlessly repeating the title, he focused intently on the ground, as if trying to recall something he couldn't quite remember.

"The Forgotten Order does not exist," he finally managed. "They are a myth and nothing more."

The tone of Vael'ehn's voice indicated he was repeating what was considered to be a widely-known fact, but his eyes revealed he was privy to at least some evidence proving otherwise.

"You were considered the best of their Order," I continued. "I was there when they turned against you. I watched as you were led out to meet your death. I witnessed you converse with Roth'Roh'Kah. I saw you succumb to his power, to his manipulation. I experienced the destruction of the Forgotten Order by your hand." It was a lie, of course; the story had been documented by Varek, but Vael'ehn didn't require that knowledge.

Vael'ehn leaned backward, his expression changing to that of his typical self again. I could nearly perceive the emotional walls he always kept around him reasserting themselves. "I did no such thing. You are creating a fantasy to-"

"You awoke on the ground," I interjected quickly, "completely unaware of what had happened. Everything around you had been obliterated, and you hadn't a clue what caused it. You had no idea where you were; no idea *who* you were."

Silenced by my statement, Vael'ehn continued to stare at me, his brain busily whirring, processing whether I was telling the truth or weaving a fantastical lie to manipulate him. I took the opportunity to continue before he could build a defense.

"You went on to inherit Kaldre'shen after your race left Xahl to track down the

Gor'tier. You decided to use it to restore your home world, but what you don't know is that your purpose - your very reason for doing everything you've done - has been implanted inside you by Roth'Roh'Kah to hide his true agenda. Long ago he tainted your father and, in turn, tainted you and your children. Roth'Roh'Kah has been playing you for a fool. You are a pawn to achieve his goals. He's trying to force his way into this world, and he's going to use you to do it."

Vael'ehn shook his head. "I would not allow any such manipulation to take place. Demons are nothing but mindless addicts, following a hunger they cannot assuage. It has been some time since talk of one having been summoned has even occurred. If what you say is true, I would have detected its taint inside myself long ago after gaining the power I now possess."

"You don't understand. You're incapable of doing so. You're following Roth'Roh'Kah's commands right now, and you don't even know it! You're manipulating Jack into further corrupting the sword - a sword that was ruined because of Roth'Roh'Kah himself! Cementing that corruption will prevent it from being used against him and allow demons easier access into this world. This is my *one* chance to reason with you before it is too late for all of us!"

"And what would you know of Jack? How were you made aware that I was waiting here for him? Did you speak with my son, Varek'ehn, before his end? Did *he* learn of this?"

"Varek tried his best to follow your instructions and, as a result, has died - possibly by Jack's hand," I lied. "You must believe what I'm telling you. Aid me in my quest. Aid me in preventing the demon invasion! Roth'Roh'Kah will never permit you to live. He'll never permit you to rebuild your home world. He will consume *everything*."

"I am supposed to accept the word of an enigma, someone I can not even scan to seek out the truth of their words?" Vael'ehn countered, showing no remorse at all for the passing of his son. "Why would I even bother *considering* such a course of action?"

"Because your daughter is still alive. There is still hope for not only her but for you as well. You may have thought your whole family was destroyed, but you're wrong."

Vael'ehn moved backward, as if my words had hit him with force. His eyes dampening, he uncharacteristically threw his cup over the ledge. Moments later, it made a small detonation far below.

"You are lying, time traveler! My daughter is *gone!* She was taken from me, as was my companion, *as was my sword!*"

"She is *very* much alive," I countered as calmly as I could, doing my best not to further aggravate such a powerful man. "Search yourself. You know it is true. Why else would you have sent your son to this time to prevent you from further falling into darkness?"

Risking everything, I decided to divulge more information only Vael'ehn would be aware of.

"Your wife's death, it was the second time you awoke surrounded by bones. Your children were gone, your shoulder was wounded, and you could not understand what had happened."

Vael'ehn's eyes widened, and he began to tremble. Slowly he reached up and touched his shoulder where the arrow had hit him.

"Vael'ehn, *you* sent your daughter through time using a Magical arrow. It was you, under the influence of Roth'Roh'Kah, who killed your wife."

Startling me, Vael'ehn exploded into a terrible eruption of nonsensical screams. "Lohn'Fallah, flight through the ages!" he yelled, shaking violently and rocking his head between his shoulders. "My daughter was sent on a flight through the ages! My daughter was sent on a flight through the ages!"

Vael'ehn's convulsing continued to increase, and he appeared to be on the verge of a seizure, but I dared not stop.

"He took everything from you! He stole your family! He forced you to kill your own wife!" I leaned forward, catching his precarious gaze for a moment. "Fight what is inside you… *Vael'curion.*"

His eyes rolling back into his head, Vael'ehn continued to yell incoherently. Shaking his head back and forth as if to clear it, he repeatedly winced and blinked his eyes, his face alternating between furious and frantic expressions. It appeared as if the thoughts of his daughter and wife had started an internal battle, the two halves of him waging war for control of his faculties.

"That's it, Vael'curion! Listen to me. You know I'm right. Fight what's inside you!"

You're pushing him too far! He's going to lose his rationality!

No, I have him right where I want him. He's going to change back into who he should be. He's going to remember what has happened and either join our side or die trying.

"And what would you have me do!" Vael'ehn yelled, his head unexpectedly snapping forward, the action again causing me to jump.

Nearly losing his sanity, he was in no way exhibiting the behavior of the calm, calculating man I had come to know. Sweat poured down his face, and the very air around him appeared to ripple with potent energy. He seemed on the verge of either passing out or detonating in an explosion of Magic.

Trying to think as logically and quickly as I could, I told him what I hoped to achieve by arriving there. "I require something of you. You have no choice but to provide me with answers to three questions before I leave you be."

Tensing and untensing his hands, Vael'ehn rocked back and forth, as if he were fighting a great mental sickness. Looking around wildly, he gritted his teeth. "I have… no… choice?"

"No, it is required of you."

"Make… make your demands… and then… and then… be… *be gone from this place!*"

Giving him no time to recover, lest I lose the upper hand, I continued. "First, I require knowledge of the dragon statues under the abandoned city of Empor'Vael. Why are two of them already broken?"

Vael'ehn, some of his composure returning, stopped rocking back and forth. Tilting his head to the side, he eyed me with uncertainty. Sweat continuing to drip from his nose, all his pretense and posturing had vanished; he was clearly exhausted from the mental anguish I had caused him. His eyes remained wild, but the change of topic seemed to have given him a reprieve. Whether or not that had been a mistake on my part had yet to be seen.

"Two? Would… would you be referring to the Droth'gon'ai? Why would you demand such common knowledge when I have mastered all there is to learn on this planet?"

Assuming he was referring to the same creatures I had, I nodded. "It is important that I be informed of the Droth'gon'ai's fate. I am not privy to the information you have. Two of them have been destroyed, and I suspect it may have something to do with demons. The statues' destruction had grave repercussions for us in the future. I need to learn more to verify my suspicions."

Vael'ehn stared into the fire, his breathing ragged. Repeatedly wiping his face, he seemed to deliberate within himself. *"Two?* Yes… yes, of course," he whispered.

Sternly he regarded me. "If I answer your questions three, you will answer one of my own. If your answer is negative, you will return to your time and refrain from meddling in matters you do not understand. Otherwise, you will be destroyed. Do you agree to these terms?"

You know what he's going to ask, and he's going to kill us when you say No.

He won't kill us. I have answers that will prevent him from harming us in any way.

Watching me nod in affirmation, Vael'ehn began to speak. "The Droth'gon'ai were, as far as the Xahl'thari are aware, the first intelligent race to comprehend the use of Magic. There were countless other races who could use Magic, of course, but the Droth'gon'ai were the greatest. Their race spanned the universe, inhabited thousands of planets, and watched over all who were lesser than they.

"Although immortal and omnipotent, the Droth'gon'ai were not heartless. They watched the suffering of beings who could not use Magic. In time they chose to give up part of their power to aid those lesser races with their existence. On many planets, the Droth'gon'ai imbued special statues, replicas of themselves, with pieces of their souls. The statues allowed the races who lived on those planets the ability to interface with Magic, granting them abilities far beyond anything they could have dreamt. Even those who could already use Magic found their talents greatly enhanced by the Droth'gon'ai's sacrifice.

"However, the statues' creation weakened the Droth'gon'ai far more than they expected, gradually removing their immortal traits entirely, until they were nothing but feeble shadows of themselves, struggling to survive with hardly any Magical abilities of their own. All that is left of the Droth'gon'ai race today are a few planets still blessed with the statues they left behind."

"Thank you for explaining their history, but I was already aware of that," I lied. "You are required to tell me how two of the statues were broken. Was it demons who destroyed them?"

Vael'ehn shook his head and laughed, the sound giving me chills. "No, time traveler, I did. As I said, there are no demons here. The act of destroying the statues should not have been possible for me, but Mor'dresh had grown far too great for their defenses. They fell without much effort on my part.

"You see, when those who oppose me learn of my intent, they will become desperate. They will seek out actions which might be deemed unthinkable. If I were in their place, I would allow the other Xahl'thari heroes to be brought back to life to stop me - an action they could certainly have made possible.

"I was not willing to allow such an action to take place, so I made the ultimate sacrifice. I destroyed the two statues I knew would prevent such an action: the statue of Xhor'thre'vzerious, which upholds Life Magic, and the statue of... of..."

The Gray dragon also mentioned Yvehn'sul'xahvon.

Who is that?

A missing dragon, apparently.

Vael'ehn paused for a moment, as if becoming confused. Searching around with his eyes, he appeared to have genuinely forgotten something he had once been well acquainted with.

"Of… its name does not matter. My lack of knowledge only proves what I sought to accomplish has finally taken effect."

Varek said Vael'ehn didn't realize how willing others would be to sacrifice everything they have. He's destroyed two of the statues because he believes his enemies may become desperate, but he doesn't realize what lengths they'll go to.

Are you insinuating other people somehow sacrifice the remaining statues to defeat Vael'ehn?

That's precisely what Wenton said they did during a final confrontation with Vael'ehn. However, if we can convince him to stop here and now, not only will the statues remain but the sword won't be lost.

I hope you're correct. Just be careful.

"That doesn't make sense. Life Magic hasn't been destroyed; there are plenty of people who I've seen use it. And…" I paused, realizing Vael'ehn had lost access to Magical knowledge I could still recall. "And… there is no other type of Magic," I lied. "It doesn't-"

Vael'ehn laughed darkly. "It does not *what?* Does not exist? It is a work of fiction I have just created? Tell me, how many forms of Magic have you been told there are. Five, six, seven? The people you meet seem confused by the topic, do they not? It is as if they are all forgetting - forgetting how to interface with Magic they have used for their entire lives, forgetting it even exists.

"You may *think* you have seen many people using Life Magic, but I suspect it is quite the opposite. You may have seen one or two, no doubt the most attuned to its use. Most who see Life Magic are awed by it, completely unaware of how potent it can be, but I tell you the truth: not long ago, its use was far more prevalent. It was utilized just as often as every other school of Magic. That is no longer the case. The denizens of this planet will soon forget that it exists. Life Magic will disappear, just as the seventh type of Magic already has."

Vael'ehn grinned, as if the idea had been a practical joke played upon everyone. "If even *I* can not remember its purpose, then all others are lost! I would not have suspected it would disappear so soon. I would have forgotten I had destroyed a second statue, had *you* not shown up!"

"And that doesn't terrify you - losing something you've always depended upon?"

Vael'ehn snorted. "As if our race was somehow entitled to the use of Magic in the first place?" He shook his head. "The Xahl'thari. We have had access to sets of those statues all our lives, both on this planet and the last. Even before traveling through the stars, we chose to channel their power into great crystalline devices to power our ships and make sure we would not go without access to our eternal crutch.

"We simply could not imagine living without them. Our culture has never been encouraged to learn of Magic in its natural state. We only began to evolve and develop occasional offspring with the proper connections after being exposed to Magic for countless years. When left to our own devices, our race is really quite pitiful - pitiful and lazy."

Startled by the revelation, I stood up. "So you just thought you would take it upon yourself to destroy the statues, then!" I yelled, throwing my hands in the air. "Just as our race had begun to *truly* connect with Magic, you've decided to destroy it because you don't feel we *deserve* it? How are we going to rebuild those connections? They'll never come back now! What kind of lesson is that going to teach anyone?"

The fury behind my exclamation was mostly muted by Rhen's timid voice.

Don't anger him by making him think you believe he is foolish!

Think of who you're yelling at right now.

It doesn't matter what I say. He isn't the type to embrace anger when it would undermine his goals. He can't risk having his question go unanswered.

Vael'ehn, appearing to recover his typical attitude, waved his hand back and forth, as if my proclamation were a fly buzzing around his head. "Oh, do not be so dramatic; I did no such thing. Magic, as a whole, is impossible to destroy. Once I gather the strength, those who follow me back to Xahl will immediately regain their abilities *and* their knowledge, as if it had never vanished.

"I simply removed the interface most of the Xahl'thari use to access it *here*. Those who have heard about the missing types of Magic will forget, then those who have seen them will forget, then those who have used them, and finally those who are well-attuned to them. I must say, everything is going according to plan, and far quicker than I anticipated."

"That's my point. Your plans fail; you don't make it back to Xahl. In essence, you *have* destroyed Magic for all of us. Even worse, what you *do* accomplish will make it easier for the demons when they arrive!"

"Yes, you keep mentioning that, but I see no demons here, nor do my plans include them," Vael'ehn stated, motioning around the campsite. "Where are your demons, time traveler? In your journeys have you seen a portal with demons pouring through it that I should be made aware of?"

"I've seen many attempts. *You* do not summon them yourself. You never even see their coming. To me it seems your part is to corrupt the sword and cause global problems that lead to the loss of our statues so we have no tools at our disposal to use against Roth'Roh'Kah once he makes his way through. In the future, almost no one knows what Magic is. All typical humans, as far as I am aware, seem to think it's a fairytale. We become weak and helpless, and it's all because of the damage you cause. We're lucky a few hidden people still exist who can interface with Magic, otherwise there would be no one to remember it at all!"

"Yes, it is a shame I am incapable of ridding myself of the others who use Wild

Magic, no matter my course of action," Vael'ehn replied, seeming disgruntled. He appeared to have ignored my comment altogether, thinking about his current plans instead.

"*Wild* Magic?" I inquired. "I've never heard of that. Is that yet another Magic you've tried to destroy?"

Vael'ehn scoffed at the notion. "Of course you have heard of Wild Magic; we have been discussing it since you arrived. For one who travels through time, you know significantly less than you should."

"Once again, that only proves my point: our race is in danger," I said, appearing more irritated by his ignorance than I should have let on.

Seeing he was frustrating me, Vael'ehn grinned. "Wild Magic is the term some use to describe unsegmented, natural Magic. It is what the most powerful Xahl'thari connect to from birth. Irritatingly, it is also what insufferable creatures such as Gnill'var use. Wild Magic, however, is far less potent than Magic bolstered by the statues, and therefore of little concern to me."

So that's what Wenton meant when he said certain people and races could use Magic innately, and that's what people keep referring to as a different form of Magic.

It's not specifically a different form. It's more like a dim, blurry rainbow. Some beings see the whole thing at once, and they always have, but it's not nearly as strong. The Droth'gon'ai created individual schools and enhanced everyone's tie to each type. Almost all of our race are incapable of dealing with it at all without the aid of the statues.

And that's why no one can access it in the future.

But what about Jillian? She could use it, couldn't she?

Well, yes. Jillian most certainly was tapping into Wild Magic. Wenton once said that Jack and she had the ties they needed. But it was revealed that they were both descended from powerful Xahl'thari. Varek indicated I had those abilities as well, which begs the question of who my ancestors were, but I'll probably never find out. And if I had to guess, based on your abilities, I'd say you're also descended from someone important.

Me? Oh, I don't think so. I don't use Magic for much of anything now, and-

But you remember Magic involving Souls, don't you?

Well of course. But until now I would have said it's not one of the six types of Magic enhanced by the Droth'gon'ai; it's just part of Wild Magic. After what you've been discussing, though, it's...

*It's as if the statue dealing with Soul Magic has been destroyed, and now you're leaning on Wild Magic to remember how to interface with the Soul aspect. And Life Magic won't be far behind. Our friend Vael'ehn here remembers less than you do, so his predicament should tell you what potential **you** have. Don't discount your abilities.*

Thank you for having faith in me, but I think you might have missed something.

What do you mean?

You said Jillian was descended from people who can use Wild Magic innately. I was attempting to point out the fact that Vael'ehn has completely forgotten part of it. A person wouldn't forget the basics of Magic if they were attuned to Wild Magic; they would only forget the parts that were amplified. But to Vael'ehn, it's as if the aspect he destroyed doesn't exist in _any_ form, Wild or otherwise.

The realization of Rehn's observation hit me like a projectile fired from a cannon, forcing me to recall Wenton's words.

"...those who cannot innately use Magic - in this case, humans - are most likely to be corrupted by dark Magic. Beings who use Magic innately do not feel ties to that sort of power; it sickens them."

Yet Jillian is bent on fighting what is inside her. So was Varek.

Varek and Jillian's mother was Demel'sa. That must be why.

Demel'sa was their mother! But that was so long ago. I don't think anyone knows of Varek's true origin. I think he claimed to have been birthed from a different woman Vael'ehn joined with. I suppose it doesn't matter now that he's gone.

I think Vael'ehn would have hidden that fact to keep Varek away from Roth'Roh'Kah after sending him through time. It was one of the details I learned through visions which convinced me he isn't truly evil.

Evil or not, he's still dangerous, Laurence.

But more importantly, you've proven to me that he isn't attuned to Wild Magic. He assumes he has those connections because he's incredibly powerful and he's never lived without them, but he's wrong. He made a mistake, and he's weakened himself far more than he intended. He's given us an advantage as long as our forces keep ties to the schools of Magic he has forgotten!

Seeing my lack of response, Vael'ehn cocked an eyebrow. "You are clearly struggling. Listen to the words I am telling you. What you have come here to prevent is no longer relevant; the other statues will not be destroyed on account of my efforts. I had no use for the lost aspects of Magic at this time, but destroying the rest would sever all but my own basic ties to them, allowing me to become vulnerable and incapable of achieving my goals. If you truly *have* come from a future where your race can not access the statues' power, it is illogical to assume it still exists in that context. You are one of the only survivors from a lost age."

I honestly don't think he's going to destroy the statues.

*It doesn't matter if he destroys them or not; it's still his fault, and that is Roth'Roh'Kah's plan. Let's say we **do** turn the statues into a giant bomb to kill Vael'ehn. We've still lost them because of what he did. It's the same effect.*

"That's not the point," I replied. "You're going to keep working toward your goal, leaving you vulnerable to anything you can't conceive of happening. You think you've anticipated everything, but I can assure you, you haven't. How did you feel when that crystal showed up with Jack? A little unnerving, wasn't it?"

Vael'ehn frowned. "Am I to understand *you* were its creator?"

I shook my head. "It's an impressive creation, but I have not found the one who designed it. I am simply a time traveler, trying to protect the future - one who has seen far more than you believe I have. My point is, any number of unexpected occurrences or tragedies could take place between now and then, and that was one of them. For all you know, you-"

Don't tell him he dies after all of this!

I know, I know. I'm trying to convince him that his plans are meant to fail, but he appears almost incapable of listening to what I say.

Have you considered that might be an intentional blockage created by Roth'Roh'Kah? You're not going to convince Vael'ehn by speculating. You and I don't have all the answers. We gave him a lot to think about. Maybe we should leave before anything bad happens.

Not until I get what I want.

Vael'ehn sighed, again becoming bored with a conversation he clearly thought was pointless. "*All I know*, is that you have arrived uninvited, accused me of creating a future that will never take place, and demanded I stop what I am doing. You have somehow gained a *considerable* amount of knowledge about me which, I will admit, *is* quite impressive, but there are large errors in what you have proposed.

"If I succeed, why will there be a future for you to travel back to? You are clearly aware I intend to use everything this planet offers for my own machinations. When I am done, it will have given itself for the rebirth of Xahl. I am not ignorant, as you seem to believe; you have all but told me my death is imminent.

"What you have failed to consider is that I have already seen portents of that death and have taken steps to make sure *your* future does not come to pass. Even this conversation has served to aid me in my success. I believe your concern to be legitimate, at least in part, but it is misplaced.

"Furthermore, if your so-called demon invasion occurs, why has it taken so long for them to make their assault? Why are you still alive? Who defended against their *many attempts* in the near-countless years leading up to your time if no one can access Magic? Surely an ignorant, helpless people would have been crushed without any resistance at all. Even *one* demon would wreak havoc among them. Did they pause to wait for a fair fight? I think not.

"Your tale speaks of some unproductive, sterile middle-ground, where catastrophes loom yet nothing happens. I think it far more likely that you are ignorant to many other events which have taken place, and you are jumping to conclusions, as one who is largely ignorant of their history might very well do.

"That being said, what has or has not happened no longer matters. Say I died. Say the demons invaded. Say the statues were lost. Say any number of situations took place. Knowledge of those events is akin to knowledge of nothing. What you perceive as a tragedy no longer exists. I am already rewriting time to suit my machinations."

Vael'ehn rose to his feet and stretched his fingers.

"I am afraid I have accommodated you long enough. It is time that you answer my question once and for all."

"No! You promised me two more answers first, and I *will* have them! I assure you, what I have to say will be well worth the wait."

"Did I?" Vael'ehn asked, clearly annoyed by my persistence - annoyed but also curious. "And if I am so inclined to humor you further, what questions would you have me answer?"

See, he won't push me.

He's only going to let you go so far.

"I've learned much about Archaeus trees since my arrival. You might even say I've gone so far as to hear one speak. Were they once a race of people - sentient people, like you and I? And if not, did you ever turn a person into one?"

Vael'ehn permitted himself a smile. "You have heard one *speak*, have you! I must admit, I was intrigued by you at first, but these questions have become quite strange indeed."

I ignored his insult. "So when you turned Jack's arm into a tree, that was something you had never tried before?"

In an instant Vael'ehn regained his serious composure. "Again, you have knowledge you should not have access to." He seemed to consider what that might mean. "It appears you *have* traveled through much of this time, but how you have gathered such information without my knowledge is a question I would very much like to learn."

Fearing the odd purple crystal following him around might prove to be an obvious source for my knowledge, I offered him a solution I knew he would be more than willing to accept.

"Let us just say that a certain brilliant invention from this time period is unearthed far, far in the future. It was a mystery to all until a certain woman learned how to operate its *considerable* number of cranks and levers. Now, *did you* or *didn't you* try that spellwork on someone else?"

Vael'ehn's eyes crinkled as he bit down on the bait I had provided him. "My Temploscope," he whispered, the corners of his mouth turning upward. Disarmed by the knowledge that I had both appreciated and used his own invention to gain my information, he continued on. "No, to my knowledge that was the first time such an action had taken place. Archaeus trees have always been as you see them, and they most certainly do *not* speak."

"And if Jack were to be damaged enough that his whole body was taken over by the tree limb, would he survive?"

Vael'ehn sighed. "I do not have time to answer hypothetical questions regarding events that have not taken place. What is the purpose of this questioning? Are you alleging that Jack, in fact, *did* grow into an Archaeus tree at some point in the future - one who speaks with you?"

I'd like to know that, too. What are you trying to learn?

I've seen several visions of the future with a tree man in them. I want to verify his identity. It could have been entirely possible that Vael'ehn transformed someone else into an Archaeus tree before we arrived. If that were the case, I needed to learn where we could find him. He is one of the last people I meet before an important battle with a demon takes place.

But it sounds as if Vael'ehn didn't do that.

Correct, Vael'ehn doesn't seem to have any knowledge regarding a person matching that description, which means the tree man could very well be Jack himself - that is, a potential version of him, anyway. Once we have altered the future, I don't think Jack will make that transition. I might be searching for useless information. Even so, Vael'ehn's answer has saved us time.

Seeing that I had again refrained from answering him, Vael'ehn rolled his eyes. "That is all I have to give you on the topic. Provide me your last question so we can end this."

It was clear I had no choice. My last question was the most important, but I had put it off until the end, as I knew it had some risk involved in the asking of it.

"Varek stole two books from Wenton's laboratory when he was fulfilling the mission you sent him on. You have them *both* in your tent."

Why did you just tell him that!

I have no ability to access his tent without him catching me. It's now or never.

If the books' existence was news to Vael'ehn, he showed no signs of it. Instead, the information had finally allowed him to piece together a part I had played in his past.

"*You!*" he exclaimed. "*You* were the one who snuck into my tent and rifled through my tomes!"

Reaching out, he appeared ready to choke me. His reaction was terrifying, but I forced myself to remain still. Any signs of fear would have given him the upper hand, showing that I was far weaker than he might have suspected.

The decision proved to be wise. Seeing my lack of receptivity to his threat caused Vael'ehn to pause. Calming himself, he continued on instead.

"And just what would you use such tomes for?"

You're aggravating him, Laurence. And now you're providing him with too much information. We need to leave, now!

Just a little longer. This is a good thing. He now believes a human was the one rifling through his tent instead of the Coadju'tahr. For all we know, that may allow that version of me a second chance to slip by his defenses when his wards are searching for you.

That doesn't exactly make me feel better.

"Yes, it *was* me," I replied. "I require them to heal someone who needs their power. I would have given them back when I was done."

Vael'ehn scoffed at the idea. "Do not lie. You would not bring back what you did not ask to take in the first place. You have made your intentions clear: you would subvert my goals by restoring the woman Jack seeks to heal and, in doing so, remove his determination to proceed by my side. I can not let that happen. I will not hand over the tomes you desire, and would strongly recommend you do not attempt to gain them through other means.

"Even if I agreed with your demand, you are too late. Your ignorance has betrayed you again. I destroyed the statues years ago. Nearly all tomes on this planet with information pertaining to Droth'gon'ai Life Magic have become illegible. They would serve no purpose to you. Her condition can not be corrected."

So that's the fate of tomes containing secrets to Soul and Life Magic; they become illegible. The ones I couldn't interpret must have contained those secrets. Even I am incapable of reading them!

But then, how would those two have been legible in the future?

I... I don't know. You have a point.

Is it possible they contained only spells a user of Wild Magic would have created, or spells written before the Droth'gon'ai enhanced Magic?

That actually makes sense. I think you might be onto something.

If that were the case though, Vael'ehn would know that. He may be trying to dissuade me from going after them by convincing me they're useless.

I chose to go along with his ruse.

"I *do* intend to restore her. The books may be useless, but I promised to correct her condition long ago, and I will not go back on my word. Your actions will not dissuade me from eventually finding a way to do so."

Vael'ehn raised his eyebrows. "So all pretense is gone. You openly admit that you are willing to get in my way. Would you have me save this woman myself? Are you so bold that you would attempt to force my hand in the matter?"

"No. What I *would* ask, is that you stop what you are doing. Let the sword go, abandon your decision to bleed this planet dry, and fight by my side. What I have told you is true; the demon threat exists, even if you *have* altered the future."

"At *your* side," Vael'ehn responded sarcastically, laughing to himself. "You must be a powerful conqueror indeed for me to accompany *you* into battle. Tell me, if I were to decline your invitation, decline to come with you and fight, *what then?* Would you attack me?"

"Of course not," I replied, denying his attempts to bait me into a fight.

Making a show of inspecting him with powers I did not have, I met his dangerous eyes. "I believe you'd best me in a duel. However, that is not my intent, even if I *did* prove capable of standing toe to toe with you. I've come to recruit you or leave.

I know full well the only reason you have listened to me this long is due to your curiosity. I have seen how much you enjoy collecting secrets."

Vael'ehn extended a hand. "Then you must also comprehend by now, I believe your requests serve none of my purposes."

Time to play my trump card.

"They serve *one* of them."

Raising his brow, Vael'ehn seemed to consider my statement. Studying me, he pursed his lips. "You promised me you would answer my own question once I answered three of yours, and I have done *far* more than that." I nodded, allowing him to continue. "You have located me from far in the future; you were capable of using my Temploscope; you are even capable of preventing me from accessing your mind. Only my own blood could perform actions such as those.

"I had thought it a flight of fantasy when you first appeared, but I return to the question over and over within my mind. You owe me an answer, and I will ask it now. Is that *you*, Vael'ora? Have you come back to me? Have I become so evil in your eyes, that you are testing my intentions before revealing yourself?" Vael'ehn's eyes appeared desperate, almost pleading for confirmation of his wishes.

Don't lie to him, Laurence; he'll be able to tell. Please don't risk it. You may be invincible in your shell, but you're doing this with my body. Please, Laurence!

I wouldn't dare to impersonate Jillian.

"No. I am not your daughter, but I *have* spent considerable time with her, and she has been a great aid in my quest. She is both alive *and* aware you exist. I have the power to reunite you, or I can choose to separate you both forever."

Seeing surprise, pain and, somehow, *hope* swell in Vael'ehn's eyes, I knew I had planted a seed within the man's heart. Whether or not it would take root or be crushed under the might of his demonic genes was another matter entirely, but it was one I could not verify until the future had come to pass.

Backing away a few feet, I pulled Ahso'lar from my belt. "Think about what I have told you, Vael'ehn. Consider the harm you are about to cause, and seek out the hidden forces that have influenced you to follow this path. When you see me again - and you *will* see me again - I wish for it to be as friends rather than foes."

Vael'ehn clenched and unclenched his hands, his expression flashing between anticipation and dissatisfaction. I had delivered my message, I had gained what I could, and I had provided a broken, manipulated man with something positive to reach for. But I had also pushed him to his breaking point; it was time to leave.

Waving the wand before me, I vanished from his sight.

With another clap of thunder, we reappeared in front of Jillian and Dreyl'vyn, inside the cave. The wand was far more powerful than I expected it to be; I felt no mental drain at all when using it.

"Where did you go!" Jillian demanded after leaping backward from the startling noise. "I was beginning to wonder if you'd gone crazy and left us forever!"

"So you *do* care about me?" I teased, smiling at her.

Jillian frowned. "More like, I'd rather not be stuck on this island forever with Dreyl'vyn." She waved a flippant hand at Dreyl'vyn. "No offense."

Dreyl'vyn shook his head. "I have been told many times I make for poor conversation."

Jillian flashed me a stern look. "You know, being on a team requires cooperation. If you're just going to head off on your own and leave us behind without considering our input, you should probably do so permanently."

"If you knew where I've been, you'd have stopped me before I left."

Crossing her arms, Jillian seemed perturbed by my remark. "Well, now that you're back, please, enlighten me."

"I went to visit your father, Vael'ehn."

"You *what!*" Jillian exploded. "You went to talk with Vael'ehn! You just risked everything we've done to have a good ol' chat with him? How on earth did you manage to escape with *your* life, let alone Rhen's! I can't believe you'd be so foolish!"

"Because he suspected I was you the entire time," I replied with a smirk. "Don't you see? My Coadju'tahr was made using Varek's Magic. Don't forget, that was what has protected me from Vael'ehn's power this whole time. It thoroughly confused him, and he may still believe I'm you, even after telling him otherwise. I knew it would buy me enough time to plant some seeds of doubt in his mind and learn a great deal of information."

"So you went there to make him feel guilty about his decisions, then?" Jillian concluded, giving me a strange look. "A man massacres who knows how many people without feeling the least bit guilty, and you're going to seek him out and have a heart-to-heart. *Brilliant...*" She rolled her eyes.

Putting my hands on my hips, I shook my head; she clearly didn't understand. "I went there to tell him the truth. Like it or not, you're *both* victims of Roth'Roh'Kah. He just happens to be far more dangerous. If we're going to proceed in attempting to wipe Vael'ehn off the face of the earth, I'd at least like him to know why. I wanted him to know the truth about what happened and give him a chance to end his madness before we were forced to do it for him. And now he has that knowledge."

"And?" Jillian asked, raising her eyebrows. "Is he off changing out of his supervillain outfit?"

"No, but he seemed far more intrigued by me than I expected, and he appeared quite conflicted. If we have to confront him face to face, it could have only helped our cause. *And*," I eyed Jillian carefully, "he is now aware his daughter is still alive, but he hasn't been told *you* are her."

Jillian frowned and shook her head. "No, you lied to him. His daughter died a long time ago."

Understanding her sentiment, I nodded and looked out at the ocean. "Yes, I'm sure you don't want to explore that road any time soon, but that knowledge could make him change his ways; keep that in mind. Should we confront him - and we eventually will - the revelation of your true identity might make him pause or drop his defenses. Even a few moments of uncertainly might be enough to turn the tides of battle."

Jillian nodded, but said nothing; she was clearly overwhelmed by the idea of facing her estranged father. Having no intention of upsetting her, I changed the subject.

"I also managed to glean some odd information from him. Those dragon statues we found, they were made by a race of creatures called, uh…"

Droth'gon'ai

Thank you.

"Droth'gon'ai."

"I know of that race," Dreyl'vyn responded. "They once spanned the stars. The Cimmerians have heard their call before but we did not respond. They are gone. Their communications faded before I was forced into this body. How many years of your time that might have been, I cannot say."

"It would have been a long time ago," I considered, watching Jillian reflect on the idea that Dreyl'vyn may have once drifted among the stars. "But that topic also brought up a valid point regarding our future and the demonic threat. Vael'ehn said I was describing some middle ground where *catastrophes loomed but nothing happened*. If he died, the sword was gone, and the Droth'gon'ai statues were destroyed, leaving us near-useless, how were we somehow safe from demons for billions of years?

"He pointed out that even *one* demon could have ruined our world, and he's probably right. The demons consume Magic from anything they can, and we would have been easy targets. If any had made it through a portal in the time we come from, they would have gained enough power to bring the rest through immediately, but that didn't happen."

"Well, there *are* still people like Wenton in the future who have access to Magic," Jillian surmised. "Perhaps they stop the threats, like the Forgotten Order once did on Xahl."

"That may be true, but there are *far* fewer people with a tie to Magic in the future, and they're working with what Vael'ehn called *Wild Magic*. It's a more basic, natural version of what people have access to here. Everyone seems to be in agreement that it's weaker than what the Droth'gon'ai imbued our world with. And if that *is* the case, I can't see it as being enough to hold them at bay. Not to mention, Wenton didn't seem to have been informed of any demon threats, vanquished or otherwise.

"No, without the statues-" I paused, an idea occurring to me. "You know what I just realized? What specific set of relics would draw demons *here* instead of a million other planets with billions of other lifeforms to consume?"

"*Oh*, I don't know," Jillian said sarcastically. "I suppose the statues might be a tempting target."

"Right!" I exclaimed. "Those statues could act like a beacon to their race! Everything is made of Magic, but souls are *far* more potent, and that's what the statues are made from - portions of Droth'gon'ai souls. For us it's probably the difference between eating dandelions and doughnuts. Both are edible, but you know which one you'd choose if you had the choice."

Jillian made an odd expression, turning her face toward the ground. Her mind had likely presented the idea of consuming souls herself, which made her uncomfortable. Unfortunately, it was a topic that needed to be discussed, so I continued anyway.

"The statues must be the reason Roth'Roh'Kah is so intent on reaching us; there aren't many sets floating around in this universe. For all we know, he could have broken through and consumed the set on Xahl after our ancestors left. Can you imagine Vael'ehn's face if he were to make it back and find them missing?" Jillian smiled mirthlessly. "But even if the demons have been successful everywhere else, Roth'Roh'Kah won't stop until he consumes this set as well."

"But we know they're sacrificed to get rid of Vael'ehn," Jillian added.

"Correct. See, I think the demonic invasion Varek is referencing never happened. Unfortunately, in the future he was intent on creating, the invasion will be *caused* by his changes. He found out about his father's past and was determined to stop Roth'Roh'Kah, but using the sword against Vael'ehn stops the statues from being destroyed. It essentially ensures that beacon is always lit, tempting the demons to invade Earth. We gain a weapon, but we also call forth an enemy.

"And that means we have a choice. We can prevent the demons from showing up, and we can do so quite easily since Varek is gone - well, easily once Vael'ehn has been dealt with, anyway. We could use the sword to stop him and *also* destroy the statues, accepting their loss as our fate. It would be a way to ensure a safe future for our race." Jillian's face scrunched up distastefully. "*Or* we use the sword to stop Vael'ehn and then determine how best to kill Roth'Roh'Kah with it, allowing us to keep the statues *and* save a ton of other worlds in the process. In that case, two questions are left: when will he make another attempt, and what should we do to prepare ourselves for when he does?"

"Wow," Jillian replied, seeming to comprehend my revelation. "But what about the two statues which have already been broken? The Xahl'thari obviously didn't break those, right?"

"Vael'ehn destroyed them, believe it or not. He said they should have been impervious to damage, but Mor'dresh had gotten powerful enough to do so. He even laughed about it. He viewed them as a threat. He suspected his enemies might bring the other Xahl'thari heroes back to life to fight him, which does sound plausible, if not distasteful."

I don't think the Xahl'thari would actually do that, though.

Nor do I. But it's something he'd entertain, so he considered it a possible threat.

"The Turquoise statue is Life Magic, and it's far less prevalent than it used to be. Given time, it's going to fade from knowledge completely. Even worse, the Purple one is proof of that concept. What I'm just going to call 'Soul Magic' appears to have completely vanished. Even Vael'ehn has forgotten, and he's the person who destroyed the statues! It must not have been used as much, or maybe it was harder to learn, but it's gone now."

Jillian sighed. "That sounds so counterintuitive. Everyone will be *forced* to forget knowledge they already know? What a stupid thing to deal with."

"Yes, it's terrible to think about, but that is our future in a nutshell. You and I won't forget about them entirely, but most everyone else will, if they haven't already. The best we can hope for is preserving the five we still have."

"Do you think you can access the forgotten Magic - since they'd still be included in Wild Magic - and bring back a bunch of people to help us fight Vael'ehn, just like he feared?"

Would she really consider such a thing?

Well, for Jillian it's probably not as strange. From her perspective she'd rather be alive than dead.

But Vael'ehn believed destroying those statues would make him safe, and he did so before he lost the knowledge of what they really meant. That means we must have no chance of doing so with Wild Magic alone.

The only way I could ever see us getting those abilities back at full strength would be to head to Xahl and bring the matching statues here, which is impossible.

I shook my head. "If you think I can use Soul Magic, you're giving me *far* too much credit; I wouldn't even know where to start. And I hate to admit it, but none of the 'lesser races' seem to have a perfect link to Magic like the Droth'gon'ai had. Without their help, those damaged schools of Magic are always going to be lacking. I doubt even the Gnill'var can bring back someone who's been dead for thousands of years."

"Well, which ones are left, then?" Jillian inquired. "Do the statues we saw under the ruins match the five in the future? I didn't get to see the dragon heads when they came to life."

Pausing for a moment to think back upon the colors, I began to guess.

"Yes, the colors of the statues *did* match. We know Blue is Arcane," I said, waggling Ahso'lar around. "A Magical arrow I saw in a vision, which seemed to manipulate time, was Grey, leading me to believe it represents Intellectual Magic. Out of the remaining three, I'm going to guess Brown and Gold-"

Grey is Intellectual as you said. Brown and Gold are as they appear: Elemental and Light.

"Rhen says Brown and Gold are Elemental and Light."

That means Red is Force Magic, right?

Yes, you're correct.

How do you know all of that?

I don't mean to make you feel stupid, but just about everyone does. Had you asked, anyone could have told you.

It's probably like learning primary colors from our time, hmm?

Yes, similar, but some of those aren't primary colors, Laurence.

Laughter filled my mind; Rhen was clearly making light of my ignorance.

"So Red is what?" Jillian asked, pulling me away from Rhen's jab. "And where are the Black and Green statues for Shadow Magic and Demonic Magic?"

"Red would be Force Magic. Unfortunately, Shadow and Demonic Magic shouldn't exist. They weren't brought here by the dragons, and they don't have statues we can break to make them go away. They're a sort of Magical corruption, like a cancer."

"Well, how do we get rid of them, then?"

"We eradicate the carriers like we would with an incurable plague," Dreyl'vyn interjected. "The corrupted schools of Magic will not be a threat if those who use them have been killed. If we succeed in that objective, we will not have to protect the other five from destruction."

"I don't think it's quite that easy," Jillian responded, patting Dreyl'vyn on the arm.

"No, it's not," I agreed, "but it *is* possible. We have to consider that objective as the purpose of our journey - defeating our threats while also keeping Magic intact. Now that we've located the statues, we have the opportunity to rewrite our future and bring Magic back for everyone."

"But, is that what we want? For *everyone* to have it? Is that safe?"

"No matter what, there will always be horrible people, if that's what you're referring to. Whether it's bombs or curses, it doesn't matter. The Droth'gon'ai gave their lives to provide us with Magic - it was *that* important to them. And I don't feel like making sure our planet continues on as a barren, non-Magical wasteland is wise when there are other planets, other civilizations, out there with statues of their own."

I can't imagine such a reality even existing. Life must be so sad where you come from.

Some might disagree, but I'm with you. I used to be very sad, and my life felt like it had no purpose. I think I've found what I'm meant to do now.

Jillian nodded in agreement. "I think there's some risk involved, but you may be right; people are able to access Magic in this time, and despite the demons, I am inclined to say there are fewer evil people overall. And it's not like we'd be handing Magic over to modern-day people, either. We'll be changing history so Magic will have never faded."

"Exactly," I agreed. "It'll be a natural progression from now into the future."

"So what should we do next? Can we go see Jack? We retrieved the wand, and considering what you just did with it, it obviously works."

I took a deep breath and pulled out Ahso'lar. "I've tested this twice now, and I've traveled to and from a hidden location without any ability on my part. It's *incredibly* powerful; I don't feel *any* mental strain. Rhen's body hasn't gotten sick, and I haven't been ejected from her mind. I feel like it might just work. There's just one thing that bothers me though: Vael'ehn said the wand was *allowing* me to control it, but it hadn't *chosen* me."

Jillian gave me an odd look. "What's that mean? You're not its owner?"

"Well, sort of," I considered. "Objects of Power bind with those that use them. In some ways they become one with each other. I don't think the wand feels that connection with me, but it also doesn't object to what I'm doing."

"Object?" Jillian repeated. "As in, it could refuse what you're asking it to do?"

"Yes, and that's what worries me."

Lifting the wand in front of me, I addressed it. "I don't know if you're aware, if you can understand me, but please consider this: we have good intentions. We are fighting against demons and evil, Magic that should not exist. If you're not willing to bind with me, that's alright, but please know that what we're doing, we're doing for the right reasons. We need your continued aid to complete our mission."

The wand, its two tiny gemstones eternally orbiting each other, said nothing.

I don't think Objects of Power talk, Laurence.

You'd be surprised what I've heard. Search it out in my mind if you want, but let me tell you, it's pretty scary.

And they may not all speak, of course, but I'm convinced they all think or react, at least on some level. Respecting this wand's abilities can't hurt. For all I know, the tone of my voice could influence its actions.

"Did… did it agree?" Jillian whispered, eyeing the wand uncertainly.

The comment caused me to laugh. "I honestly don't know. There's only one way to find out. If you're leaving the decision up to me, I say we head to the tournament."

Jillian eyes grew wide. *"Really?* Right now?" The impact that she might be reunited with Jack in a matter of minutes clearly hadn't sunken in until that very moment. "What time period during the tournament are you looking to arrive in?"

The statement was one I hadn't expected.

Damn. I have no idea what is taking place at the tournament right now.

I don't even know where Jack is by this time. He might not even be there!

But you've teleported through time before. You've traveled all the way to the future and back. Why can't we just go to that specific time?

This is far more complicated. I've never taken people with me through time before, and I've certainly never pierced through a shield while doing so. For all we know, it could be programmed to thwart ideas like that.

I don't think we have a choice.

You're right - we don't.

"I'm thinking of the moment when the winners are about to leave but haven't done so yet," I responded. "Everyone will be gathered together, the tournament grounds will be empty, and it'll be the perfect opportunity to introduce ourselves."

I turned toward Dreyl'vyn who, despite his smaller form, did not look the least bit friendly. "It will be important that we do not threaten them, Dreyl'vyn. No one is going to expect us to pop in, not even Wenton. That's specifically what the barrier protects the tournament from. For all I know, we might be the first to defeat it - aside from Doug-Bug, that is."

Jillian seemed intent on making sure there was no room for confusion. "Alright, Dreyl'vyn, that means if they attack or hurt you, you can't touch anyone. They're all going to be on our side, even if they don't look like it at first."

"They will not comprehend we are of no threat until we are given a chance to explain ourselves," Dreyl'vyn concluded. "I understand. I am ready."

"Are *you* ready for this?" I inquired of Jillian, who nodded. I shook my head. "No, I mean, are you ready to see Jack? He's gone through a few changes since the last time you laid eyes on him."

"*Changes?*"

"Yes, changes," I cautioned. "Let's just say there's a reason I knew so much about those Archaeus trees and their effects on humans. Picture a blue tree limb for an arm, and you won't be far off."

Jillian made a perplexed expression, as if the mental image she had chosen hadn't made any sense at all, but nodded anyway. "Whatever's happened to him, it can't be worse than what's happened to me. Whenever you're ready, just go for it. I'll deal with what I find when we get there."

Lifting the wand above my head, I attempted to steady myself in preparation for what might be a strenuous teleportation through both time and an impenetrable shield. Picturing the moment when I hovered inside the tournament grounds, preparing to leave with the other winners, I focused on an area farther out from the gate, an area I knew would be unoccupied.

"Alright, here we go."

Bringing the wand slowly downward, I pointed it at our feet. Immediately it crackled to life, a shower of blue sparks exploding around its tip.

"Ahso'lar, please take us to the tournament!"

CHAPTER
Fifty-Eight

-ROAD TO RUIN-

We exploded through the tournament barrier, our arrival shaking the earth. Once nearly invisible, it rippled and wavered from our assault before regaining its prior integrity. The energy expelled from the wand was truly immense and threatened to collapse the monumental castle standing high before us. Near the gates, people dove for cover, save for Jack and Wenton, who raced toward us, their weapons drawn.

We made it!

Yes, but we're not safe yet. Hold on!

"Escorts, back inside!" Wenton yelled to Payton and the others, who took off running.

Lifting me off the ground with an unseen force, Wenton held his staff high in the air. I found myself struggling to retain my focus, the world around me becoming a blur of sound and colors. Surprised that we had not only made it through the barrier but had again arrived exactly *where* and *when* I had imagined, I was completely caught off guard.

"Wait!" Jack yelled. "Wenton, wait!"

Sprinting forward, Jack came face to face with Jillian, whose eyes had already begun to spill over with rivers of black tears.

"Jill?"

Mor'dresh fell from his hand but did not hit the ground. Instead, it hovered off to the side, seeming to approve of the reunion.

Do you see the sword? See what it did?

Yes, I do.

If I'm correct, my Coadju'tahr - being an Object of Power - has just passed all knowledge of our journey to Mor'dresh. The sword has learned what I intend to do, it has welcomed our arrival, and it's about to start working with us. Or...

Or what?

If I'm wrong, something horrible is about to happen.

Jillian and Jack leapt into each other's arms.

"Jack! I knew we'd find you!" Jillian cried. "We did it! We saved you just in time!"

"I'm fine, babe! There wasn't anything hurtin' me in here, but I'm so glad you're okay!"

Without thinking, he raised his bark-covered arm, meaning to brush her hair back. Jillian stepped backward in surprise but quickly recovered. As Jack fumbled with his words, desperately trying to explain what had happened, she smiled and slid her hand along his gnarled appendage, gripping his talons tightly. Upon being touched, the soft blue glow within his arm momentarily increased.

"No, it's okay," she said, watching the illumination with overt interest. "I just didn't expect to see it; it took a moment for my brain to process what I was actually looking at." She frowned. "That tree did a number on your arm, didn't it?"

Jack laughed. "You got no fuckin' idea. But you shoulda seen me before it gave me that arm." He made a slashing motion at shoulder level with his finger, indicating an amputation. "And wait 'til ya see the side of my chest. It's like body armor!" Watching her brow furrow, his cheeks darkened. "*Oh*, uh, sorry if I'm… ugly now."

"Oh, no, it's not that at all," she replied with a tired smile. "We've just both been through so much in such a short period of time. I mean, have you taken a look at *me?"* She waggled her fingers in front of him, the blackened, vein-covered digits immediately catching his attention. "Talk about *gross*."

Jack grabbed her fingers and pulled them down to hold them in his hands. "Well, you gotta admit, we still make quite the pair." He laughed. "But honest, you look really good. You're not gross at all; way better than when I last saw ya. And that red hair… and… your skin and eyes are… ah…" Jack seemed to trail off into a sort of stupor, but shook his head, managing to clear the sensation.

Jillian, noticing the effect, grimaced and took a step backward. "Yeah, well, there is a story behind that, and it's not a good one. You need to be *very* careful around me now. What you're experiencing isn't natural. It's important you guard yourself against my-"

Jack reached forward and pulled her close to him again. "I don't care," he stated firmly. "You're here, and that's all I wanted. I didn't know where you were, or if you were even alive. Whatever's happened, it doesn't matter. You found me, you're safe - that's what counts."

I couldn't help but notice that, despite being excited to see each other, the two didn't seem quite as emotional and thankful as I thought they might be. Both shared a certain sadness in their eyes, as if they knew nothing would ever be the same, saying and acting out what they thought they should have felt but not quite meaning it. Whether it was the violence and pain that had hardened them to the softer side of humanity, or whether each saw a monster standing before them, something inside the pair had clearly been damaged.

As much as I didn't want to admit it, a part of myself seemed satisfied upon noticing their small hesitations. For once I felt as if I had been given a chance to explore my own feelings with Jillian instead of dealing with the ever-present threat of their reunion.

You should be ashamed of yourself.

I am, Rhen. But I also can't help but feel how I do.

Can't you see it's her demonic hold on you?

Haven't you considered that?

Every moment of my life. But the feelings are still there, no matter their source.

The two continued to fill each other in on the events leading up to their reunion, but I had my own struggles to deal with. Wenton, still holding Rhen's body within his spellwork, turned his gaze back upon us. With it came a peculiar intensity. Blearily, I wavered back and forth, both my offensive and defensive capabilities seemingly just out of reach.

"I see that she is Lady Jillian, whom Master Jack has spoken of, but there are still questions to be answered." Wenton demanded, his voice firm and authoritative. "Who are you, and how did you pass through an impenetrable barrier?"

Releasing Rhen from my mental hold, I returned to the Coadju'tahr. Regaining my focus, I drifted out from her belt and down toward the Gnill'var. Raising his bushy eyebrows, he stared in surprise at a crystal identical to the one which still hovered by Jack's side. Knowing just what to say, I quickly summoned words which would cement our intentions in his mind.

```
          Don't feel too badly.
     Life has a way of drawing us all
      back together when we need it most.
```

Letting out a slow breath, Wenton nodded and set Rhen down. The words, of course, were those he had just uttered to Jack minutes before our arrival. I had remembered them well through my entire journey.

Turning his attention toward Dreyl'vyn, Wenton called out to Modera, Cindee, Dael'yan, and Walther, who had surrounded the shriveled giant. Pointing their weapons and hands up toward him menacingly, the group clearly had no notion of Dreyl'vyn's true capabilities.

"He is not our enemy - *whoever* he is."

"His name is Dreyl'vyn of the Cimmerians," Rhen announced. "You can call me Rhen, and the man inside the floating crystal before you is Laurence. We are here as friends of Jillian and Jack."

Wenton turned back toward me. "*Laurence?* Not Steve?"

```
        No, my name was never Steve.
            That was Jack's idea.

      I couldn't communicate properly
        until I learned more of Magic,
   and there were far more important matters.

   I have come from the future - your future.
    We are here to stop you all from leaving.

       Please excuse me for a moment
        while I attend to another task.
```

As Wenton eyed my floating, enchanted words with overt curiosity, I drifted over toward my past self. Knowing full well he was not attuned to Magic potent enough to produce words of his own, I had one action in mind: touching him. I wasn't sure whether it would produce a vision, transfer information, or allow me to contact his consciousness like I had done with Rhen; but I was about to find out.

As I moved closer, my duplicate backed away, clearly unsure of my intentions. Before he could react, I shot forward, our two crystalline forms clinking together like champagne glasses. No vision presented itself. Instead, Laurence's consciousness pushed against mine, the two wills drifting back and forth between forms, waiting for one to advance against the other.

Hello Laurence. Enjoy the tournament?

You have changed greatly since we last passed each other.

You know who I am.

Well, our Coadju'tahrs *are* Objects of Power. What did you think would happen when you came near me? I saw everything that happened to you, everything that would happen to me. Even now, I'm being fed your knowledge.

But why are you here, then?

The truth was, I had begun to feel a trickle of imagery flowing from Laurence's Coadju'tahr since our arrival, but it appeared to be events I had already lived through. Even so, I still found it far more effective to seek out the specific information I was looking for.

What else was I supposed to do? You told me I failed. You told me we had been given a second chance. Everything relied on events playing out as they had, so you would remain free to do as was needed.

So you've reenacted every event that took place before?

Every detail, step by step. Even the failures, which were quite embarrassing.

*Well, to be fair, those failures weren't exactly your fault. I feel you - **we** - did the best with what information we had been given. But that doesn't matter now. Jillian, Dreyl'vyn, Rhen and I have come to join you all before you head out and meet your end. We're going to team up against Vael'ehn and stop-*

*Laurence? Are you listening to me? **Laurence!***

I could feel my prior selves' attention drift away from my thoughts and focus upon

Jillian instead, his mind swimming with intense emotion for her. Laurence's infatuation also washing over me, I found myself filled with irritation and bitter jealousy. Not only did he seem to have no interest in listening to me, but he also appeared to believe he had some sort of chance at attaining a relationship with her.

How can you possibly ignore me at a time like this! And for what - daydreaming about Jillian? She is not for you. What could she possibly see in anything you have to offer?

What do you mean? I wasn't-

Of course you were! Don't lie to me. I can feel your emotions. I can feel the thoughts you have for her. I'll save you the trouble and heartbreak. You will never have her!

Why not? You should know more than anyone how I feel about her.

Yes I do, but you are Laurence no longer. I have risked everything for her, endured immense pain for her, and she has done nothing but deny my every advance. She believes I am delusional because of her condition. Besides, should she one day choose a version of Laurence, it would not be you, a lesser version. I am sorry, but you need to accept that your emotions are not important. The outcome of this mission is what matters-

No! My emotions **are important! I am just as much of a person as you are! How can you show up and treat me like a stranger, treat me like I am not even myself, when you know exactly what I am feeling!**

Which one of us is greater: the one who blunders through time, causing all sorts of havoc? Or the one who does what he's supposed to, watches people he could have saved die, fails to grow in power - all in an effort to preserve the timeline and give everyone another chance?

Did you just think you would stroll up to me, tell me what I'm supposed to do with the rest of my life, and convince me to follow your every command? You may be from the future, but I know everything you know. You are-

I must admit, I'm starting to find myself wary of your intentions. You've begun to convince me your further participation in this plan is going to cause nothing but trouble. You need to listen to me and put your feelings aside. This is going to proceed how I have decided it will, or everything will be lost again!

Wary of *my* intentions! Look at what this has done to you! You've barely contacted me, and already you're telling me what I can and cannot do like I'm some sort of robot! There's no humanity left in you! When I get back to my body, maybe I should tell Jillian who *you've* become so she knows the truth!

Your body! **Yours?** *Why would you ever conceive that I'd let you have **my** body, should I ever make my way back to it?*

What right do *you* have to claim it? You forfeited yourself when you went back in time! I am the original. You are just a copy of me, and a poor one at that!

*Forfeited myself? Hardly! I made it farther than you ever did. I made a sacrifice far greater than you could ever conceive! That sacrifice is why you are a relic, and I have survived to correct what you have done! I have grown more, achieved more, reached for everything you have not. I am not the copy, Laurence - **you** are. A copy is never greater than the original.*

I would not follow you anywhere! I'd just as soon meet my fate and fail again than follow the path a corrupted person has laid out for me, even if it *is* a version of myself! I'll continue on with *you* emblazoned upon my mind as an example of what *not* to become! That knowledge will increase *my* chances of success a thousandfold. You-

My conversation with Laurence had allowed me to come to a conclusion: he did not see me as having a place in what he perceived as his timeline. Feeling what he felt, I knew he had also come to a decision of his own: he would attempt to eliminate me the first opportunity he found. However unlikely the chances of his success may have been, I could not risk allowing him to try.

Reaching out, I pushed inward upon my duplicate, pressing him back into his body and crushing him inside it. He may have offered more resistance than the woman in the restroom had, but it was nothing compared to the power I had gained. Slowly but surely, he weakened and faltered under my immense mental strength.

Laurence! No! Laurence! Please... look at yourself... see... what you've... become...

His life force failing, Laurence began to drift aimlessly in the air, but I did not stop. As his consciousness disappeared, I sensed the power contained within his vacant form and pulled it toward me. His Coadju'tahr was stripped entirely of Magic, leaving only a grey, inert stone behind, which crumbled to dust. I swelled with Magic - *potent* Magic. My crystalline form crackled with incredible strength. I felt I could accomplish anything.

No one will take what I have worked so hard to achieve!

No one.

I turned my attention back upon the group, only to find Mor'dresh watching me intently. It needn't have spoken to remind me of what it had once said: "The stone, devoured by itself." I had just unwittingly participated in the sword's own prophecy.

Determined to ignore what that might mean, I drifted over to Rhen, who was conversing with Wenton. Slipping into the pouch on her belt, I pushed into her mind, stealing her body away.

Laurence, I was talking!

I'm sorry, but we don't have time for pleasantries. We have to keep moving. Vael'ehn has to be dealt with before he unravels what I've worked so hard to achieve.

What happened to your-

Apparently two identical versions of my form could not exist in the same time.

When I touched him, his consciousness blended with mine.

He *couldn't* **exist, or you didn't** *want* **him to exist?**

Search for the truth if you want to, but don't look for answers you aren't ready to accept.

"Wenton, we do not have much time. This is Laurence speaking now. I have taken control of Rhen for the moment to expedite our plans. We have to move. Our next step is to travel far to the southeast and visit the Retrogrades before Vael'ehn recruits them for his cause. We will be required to wage war against him, and I have knowledge I can trade in return for their services."

"Taken control of her?" Wenton responded in a startled tone. "Laurence, that is dangerous Magic! You shouldn't be dealing with-"

Reaching out, I grabbed Wenton's robe and pulled him closer. "Perhaps that's why we are in this predicament to begin with, *Wenton*. People have never been willing to go as far as this situation requires them to. *I am.* You should not be concerned with the details of my methods when they will earn the results you are looking for. Or are you so ashamed of the Seekers you employ, that you cannot bring yourself to see my value?"

Wenton backed away a step, pulling free from my grasp. Motioning out into the distance, he seemed to be signaling toward something that wasn't there.

"I would be careful how you react in my presence, Laurence. Two of the Seekers I am so *ashamed of employing* are watching you. You have attracted their attention. They have not interceded at my behest, but I assure you, another mistake like that and I *will* pull them right through that barrier. And I might add, they do not take kindly to the mistreatment of the one person on this planet who has shown them a kindness. The others have never agreed to the inclusion of Seekers upon these grounds, but I assure you, I am *quite* open to the idea. Do *not* push me."

I stared out into the distance. As far as I could see, there were no Seekers present.

Is he bluffing?

What purpose would you even have to confront him on such a bluff! Let this go before it gets out of hand!

"I'm… I apologize," I offered. "I got carried away in the moment."

"Naturally," Wenton replied, eyeing me carefully. He motioned toward the area where my duplicate once floated. "Is it your twin who aggravated you? What happened to him?" His tone indicated he already knew the answer.

"He did indeed. But he's merged with me now; we have combined our power."

Don't lie to him, Laurence.

Well, it's true - in a way.

I laughed coldly to myself.

Consuming someone isn't the same as keeping them alive!

Isn't it though? I'll use his power to my advantage. He wasn't strong or talented enough to do anything on his own, and he resisted everything I asked of him. He would have held us back and tried to kill me. Now he'll contribute to our cause instead.

Sighing, Wenton gave me a cautious glance before staring out into the distance. "I am not going to claim to be an expert on the Magic you appear to possess, Laurence. It is strange to me, and I've never used it before. I will offer you these words of caution: be careful how far your convictions carry you, lest you find yourself swept away by them."

Turning his attention toward Jillian, he frowned. "There continue to be *several* matters which concern me in regard to what has transpired. The Seekers informed me of what they found at the village of Duff. Tell me, was it I who sent you and Jillian back from the future?"

"Why would you say that?" I responded, not at all prepared for his conclusion.

"Jack seemed disinclined to mention just *who* sent you backward, nor did I press him on the matter. At times, foreknowledge of a person's actions can have adverse effects on a situation, so it is often best to leave such topics alone. But seeing you all here, I understand why I have had such strong convictions to advance through time. Traveling to the future could have aided greatly in the correction of this tragedy, but if it was I who had done so, that would also have certain implications."

"And what implications would those be?" I asked, trying my best not to indicate he had correctly ascertained his participation in the portal's creation.

Receiving nothing from me, Wenton's frown deepened. "If it was I who sent Jack backward in time, there are several courses of action I could take. My first inclination is to ignore your sudden arrival and head to the future. The part I played in sending you back would have led to this moment. That means I should depart and repeat that action, despite what I have just learned."

The revelation startled me, as I had not questioned that line of reasoning before. Wenton was insinuating that, should he choose to stay, there would be no one to aid a future Jack and Jillian. Should the need arise, if I were to travel to the future again, I wouldn't find the pair where I expected them to be. For that matter, Wenton's entire lab would be missing. Not a single event would have turned out the same as it had.

"What if you *were* to decide on a different course of action?" I asked. "Why not just ignore this giant loop, since we're changing the future anyway?"

Seeing that I had inadvertently acknowledged his reasoning had been correct, Wenton nodded to himself. I needn't have told him he had traveled to the future and aided our group; he already deduced it.

"*If* I were to stay here and refrain from traveling to the future, this might be the last time these events take place. Before I met any of you, before I sent you back in time, it is now clear I *did* make the decision to head to the future on my own and search for the sword. Considering your presence - and I am referring to the fact that there is a duplicate of you - only further complicates events. After Jack completed the tournament and left, I must have decided to ignore what I learned and follow my prior path a *second* time."

Again, Wenton's conclusion gave me pause.

"Wait. I traveled back to the future to follow Jillian. The version of you from *that* time traveled to the future after meeting Jack and I? You're saying you played out your part in those future events, despite having new knowledge of what it meant? You could have made countless changes to aid us!"

"*Could I have?*" Wenton shrugged. "I cannot say for sure, as I have not taken that trip, but being myself, I *can* say that keeping the timeline intact would be the course of action I would likely choose. There are too many parts in play to risk altering my own choices in favor of what I *think* might help." He motioned toward everyone around him. "If I were to die in a battle with Vael'ehn and your new plan were to fail, there would be no certainty of what you might find, should you choose to try again."

So that's my new dilemma. Do I convince Wenton to head to the future as a safeguard, maintaining Jack and Jillian's recruitment to our cause, or do I keep him here to bolster our numbers, knowing that if we fail and he dies, I will not have another chance to seek his aid in the future.

Nothing would prevent me from heading back in time; I'd simply be starting over with a larger amount of unknown variables. And I might not need him again, given my knowledge and power.

You need to tell him everything that has happened so he can make a wise decision. He is your best choice for guidance.

Do I though? What can he possibly tell me that I don't already know? Think about everything we've learned. Besides, I'm not a helpless failure anymore. Technically, I know more than he does.

Laurence, don't assume you can control every aspect of this. Time is too complex; you can't possibly predict every outcome. You should seek out as much help as you can. His perspective on this matter has already managed to surprise you in the last few minutes alone. I know; I can feel your emotions.

I don't need help from anyone or anything if they're set on going against what I deem the right course of action. It will slow us down and muddle our results. That's how I'll know if he should stay or not.

I don't think that's wise...

"How do we know that we haven't made enough progress since the last attempt to achieve victory now?" I asked. "What if losing your assistance results in another loss? What if something happens to me, and I'm not able to contact you after you leave, rendering your assistance useless?"

Wenton scratched a tufted ear in thought. "If I were to travel to the future again, refrain from sharing my knowledge of these events with Jack, and you do not arrive from the past to intercept us, a similar series of events resembling the first timeline may take place. However, if I never travel to the future in the first place, we will have *no* idea what might occur, as Jack will acquire no guidance in regard to the sword. There are too many variables to ascertain at that point."

*If I **do** require another chance, and Wenton isn't there, Mor'dresh would at least learn all that has happened from being in close proximity to me. The sword will aid me and make sure we can complete another attempt.*

The sword will... *aid* **you? Have you lost your mind!**

It's not as evil as it seems, Rhen. I'm telling you, it's trying its hardest.

Oh, for the love of all things Magic- Even if it is, you cannot stand there and consider Mor'dresh a suitable replacement for Wenton!

"Well, things haven't gotten worse," I replied, shaking my head. "We *are* making progress. We're right on the verge of winning, even though our first attempt failed. In fact, we might be closer to winning *because* our first attempt failed; it could have been a necessary step. I say you stay here and fight with us."

Wenton didn't seem quite as convinced. "Are you so sure that you'd risk a future timeline for your possible success?"

We are better off with a safeguard, Laurence.

From his response, it doesn't appear as if I have a choice.

I took a moment to consider the meaning of his question, doing my best to read the unsaid words held within his secretive Gnill'var eyes.

"There is no reason to discuss this further," I announced. "You would be wasting your time by discussing any idea which opposes what I intend to do. I suspect you've already made up your mind. If you're traveling to the future, your actions are no longer a concern of mine."

Motioning to the others, who were attempting - and failing - to have a productive conversation with Dreyl'vyn, I encouraged them to come over. As everyone gathered around us, Wenton regarded me with a nervous expression; he was clearly uncertain about my decision.

"My name is Laurence, and whether you know it or not, I am the one who controls the purple crystal. I am speaking through the body of a woman named Rhen in order to aid me with my communication. I have brought you all together to wage war upon Vael'ehn, preserve Magic from its destruction, and prevent our world from being besieged by demons."

"Demons?" Wenton whispered, confirming my suspicion that he indeed had no knowledge of a future assault by Roth'Roh'Kah.

Walther scoffed. "Arriving in this place was no doubt a tedious task for you to perform, but I have somewhere to be. If you haven't noticed, I've just won this tournament, and my career is waiting for me. There are countless people on this planet. Surely you can rouse a few of them in my stead to fight just *one* man."

I grinned darkly at Walther; I had forgotten how self-absorbed he could be. "We will need far more than a few men, Walther. We are heading to the Retrogrades' stronghold. I have information they want, information they will trade *anything* for. I am about to become the leader of a grand mercenary army - an army that will mark the end of Vael'ehn and secure our future forever. We need every person we can rally. Vael'ehn is incredibly dangerous and unstable. If we don't stop him now, far more people will die before this is over."

"Buh-buh-buh-buh…" Dael'yan began, but Modera pushed him backward.

"Not now," she growled, "the grownups are talking." He eyed her with an annoyed expression, but she ignored him. "Walther may be too busy with his brittle bones and dusty books, but I'm not so keen on the education I've just been assigned." She shot Wenton an indifferent expression. "What do you have that the Retrogrades want?"

"I have knowledge on how to attain a great ship that sailed the seas long ago."

Wenton's eyes grew wide. "Are you referring to *the Ridden?*"

"Yes. I know where it is, and I'm going to give them access to it. Don't worry, it's ruined and sunken, and they will not have time to repair it until after the war is over. When we are done with our assault against Vael'ehn, we will wipe out any Retrogrades who survive. It will be another great victory for the Xahl'thari race."

Walther laughed. *"Oh?* And just how might you wipe out the army you've hired to fell Vael'ehn?"

"With three weapons of legend," I replied, causing his smug expression to drop. "Jack carries Mor'dresh, Call of Darkness. Without Vael'ehn in the way, we *will* restore it to its proper state. I have in my possession Ahso'lar, Touch of the Unknown." I withdrew the wand. "And Cindee…" I turned toward the small girl and kneeled. "You, my dear, have something *very* special."

"I… *I do?*" She looked up at Jack, who shrugged. "I just have my wand, and that's all."

I shook my head. "No, Cindee, that is not just a wand; that is Khalla'lar, Touch of Life, crafted from the shards of Khalla'sall itself!"

"Khalla'sall," Wenton mouthed. "That sounds so familiar."

"It should," I replied. "It is The Weapon of Legend tasked with manipulating Life

Magic - a Magic brought to our race by the Droth'gon'ai."

"Yes, of course. Life Magic," Wenton agreed, clearly feeling foolish. "That is very strange. For a moment the story of Khalla'sall-"

"Was absent from your mind, and you felt confused," I finished. "That does not bode well for our future at all. The effects are slowly taking hold, even on you."

"Taking hold?" Wenton repeated. He stared at me for a moment, deliberating with himself. At last, his eyes widened as his brain connected the dots. "Something has happened to the Droth'gon'ai statues, hasn't it? Have you located them?" I nodded. "How many statues were there?" he demanded.

"There are five statues now, where seven once remained."

"What does that mean, Wenton?" Cindee asked. "I remember Life Magic just fine, don't you?"

Wenton turned toward her, his furry face managing to grow pale. He stared down at the small wand in her hand. "Yes, of course, yet for a moment all but my basic ties to healing Magic had begun to wane, and I genuinely forgot Khalla'sall's story. Something is happening to the statues, causing those links to be severed. My race has a natural ability to reach out and touch Magic, but the Droth'gon'ai made those bonds far greater.

"As we continue on into the future, almost all Xahl'thari will forget those parts of Magic entirely, including their own stories, history, and everything once tied to it. Anything built using that Magic will no longer be supported. Their documentation, the heroes who represented them, entire territories, even the parts it played at the tournament for many, many years - all gone.

"The races who were attuned to Magic before the Droth'gon'ai will revert to their non-segmented, basic versions, acknowledging Magic as a singular concept. Soon, this entire planet will forget Droth'gon'ai Life Magic and… and…" Wenton looked up at me again. "You said *two* were destroyed, but five still remain?" His eyes grew wide. "I am only aware of six schools of Droth'gon'ai Magic. One is already… *gone?*"

Grimly, I nodded. "We have lost our link to Soul Magic."

Wenton turned his gaze toward the ground, his eyes filled with both surprise and sorrow. "Of all things Magical… I am aware that Magic can manipulate souls, of course, but I have no recollection that it was ever part of the enhanced schools brought to us by the Droth'gon'ai. If you had asked me about it a few minutes ago, I'd have sworn it was a lesser, almost forgotten aspect of Magic that is seldom used - possibly even ignored - by Xahl'thari. That part of our planet's history, even *their* planet's history, has vanished entirely. We are now truly ignorant."

"The other statues are safe for now," I offered, "but Vael'ehn has destroyed those two in order to prevent heroes who have died from being brought back from the dead." Seeing several people eye Jillian, I added, "In a natural state, of course."

On the verge of tears, Wenton turned back toward Cindee. "Leucinda, that wand - if it is what Laurence says it is - is one of the most important objects on this planet right now. Someday it may be the only item left that interacts with the school of Life Magic, and you will have the greatest chance of maintaining your enhanced abilities and knowledge."

Cindee frowned. "But it's not; it's just a wand my father gave me. It's not some grand wand forged from Khalla'sall; it's just like every other wand people have access to."

Smiling, I withdrew the small scroll we had found with Ahso'lar. Handing it to Cindee, I patted her on the shoulder. "In a moment I think you will realize what your father *really* gave you all those years ago. He was correct; it was meant to do far more than be buried in the dirt." I winked, her father's words causing Cindee's eyes to grow wide in acknowledgement.

Standing, I regarded the group again. "It's not all bad news. I've learned that Vael'ehn is not like the Gnill'var, other races, and Xahl'thari heroes; he has no link to Wild Magic."

"How have you come upon that information?" Wenton inquired. "He's incredibly powerful; that seems unlikely."

I waved the question away. "That doesn't matter. Suffice it to say, I know for a fact he has no idea what Soul Magic is, and as Life Magic continues to falter, he'll forget about that too. I'm determined to use such knowledge against him; I just have to figure out how.

"But we can't speculate on that yet; it's time to leave. We have to visit the Retrogrades before Vael'ehn does, and by choosing this moment in particular to intercept you all, I fear I have cut our timeline *quite* close. The information I have is only valuable to us if we get there first, otherwise we'll have an entirely different war on our hands. From prior experience, I can say it does not go so well."

Wenton stepped forward to address everyone. "I can neither approve nor reject the validity of that plan, as I have no idea how the Retrogrades will react. Whatever you all decide, I cannot come with you; I have some business to attend to."

His expression was filled with determination, and I knew precisely what he had decided. Long ago I wondered what would cause Wenton to traverse billions of years into the future. Now I knew it was his selfless determination to aid those around him. He would make sure that no matter what, we would not fail.

I sincerely hope we do not need you here, Wenton, but I'm sure we will.

I still feel this is the safest course of action; even you are not certain this will work. If there is no guarantee, we need a backup plan in place. He will provide that.

In the future, Wenton clearly existed in a weakened mental state, living in a time when no statues existed, his abilities relying entirely on Wild Magic and what little the fragmented dragon busts in the basement afforded him. As to what supplies he would bring with him, what he would remember from the past, and how much the new information he had garnered would do to aid those debilitating circumstances, I had no idea.

Hopefully he arrives to find we've written a new future, one free of demons and Mor'dresh's corruption; one where the dragon statues still stand and Magic continues to flourish.

"Will you at least lend us the use of your Seekers?" I inquired.

Wenton shook his head. "They are not the type of creatures who work well with others. They are dark and twisted and listen to no one. I have aided them in redeeming themselves, but do not think for a moment they are a group who are willing to rally to your call. They tend toward being discrete, only gathering when I require it of them. I am hesitant to inform the Seekers of your potential upcoming battle, as their spellwork is not of the type that puts much emphasis on the protection of allies. Calling in a large group of them is dangerous. You are just as likely to come under fire from their nightmarish spells as Vael'ehn is, and I cannot condone the loss of *any* of you."

Again glancing toward the area Wenton had indicated the Seekers might be, I frowned. "What will happen to them after you depart? Isn't it dangerous to leave them unchecked?"

"They have all been subjected to a series of spells. We know where they are and what they are doing at all times. At any moment we have the ability to end their lives if they are not living up to the arrangement they have agreed to. As of yet we have had no incidents at all, but the safeguard remains. There are others I will put in charge of their care. Whether or not this program continues on in my absence, I cannot say, but their lifespans are not very long once they have chosen to refrain from transferring the life force of others into their bodies."

"So it will work itself out."

"That is one way to put it," Wenton replied.

Reaching forward, I extended my hand and shook his fur-covered paw. "Well, we need to be on our way. Enjoy the time you have with Renault," I said, causing Wenton's brow to wrinkle in confusion. "And don't forget your birthday. I won't be there to remember it for you."

The statements made no sense to him, of course, but I didn't care. The future was useless to me; it was useless to all of us. Where he was going would be rewritten with the next few hours' worth of events.

I will achieve what I intend to. Redoing all of this a third time with even more people and more variables in play isn't a viable option.

With all my heart I hope you are right, Laurence.

Stepping back, I raised Ahso'lar in the air.

"*Wait*, shouldn't we like, discuss this more or somethin'?" Jack asked.

Shooting him a fraudulent grin, I waved the wand. Our group vanished, leaving Wenton alone on the field outside Castle Ahr'bor'ahk.

With a clap of thunder, we arrived high above the Broken Peninsula tree line. Stunned by where we had appeared, I began to plummet toward the horrific, carnivorous trees below. Cindee and Dael'yan screamed as the entire group began a rapid descent. Collecting myself, I spread my arms, suspending Rhen's body in mid-air. One by one, I grabbed those around me, saving them from certain death.

To my horror I realized that Jillian and Dreyl'vyn - the two people I spent significant time with most recently - had been teleported first by accident. Whether it was due to the wand's familiarity with them or if it had been caused by some fault of my own, I couldn't say, but by the time I gathered my wits, they had already disappeared through the canopy below.

Rushing downward, I tore away the branches with little regard to the plants' wellbeing; as far as I was concerned, they were a blight upon the land. Uprooting an entire tree blocking my way, I threw it high into the air. It would have collided with several members of the group, had Jack not managed to slice it in two at the last minute.

"What the fuck're ya doin', man!" he yelled.

He's lucky I saved him from falling. What would happen if I had dropped him, just tossed him into the trees? I wonder, would the grove accept him as one of their own due to his arm, or would he still be in danger?

Why would you even consider such a thing!

Oh, I meant nothing by it.

You know that's not true. You resent him.

Rhen, stop antagonizing me! If I wanted your opinion right now, I would pull it from your mind!

Landing on the ground, I saw that there were branches and debris littered across the forest floor. In two crumpled heaps, near where we had made our descent, lay Jillian and Dreyl'vyn, severely injured from the fall. Surprisingly, the trees appeared to want no part in touching either of them.

They must consider their bodies to be tainted.

"I'll save you!" yelled Cindee, withdrawing her wand, but I lifted her up off the ground, causing her feet to pump comically underneath her.

"Dreyl'vyn is immortal," I called, "and Jillian is no longer a human. All of you stay away from her. *Jack, I mean it!*"

What if Leucinda can repair her body?

I honestly don't know if Life Magic can heal Jillian's body or not, but she could turn at any moment. It isn't worth risking Cindee's safety to find out. We're about to go to war, and her abilities are too important. We have a system that works, and we should stick with it.

Disregarding my warnings, Jack had already moved toward Jillian's shattered body. Knowing full well he was just as likely to harm her as he was to be consumed by her, I threw up a barrier, buffeting him backwards.

"*Dude!* Let me through!" he exclaimed, turning to face me with tear-filled eyes. "I can see her breathin'! We need to help her!"

"You can't touch her," I replied sternly. "She'll consume you. Things have gotten *far* worse for her since the events down in Wenton's undercroft took place. Her appearance means the opposite of what you think." Seeing I hadn't convinced him, I added, "Remember when you held Balrick back from touching Matteus? Don't be foolish by making the same type of mistake he would have."

"I'm not giving you a choice," Jack growled, his darkened emotions seeming to rise up through his dismay. Walking forward, he confronted me, face to face. "You need to get the fuck outta the way and let me n' Cindee handle this." He reached for the sword but, thankfully, it refused to pull free from it sheath.

*As if you have **any** experience with keeping her alive…*

Annoyed by Jack's audacity, I felt he needed to be taught a lesson.

Laurence, please! Don't do this!

No, he's asking for it.

Extending a hand toward Jack, I made a crushing motion, imagining his heart withering under my touch. Instantly his skin turned white and he stumbled backward. Anger boiling over inside him, he still managed to lunge for me.

As his wooden talon made contact with my skin, it flared brightly. Paralyzing electricity coursed through my body as the appendage began to absorb my power. My world turning black, I collapsed under his weight and lost control of Rhen.

Desperately she cried out to the group. "Don't kill me, ple-"

Rhen's words were cut off as I merged with her body again. Crying and pleading filled my mind; intense pain soon followed.

Laurence, you're not thinking clearly! He's going to kill me! I don't have a crystal to run to! Please calm down and think about what you're doing!

"You two stop it!" Modera yelled as Jack writhed around, trying to break away from her and Dael'yan, who had just pulled him off me.

"I'm fine," Jack replied, shaking the two off of him.

"We have more pressing matters than your rivalry," she added, motioning toward Jillian and Dreyl'vyn.

"Jack, don't!" I called.

Unsheathing Mor'dresh, Jack pointed it toward my throat; it clearly did not believe his threat was genuine. "You come after me again and I'm puttin' you down."

I laughed darkly. "Mor'dresh has gained too much integrity to let you kill an innocent woman." Dodging the sword point, I stood up. "This body is under my control, but Rhen has no part to play in my decisions. You wouldn't want to hurt yet *another* person who doesn't deserve it, *would you?"* I teased, walking away from Jack while running a finger along his rough wooden arm.

"Besides," I called as I made my way to Jillian, "there is only one way to save her, and it doesn't involve either of us. Unless, of course, *you're* volunteering to die for her instead."

Jack gritted his teeth as he watched me. "If I have to, *I will."*

"Don't tempt me," I replied in a harsh tone, the thought of his death sounding quite appealing after being attacked.

"You weren't such an asshole when you were missin' a body," Jack growled.

Laurence, wait. Just a moment, please. You're making everyone resent you. They're not going to follow a leader who acts like this.

What do you want? It seems you're always in the back of my mind, nagging me. You used to be so helpful.

You used to be so logical, you fool!

You need to stop taunting Jack! These people are on your side. Do your best to help Jillian and Dreyl'vyn, and then back off. If you make an enemy of everyone, you're not going to have an army.

I wouldn't really kill him…

You just tried to! You just tried to crush his heart!

I would have let go when he learned his lesson.

Are you so sure?

If you don't believe me, then search my emotions.

I did. That's why I don't believe you.

Ignoring Rhen's inflammatory comments, I moved closer to Jillian. The fall had not been kind to her undead body. She had broken both her legs, dislocated an arm and, from the looks of it, damaged her spine. She writhed on the ground, her mouth wordlessly opening and closing as her wild eyes searched the area. At last, they met mine and paused.

She's desperately calling out to me for aid.

She's not calling you, Laurence; she wants to feed on you!

Nonsense.

Bending over, I regarded her. "Don't worry, my dear, I'm here to save you. I would never let you die; you're far too precious to me."

Silently Jillian reached for my face, but I forced myself to back away.

Levitating her off the ground, I rotated her body, placing her on top of Dreyl'vyn. Having landed on his head, he had fared much worse from the impact. His skull caved in and neck broken, his body twitched uncontrollably beneath her.

Immediately Jillian opened her mouth, initiating the dark ritual. Little by little she drunk in the intense orange orbs which composed Dreyl'vyn's immortal life force. With every moment that passed, her skin improved in complexion, and various pops and clicks were heard as her skeleton realigned and repaired itself.

"I'm going to be sick," Cindee cried, running behind a fallen tree to vomit.

Eyeing her as she did so, Walther made a disgusted expression. "It's like she's never seen a cannibalistic monster sucking the life out of someone," he commented sarcastically.

"She's doing what she has to in order to survive," Jack defended. "That Dreyl'vyn guy is too fucked up to live. At least she's gonna be okay now."

"Oh, he'll live, too," I said, "but it'll take him a while. He's not going to look pretty, but he'll be back in action soon enough." Seeing the group's odd expression, I continued. "As I said, he's immortal. It doesn't matter what happens to his body; his soul can rebuild it. It's a good thing we have him around for Jillian's sake, otherwise we'd have to consider other options."

You'd sacrifice one of them for her, wouldn't you?

Yes, I would. In a heartbeat.

Just in case you've forgotten, Varek used that strange mixture on Dreyl'vyn to limit his abilities. He may not recover this time.

If that's the case, I'll sacrifice Walther. He's old and arrogant, and I don't like him.

I was referring to the risk you're putting Dreyl'vyn in!

You can't treat people like food!

I can do whatever I want to as long as we meet our objectives. Besides, Walther is useless. Why do you think I insisted he come with us? He's a preventative measure in case we lose Dreyl'vyn.

You can't be serious…

Seeing that my comment was met with surprise and disapproving glances, I eyed Jack. "Don't act like you wouldn't do the same thing for her." Finding the response I had been looking for in his eyes, I smiled. I knew he would act as I had, but didn't have the courage to admit it to the others. "That's what I thought," I said, turning back toward Jillian.

In the few moments since I had last inspected her, Jillian had entirely rebuilt herself, once again leaving behind the withered corpse of Dreyl'vyn. Her injuries did not horrify me as they once had; I knew from experience she would rise and rejoin our group.

And if Rhen is right and Dreyl'vyn doesn't follow suit, so be it.

As if listening to my call, Jillian unsteadily clamored to her feet. Standing above Dreyl'vyn, she regarded me with the purified face of an angel. I couldn't help but smile.

A fallen angel, maybe.

Is that dark humor, Rhen? Maybe there's hope for you yet.

I was being sarcastic. You're admiring her negative attributes. What makes her so flawless is what kills other people.

And I'd bring her a steady stream of people to consume if it meant looking into those eyes every day.

I have no doubt you would.

"I appreciate your effort, Laurence," Jillian said, turning to stare down at Dreyl'vyn with a guilty expression, "but I wish you wouldn't have done that. He's not the same as he was before. Is he going to be alright?"

I leaned to the side to view Dreyl'vyn's emaciated carcass. "I should think so. He's always told us he's been through worse, whatever that might mean. If we give him a while, I'm sure he'll be back up on his feet. I can't imagine Varek's concoction could completely negate the abilities of a being as powerful as a Cimmerian."

"Can I try to heal *him* at least?" Cindee inquired.

I gave her a warm smile. "I appreciate the offer, but his condition is not what you think. He'll rebuild his body at no cost to him, while you would be using a limited resource."

Cindee turned her large, sad eyes up toward me. "What if he doesn't?"

I knelt down and placed a hand on her shoulder. "Then we'll have given him a gift he's been searching a long time to find."

Cindee didn't seem to understand but, having no idea what Dreyl'vyn was, refrained from pressing me on my decision. Instead we followed Jillian back toward the others, where she hugged Jack.

"I'm sorry you all had to watch that," Jillian said to the group, remorse and embarrassment evident in her eyes.

Jack snorted. "Honestly, I've seen far worse from this sword. I'm just glad you're back and ya didn't have to kill anyone to do it. While we're waitin' for ol' Drelly over there to recover, why don't I introduce you to everyone? We haven't had much time to talk, and after we start movin' again, we prob'ly won't have another chance."

Summoning a campfire and a half-dozen wooden seats, Jack threw a severed branch from an Archaeus tree onto the blaze using his wooden arm. Upon touching the fire, the branch ignited in brilliant blue flames, burning far more heartily than typical wood. Touching the branch had no effect on the appendage, and Jack clearly knew that would be the case. Whatever part the arm now played in his anatomy, the pair somehow operated symbiotically but separately.

Sitting down, Jack motioned for the others to do the same. Absently I noticed he hadn't summoned a seat for me to use, but I didn't care. Aside from Jillian and Dreyl'vyn, none of the company appeared to like me.

And for good reason.

I may shock them, I may even disgust them, but I am doing what is right, and they will thank me when they see what I accomplish.

"Well, this is Jill, as you all know," Jack began. "And before we go try to ally with of bunch a monsters, I think you all should hear the story of why we're here first. Then we can decide if that sounds like a good plan."

What felt like an hour or more passed before the group had been brought up to speed. Watching as Jack took the lead felt silly to me, as he was in no way fit to do so. Therefore, I interjected wherever I felt it appropriate, as out of everyone, I had experienced the most.

A leader who has no idea what he's doing isn't fit to lead at all.

He isn't fit to do so, or you would rather not deal with an opinion other than your own?

*This is **my** plan. He's only involved for his part to play with Mor'dresh. I need its raw power, otherwise I'd have left him behind.*

Incoherent groaning from behind the group caused us all to turn. The noises signaled the return of Dreyl'vyn who, appearing far worse than usual due to Varek's meddling with his regenerative abilities, stumbled toward the group.

His dried, jerky-like appearance did not sit well with Dael'yan, who seemed disturbed. "Thuh-thuh-thuh-that muh-man looks like huh-he's muh-made of scuh-scabs."

Jack laughed at the statement. "Well, you're not wrong." Turning, he grinned at Dreyl'vyn. "Good to see ya up and about, Drelly!"

Dreyl'vyn's black orbs eyed Jack with uncertainty. "I am not familiar with the term *Drelly*," he croaked, his hollow voice reverberating in his chest like a washboard.

"It's a bastardization of your name," said Walther humorlessly.

"It's a term of affection," Jillian corrected, shooting Walther a dissatisfied expression. "If you like someone, you make up a nickname for them, Dreyl'vyn. Jack is showing that he likes you."

"What evidence has Jack based such a decision upon?" Dreyl'vyn asked. "He has not yet accompanied me into battle."

"Well, for one, you saved me from dying again, ya big lug!" Jillian teased, slapping Dreyl'vyn on the thigh. It made a thick, wet noise, which caused Dael'yan to grimace.

"So why are we here?" Modera asked. "I know where *here* is, but I'll be damned if I've ever wanted to travel to this forest."

"Yeah, why'd you bring us back to these fuckin' things?" Jack agreed. "And why'd we arrive in the air? We almost died!"

"This situation wasn't intentional," I admitted. "It took me a moment before I realized just what had gone wrong. Weeks ago, while Jack's arm was being... *repaired*, I had spotted a black fortress in the distance. At the time, I had no idea what it was, but while visiting No'ahn, she laid out a map on the table.

"Below the Vaelcurian Empire was a wall, and there was an area marked as *Retrograde Territory* beneath that. Further south was the Broken Echelon Peninsula, where the Archaeus trees grow. Having already traveled both above and below the Retrograde's territory, I knew that the fortress I spotted had to be owned by them.

"I will admit, however, it is my fault alone that we arrived *above* this spot in particular. It was naïve of me to assume the wand would bring us directly to that fortress. The picture I had been imagining in my mind was from the only time I had seen it."

"So we appeared where you first spotted it then: in the air," Jillian concluded.

I nodded. "Yes, exactly. This forest is still quite a distance away, so we have some traveling to do, and the Retrogrades are no doubt going to get in our way. I'll have to shield us as we enter the area. Killing them off won't increase our chances of appealing to their good side. We need to track down their leader and explain ourselves quickly."

"So what are we waiting for?" Modera inquired.

"Well," Jack begun. "Is that a *good* idea?" He surveyed the group. "Laurence took off without askin' anyone what they thought of all this." He flashed me a disgruntled look. "I think we should take a vote, don't you?"

Does he really think he can come in here and start telling me what to do? This isn't a democracy.

Why don't you just give them a chance before assuming they'll disagree with you?

Because even if they **do** *agree, they're agreeing because Jack asked them to! There is no choice in this; we're going there no matter what.*

Cindee stood up. "If what Laurence says is true - that Vael'ehn convinces the Retrogrades to follow him because of that giant boat - I don't really think we have a choice. If we don't band with them, we're going to face them *and* Vael'ehn. If we go ahead with Laurence's plan, the tables will be turned.

"I *do* believe we should refrain from heading out on some grand quest to attack him though; he's too crafty. I feel we should travel to Toriash'ahn and explain everything we know to the Grand Magus. Hopefully he will decide to join us as well. The more people, the better."

There's no point in going to Toriash'ahn. We've made an enemy of that entire city. Besides, the Grand Magus isn't going to agree with my methodology, and I don't need yet another loud voice contradicting what needs to be done.

The fact that they might not appreciate those past events is valid, but we can handle that decision after we deal with the Retrogrades.

One step at a time, Laurence.

Fine. But we're not going to Toriash'ahn.

"That's a good point," Jack replied. "Okay, is everyone alright with goin' up and talkin' to the Retrogrades, gettin' 'em on board with our cause, and then headin' to Toriash'ahn?" Seeing everyone nod in agreement, Jack turned toward Dreyl'vyn. "Are you feelin' well enough to travel?"

"It will take significantly more time for my form to recover completely," Dreyl'vyn replied, his voice already managing to attain a significant increase in volume. "It does not make sense to wait here when we are attempting to avoid battle in the first place."

Nodding, Jack stood and turned toward me. "Is that fair?"

"Fair enough for now," I responded.

Judging by his expression, Jack wasn't entirely pleased with my response but ignored it. "Alright, then how're we gettin' up there?"

I pulled out my wand. "Everyone move in closer. I'm going to levitate and protect us at the same time. There is no sense in walking through this forest of death, only to be faced with a body of water to cross and countless Retrogrades on the ground."

As everyone gathered near, I cast a giant sphere around the group, scooping up the dirt beneath our feet as I did so. Slowly rising out from under the trees, we left a concave depression in the soil beneath us.

Realizing the combined weight of everyone seemed far less strenuous than it might have been in the past, I smiled to myself.

See, Rhen? The other Laurence is helping us to succeed even as we speak.

CHAPTER

-BLACK METAL TOWER-

As we neared the fortress, I could see I had indeed been correct. Built from roughly-forged, riveted metal, it loomed up in the air before us. Massive, crooked watchtowers stretched around the structure, peering over the landscape. Beneath them, familiar rows of rusty siege weaponry and gargantuan machinery stood, completely exposed to the weather.

Where are all the Retrogrades?

There doesn't seem to be anyone here at all.

And it was true. The area they controlled stretched on and on, taking up acres worth of land. However, the Retrogrades, of which I had assumed there would be plenty, were curiously missing.

"Are you certain this is the correct location?" inquired Dreyl'vyn.

"Not entirely," I replied. "But it is the only location I have had experience with that *should* have been filled with Retrogrades. It *is* their territory after all."

"Why didn't you just ask Wenton where they'd be? He was right there. He would have known," Cindee asked politely.

I didn't bother with a response. The suggestion would have made things easier, but I had been certain the fortress was the spot we needed to head toward. Still, I wasn't convinced we should leave without investigating it further.

Who would abandon such a giant stronghold? I can't imagine they have another location more secure than this.

I don't think they would; I bet a few are still down there somewhere. Perhaps it's a trap, and they're waiting to ambush anyone who might arrive.

"We're going to head down and investigate it," I concluded. "If they're not here, there may still be clues as to where they've gone."

Panic swept through me as I considered another location they might have headed toward. I found it so unsettling I nearly dropped the entire group onto the earth far below.

What if Vael'ehn has already recruited them! What if they're already on their way to the Citadel?

Would he have had the time to do so?

No, no, you're right. Vael'ehn would have had no reason to come here until he saw Jack start on his journey away from the Citadel. For all Vael'ehn knows, Jack is still inside the tournament. He wouldn't have even been aware Jack was preparing to leave.

Landing in front of a towering iron door, we peered around at the deserted construct. Vehicles, which from high above appeared stationary and abandoned for years, had instead been freshly moved. Wheel ruts and heavy boot prints had been pressed into the soil in all directions.

"This has not been left to be reclaimed by the earth," Dreyl'vyn announced, taking notice of the same signs I had.

Walther nodded. "The Cimmerian, *although loud*, is correct; this could be a trap."

Jack withdrew his sword. "Well, if this is a trap, then they're in for a surprise. Three Weapons of Legend - I'd like to see their faces when we tear em apart." He grinned at Jillian, who seemed surprised by his reaction.

"I guess things *have* changed a lot since I've been gone," she commented.

It was true. Before she made her way there, both Jack and I had been through several traumatic events. But Jack was faltering in his convictions, whereas I was growing in power and determination. I was going to set things straight once and for all, and I knew it.

It's only a matter of time before she realizes Jack isn't who she thinks he is. He'll prove that to her himself. I have nothing to do but wait. And then… then I will be there for her when she needs love and support.

Laurence, clear your mind. Think rationally. Jack isn't the only person suffering from delusions here. At least he has the sword as an excuse for his behavior. Laurence, you're-

Enough of that! It's not the sword, it's him!

"Then let's remain on our toes," Cindee said in her melodic, small voice. "It's only a trap if we aren't ready when they spring it on us. Everyone get their spells ready for when Laurence opens the door."

Nodding, I took a step in the direction of the massive tower looming high above us. Reaching out toward the immense gate, intent on forcing it to rise, I instead leapt backward, swinging the wand out from my belt. Before I could cast a spell, the massive obstacle shuddered and began to rise on its own.

"Get ready!" I yelled.

But as the gate continued, only a lone silhouette appeared in the dim light within: a large but hunched form, barely taller than a man. Stepping forward, the stranger was revealed to be an old, bipedal reptile, heavily scarred and cloaked with tattered garments.

"My name is Mohrn," the reptile croaked. "Welcome to Black Metal Tower, home of Draughon, leader of the Retrogrades, overthrower of all who oppose him, crusher of bones, and whatever else he wants me to introduce him as."

"Black Metal Tower?" Jack snorted. "Not much for creative names, are you?"

Mohrn eyed Jack wearily, humor failing to rise from his dull eyes. "No, we are not. Please follow me inside. Draughon will be interested to hear why you have come."

As we walked inside, Modera scrunched up her face. "So you just let strangers walk inside your fortress, then?"

Mohrn shrugged. "Most who would attack us do not attempt to knock first."

Leading us out into a vast, empty chamber ringed with doorways, we stepped up to a crude throne crafted from a single broken slab of rock. Upon it sat a large, one-eyed Retrograde with deep gashes covering most of his skull. The wounds had healed long ago but had left him with a less than desirable complexion, even for a war-torn reptile.

Standing, the leader spread his arms. "Welcome to Black Metal Tower. I am Draughon!" he proclaimed, his reptile-like lips mostly reproducing the human words correctly. "Mohrn, you can leave us now."

Mohrn grunted and walked away through one of the doorways.

Regarding us individually, the lizard ruler raised his one good brow. "Our instruments located you before you arrived. Quite an arsenal you have at your sides," he concluded while staring at Jack's sword. "If one wanted to sell such an item…"

"Not for sale," Jack replied, seeing Draughon's overt interest in the piece.

Draughon let out a crude laugh. "Of course not; I did not assume you to be a fool. But one question remains: why are you here?"

"Why *aren't* you here?" Walther countered, almost accusatorily. "For such a grand army, you seem a little light on troops."

Again Draughon laughed. "Old Mohrn is far more dangerous than he looks!" he announced sarcastically. Receiving little response, he continued. "We *are* stretched thinly these days, but there is a vast network of tunnels under these mountains. If I thought your visit was… *not* of the speaking variety, you would have been met with a less than pleasant reception, I can assure you."

"Thank you for seeing us on peaceful terms, then," Cindee commented brightly.

Stepping forward, I regarded the lizard. "We have come to see you on this day with the purpose of discussing recruitment. We would like your army to join our cause. I have heard rumors that, *for the right price,* you might be willing to, say, *remove* someone distasteful from this planet."

Draughon gave me a toothy grin. "You'd like to hire an army for just *one* man? Who would be so-" His mirthful expression fell from his battle-damaged face. "You'd seek to destroy Vael'ehn."

"You seem to be well aware of who he is," I replied, feinting that I had neither knowledge of their assaults on Empor'Vael nor their future agreement to besiege the Citadel.

Draughon grimaced. "I should hope I would recognize my own creator."

The statement caught the entire group off guard.

"Vuh-Vael'ehn is your fuh-father?" Dael'yan asked.

Draughon regarded Dael'yan's speech impediment with a curious expression before replying. "In a way, boy. Have any of you been told why the Retrogrades suddenly appeared on this planet, having never been encountered before?" Everyone shook their heads. "It is simply because our race did not exist before then."

"Are you insinuating you arrived from a different time or dimension?" I inquired.

Draughon shrugged. "In a way, I suppose. Deep under Vael'ehn's wealthy city, he kept a secret. The reason he built upon that location in particular was because it would hide what he wanted no one else to find: the Droth'gon'ai statues." Seeing Jillian's expression, Draughon nodded. "Oh yes, girl, I am aware they exist there -

far more aware than any of you, I am sure. Vael'ehn used those statues to create *us* - a hideous amalgamation of the past, the present, and the future, all fused into one disgusting abomination." He watched our reactions closely, deriving a small pleasure from our astonishment.

"You might have been persuaded to believe that we did this to ourselves; that we, the demented barbarians that we are, were so horrifically insane that we mutilated our bodies for some unknown purpose. I assure you that is not the case. We are reptiles, we are robotic marvels, we are gene-spliced abominations - we are *many* such things. And we are such, for we were conceived as such. Vael'ehn created us for *sport*. He made a group of detestable villains to fight in his circle of blood."

"*Jesus Christ…*" Jack whispered to Jillian. "That's fucked up."

Silently, she raised her eyebrows and nodded in response.

"But if Vael'ehn made you, why did he make so *many* of you?" I asked. "He's not stupid. He wouldn't have created an army powerful enough to risk overthrowing him."

Draughon grinned darkly, an expression which mimicked Vael'ehn quite well. "He did not; *I* did. I was not as *witless* as he expected I would be, and I was not content with my life as a gladiator, my destiny to become a sacrifice for the satiation of the crowds. I escaped from my bonds and found my way to the statues I had once crawled out from. I reactivated the spellwork that Vael'ehn had started as best I could, and let it continue until an army of our race poured out from within.

"Not all were like me, of course; I had little idea of what was required to maintain the spell. With each repeated creation, the spellwork degraded, and the warriors became more massive and less intelligent until they resembled nothing but giant, ignorant reptiles. Those who could communicate, however, identified me as their leader, and I unleashed their fury.

"We swept through the streets, destroying all we came in contact with until nothing was left. And when it had all burned to the ground, I gave them direction,

I gave them *purpose*. I continued to lead them and formed them into a great race. *We* will inherit this planet and outlast all who call it theirs."

Did Draughon just admit to having created dinosaurs by accident?

What's a dinosaur?

They're massive reptiles that once covered this planet in the future, but were long gone by the time I come from. I had seen some held in cages when the Retrogrades were marching on the Citadel of the Shattered Moon. There might be more roaming somewhere.

Oh, yes, there are big reptiles as you say, but there aren't large quantities of them.

Not yet, but trust me, they reproduce and evolve into all sorts of creatures.

"That's nuh-nuh-nuh-nuh-not very nice," Dael'yan said. "Wuh-wuh-we aren't all muh-mean puh-people, yuh-you know."

Draughon shook his head. "What is wrong with you?"

Dael'yan frowned and hung his head.

Draughon, receiving no response, carried on. "You might be naïve enough to believe your race might accept mine, but I assure you, people such as Vael'ehn would not allow that to happen. Either our race or theirs - one shall go extinct sooner or later."

"Would you like to know which one?" Jack asked, seeming to follow my line of reasoning.

"Draughon gave Jack a knowing smile. "We all make our own fates, Xahl'thari."

"So you have no love for Vael'ehn," I interjected. "I should then assume you will aid us in our cause."

Draughon shook his head. "To go after such a man would mean the death of *many* of our race. Such a loss would be near impossible to offset. There is nothing on this planet worth that type of pain, and we do not reproduce as you do."

"Nothing?" I replied. "What I have come here to show you will be worth much more than you will have to endure. It will purchase you as much power as you want, and then some."

Draughon raised his brow. "As much power as I want, you say? I suspect there is nothing on this planet that would meet those qualifications, but by all means, show me what you have." Turning, he called over his shoulder. "Mohrn. *Mohrn!*"

Nearly a minute later Mohrn lumbered back into the room. He appeared not at all concerned by Draughon's urgent tone.

"What do you want, Draughon?"

Draughon eyed him suspiciously. "What took you so long?"

Mohrn frowned. "I am old, Draughon. My bowels give me little notice before emptying themselves."

"This is no place to discuss your urgent bowels!" Draughon exclaimed, slamming his fist down on the fractured throne.

Mohrn shrugged. "On the contrary, your repetitive demands remind me very much of my urgent bowels. Now what do you require of me?"

"Where are my Electronicles, Mohrn? I need them. This newcomer has something to show us," he announced, motioning toward me.

I raised my hand to interject. "What I have to show you is quite far away. You won't need your device; I can show you myself. It will take just a moment, and then we'll be back."

As Mohrn handed a strange set of binoculars to Draughon, he grinned. "I suspect we will still need these," he concluded, stepping down from his throne. "But by all means, take me to where-"

Draughon had no time to finish his statement; I had already waved the wand. With a familiar clap of thunder, we arrived at the base of the hill I had portalled onto long ago. Or rather, it *should* have been the base of a hill. Before us lay nothing but a humungous, v-shaped chasm leading far out into the ocean where the hill had once stood.

Where is it? Where is it!

Where is what?

The ship! The Xahl'thari ship! It's gone!

"I…" I started. "There was a ship here not two weeks ago, buried under the ground. We intended to give it to you in trade for your services."

"A ship?" Draughon repeated. "I see a depression where something tremendous once lay, but someone appears to have arrived here first and completed the heavy lifting for you. Might you know where the ship was brought to? Perhaps we can inspect it there."

"Vael'ehn," I growled. "He must have taken it! But where would he have stored it?"

I looked around aimlessly. The wide expanse of the crater floor went on for miles around us, the ocean stretching even further out before us. The gorge the ship had left behind was positively enormous. What I had once assumed was a substantial portion of the ship sticking out of the ground must have only been a small piece of the bow. Wherever it had gone, it would be easy to spot, and that meant it was nowhere near where we stood.

Could he have moved something so large?

If you had seen the rock giant he created, you'd have no problem believing he could move a ship, no matter how large it may be.

Disappointed in myself, I waved the wand, teleporting us back to Draughon's throne room.

With a crack of thunder, we reappeared in front of everyone, startling all in attendance.

"I'm sorry, Draughon," I said, staring into the battle-hardened lizard's good eye. "We need you on our side, and I thought I could provide you with something truly worthy in return. Now I must ask you to aid us in good faith that, afterward, I will make it right for you and your people."

It was a complete fabrication; I had no intent of doing anything for him.

Draughon smiled. "If it allows you to rest better at night, do not feel sorry for me; I already have a ship."

I shook my head. "You don't understand. This ship was the one you spent so long trying to access: *The Ridden.*"

"Yes, the last of the five ships the Xahl'thari built before their arrival on this land," Draughon said. "Come, look into my Electronicles." He reached forward, offering the device to me. "It does not matter what direction you look into them; they are already adjusted to view what I want them to."

Accepting the offering, I held the gadget up to my eyes. It began to buzz and glow from some sort of power source inside. Slowly, the eyepiece crackled to life, and a grainy image was displayed. In front of me lay a wide ocean inlet, what I guessed might have been Herien Bay. Taking up a large portion of the bay, floated an impossibly large ship. Far larger than an aircraft carrier, it dwarfed the land around it. Unlike anything we might equate to a modern sailing vessel, it didn't seem to have a deck, nor did it have sails, but a ship it was.

Removing the Electronicles from my face, I felt cold and sick. For a moment my eyes met with Jack's before turning back toward Draughon.

"Where did you find your ship, Draughon?" I asked, already dreading the answer.

Draughon shrugged casually. "Vael'ehn was here not long ago, the ship waiting out in the bay, ready for me to commandeer. He had but one request: should a group of travelers arrive, I need only agree to wipe them from existence, and the ship would be mine. You must understand, eliminating seven travelers certainly seemed far preferable to dealing with the likes of him.

"You all seem to represent something better than what I have seen of your race, but your future has no place for us in it. After Vael'ehn completes his task, he will leave the bones of this planet behind, free from the rule of Magic users. He cares not what happens to it after he has gone. In the midst of ruins, *we* shall rise to power."

And without Magical knowledge, technology would be the ruling force on the planet.

What is technology?

It's all the light-up mechanical inventions they have, like his Electronicles. They're from the time period I come from - at least, in part.

"Vael'ehn is mistaken," I announced. "He *thinks* he's going to reforge his planet, but his actions will create a way for demons to access this world. When they arrive everyone will be killed."

Draughon shook his head. "We have made… *special* arrangements," he replied, as if that explained anything at all.

Is he working with the demons?

I sincerely hope not.

"Why not tell us of those arrangements in the first place?" I questioned. "Vael'ehn has clearly made a mistake. With that ship already in your possession, and our forces here to aid you, we can surely deal with him more effectively now."

Draughon offered another reptilian shrug in reply. "I am sorry, but business is business. Even with the likes of one as corrupted as he, I intend to honor my word."

Withdrawing a massive, crudely-forged axe, crafted from what appeared to be a large spinal column, he grinned.

"This weapon was created from the bones of one who came before me. It was he who freed me in an effort to save the Retrogrades. He is the reason I was able to create my army, but he did not have a taste for war. Now he has no choice but to draw blood." Taking a step forward, he pointed the axe at me. "This delightful conversation has given me time to surround you with *all* our forces. There is no way out, I'm afraid."

On the word *afraid*, Dael'yan let out a cry. Turning, we watched as he was lifted into the air, a gore-covered spear protruding from his chest. Beneath him, an imposing reptile slithered out from under a large stone, which had once made up part of the floor.

Spinning on her heel, Modera unsheathed her blades, disemboweling the creature in one beautiful, fluid movement. Immediately it let go of the spear, and Dael'yan dropped hard upon the ground, blood gushing from the lethal wound.

Frantically Cindee raced over to heal him, but she was knocked backward by another lizard, who barreled in from the opposite direction, crushing Dael'yan under his foot. In seconds, hundreds of Retrogrades had poured through the doorways lining the cavernous room. Our only saving grace had been that most were so large, they had to make their assaults single-file.

Watching Draughon cackle with delight, the hordes of reptiles colliding with us from all sides, fury built inside me - fury toward Vael'ehn for going against my warnings; fury toward Draughon for wasting my time and being too stupid to realize the mistake he had made; fury for allowing myself to be put in such a position again.

"This is *not* where we meet our end!" I yelled.

Leaping into the air with inhuman agility, Draughon descended upon me, his axe ready to split me in two. Instead, the weapon shattered into several pieces as it collided with an invisible barrier I had cast. Surprised, the giant lizard caught himself just in time, springing backward onto his throne. Tossing the remnant of his weapon to the side, he bared his claws, ready to attack me again.

Extending a single hand, I reached out toward the Retrograde leader. Draughon's progress was cut short. He found his body pressed inward on all sides with no hope of escape. Writhing as he rose from the floor, he growled and gnashed his dagger-like teeth.

"The only blood your weapon will taste today is your own!" I yelled.

Squeezing, I crushed his heavily-worn body between giant, unseen fingers until he was nothing but a bleeding mess. Launching the heap of guts across the room, it collided with a half dozen enemy soldiers, bowling them over backward.

Pleased with my effective spellwork, I spun to see the entire group engaged in combat. Determined to aid our faction's efforts, I lifted each of their assailants into the air before tearing them into dozens of pieces, their blood and entrails spattering those below. Discarding the decimated corpses, I reached out for still more, and more after that, the body count reaching well over a hundred in just moments as Retrogrades continued to pour through the doors to meet us.

The floor awash with blood, my vision blurring from streams of sweat, I pushed onward, ignoring the signals my body was telling me. Hundreds more fell, ripped to bits without knowing who had ended their lives.

L-Laurence... I... you're pushing me too hard.

No, we can do this. We're going to kill them. We're going to kill them all!

Whirling in circles, I watched as the group fought against the insane warriors, each one taking on several at once. Jack, swinging Mor'dresh in large arcs, slung ribbons of red high over his head. Jillian, savage and hell-bent, dismembered Retrogrades with her demonic claws. Dreyl'vyn, only a shadow of his immense size, stood unopposed, crushing those around him with impossible strength. Modera, a whirlwind of blades, mutilated all around her until their bodies proved incapable of standing.

But of Walther, there was no sign.

Where is Walther?

There, underneath the heavy foot traffic, Walther lay with a large axe protruding from his chest. The contents of a crushed potion bottle sizzled in his hand, scorching his flesh. Cindee pulled frantically at its handle, the gargantuan weapon standing far taller than she was. Desperately she screamed for help, but no one could hear her over the din of battle.

Reaching out toward her, I summoned the axe back to me, pulling it free from his chest. Cindee, following the weapon's path, brought her eyes up to meet with mine. Everything around us seemed to slow. In a moment I saw the last untainted bit of goodwill the world had left in it. Her eyes, pure and filled with anguish, cut into my soul, the expression filling my mind with confusion and guilt for what I had forced her to participate in.

As the axe met my hand, I lost focus, its weight sending me staggering backward.

Laurence, are... are you alright?

What's the matter with me? Rhen, I-

My head swimming, I stumbled into yet another group of Retrogrades, who swung wildly, knocking me to the floor. Withdrawing Ahso'lar, I pointed it in their direction. Nothing happened. Rolling to avoid a series of crushing blows, I tried again to no avail; the wand would do nothing to defend me.

Why aren't you helping me!

Again, a Retrograde brought its axe down, narrowly missing my head. Returning the wand to my belt, I forced the reptile's weapon upward, breaking its jaw. Swinging the axe around with the flick of my wrist, its edge embedded itself deep into the face of another, nearly bifurcating its head. Levitating the deceased Retrograde off the floor, I threw it down onto yet another with such force, its spine shattered. Summoning the axe, I sent it whirling across the battlefield, where it pinned a combatant against the wall. Turning on still others, I tore them limb from limb, refusing to allow them a single moment to regroup.

Please... Please...

Not yet!

Corpses continued to pile up on top of each other, our small band slaying hundreds for each one of us who still stood. Yet the numbers of Retrogrades hadn't diminished at all. Instead, the room continued to fill, reptiles practically waiting in line to get slaughtered. And I stood before them all, my chest heaving, my body covered in blood from head to toe, my feet slipping in the gallons of gore coating the stone floor.

"You all want to die? Then so be it!" I yelled, the air around me rippling with devastating power.

Faintly, far in the back of my head, something began to trickle forward - pain, fatigue, nausea. Looking down through blurry, blood-tinged vision, I saw that my body had been covered in cuts, gashes, and welts. My own life fluids merged with that of my enemies, saturating the thick leather I wore. Teetering back and forth as I tore yet another lizard man in half, I realized my body was near the end of its capabilities. Soon it would fail from exhaustion; soon I would too.

Laurence... your hold is... too strong.

This is not... your body. It is... me...

We... we have to leave. There... are too many...

Please... get the others... get out!

Realizing I could no longer ask more of the frail form, I blasted a dozen Retrogrades backward with a wall of Magic before sprinting the opposite way toward where I last saw the group.

As I neared, they too appeared to be flagging. Walther, once again on his feet, threw a bottle in the face of a reptile, causing its skin to erupt into boils. Cindee, whirling her wand over her head, continued to summon orbs of turquoise light around him, further repairing his once-grave wounds.

Wait, what happened to Jillian?

Where is Jillian!

I can't spot her from here.

Feet from me, Jillian leapt out from behind the corpse of a massive Retrograde whom she had just consumed, landing on a second. Tearing half its skull away, she absorbed thousands of turquoise and purple particles from its mouth before its body hit the floor. The last remnants of her human face disappearing under stains of black, she peered around with blazing green orbs, her expression ravenous.

Noticing my presence, she motioned in my direction, but instead paused, doubling over in pain. Crying out in an otherworldly language, she clawed at the ground as visceral, black wings ripped through her clothing and spread out behind her. Horns tore through her skull, curling up and over her head. Long jagged claws extended down from what could have once been mistaken for fingertips. Horrific hooves ripped through her boots as her legs broke and bent backward.

Jillian… No…

She's turning into a demon, Laurence!

Kill her before she recovers!

With one powerful thrust of her imposing, bat-like wings, Jillian launched into the sky, continuing to cry out as she peered down upon the battleground. Nearly everyone gaped in horror at what had befallen their ally; even some of the Retrogrades turned an eye toward her menacing ebon form.

Jack, however, appeared unwilling to accept his girlfriend's fate. "Jill, stop! I know you're still in there! Come back down to me! We can fix you!"

His efforts to reason with the demon were cut short as he was assailed by yet another wave of Retrograde foes.

"Esaeu lizz ozz xa aoqar xes ya legus!" Jillian roared, running a finger down the length of our group from high in the air.

Sprinting forward in a heroic gesture, Cindee slid under Dreyl'vyn's legs as he bowled over a line of reptiles. Extending her wand upward, she pointed it at Jillian.

"You will be freed from your maladies, Jill!"

Closing her wings, Jillian dropped upon Cindee like a hawk diving on a field mouse, her small body giving the demon no resistance at all. Grabbing the tiny girl by the throat, she squeezed, choking her.

Dispatching the last of his foes, Jack turned back toward the pair, his eyes widening in horror. *"Jill, no!"*

Tears in his eyes, he slung Mor'dresh across the battlefield with all his might. Spinning with deadly precision, it cut a Retrograde in two before slicing cleanly through one of Jillian's wings, severing it at the shoulder blade. Arcing upward, Mor'dresh continued its deadly boomerang-like movement as it returned to Jack, who somehow caught it without amputating his hand.

Sprinting toward Jillian, he swung again, cutting deep into her arm. Screaming in agony as the weapon separated her flesh, she rolled to the side, a repeated swing missing her head by inches. Somersaulting through the air, she landed behind him, her wounds trickling arcs of black ichor across his face. Swiping upward, she cleaved into Jack's wooden arm, her talons glowing with some sort of unholy green Magic.

Whirling on his heel, Jack motioned toward Jillian's chest, intent on taking advantage of the opening she had provided. Instead, he stopped dead in his tracks; his arm had been cut in two, revealing a strange wooden core. Whatever power Jillian had summoned, his enchanted armor stood no chance of deflecting it.

Jack's hesitation was all Jillian needed to re-center herself. Dodging another pair of sword thrusts as he attempted to press on, she unexpectedly sprung forward, grabbing ahold of his wooden shoulder. Using her terrible might, she tore the entire segment free from his torso.

Jack stumbled backward, blood erupting from the catastrophic wound. Somehow remaining on his feet, he stared at his chest where wood once resided, his eyes filled with disbelief as crimson fluid began to coat the floor. Mor'dresh fell from his remaining hand, clattering against the floor.

The trauma was beyond severe. Raw, frayed musculature lay revealed where bark had once met up with flesh. Several bones, broken or dislocated, hung at unnatural angles. Internal organs, some converted entirely to wood, hung from his open chest cavity. Severed root tendrils wriggled under his skin, frantically seeking to seal the incomprehensible injury.

Jillian leapt upon Jack, easily knocking him off his feet. Landing on an uneven, toppled stone, their combined weight catapulted Jack's severed arm through the air, where it landed at my feet. As if in a dream, my eyes lowered from the scene unfolding before me to where the wooden appendage lay, blindly grasping at the floor.

What is happening?

I thought I had planned everything perfectly. This isn't how this should end…

It will only end if you don't do something!

Put her down before my body fails you!

Finish this! You know what needs to be done!

Rhen's demands forced Wesson's words back into my mind.

"When the moment arrives, you will feel its coming. Do not tarry in what you know needs to be done."

Tears rising inside me, I knew what the old Gnill'var had *really* prophesied before his death. I knew what the visions I witnessed had meant. I knew the one task I had to perform. Reaching downward, I lifted Jack's enchanted appendage from the ground. Still alive, it snapped back and forth, attempting to grab me. Pushing Dreyl'vyn and a pair of Retrograde foes out of the way with my mind, I slowly walked up behind Jillian, who was ravenously feeding upon an unconscious Jack.

Nearly blinded by the tears pouring from my eyes, I drove the wicked wooden appendage into her back with all the strength I could muster. The sharpened talons slashed like knives, doing their work all too well, tearing through her body and out through her chest. Bits of her blackened heart spattered the ground as ebon fluid poured from the wound.

Screeching and flailing, Jillian launched away from Jack and spun through the air, beheading a Retrograde with her razor sharp claws in the process. With one last roar of agony, she collapsed to the ground behind a group of mutants, who furiously began to pummel her broken form.

Turning, I stared down at Jack, who had somehow regained consciousness, albeit barely. The rivers of blood had been constricted down to a trickle while root tendrils continued to stitch themselves into his body. Even so, I could see the injury was beyond repair unless Cindee aided in his recovery.

My eyes trailing toward where she stood, I saw she had again been assaulted by Retrogrades and was unaware of what had just transpired. I motioned to destroy them, but Jack grabbed my ankle. His skin pale and cold, tears running down his cheeks, he reached over and picked up the sword with his good hand, somehow finding the strength to slowly rise again. Staring desperately into my eyes, his expression told me without words what he intended.

"This is my ending," he whispered. *"Run."*

Quickly I glanced down at Mor'dresh. It returned my gaze evenly, coldly.

Do something. Save us.

The sword made no reply, its intent already decided.

Turning, I began to sprint toward the nearest doorway, but something caused me to stop in my tracks. My legs, feeling as if they had been nailed to the floor, refused to take another step.

No. You. Don't!

Rhen, no! His spell will kill us!

Enough of this! You won't abandon your friends!

I won't let you escape while leaving them behind to die!

To my horror, I felt my consciousness dragged to the back of Rhen's mind. In my emotional weakness, she had seized the opportunity to trap me within her will. Watching helplessly, I sunk deeper into her subconscious as she turned and ran back toward the others.

Mentally pulling them from battle, Rhen lifted the entire group up and through the nearest door. Knocking the closest wave of Retrogrades as far backward as she could, she summoned a small blue shield around the doorway, protecting our allies.

How… how are you able to summon such power?

I swore I would never be the cause of a tragedy again!

Today, I find my redemption.

What do you-

A blastwave hit us from behind. Jack, his life force fading from him, had driven Mor'dresh into the ground. Using all that remained of his strength, he asked it to enact one last destructive spell. A tsunami of Magic raced outward from the sword, consuming everything in all directions. Retrogrades, their weapons, Draughon's throne, the walls, the roof - nearly the entire tower was vaporized.

As the wave collided with Rhen, she too was blasted backward. Ignited by Magical fire, she landed in a crumpled heap, far from where she had once stood. Her actions, however, had given the rest of the group the protection they needed. Sizzling and blackened, the crumbling archway stood in place. Everyone had survived the catastrophic spell - everyone aside from Jack and Jillian.

Rhen?

Rhen!

Searching Rhen's mind, I realized she was no longer present. Digging in every crevice of what used to be her consciousness, I found nothing but darkness surrounding me.

Rhen, no! Where are you?

Please don't leave me!

…Rhen?

It was too late; Rhen's sacrifice had been made complete.

She had died to save us all.

CHAPTER Sixty

-CADAVEROUS CONFLICT-

Straining with all my might, I forced the vacant body to respond to my will. Twitching and shaking, much as Jillian once had in Wenton's dungeon, it staggered to its feet. Dragging and tripping, I pushed the burned and blistered corpse toward Jillian's demonic remains, calling out to her as I shambled along.

"Jiii… Juuuh… Jiii… Juuuh… Juuuh…" The body moaned over and over, refusing to utter the single name I most desired to say.

As I neared her corpse, the air electrified. Vael'ehn appeared between us, separating me from my goal. Taking one look at my mutilated form, his eyes widened. Seconds later the expression changed to that of amusement.

"Well, well, well, time traveler, it appears you have seen better days, hmm?" he taunted.

"Vael'uuurnnn…" The body moaned as I attempted to reach for him, fury saturating every ounce of my being.

Vael'ehn stepped out of the way as I tripped and fell next to him, cracking the corpse's skull open on a stone.

"You are a sad sight to see," he whispered, kneeling next to me. "Today it seems I have removed *many* threats in one stroke. Jack, the Retrogrades, you - even a demon, of all things! Was that your invasion?" He pouted his lip. "I suppose I owe you an apology, but you must admit, it *was* a little smaller than you let on."

Vael'ehn looked around, taking in the destroyed remains of the tower and all who had perished within it. He spotted what was left of our group on the opposite side of the crater, Cindee frantically trying to heal them. Appearing to view them as no threat at all, he smiled and regarded me again.

"What a success this was indeed!" He leaned closer to my face. "But I am a fair man; I will give you one last chance to redeem yourself. Make your death worth something. Tell me where my daughter is before I end your life."

In one last act of defiance, I forced the corpse to grin. "Haa... haa... haa..." It moaned from its broken, burned mouth.

Extending my arm, I pointed toward Jillian's body. Casually, Vael'ehn turned his head toward the corpse.

"Yes, I see you finally found your-"

He paused, his smug expression dropping from his face, as if an otherworldly sense had alerted him to something I could not see. Taking several long strides across the war-torn room, he slid on his knees next to Jillian's body.

"*Vael'ora?*" he whispered.

Surprisingly, Vael'ehn began to weep. His body heaving, he shook as tears pattered the charred remains of his daughter.

"What have they done to you, my child?" he asked of the departed form. "You have become such a horror! Was the time traveler correct? Will demons take everything from me?" He ran the back of his finger along her blistered, ebon cheek. "Or have they already succeeded in doing so?"

His eyes trailing down her body, they stopped on the enchanted arm, which protruded from her chest. Somehow, it hadn't been charred at all, instead appearing quite healthy. Small leaves sprouted from its fingertips, the power of Jack's final spell no doubt pumping it full of Magical energy.

Growling, Vael'ehn turned his head in the direction of Jack's corpse, which I had neglected to pay any attention to. To my astonishment, Jack still knelt where he had cast his last spell. His body had been replaced in full by an Archaeus Tree, his form still vaguely familiar in the shape of its trunk.

Branches sprouted from his shoulder and head, and dozens of leaves had already begun to tilt toward the moon, little orbs forming under each one. What had once been his arm extended downward to clutch Mor'dresh in a hand-like burl. His expression wiped from his featureless face, Jack's head still tilted toward Jillian's body, his last thoughts focused on her.

Vael'ehn laid his daughter on the ground, his face menacing and cold. Marching toward Jack, he knelt down to meet him face to face.

"You have murdered my daughter, *boy*. If your foolishness had not done you in, I would have tortured you for a thousand centuries!"

Receiving no response, he turned his gaze toward Mor'dresh. Appearing not to see the results he had hoped for, he frowned; the sword had changed drastically in color.

"Your sacrifice has greatly lessened the power of Mor'dresh. It will require the absorption of *many* more souls to correct this." He turned a murderous gaze on the others. "But your friends will be an excellent start."

As Vael'ehn reached out to free the sword from the burl, light erupted from the artifact, bathing the area in a blinding wash of golden rays. His hand smoking, he yanked it away, staring down at a palm which had been horribly burned.

Sneering, he yelled at the sword. "How is this possible! You have murdered everyone here!"

Again, he reached forward, forcefully trying to destroy the burl. In response, Mor'dresh blasted him with a second, focused beam of light, throwing him several yards away. Landing on his back, Vael'ehn shook with fury.

"You dare defy your master!" he yelled, pointing at the weapon as he scrambled to his feet. "I *will* have you! You *will* succumb to what is inside you. It is inevitable! It is your destiny!" Calming somewhat, he lowered his voice. "In time, you *will* return to me."

Vael'ehn walked back to Jillian's corpse. He again began to cry through his rage, the two emotions blending all too well upon his face.

At that moment, something caught my attention. From around the room, shadows shifted in the moonlight, as if someone had just tilted a lampshade. Something in the darkness filled me with a sense of unease. We were not alone.

Behind Vael'ehn, a Retrograde opened its eyes. Hanging from a massive stone block, which had once comprised part of a wall, an axe lay buried in its torso. It was anything but alive; I knew, I had killed it myself. The bloodshot, cold eyes flickered down toward the weapon. With jerky, inhuman movements, the reptile reached out and pulled the axe free. Landing on the ground, it lumbered forward, swinging with impossible strength.

Vael'ehn, far more perceptive than most, spun around just in time, passing his arm across the lizard's torso. Whatever spell he had used dissected the creature into a series of macabre segments. It fell to the ground before him, still animated, growling and writhing. Without legs or arms, however, it posed no threat.

Frowning and wiping tears from his face, Vael'ehn looked around. Dozens of Retrogrades had risen from the ground, most of which were missing limbs, heads, or worse. As one, they stalked toward him. With a wave of his hand, he sent the risen warriors tumbling out into the distance, as if they were nothing.

"So Wenton's lap dogs have come for me again!" he called. "Have you not heard what I did to Gehr'ret? Surely, none of you were a match even for him!"

The wind stopped and the ruins grew quiet. The entire area dimmed, as if the moon itself were shying away from what was about to take place. The shadows crept inward, rising from the floor and taking on solid form. Two, three, a dozen, and more - Seekers materialized in all their horrible glory, stalking toward Vael'ehn with their inhuman, insectoid strides. Disgusting, sagging, bereft of eyes;

Gehr'ret had clearly been the most powerful of them all, for his body had remained in far better condition than theirs.

"Vekh'lesh," Vael'ehn called to the one nearest him, a false smile upon his lips. "So good to see you."

"The greater your enemy, the greater your smile, I see," Vekh'lesh returned, his voice sounding like the last breath pressed from a corpse.

Vael'ehn pouted his lips. "How is that any way to speak to your teacher?"

Vekh'lesh motioned toward the rest of the Seekers. "Am I supposed to be thankful for what you taught us, what you *cost* us? And now you spend your time in the company of a demon, your tears dampening its remains."

"You have spent too much time with that old, miserable Gnill'var," Vael'ehn returned. "He has convinced you to refrain from collecting the life of others. It has indeed cost you much, *weakened* you much."

"He who steals the life of another is far weaker than I will ever be," Vekh'lesh countered.

Vael'ehn glanced toward Jillian, a dark smile creeping across his features. "Let us put that ignorant rhetoric to the test."

Immediately the group of Seekers shook as Vael'ehn's invisible assault pressed against their bodies. Raising their hands, Vael'ehn in turn was forced to steady his feet. Around the group of sinister spellcasters, the area continued to dim. What sounded like disembodied voices cried out while wisps of shadow coalesced and began to drift around the room.

As they made their way ever closer to me, the shadows took on the form of wretched spirits, bent, distorted, and writhing in agony. Words began to spill from their wailing maws - horrible words, beckoning words, tempting words, words not meant for human ears. The shadowy apparitions pleaded, *demanded*, that I give them my life. Soft like silk, I could feel a razor edge hiding just underneath their moans, ready to flay the life from me.

Recoiling backward, I tried my hardest to picture Vael'ehn, convince the shadows it was he they sought. Begrudgingly they pulled away, not by my will but at the behest of those who had called the spell into being.

Swirling into tighter and tighter whirlwinds of death, the shadows descended upon the group of spellcasters, seeking to entice, seeking to consume. As they swirled about Vael'ehn and the others, I realized it was not a single spell controlled by any one man; it was a series of spells, summoned by many, and both sides were fighting each other to control them, to direct them.

Closing in, the shadows began to bite into the flesh of the Seekers, pulling with them wisps of turquoise. Impregnated with the brilliant color, the specters rose, conjugating above the warring parties. Again and again more shadows struck, leaving behind wounds that were not wounds, black lacerations bleeding life instead of blood. Vael'ehn himself suffered from dozens of his own, but his expression told me everything; he was winning, and his prior pupils were too weak to take him apart.

Before long a few of the most frail fell, their bodies riddled with shadow fissures. Those still in control found themselves stricken by even more vampiric threads. One by one, they too began to collapse. In the end it was Vekh'lesh who stood toe to toe with Vael'ehn, the two exchanging blow after blow. Their bodies had become a crosshatch of horrible incisions, and their life force flowed into the air like blood in water.

His power coming to an end, Vekh'lesh crumpled to his knees, his macabre, disgusting face turning toward me. "It wasn't until I lost my eyes, that I truly saw the magnitude of my mistakes," he whispered. And with those words, he fell.

Vael'ehn called down the mass of swirling shadows and turquoise orbs. Looking into its depths, I could see he was tempted to use it on himself, rebuild what he had lost. He appeared frail, weak - far worse than I had ever seen him. And yet he was also satisfied, content with the knowledge that he had attained something precious, something which might rectify a great tragedy.

I knew in that instant it was our group's most opportune time to attack him;

Vael'ehn also appeared to acknowledge that truth. Even so, he smiled, somehow sensing that I lacked the will to make a move. And it was true; I found myself incapable of action - not due to Rhen's body but because I knew what he had in mind. Vael'ehn was about to resurrect Jillian using the life force flayed from the Seekers and himself, and I wasn't about to stop him.

I know you don't approve, Rhen, but he is weak. The act of resurrecting her will only weaken him. We will get our chance for revenge, but not before I make sure she's brought back into this world.

Vael'ehn called out toward our group, whom Cindee had nearly finished healing. "You will *all* die. When I resurrect my daughter, we will come for you. Mor'dresh *will* have your souls."

And then he vanished, taking the swirling orb and Jillian's corpse with him.

Rhen's body failing to rise from where it had collapsed, I finally accepted the inevitable; it had been lost. Pushing backward, my vision swelled to that of the Coadju'tahr. Sliding out from where it had been stowed, I stared down at what was left of her. Missing most of her clothing, skin, and hair, I was surprised the body had responded to my summons at all.

It's alright, Rhen. I know you were worried I'd hurt your body, but we'll find another one. I promise.

Cindee and the others walked toward Jack. Covered in dirt, sweat, and blood, they appeared exhausted, but Cindee's Magic had relieved them of their wounds. In fact, due to her extensive use of Healing Magic and the toll it had taken on her, she appeared to be the worst of them all.

"I still don't know why you wouldn't let us attack him while he was here," Modera muttered.

Cindee turned and eyed Modera as if she were an ignorant child. As I watched her, I knew the violence and tragedy had slowly begun to harden her emotions. She carried a commanding expression set deep within her once jovial, bright eyes

- one I suspected might remain for the rest of her days. Although only half the height of her comrades, it no longer felt as if she were begging for their attention.

"Do you have any idea who Vael'ehn is, how inconceivably dangerous he is?" she chirped, her small voice somehow carrying all too well across the ruined structure.

"Well, yeah, but-" Modera started, but Cindee cut her off.

"All of these creatures we fought here, they were created *by* him. Those Seekers were trained *by* him. He's more powerful then all of them combined, Modera, and if we would have stepped out there, we'd have had our lives torn from our bodies.

"If I interpreted their discussion correctly, Laurence convinced Vael'ehn that Jill was his daughter. I don't know if there is truth in that or not, but it was certainly fortunate for us; he was far more preoccupied by that than revenge. *We* were lucky today. *We* escaped, not him."

She turned to face the tree that had formerly been Jack. "And if Jack hadn't sacrificed himself, he would have also taken Mor'dresh, possibly given it to another victim to finish tainting it. But if I didn't know any better…"

She sheathed her wand and walked in the direction of the tree before reaching out toward the sword. Closing her eyes, she gingerly poked at it with a finger, expecting some sort of pain. Instead, the sword made no response. Letting out a breath, Cindee wiped her forehead.

"*He did it,*" she whispered.

The sword's prophecy - the first words it had ever pressed into my mind - came rushing back.

"The Marris line, extinguished.
Kaldre'shen, its light expended.
The stone, devoured by itself.
The demon deceived, destroyed.
The Marris line, extinguished."

Jack had been murdered, Mor'dresh had fallen into darkness, I had killed myself, Jillian had died, and Jack had suffered a second death - five events which would lead to the purification and restoration of Kaldre'shen.

It... knew what it would take to make it this far, what it would take to restore it.

"Did *what?*" Walther muttered, reaching for Jack's burl, intent on freeing the sword. For whatever reason he seemed to think he, of all people, should be allowed to retrieve it.

Quickly I rushed forward, shoving him away. Stumbling backward, Walther eyed me with a fierce, perturbed expression.

"What is this! The crystal again? Where did *you* come from?"

In response, I threw up a rippling wall of letters.

`That is an Archaeus tree.`
`It will consume you.`
`Do not touch it!`

The truth was, I hadn't been completely sure if the tree would hurt Walther or not, given it had been made *from* Jack. I assumed it might, but more than anything, I simply didn't want to give Walther access to the sword. He was far too selfish and arrogant.

Walther, despite showing signs of continued annoyance at being pushed away, eyed the tree with far more respect. "What did Jack do? *Besides* change himself into a tree."

Cindee poked the sword a second time with her finger, again with no response. "I'm not an expert on Objects of Power. Truthfully, I know almost nothing about them. My friend, Balrick, was the one who studied that stuff. But Jack sacrificed himself for all of us just now. He impressed his good will upon the sword with every ounce of life he had left, and he convinced it do something Vael'ehn never would have expected." She looked up at Walther, her eyes wide. "I think he may have converted it. I think it's begun to revert back to Kaldre'shen again. Maybe not entirely, but it *has* changed. Look at it; it doesn't even have the same appearance."

And it was true. While the sword still retained much of its original form, some of its most distorted features had lessened, and the blade had lightened from near black to almost gold in color. So, too, had the gems changed. No longer did they contain a black, undulating ink. Instead they had lightened to a cloudy, brown-gold hue.

"But without touching his hand, I'm not sure how to take it," Cindee considered, eyeing the sword from multiple angles.

Focusing on the ground surrounding the weapon, I tore away the scorched remains of the stone floor and the dirt beneath it until the entire weapon lay revealed. With some trepidation, I reached out to touch the hilt with my mind.

Could it be Kaldre'shen is now ours, Rhen? With our invincibility toward Vael'ehn, and the sword not only in our possession but also resisting him, we can achieve everything we've-

As I made mental contact with the weapon, I felt its attention turn from the others to me. Buffeted backward, an immense, almost unfathomable force held me at bay.

Mor'dre- I mean, Kaldre'shen, it's me! I'm here to help.

Kaldre'shen continued to hold me in its grasp.

Where the light shines, the shadow must flee.

I... I don't understand.

Reaching forward, Cindee firmly gripped Kaldre'shen's guard with her small hand and pulled downward. She was rewarded for her efforts as the sword slid free of the tree's grasp with little resistance. Awkwardly hoisting the comparably massive

Kaldre'shen into the air, she watched it reflect the moonlight from above, amplifying its brightness as it did so.

I attempted to pull the sword from her grasp, but Kaldre'shen kept me at bay. I watched in horror as Cindee turned away without the slightest resistance on my part.

How is the sword able to nullify my attempts!

How is she so powerful that she can wield it?

Cindee offered the sword to Dreyl'vyn. "You should be the one who carries this."

Dreyl'vyn stared down at it, confused. "Why do you offer me such a weapon?"

"Yes, shouldn't one of us carry such a powerful object?" Walther agreed.

"He *is* one of us," Cindee scolded. "Who did we stand by and fight the Retrogrades with? Did you not see how many he took on, protecting us from danger; or did you spend so much time on the floor, *injured*, that you missed his assistance?"

She regarded Dreyl'vyn again. "Because it's influenced by the desires of the people who use it, Dreyl'vyn. It's a Weapon of Legend, and it should be far more resplendent than it is right now. It may have resisted Vael'ehn, but I think it's right on the verge of tipping toward either direction. I'd rather keep it how it is now than risk having it turn evil again. You don't think with emotions like we do. You won't influence it."

"That is wise of you," Dreyl'vyn responded. "I see now why you are the leader of this company." Reaching down, he bent low and accepted the weapon.

Cindee seemed ready to protest Dreyl'vyn's compliment, but seeing that no one had disagreed with him, she clamped her mouth shut. Walking over to Rhen's body, she pulled the wand free from under the corpse. Staring down at the two blue gems, which continued to slowly orbit each other, she considered for a moment before turning back toward the others.

"Walther, Wenton said you are adept at using the Arcane," she announced, her eyes betraying a small uncertainty. "I'm going to allow you to use this wand, but it is not yours, and its use comes with a price: you need to continue on by our side. You cannot go off to your old career. We need you with us, and you need a weapon. We can't have you throwing potions this way and that like you have been. They obviously have a use, but you almost died several times."

Surprisingly, Walther had no smart retort to shoot her way. *"Me?"* he whispered, shock evident upon his face.

As Cindee laid the artifact in his hand, tears welled in his eyes. Somehow it, too, appeared to accept its fate - an action I never would have thought possible considering who it had been given to.

It ignored my efforts, but it accepts the hands of that old fool!

"I… *I am sorry*," Walther replied, his lip quivering.

"You *need* to accept it, Walther," Cindee replied, mistaking his apology for rejection.

"I… I will," Walther replied. "I mean, I am sorry for who I have been. I have acted as if you are all excrement, and yet you…" He stared down at the wand. "And yet you would treat me like an equal and bestow upon me this power. It is hard to accept."

Cindee pointed a finger up at him. "I'm doing this because I think you're the one who can use it best, and we *really* need its help right now. Don't make me regret that decision. I appreciate you trying to be a better person though. Thank you."

Regarding the scene of the battle, Cindee paused to deliberate.

"The Retrograde threat seems to have been dealt with, at least for now. Who knows how many of their forces we eliminated tonight and how many are still out there, but we *did* put a huge dent in their numbers, and we even killed their leader. That has to count for something.

"Vael'ehn has also lost his greatest weapon, perhaps for good, but we paid for its acquisition with *our* blood. In doing so we have lost four great allies of our own. Jack was a friend who I cared very much for. Jill brought out the best in him, despite the path she was led down. Rhen, I did not know well, but she was clearly of great aid to all of us. Dael'yan… may we forever hope to be as innocent, loving, and selfless as he was." Looking over toward Dael'yan's charred corpse, which had been repeatedly crushed into the ground during the battle, she sighed.

"I in no way mean this as an insult, but can we not revive Dael'yan?" Walther inquired. "You did so for me, and I am forever in your debt."

Cindee, nearly losing her composure, did not reply at first. Fighting to keep tears from spilling from her eyes, she regarded Walther with an expression of painful determination.

"At the tournament I was told I could not save everyone. By the time I was able to make my way back to him, he was gone, and everyone else had taken wounds of their own. There might have been some small chance of bringing him back, but I felt it was a far greater risk to allow you all to fight without my aid." Staring down at Dael'yan's corpse again, her lip quivered. "I will never forgive myself."

Modera shook her head. "Don't say that; you did the right thing. If you had risked devoting your attention toward him, then one of us - maybe even *all* of us - could have died instead. You can't focus on what happened to him. We need to start planning for the future. Vael'ehn thinks we've killed his daughter. True or not, that makes him more dangerous and unpredictable than ever. We should get moving before he decides to come back."

Wiping tears from her eyes, Cindee nodded. "As much as I find myself unable to accept that inside my heart, you're right; we need to teleport to Toriash'ahn and explain all of this to the Grand Magus. He'll help us figure out how to track Vael'ehn down and stop any further calamities from befalling us." Motioning toward Walther, Cindee extended a hand. "If you would do the honors, Walther, you're the one who can take us there with the least trouble."

Walther nodded and stepped forward to begin, but as I glided forward to join the group, Cindee raised her hand, motioning for me to stop.

"You will not be coming with us, Laurence," she announced, her expression again impassive. "I've watched you go from someone I felt sorry for, to someone who has been a great aid to our cause. But now... now you've become someone I fear. You may deny it, but I believe I watched you consume a version of yourself before you took over Rehn's body. For all I know, she was a victim of yours as well.

"The spellwork you used while fighting the Retrogrades was savage and violent, and the horrible grin on Rehn's face while you fought them told me everything I need to know. You have been corrupted - maybe not completely, but enough to put us at risk."

Corrupted?

*She can't deny our part in this, Rhen. This is **our** plan!*

You need us!
You will fail without us!

Gliding forward again, I was physically stopped by Cindee, her powers somehow holding me against my will. She shook her head, determination splayed across her features.

"*Us?* Laurence, I don't believe you have a solid grasp on what has happened. You've just suffered through a serious trauma. Rhen is gone; she sacrificed herself. You need to stay put. We certainly do not need *your* aid. You have to stay far away from Kaldre'shen until it has been purified. You're too much of a risk, and you might taint it. It can't be allowed to revert back to what it was. I'm sorry for what has happened to you, but you've fallen too far into darkness."

Stunned by Cindee's comment, which mirrored a sentiment once spoken by Rhen, I backed away, as if I had just been slapped. For a moment I had considered fighting against the diminutive girl, forcing her to abide by my will, but somehow her words had defeated me without a single spell being cast.

Fallen into darkness?

Cindee motioned toward Walther. "Go ahead. Just the four of us, Walther."

As Walther waved the wand over their heads, the group vanished with a clap of thunder, leaving me behind in the decimated remains of the fortress. I could have overpowered them all, taken everything from them, but with Cindee at the helm and the sword again resisting me at every turn, I could not find the strength to do so.

Why is such a small girl capable of completely disarming me?

You know what, Rhen? It doesn't matter; they see me as a villain anyway. I have to prove my methods first, then they will learn what I have done for them, the sacrifices I have made for this planet.

*You are wrong. She is wrong too. I have **not** fallen into darkness. I will prove I can justify to you both what I have done. I will set everything right.*

Staring at Dael'yan's burned remains, which resembled little of the young man he had once been, I found myself more resolute in my convictions than I ever had been. He represented the epitome of what had gone wrong with each and every person I had met, the fate of the world if I left it in the hands of others.

Everyone on this planet is naïve. They are too focused on what they consider to be right and just. They are all unaware of what needs to be done to accomplish the impossible.

A person has to fight fire with fire; it is the only way. Without my actions, the group wouldn't have found Ahso'lar, and they certainly wouldn't have regained Kaldre'shen. Jack, Dael'yan - they were both useless in the end. I've let people muddle my results.

Jillian is the true tragedy. If Vael'ehn can't bring her back, I will mourn her loss for the rest of my days.

You were wrong about that as well; she would have warmed up to me if given enough time without Jack. When I saved her in the forest, I could see it in her eyes.

Turning my attention toward Jillian's severed demonic wing, the realization of how those events had unfolded spilled over into my mind. What I had seen in my repeating vision had finally come to pass. In Wenton's room there had been a table, and on it had lain the corpse of a demon. Looking back upon it, I now knew the body to be Jillian's; she had been prophesied to die. I was right to assume Jack was in danger, but I had not expected to cause the final blow to her myself.

And with Jack's severed arm, of all things.

Disastrously, many details had changed from the vision, proving it would never take place in the reality I had created. Wenton was no longer there to guide the group, Dael'yan had died a brutal death, the wooden man had never joined our force, and Dreyl'vyn was no longer the towering giant he had once been. I wasn't even part of the company myself, for that matter; I had been shunned. Worst of all, despite having fulfilled my apparent destiny, Vael'ehn had stolen Jillian's corpse and taken it with him.

Wenton must have remained here in that version of the future. His presence alone may have forced Vael'ehn to leave before he could capture the body. Vael'ehn may never have found out Jillian was his daughter, for all I know.

But you know what? I think the cost was worth it. His mourning could still turn his emotional state against Roth'Roh'Kah, if it hasn't already. And now he can resurrect Jillian. Without Life Magic and Soul Magic, I don't know what he plans to do, but if anyone has a chance of finding a solution, it's him.

Focusing on the tree, I stared up at its trunk.

*So you die again, this time by sacrificing yourself. Why wait until everything was ruined before choosing to be selfless? Jillian didn't have to turn, didn't have to be killed, but you **had** to procrastinate.*

You forced me to kill her!

*I should **not** have been the cause of her death!*

Angrily I lashed out at the tree, attempting to shatter it with my power. Infuriatingly, it was in no way harmed, instead absorbing every ounce of what I poured into it. Within seconds it grew both taller and healthier, its leaves swelling and doubling in size. It would clearly grow in that spot for all time as an eternal reminder of the pain Jack had caused me.

For all I knew, it would reproduce, spreading its infernal saplings across the land until everyone was burdened by their existence again. If I ever returned to the future, I might find millions of its descendants infesting the countryside, forever making certain that the tragedies of this day would live on, no matter where I traveled.

*You have somehow managed to be the reason for my unhappiness before **and** after your death. I should just travel back and erase everything you did!*

Unfortunately, such an action wasn't prudent; Jack's choice brought with it a serious complication. He had managed to remove most of the corruption Vael'ehn had instilled within Kaldre'shen. It was finally at a point where, with enough positive reinforcement, it could rid itself of its taint altogether. It had even gone so far as to defy its old master twice, physically harming him in the process - something it couldn't muster the strength to do in the past.

However, Jack had only given himself up for the rest of us when the situation appeared most grim. He was gravely wounded, Jillian had died, and Retrograde forces were pouring in from all sides. Without making the conclusion that our situation had become utterly hopeless, he would never have chosen the path he had and, thusly, wouldn't have purified Mor'dresh.

What he had stumbled upon was the key to our success. It remained with him alone, and no other could provide it. But with it had come a cost: time-traveling back to any point before his sacrifice might cause more harm than good. As much as I was tempted to head back and thwart Jillian's death while also giving us a greater fighting chance against our foes, that action would prevent Jack's sacrifice and create an opportunity for Vael'ehn to thwart us when he arrived.

The sword may have wanted to change, it may have even tried to change, but it was still burdened by Vael'ehn's treachery. If brought within the presence of its master - under different circumstances, while still corrupted - we had no way of guaranteeing it would act appropriately. It had, after all, killed Jack once before.

Instead, the Retrogrades had been dealt a fatal blow, and Vael'ehn no longer had access to the sword. Even better, he was in a distraught emotional state, making him incredibly vulnerable. After trying, and hopefully succeeding, to resurrect Jillian, we could use Kaldre'shen to kill him. That act alone would surely finalize its purification, and we would be free to turn our efforts toward Roth'Roh'Kah. It was the exact outcome I had been looking for, and it had happened far more quickly and easily than I expected. But Jack had created success through a nearly unbearable sacrifice.

This just doesn't feel like a victory at all without Jillian by my side.

I should have watched her far more closely during the battle, prevented her from feeding.

I wonder if Jack would have made the same choice if a Retrograde had mortally wounded him instead of her.

I could travel back in time and isolate him in the middle of a group of enemies, force him into desperation!

But could a Retrograde do enough damage to him?

I could tear off his arm myself!

The truth was, the risk was far too great, and I knew it. If it hadn't been, my determination to save Jillian surely would have teleported me back through time without any further consideration. But there I hovered, furious and alone, my resentment and conviction building inside me.

Damn it, Jack! Why couldn't you have chosen to die before she changed? I would have kept her safe until I found something to remedy her condition. Dreyl'vyn could have restored her over and over again - forever, if need be. It didn't even bother him!

I'm glad you're dead, Jack; you deserve it. I will never forget the pain you've put me through - you **and** the others. I'm better off without the lot of you! Now I'm free to do what needs to be done from this point onward.

I can head to Toriash'ahn myself, learn of their plans, and find out where Vael'ehn has gone. I can sit back and let the Xahl'thari forces wear him down. Each and every one of them can die for all I care.

When I make my move, I'll ensure Vael'ehn perishes by the sword, even if I have to guide Dreyl'vyn's hand with my own power. I will prove my greatness to Kaldre'shen, prove I am worthy of wielding it against the demons.

This planet is full of people too ignorant to do what needs to be done. Earth requires a guardian, someone who is willing to make the decisions innocent people cannot, someone to make sure this kind of tragedy never happens again.

And that person will be me.

I will seek out and destroy all knowledge of demons - anyone who has ever communed with them; anyone who has dealt in demonic Magic. All threats must be eliminated without compassion, without remorse. There will be no more opportunities for evil to take root in this world.

If Roth'Roh'Kah ever manages to show himself again, he will be met with absolute brutality. *I* will be waiting and ready for him. *I* will turn his own sinister spells against him. He will wish he had never learned of this planet. And then, *I* will crush him.

After he has been dealt with once and for all, and the planet is finally safe, everyone who still lives will see it was I, Laurence, who protected the Xahl'thari and brought Magic back to the world.

EPILOGUE

Laurence stared at me in silence for a long while. His face had gone pale, and it seemed, at least for the time being, his eyes had stopped burning with power. For nearly an hour he had been crying as he retold the last details of his story, and tears had soaked the top of his robe. Finally, as if he had conceded defeat, he looked away.

"When you said pain was powerful, but regret was far more dangerous, you were referring to Jillian's end, weren't you?" I offered, trying to break the silence, which had begun to hang over me like a smothering blanket.

Laurence turned his eyes back upon me. He appeared weak, tired, as if the very fibers of his being were losing their cohesion. "She did not deserve what was put upon her. She did not deserve *any* of it, and it was *my* hand that forced her to leave this existence." He let out a long, measured breath. "And now you have begun to learn the truth. I wonder, do you still think I am similar to Wenton?"

I had secretly dreaded the prospect of Laurence bringing up that question again. At one time I had thought it a silly thing to ask; I had assumed him to be more like Wenton in that comparison. As the tale unfolded, however, I saw that he had begun to unravel, the events he had seen and endured playing upon his psyche.

"Well, I don't think you're similar to Vael'ehn."

Laurence laughed humorlessly. "I can tell when someone is lying, and I can tell when someone fears for their life; you are exhibiting both of those traits. You'd rather offer me what I want to hear and continue to breathe, than use your last breath to speak the truth."

He had summed up my emotions exactly. What Laurence had done was hardly absolvable. Killing one's self, it could be argued, might not be murder at all. Then again, killing one's self might be the worst form of murder. The person he had murdered had also been the original; the corrupted facsimile had dispensed with a more legitimate heir to the time period - at least from my perspective.

Worse, what he had done to Rhen could be considered mental rape or assault. She was held as a hostage up until her last minutes, when she finally overthrew him and saved the group. Her death, all the prior murders - they were awful to hear, but it seemed, if anything, that was precisely what Laurence wanted me to admit to him.

"If you want the truth, then yes, you're exactly like Vael'ehn," I managed. "Technically, you're worse. He was corrupted by demons and brainwashed into doing what he did. From what you've told me, he was loving, passionate, and had a bright future. But you - you became the monster you thought you were hunting, and now I'm having trouble justifying why you're the one who made it through alive."

Surprisingly, Laurence nodded in agreement with my charges. "You have kept your eyes open and seen the truth, Viktor. In order to detail our past properly, that is what will be required of you." He held up a finger. "Be careful when you copy down what you have learned. You cannot side with or against those you have heard about. You cannot pass judgement on what has been done. You must simply report on that which you have been told. Right or wrong, it is our history and must be documented as such.

"You *are* correct, however. While seeking to prevent the death of someone I loved, I have become death myself, and I have done a great many things you would find hard to accept while trying my best to achieve the results I knew I would attain."

"Are you insinuating you achieve those results? Is everything you have done worth it? *Did* you become the guardian of this planet and keep it safe from demons? Last I checked, I don't see demons anywhere, but I also don't see Magic. That is, except for the Magic *you* use, and now I can't help but question why that is. Did you take it all for yourself?"

Laurence smiled humorlessly. "No, I can assure you, I did not - take Magic for myself, that is. In the end, I have become far weaker, a shadow of what I once was, and for good reason. Did I achieve the results I wanted? No, I did not. Did I set into motion that which needed to happen and justify what I have done? I think that is an answer only those who read your words can decide for themselves. After all, the story has yet to be finished."

I opened my mouth to reply, but Laurence once again vanished, the act frustrating me more than it ever had. But I did agree with him on one point; those who read his story *would* have to decide if what he had done was worth it in the end. As for me, I had no choice but to pass it along untainted; I found myself compelled to write down exactly what he had told me, word for word. He may have suspected otherwise, but the spellwork lacing his tale wouldn't have allowed me to change it to suit my own interests even if I had tried.

In regard to whether or not I remained unbiased, I had already made up my mind. Laurence hadn't caused nearly as much damage as Vael'ehn had, and to be honest, Vael'ehn wasn't as much of a villain as he first appeared, despite what he had done. As to what side either one would eventually fight on or what ideals they would fight for, the lines between the two were starting to blur. One was quickly becoming the other, and I suspected the parts they played would not be nearly as defined as I had initially assumed.

That night I would find myself incapable of sleep - not because I was shocked or scared, but because I was disappointed and suspicious of Laurence's intentions. Within minutes of his departure I had begun to document what he had said. Of course I was eager to write down everything I could in order to avoid the sickness that had accompanied my prior lack of writing, but more than anything, I was anxious for his return.

Once and for all, I needed to know the truth not only about the story I was being told, but also the two men involved. I suspected neither were what they had once appeared to be. No matter the horrors I was destined to reveal, I would remain vigilant, spreading the story of our forgotten history. Whether it be tragedy or triumph, it mattered little; our race had remained ignorant for far too long.

This narrative takes place over five volumes,
and I have just begun to discover the truth.

Please return with me to reveal what Laurence has brought to pass after parting
ways with his former allies in the fourth part of his epic journey:

VAAL'BARA
HISTORICAL SOCIETY

- Volume Four -

The Breath of Those Forgotten

CPSIA information can be obtained
at www.ICGtesting.com
Printed in the USA
LVHW090918140520
655573LV00012B/357/J